Shadow in the Wind

Charlotte Ann Minga

Copyright © 2012 Author Name

All rights reserved.

ISBN:1479335533
ISBN-13:9781479335534

DEDICATION

Shadow in the Wind is dedicated to childhood memories and my dad, Thomas E. Minga, Sr. who gave me the gift of laughter and adventure; and in memory of my mom, Mary Afton Weaver Minga who gave me the love of literature and taught me the joy of playing with words; and in memory of my brother, Thomas E. Minga, Jr. who was the music of my life and taught me to see the absurdities around us and the humor to survive them. I am eternally grateful for the privilege and blessings of going along on the magical ride of our parents' lives and adventures together.

ACKNOWLEDGMENTS

First of all to my amazing husband, CJ, who has been my partner, encourager, my sounding board, and a great coach – thank you for rescuing me from the ruins. I love you dearly. You truly are my dream come true.

To the incredibly gifted Bradley Franklin Austin of Rocketbox Studio in Kansas City Missouri who designed my cover. You took the image in my mind and made it real. I appreciate your talent as a photographer but I am most blessed to have you as my son-in-law and friend. I love you deeply.

Acknowledgements are very much like invitation lists to a wedding. I have never known where to start and with whom to end. This novel as been decades in the writing and along the way I married (twice) and had three wonderful, brilliant, amazing, and beautiful children and am now going on an even dozen wonderful, brilliant, beautiful, and amazing grandchildren. So many people have a part in making this first novel what it has become. Shadow in the Wind was born in a stack of spiral notebooks, grew through an electric Brother typewriter (with carbon paper that I am sure was the spawn of Satan) and then an IBM Select II; it came of age through a Tandy computer with Xanadu integrated software and to fruition in this Dell Laptop. I am eternally grateful for all who have encouraged me, touched my life and helped me to grow. I sincerely hope each and every one of you know who you are.

Charlotte A. Minga

CHAPTER ONE

The Sniper paused on the path he had traveled for the last fifteen minutes, glancing around casually. The eager spring sun struggled to climb the morning sky, determined to burn through the mist and casting long shadows toward the west. He breathed heavily, not as much from exertion as anxiety. There was something about the hunt that always brought ambivalence and exhilaration sweeping through his mind and into his body.

He veered off the trail and then made his way through the underbrush. His movement through the trees silenced the birds that were cheerfully greeting the morning just moments before. Slung over his shoulder was a finely stitched leather case that protected his M-16 from the branches and brush that now caught at him as he plunged through the fragile spring growth. The morning rays of the sun danced to the tune of the gentle breeze in elongated distortion under his steps as he made the now familiar trip to the outcropping of rock that overlooked the winding river below.

He paused for a moment to suck in the thin mountain air, feeling its cold bite as it filled his lungs. Although he trained his body for the rigors of the hike, he was still training his mind to overcome the anxiety of the hunt. Perspiration beaded on his forehead and his hands were clammy. He brushed the sweat from his brow with his shirtsleeve and wiped his hands on his pants as he peered through the newly budding branches that rose above the rocks.

From a pocket he pulled a headband and positioned it on his forehead to prevent perspiration from getting into his eyes. The chill in the spring morning made him all too aware of the nervous sweat. He then dealt with the hassle of tugging on the exquisite hunting gloves, thrusting the fingers of one hand into the webs of the fingers of the other. He was keenly aware of the time as he glanced at his watch.

Below him, the river was rushing from the cascading falls below Hawthorne Manor and broadening into the swells that the valley allowed. About a quarter of a mile further downstream, there was another series of step down falls and the river constricted once again into narrows, creating not only white water rapids but also dangerous undercurrents as it plunged through the last ravine before the valley spread out toward Oak Meadow. From there the river spread out in the wide valley becoming ten miles of lazy waterway winding through the cluttered riverfront of Crystal Springs before winding through the mountains to Edgewater, another twenty miles downriver.

He slung the case to the center of his back, braced himself before hefting himself up on the first outcrop. He hesitated a moment to regain his balance before crawling across the top to peer over the side. He would never get used to the fear that rushed through him at this point. He peered between two boulders that were locked in an ancient embrace and could see the river below.

After taking several deep breaths that should have calmed his nerves but didn't, he pulled a wooden object from the inside pocket of his parka and studied it briefly before carefully securing it into the V made by the fused rock. He leaned back a moment, aligning the wood with the river below. It was all about trajectory. He heaved a sigh and then reached out and tested the support the rocks provided for the block of wood with the swivel securely screwed into place.

He'd spent weeks studying the habits of his prey and getting the math right. He eyeballed the line of fire again. With the spring coming and the activity on the mountain increasing with the end of the brutal winter, he was running out of time. If he did not act now, he would lose his chance to act at all.

He swung the case from his shoulder and laid it on top of the waist-high boulder. As he leaned forward he thrust his arm out so he could see the face of his watch. With an ominous intensity he unzipped the case and pulled out the rifle, stroking it almost affectionately before attaching it to the stabilizing mechanism screwed into the wood.

He heard the familiar sound on the gentle morning breeze and his head jerked up quickly. He looked through the canopy of tender leaves and his heartbeat quickened as he caught first sight of his prey coming toward him along Sutter Trail below. Although it would be several minutes before his target was in his crosshairs, he felt the urgency.

The sun flashed off the rich bronze coat as his prey made the tight curve along the path effortlessly. He waited while the twists and turns were taken with powerful grace and beauty that always impressed him. He felt a twinge of sorrow that such beauty would be destroyed, but there was no other option left to him now. He checked the swivel pin on the handmade gun stand and tested the movement back and forth by fixing the sight carefully and tracking his mark skillfully through the high-powered scope.

There was no wind this morning. The tender new twigs in the trees above him were still. It was so quiet the sound of the river rose to his ears and seemed to synchronize its flow to the rhythm to his rapidly approaching target.

"Such a creature of habit," he murmured with a self-satisfied smile. He could hear the deep growl as the graceful rush of bronze passed below him. He moved the laser crosshair from the side of the sleek body and locked the scope onto the flank as he held his breath and his finger began squeezing the trigger.

Nicole Emerson paused at the crest of the last rise in the well worn path between the Manor and the glade. The Emersons were nothing if not pragmatic in the naming of their holdings. Their Scot and French heritage seemed to be in play wherever they were. Hawthorne Manor, named for the wild flower indigenous to the area was usually referred to as simply The Manor. Much like the MacIntosh Lodge. Once the only trading post between the colonies and the great wilderness it had first been known as Journey's End Trading Post. The name was changed to Journey's Inn around the turn of the nineteenth century when the Upper Lodge was built and the Inn expanded. Now, into its third century in the family holdings, it was known most commonly as just The Lodge.

She took in the scene, listening intently for any indication that the workers had arrived. She could hear nothing but the birds in the trees greeting the new morning. She stepped from the path into the high side of the meadow where it sloped toward the river. She paused to catch her breath and watched the river a moment as it flowed easily past, cresting occasionally in the gentle breeze.

She turned her attention back to The glade and heaved a heavy sigh of contentment. The tall grass, still brown from the winter, had been flattened by the unrelenting movement of the bull dozers, dump trucks, and workers' vehicles. The heavy equipment was lined up across the glade at the end of the newly cut road like monstrous metal creatures, waiting for their next chance to get at a piece of the mountain.

There was still the cove to be excavated and then graded and huge piles of gravel had been brought in the day before and dumped in strategic spots along the freshly cut gash that would soon be a real drive coming into the site from the old highway on the back side of the mountain. In the early morning light, the equipment had a surreal dewy sheen that belied the dirt encrusted treads of their tires, the dust-covered metal of their bodies and the ear splitting noise they brought to the glade.

Nicole crossed to the small modular shed that was being used as a construction office at the moment and would be a garden shed when the house was complete. She opened the unlocked door and then reached for the inside of the frame, using it as leverage to pull herself in. She stood for a moment over the blue prints, spread out over the drafting table, and studied the plans.

She breathed in a deep breath and let it out slowly. She had been living at The Manor for almost a year and a half. She could not have known what she was getting herself into when she was caught up in the whirlwind romance across the northern provinces of Italy, but she had adjusted her lifestyle as much as she was willing to what was expected of her as the newest addition to the Emerson clan.

She pushed the thoughts of The Manor and the family from her mind as she turned and hopped out of the shed. Between herself and the river, she could see the stakes and iridescent orange string outlining the footprint of their new house. She took a short breath and trudged to the house site. She paused for a moment studying the outline.

The trees that had been felled were in various stages of recycling. The hardwood had been separated from the pulp and some of the older, more gnarled and mature trees were being cut up for firewood. The younger trees, those with fewer branches and straighter trunks were going to be milled for later use.

She walked along the outer perimeter of the string, making her way around the charred remains of the limbs, branches, and leaves that had been burned, and wound up at the far end where the freshly graded dirt was soft under her feet. There was a new towering pile of tree limbs and branches with wilting leaves drying up and dying in the glade to be burned.

If there was one thing the Emersons and the MacIntoshes had in common, it was how to make the best use of the mountains' resources. Little would go to waste. The trees that had come down to build the new house would be added to the next MacIntosh milling. Nothing would go to waste.

As she came full circle back to the shed, Nicole made sure the door had latched before turning back toward The Manor. She stood in the center of the glade and pulled her camera from her jogging suit pocket. She started snapping pictures for her scrapbook.

With a heavy sigh, she headed back, in no hurry to return to the family dynamics but she needed to get into the shop. She had received notice the afternoon before of a shipment arriving at the warehouse that had been unpacked, inspected, and logged into inventory. The consignment would be transferred to the shop and needed to be unpacked.

Nicole made unintentional rivals and discovered unexpected allies in the Emerson family mix. The problem to her was the presence of rivals and allies in a family at all. Nothing in her life as an only child prepared her for it. She felt the heaviness of heart and subtle dread begin to nag at her as she thought about returning to The Manor. Her morning jaunts along the garden trails began soon after moving in and now she added a daily trip through the garden paths and along the mountain trails to the site. Her escapes were blessed respites from the drama of the family relationships. She was giving her best effort to understand and relate to Cameron's family, but she didn't think she was doing a very good job. She could always feel the eyes watching and the ears listening.

Nicole picked up her pace as she glanced at her watch and was soon jogging slowly back to The Manor. The trail carried her along the path of the river for quite a while before it veered back into the woods. She felt the wave of nausea sweep over her just as she reached the orchards at the back of the estate and could feel the nagging headache taking hold of her again as well. They were becoming her daily companions.

Trevor Cantrell shifted the thick leather strap of his test case from his hand onto his shoulder, shrugging it to his back to ride alongside his rifle as he followed the mountain trail over the tunnel that had been cut through the mountain for the old county road. Sutter Trail had once been a foot trail through the upper pass of the mountains, following the river's path into the valley. Horses gave way to wagons and eventually, when the road was cut through for the first automobiles, it was the path of least resistance.

He'd already been out for an hour, leaving the cabin just as morning light was beginning to thin the darkness. He was so familiar with the routes leading to his well established test sites he needed very little light to navigate. Each morning, as the spring crept onto the mountain and the days became longer, he was able to leave earlier and expand his test area into the late afternoon.

Below him, Sutter Trail was obscured by the rising mist that was boiling out of the cold mountain spring water into the warmer morning air. From this vantage point he could see how the blacktop followed the side of the mountain, making a loop and turning back under itself as it descended the mountainside. Farther down he could see the road as it straightened out and disappeared into the next tunnel before it traveled alongside the narrows.

He left the trail behind following a stream as it cascaded along the ancient creek bed, plunging off the edge of the mountainside, and dropping in a twenty foot waterfall. Trevor stopped at the edge, watching with an awe that never waned as he stared down at the scene.

This stream had rushed from the upper elevations for eons, bringing the thawing snows to the lower elevations, exposing the huge boulders more each spring. The rock around the top of the waterfall was now a smooth mantle. He studied the whirlpool created in the surreal morning light. It was an ever changing view that mesmerized him.

From the top of the flat boulder, a footbridge was secured by massive steel rings and threaded cabling to both the rock, the surrounding ground and tied off around ancient tree trunks on both sides of the river. The work was a novelty of the MacIntoshes. Since the only other way to get across the river was either driving down to Oak Meadow or up to The Lodge, the bridge was a godsend when his advisory committee suggested he should include testing from both sides of the river to defend his masters thesis.

The sun was just peaking over the mountain crest behind him as he stepped from the solid foundation of the boulder onto the suspension bridge. He paused as it dipped slightly under his weight and gave himself a few seconds to sync his balance to the slight swaying. As he left the shady side of the river and made his way downstream, the thin sheen of morning dew that had collected on his outer garments sparkled like tiny crystals in the climbing sun.

He shifted his gear, allowing the test case to tumble from his back, lifting his arm to catch it in the crook of his elbow in one practiced movement. He fell into a steady pace as he moved along the trail, taking mental note of the fresh footprints of animals in the soft forest ground. They were his best guide to locate new waterways. The melting snow found innumerable ways down the mountain.

He hefted his shoulder, repositioning the rifle on his back and shook himself slightly, pausing from time to time to orient himself to his surroundings. He found landmarks and took his time trekking through the unfamiliar territory to locate all the necessities of surviving in the wild – shelters with no sign of animal presence that would be safe during sudden storms, and evidence of dry creek beds he could expect to find active as the spring rains came but could be used as safe conduit through the mountains during dry spells.

He watched for the tributary streams where he established the new test sites and systematically took his samples. Last week he tracked the first stream into the high country and came out just east of The Lodge. Then he tracked the stream down river, discovering it meandered along to another tributary. At some point he would track that tributary back to its source, but for the moment, he was still mapping the original waterway. About a quarter of a mile down, this waterway went underground for another quarter mile before resurfacing just above the narrows and making a less than dramatic entrance into the river than the waterfall behind him.

He made his way purposely along the trail, seeing the stream as it converged along the same ridge and into the creek bed along side. He studied the stream's course with a practiced eye, evaluating the water's flow rate without a conscious thought. He spotted his test site number W28 and made his way purposely toward it.

He placed his case in the clump of winter dry grass where he had created a nest for it. He flipped the top open with a skillful ease and reached for the next empty test tube, already prepped and ready. Wrapping his left arm around the strong trunk of a sapling, he leaned out over the rushing water of the mountain stream, lowering the tube just enough to capture a sampling of the water tumbling merrily over the rocks, scattered limbs, and branches that were collecting along the banks with the spring thaw. With trained ease he pulled a plastic cap from his parka pocket, popped it into the test tube and grabbed his shirt tail that he left dangling below his parka to use as a drying towel. He then dropped the tube back into its spot in his test kit.

As he reached to pull the case cover closed, an unmistakable sound became a thundering echo across the mountains around him. His head shot up as he instinctively snapped the kit closed and secured the clasp, pulled it from its nest, and mechanically rose to his feet in one decisive movement, falling unconsciously into the combat mode that had become second nature to him.

He shifted all his gear instinctively, allowing the rifle to drop from where it rested over his back into the crook of his elbow, shifting his backpack more squarely between his shoulders, and pulling the strap of his test case on top of his left shoulder. His hand reached backwards for the stock of the rifle in the same fluid motion that brought the weapon into ready position. His eyes searched the immediate area around him from a deep seeded training as his mind was processing the fact that a rifle shot had traveled some distance before reaching his highly trained ear.

Right on the heels of the fading echo of the shot, a cacophony of noise screamed through the mountains. It took a moment for him to realize what it was, but as the realization hit him, he left the stream and plunged off the trail, pausing only a moment to verify his bearings before heading toward the river. He moved differently now, traveling through rough terrain and unknown areas. With quick, defensive actions that watched for any movement around him in the woods, he arrived at the river's edge on a bluff high above it. With inherent intuition and innate training, he began moving downstream, making his way carefully around the natural obstacles along the way until he reached an animal trail that he knew would take him to the river's edge in the most direct way.

৩~৫

The Sniper saw rather than heard the back tire explode before he heard the sound of the shot echo off the adjacent mountain and charge back at him, obscuring the sound of what happened below. He watched as the Jaguar jerked violently to the right, heading directly into the rock face of the mountain. He cursed and dropped the rifle; not even hearing the sickening grating of the weapon as it slid down the ragged rock to the dirt at the base of the outcrop. As the Jag grazed the rock face below with a sickening sound of metal screeching against stone, he crawled higher up the boulder for a better view of the drama playing out below.

He held his breath as the Jag veered sharply back to the left. Obviously, the wheel was yanked in an effort to regain control. He could see the mangled passenger side, the freshly carved gashes gleaming bright silver through the customized bronze paint. The Sniper closed his eyes as the hub cap started rolling along the road and the wheel hub tore into the pavement with flying sparks and a metallic scream as the tire was shredded. The repeating thud of the flapping rubber hitting both the road and the car chassis followed the echoing of the collision through the mountains. He watched in silent relief as the car left the blacktop. The shriek of the Jag tearing through the metal railing joined the earsplitting noise and bounced back at him in accusing intensity.

His breathing became labored; sweat poured from his forehead, soaking the headband and dripping down the side of his face as the Jag became airborne. Inertia propelled it off the mountainside and out over the river. The car seemed to hang in mid-air for a heartbeat. In that moment, the condemning echoes rumbled away, leaving the mountain eerily still except for the sound of the rushing river. Time seemed to stand still as he watched the front end begin to dip and then the car dropped like a stone.

He exhaled sharply as the Jaguar fell below his line of vision. As the car hit the surface of the water it sounded like a second gunshot with renewed echoes rising from the ravine. The Sniper caught sight of the car again downstream and watched as the river sucked at it, the current snatching it and drawing the car into a macabre spin as though playing with a newfound toy.

The car made a one hundred eighty degree turn and for a fraction of a second, an optical illusion caused it to appear to be coming back upriver toward him. He felt bile rising in his throat as the reflections of the sun caught spots on the car, sending out flashes of light that were blinding. He raised his hand to shield his eyes and watched intently as the undercurrent of the river continued sucking it under.

The Sniper realized sweat soaked his shirt as he backed down off the boulder and pulled at the gun mount to dislodge it. As he pulled it free, the gloves caused him to lose his grip on it and it toppled over the boulder. He cursed as he leaned out over the cliff watching as the mount hit an outcropping of shale and he heard the wood splinter, the sound of the metal swivel clattering on stone before bouncing again, rolling end over end until he lost sight of it. He hesitated only a moment before scrambling off the boulder, retrieving his rifle and shoving it back into the case. He was soon retracing his steps in a headlong rush through the branches and twigs that seemed to be reaching out to grab at him.

He glanced at his watch. He was less careful making his way once he reached familiar ground. He picked up his pace. He'd made the return trek in nine minutes fifteen seconds this morning. It had to be the adrenaline rushing through him. He spotted the rock formation he knew all too well and climbed up the first scattering of rocks to a natural enclosure hidden among the formation.

Sitting open in the space was an old metal guitar case. He'd bought the guitar from a pawn shop when he was in college. He pulled the rifle from the case and broke it down, placing the pieces quickly into the case. At the base of one of the larger rocks was the gaping hole he'd dug out once he realized there was only one thing to do. He shoved the rifle and guitar case into the hole under the rock, then pushed the large clods of dirt mixed with dead leaves and smaller stones into the cavity and over the case.

He crawled out of the rock formation, glancing around quickly to make sure no one was around and then made his way away from the area as quickly as he could, moving through the morning shadows with a practiced nonchalance and carefully affected ease. He was again nothing more than another early morning hiker along the many scenic trails.

CHAPTER TWO

Nicole sank onto the weathered concrete garden bench and closed her eyes, leaning her face carefully against the rough bark of the tree beside it. She took several deep breaths, raising her hand up to wipe her brow and then wiping her hand on her pants' leg. She lifted her head from the tree and tilted it backwards, willing the nausea away. She could taste the bile as she swallowed hard and then heaved a heavy sigh of relief as the nausea eased and her head quit spinning.

She would pay a price for her jog back from the glade. She opened her eyes and struggled to her feet as she brushed the seat of her pants, beginning to feel the morning dew that was soaking through. She made her way through the apple orchard and to the gate into the back gardens. There was new straw packed down in the beds. In a few weeks Douglas would supervise the grounds men as they uncovered the beds. The conservatory would be emptied of the plants and flowers that were carefully tended through the deadly winter. Soon the beds would become vibrant mazes of spring flowers.

She made her way along the garden paths and their Halloweenish specters of hay and ghostly trellises in the formal garden. These were filled with evergreens and once the threat of frost was over, blooming plants and flowers would be woven into their midst to bring summer joy to the area. The paths here were cobblestone, so her pace was slowed as she made her way to the lower level entrance and the east wing of The Manor. As she carefully crossed the stones, she noticed that several of them had been dug up and reset, the new sand a stark contrast to the older, weathered mortar. By the time they were using the gardens, the repairs to the cobblestones would be barely noticeable.

Nicole shivered slightly as she pulled open the heavy, metal studded door in the south turret, pausing a moment before making her way up the stairs that protruded from the outer wall like some Hollywood set. The first time she saw the turrets, she fancied she would soon see Errol Flynn and Basil Rathborn's exaggerated shadows in a duel of swords. During one of the generations since the building of the replica of a Scottish castle in the early 1800s, wrought iron banisters were added to the stairway for safety. The deeply worn stone steps, however, were still subject to the damp and Nicole had slipped more than once, banging her chin into the sharp edges.

She made her way to the first landing, scotching her heel against the wall before tugging at the other massive door. Since the opposite side of the wing belonged to Sadie, Cam's older sister who spent most of her time overseas, she and Cameron usually had the floor to themselves. Still, there was something about the ancient design and materials imported from Scotland, along with the stories the Emerson kids loved to tell about hidden passages, dungeons, and secret rooms that made her uncertain that someone wasn't always near.

Once inside their suite, she took a deep breath and began stripping off the damp jogging suit as she crossed to the dressing room. The house had gone through extensive renovations over the years and what was once a bedroom was now a massive bathroom with all the modern amenities anyone could want.

She turned on the shower and as she waited for the water to heat, she gathered a towel and her robe and slippers from her closet. With a deep groan of satisfaction, she stepped under the warm spray and stood as the hot water filled the shower stall with a warm steam that engulfed her in a world of muffled solitude allowing her to escape all things. When she felt the water beginning to cool, she reached for the soap and her washcloth, breaking the spell of the steam and turning her mind to what she needed to accomplish that day,

As she stepped from the shower, she pulled the plush, oversized towel, custom made in one of the textile mills recently opened under the Emerson banner in Germany, from the towel rack and wrapped it around herself. She pulled a smaller towel over her head, bending forward to catch the heavy, wet hair in a practiced twist that landed on top of her head. She was tucking the back edges under when the nausea returned with a vengeance she was unable to force back. With a lunge across the room, she dropped to the floor, hanging her head over the toilet just before she lost everything that was on her stomach.

"You okay?" Mae asked, coming into the bathroom and grabbing a wash cloth she wrung out under cold water.

Mae Chandler had been with her as long as she could remember. She was first a housekeeper for Janet and Drake Quinn before Nicole was born and after Nicole came along, with her parents traveling the globe on buying trips, Mae became her second mother.

Nicole reached for the washcloth and sat back on her haunches, staring at the wall behind the toilet as she waited to see if the bout of nausea was over.

"I think so," Nicole said, wiping her mouth with the cloth and then rolling over onto the floor.

"You went jogging this morning," Mae stated, her expression leaving no question about her disapproval.

"No," Nicole replied shortly before she could restrain her irritation. "Not really," she amended in a softer tone as she got to her feet and followed Mae into the bedroom. "How did you get in here?" she asked as she dropped onto the edge of the bed.

"It's a yes or no question," Mae said evenly.

She pulled the pillows from the bed, setting them on the chaise lounge near the window and was pulling the sheets up and straightening them out as Nicole got up and moved toward the antique Queen Anne wardrobe that towered ten feet against one wall. It was one of the few pieces she brought to The Manor when she moved in.

"I jogged through the back garden," Nicole admitted, pulling her panties on and then her bra. "That place creeps me out. I don't know what it is about it…"

"Once they finish the road, you might think about driving around to the house site."

"It's so much quicker through the woods though," Nicole sighed returning to the closet and standing in front of the hanging clothes, deciding what to wear. She reached for a pair of jeans and a comfortable sweater.

"You *are* going to come across a bear on the trail one of these days," Mae called. Nicole could hear Mae's practiced fluffing as she placed the pillows on the bed before dragging the bedspread across them.

There was no point in confessing to her once childhood nanny and now personal attendant that had already happened. As she rounded a turn in the trail last summer where a bank of wild blackberries grew she came upon a young cub enjoying the first fruits. Her startled scream turned out to be the recommended action for the occasion.

"Don't forget you have to take your car in for service," Mae said as she joined Nicole in the closet and opened the two hampers sitting side by side beneath the window. She pulled the handful of Nicole's dirty laundry from the depth of one and dropped it on top of Cameron's in the second hamper before scooping it up and heading toward the hallway door.

"Cam took it in," Nicole said off handedly. "I wasn't sure I'd be going anywhere when I woke up this morning."

"The shrimp last night?" Mae asked, raising an eyebrow before opening the door.

"Yeah," Nicole nodded, crossing the space between them and kissing Mae's cheek with a slight smile. "That's as good an excuse as any."

༄

Riva, the Emerson housekeeper, looked up from her preparation for lunch as Richard Weston pushed through the back door. She smiled and nodded slightly as he tossed his empty water bottle into the trash bin and reached for the towel tucked into his waistband and mopped the slight sheen of sweat from his face.

"Have a good run?" she asked as he crossed the kitchen toward the back hallway that would take him to the third floor and the suite he shared with Holly, the oldest Emerson child.

"Very," Richard said with his charming smile breaking across his face. "Three trips around the north lawn is exactly two miles. I see that Douglas has been doing some repairs."

"This wet winter has been hard on the gardens," Riva said with a heavy sigh. "He thinks we've lost several of the hedges along that north end."

She moved a step out of the way as he stopped at the kitchen sink to wash his hands. No one else would have dared get in her way in her kitchen, but he was one of her favorites.

Richard had been married for six years to Holly, the eldest Emerson child, who was known more for her free spirit and love of the jet-setting life than anything else. To the family's disappointment, he had been unable to tame her wild ways. She spent her time with friends neither of her parents approved of while enjoying the trust fund she inherited from her grandfather when she reached her thirtieth birthday.

Richard and Holly met on New Year's Day morning in a small cafe on the Seine in Paris. She was one of the few in the "City of Lights" who did not appear to be hung over and completely wiped out from the New Year's Eve festivities of the night before. Richard was with a Belgium company and had just arrived in the city as advance mad for a conference that was to begin the following day. He stopped at the café for breakfast and his life changed forever.

Holly Noel Emerson was someone who could never be described, she had to be experienced. There was no understanding or explaining her. Some, the more gracious and forgiving, called her a free spirit and bohemian. Others, the ones who made the mistake of crossing her or even worse – boring her – called her other things that were usually unrepeatable in polite company.

Richard managed what no one else had. He did not bore Holly, though no one who spent time with him could completely understand why. When Holly brought him home the following Christmas, everyone in The Manor was stunned. He was not covered in tattoos, there were no outstanding arrest warrants on him, and he had never made the news in spite of the fact they had been seeing each other exclusively since they met.

With the skill that only Holly possessed to keep her private life private, she kept Richard to herself. Holly discovered the secret of the world's truly elite. As much as celebrities complained about the invasion of their privacy and the constant attention received with their images splashed across the covers of rag sheets and magazines, it was their life's blood – or at least their career's life's blood.

Holly managed to avoid the world's paparazzi because she never let her travel plans be known. She considered herself a citizen of the world, and she traveled under several passports issued to her due to her status as a member of the Board of Directors of the Emerson Foundation on the private jets of friends. She thought of it all as a globe hopping game. Every morning when she got up, she put on a character as though her life was a play and she was always the star.

Holly hit on the subterfuge when she was sent as an Ambassador of the Foundation to the tiny African country of Eritrea. With the language barrier, there were problems translating her name to the children. After several futile attempts by the translator to teach the children her name, Holly pulled a ring from her finger and shown it to the children. It was a ring of delicately etched gold holly leaves with tiny ruby clusters as berries, given to her by Cameron one Christmas. The translator chose an indigenous vine similar to holly and thus she received her first pseudonym which translated back to English as Ivy in the press release of the country's press secretary.

The story was published because of the human interest behind it. It also gave Emerson International some cover. With a few carefully placed stories in publications of little interest outside of a small groups of people directly involved in obscure charities and causes, celebrity hunters concluded that when Holly dropped off the radar, as she did often and for extended periods of time, she was probably in some remote area taking care of the Foundation business.

Richard was an international financier who specialized in market analysis and had a source of income of his own, also an exception for the men Holly usually brought home. They were married in a very private ceremony in the small chapel on The Manor grounds on New Year's Day, the first anniversary of their meeting. After a few months of globetrotting to Holly's favorite haunts, they returned to Oak Meadow.

Richard planned to settle down and have a family but Holly's wander lust that seemed to be a part of her DNA boiled over and she took off. She would be gone for a few weeks or months at first, coming home sporadically for family birthdays and holidays. As they settled into their marriage and Richard accepted a position with Emerson International, her trips away from home became progressively longer in length.

Richard began lending a hand with the long range planning and then the Emerson International expansion into the European market. Within the first few years following their marriage, he became Gregory's right hand. In the years since, he had become an integral part of not only the family, but the company as well.

Holly had not been home in several years, now. Not since she came home for Christmas and got into an ugly argument with Vanessa, Garret's new bride. Vanessa was a no-nonsense social climber who expected to be first lady of the state sooner rather than later; and First Lady of the land at some point down the road. Everything about Holly irritated Vanessa, especially her irresponsible habits and cavalier attitude about the family image. In the typical Holly reaction, she canceled her plans and hung around The Manor for the express purpose of making Vanessa's life miserable.

While on a white water river rafting trip at The Lodge, Holly spotted a college student who was doing an internship with the Mackintoshes. Nate Caulder became the perfect toy and ploy for Holly to drive Vanessa over the edge, who finally packed up, with Garret's blessing, and went on a vacation with her sister. With Vanessa gone, Holly quickly became bored and it wasn't long before they awoke one morning to find her gone.

There was great surprise, however, when it was discovered that Nate left with her. He called the registrar's office and told them he was leaving the country and planned to continue his studies overseas. He told them he had the chance to do an internship in the mountains of Spain and could not turn it down.

Richard stripped his jogging suit off and tossed it into the laundry hamper inside his dressing room. He turned on the shower, stepping under the cold spray to shake the heat of the run from his body and then breathed a deep sigh of contentment as the cold water turned to a steamy spray.

Within half an hour, he stepped from his suite, dress shirt crisply starched, pants crease razor sharp, with the only casualness about his appearance being his unbuttoned shirt. After he ate breakfast, he would put on his tie. With a final glance in the full length mirror across from the door to their suite, he started down the hallway toward the back stairs. A slight noise caught his attention and he stopped, lifting his head to indentify the sound and then walking toward the front foyer.

≫≪

Gregory Emerson stood on the catwalk outside the penthouse offices of Emerson Plaza overlooking the atrium below. He glanced at his watch, twisting it absently and turned to walk back into the conference room and pressed the intercom button on the phone, waiting until Ellen's voice responded to the page.

"Yes sir," her voice came through the speaker.

"Have you heard anything from Cameron?"

"No sir. I've called him twice in the last twenty minutes," Cameron's assistant announced.

Gregory glanced at the bank of clocks on the wall. There was one for each global time zone. Cameron should have been there and it wasn't like him not to call if he was delayed.

"Thank you, Ellen," Gregory replied absently as he pressed the button again to disconnect the line. He reached for the handset and pressed a speed dial button. He heard Cameron's cell phone ring once and go straight to voice mail. With a sigh, he pressed the intercom again and Ellen instantly answered.

"Call Joan and have her bring me Cam's file. I need to brief it in case he's not here when the meeting starts."

Gregory headed back to his office and settled into his chair. Reaching for the phone he pressed in a number. The phone on the other end was answered during the first ring.

"Stafford County Sheriff's Office, this is Connie."

"Connie, this is Gregory Emerson," he announced as he leaned back in his chair and glanced at the clock positioned prominently on his desk.

"Good morning, Mr. Emerson, how are you?"

"I'm fine, thank you, but I've lost Cameron. He drove in this morning and should have been here by now. We've been trying to call. He was bringing his car in for service and I'm wondering if he ran into some car trouble on the Trail. His cell phone is going straight to voice mail. Do you have someone who could check it out to make sure he's not stranded in one of the dead spots and in need of a tow?"

"Of course, sir," Connie replied as soon as he paused to take a breath. "We'll check it out."

"Thanks, dear," Gregory said absently as he reached for the thick file as Ellen entered his office. He was already turning his focus to the meeting that might have to start without Cameron.

In Oak Meadow, Connie heard the dial tone as Gregory disconnected the line and she dropped the receiver back onto the phone. She looked up to see Jake standing in the door of his office where he appeared when he heard Gregory's name.

"Mr. Gregory asked if someone can see if Mr. Cameron might be broken down on the Trail."

"Check with the units... if nobody spotted him coming through town have Jane run up the Trail and see if he's stranded."

Jane Adler left her patrolling along the streets where vacation homes offered a varied collection of everything from single-wide mobile homes to expensive gated communities and headed out of town toward the river. She was the rookie on the Stafford County Sheriff's force and this was a rookie's errand.

She was out of Oak Meadow in a matter of blocks where the road changed from the wide double lane quickly into a narrowed mountain road that often demanded one vehicle to pull over to allow another room to pass as it wound through the vast Emerson estate.

Jane graduated among the top two percent of her class from the university with a criminal justice degree and the Emerson International's security detail tried hard to recruit her, but she opted for Jake Clairborne's department instead. She had her eye on state law enforcement and believed that one day very soon Garret Emerson would be governor. She was hooking her wagon to the Emerson star and definitely could see a gubernatorial detail in her future. It was a judgment call, but she was betting it would be easier to move from the Stafford County Sheriff's office into state law enforcement than from the private sector.

She headed out of Oak Meadow along Sutter Trail and made her way up the torturous mountain road. As she made the sharp turn just above the river's descent into the narrows, a sick gnawing feeling started her stomach churning as she spotted the jagged tearing in the asphalt and then the hole in the guardrail.

She eased her squad car to the side of the road, mindful of the fact others from The Manor might be coming along. She pressed a button and the soft glow of the hazards lights danced on the top of her squad car. She reached for her radio as she crossed the upcoming lane and stood at the edge of the pavement. The quiet of the mountain was disturbed only by the twittering of birds in the tops of the trees and the murmur of the river rushing along below, offering a bizarre contrast to the ghastly hole ripped through the guard rail leaving an uncommon unobstructed view of the river below.

She spotted the fresh scrapes on the rock face as she turned around and crossed the road to run her hand along the newly scarred stone, glancing back over her shoulder. She could see the flecks of bronze paint once she looked closely. She crossed the road again, stepping as gingerly as she could onto the shoulder along the bluff over the river and clicked her radio twice to see if she could raise Connie. She stared over the edge, knowing before she did, she would not see anything. There was an outcrop of rock and then a steep drop-off into the river.

"Come in," she heard Connie's voice from the radio, eerily floating away on the rising wind moving through the river ravine.

"Connie," Jane said, cupping her hand around her mouth and speaking directly into the microphone to cut the interference as much as possible, "I'm about three miles up Sutter Trail. Alert the rescue team. Everything indicates that we have a car in the river up here."

Jake stopped in mid-stride as he crossed the room, turning to listen to the static filled transmission. As he left the room, he heard Connie on one frequency alerting the other deputies and he returned to his office to call the fire station across the street to sound the alarm.

Charlotte A. Minga

CHAPTER THREE

Nicole Emerson emerged from the suite and paused at the top of the sweeping stairs to listen to the early morning activity of Hawthorne Manor. She knew her father-in-law had already left for the office; she'd heard the helicopter as it swooped down to the helipad on the south lawn on her way through the gardens. She inhaled quietly as she wondered where her mother-in-law was. The house seemed still, but she knew better. The Manor never really slept. She was never really alone.

Gregory and Helena Emerson seemed formidable to Nicole. She still felt the watchful and wary eyes of the entire Emerson clan. As far as some of them were concerned, she blew in like a bad wind and swept Cameron away from the plans they had for him as far as a wife was concerned. Although they were cordial and appeared accepting, Nicole felt as though she was always on review and never meeting their expectations for the wife of an Emerson heir.

Her trip to the site had taken a toll on her and she was not feeling at all well this morning. Her large gray eyes were magnified in her pale, drawn face as she took the first steps down the foyer's sweeping staircase. She grasped hold of the banister to steady herself and took a deep breath to try to stymie the nausea.

The grand staircase was a double stairway, curving from the east and west wings, merging at the mezzanine as one flight to the first landing inside the massive entrance hall. A thick burgundy carpet runner cushioned her steps, shielding her for the moment from those in the house, but she could not escape the watchful eyes of the Emerson and MacIntosh ancestors peering at her from the portraits along the upper gallery; their stiff, formal faces and some whose eyes followed her every move with obvious disapproval. Nicole was amazed at how confined and restricted she could feel in a house that could hold its own with any royal estate of any existing monarchy.

At the bottom of the stairs she paused to stare out of the heavy leaded windows that flanked the double front doors. The lawn spread out from the house farther than she could see, with carefully maintained beds and ancient trees that stood like sentinels lining up to protect the winding drive that meandered up through the manicured front lawn more than a half mile from the stone entrance. Tall metal gates always prevented the real world from invading the Emerson realm and it was more and more common to see teams of Emerson International guards manning the stone gatehouse these days. She felt the twinge of nausea hit her again and she sighed deeply.

"Thinking of making a run for it?"

Nicole gasped and whirled around, seeing her brother-in-law, Richard, leaning against the doorjamb of the back hall. She did not know he was in the front wing of the house and felt a flush as it rose from her neck into her ashen face. Most of the family moved about through the back halls and staircases, but Nicole was unsettled by the stone staircases in the turrets as well as the long, dark, halls that linked the three floors and four wings of the house. She preferred the sunny openness of the foyer.

Richard was a tall, thin man with blonde hair, fair skin and gentle manners that always put Nicole at ease. He was dressed in his suit pants and dress shirt which told Nicole two things. First, he was done with his morning run along the winding paved paths through the extensive back gardens; and secondly, he had not had breakfast or he would have his tie on and his suit coat in his hand. He was as predictable as the loud ticking of the enormous grandfather clock on the mezzanine above. She caught the subtle sardonic look in his eyes at her expression and wondered what he read on her face.

"You're still here!" he commented, stepping aside to allow her to leave the stairs and join him in the hall. "I thought I saw you leaving for the shop."

Nicole sighed softly and returned his smile, reaching behind her head to gather the long, thick blue-black tresses over her shoulder. "I'm just really not feeling well and Cam had an early meeting."

Richard quickly became her favorite among her new relatives. He had an easy charm and a personality that made her feel she had always known him. He seemed more a son to Holly's parents than she was a daughter. He was vice president of Emerson International's export division. His expertise in international trade and finance was legendary. He was given credit for much of the company's phenomenal success in the international expansion of the last few years.

After experiencing the dominating hierarchy of the Emerson clan, as well as Vanessa's combative and acerbic personality, along with Andrea's childish jealousy, Nicole had to admit she could sympathize with her husband's oldest sister even though she had yet to meet her. She wished more than once she could just pack up and take off for a while.

Nicole was an only child and had come along later in life for Drake and Janet Quinn. As gregarious and outgoing as the Emersons were, her parents were quiet and tranquil. They were always calm. No matter what was going on around them, there was a stoic steadiness and sober mindedness she had taken as the norm until she began moving out into the world and discovered they were the exception, not the rule.

Not only was she not used to the dynamics of a large family of six competitive siblings, but she had also been raised with a more independent attitude. While Gregory Emerson carefully plotted the future of not only his business empire but also each of his children's careers with as much attention to detail and execution; her parents allowed her to chart her own course and follow her own aspirations. She learned that was something never considered in the Emerson clan.

Sadie, Cameron's second oldest sister spent most of her time in the Zurich office and Nicole barely knew her or her husband, Ben Faraday. They came home for holidays and family events, but those only ramped up the kinetic energy of The Manor. When the Emersons filled the house from rafters to basement, it was an experience that left Nicole completely overwhelmed.

Thank goodness Garret and Vanessa were now living in the capital where he was being groomed for political office as a junior partner in one of the state's most prestigious law firms. Vanessa was the consummate politician's wife and spent every spare moment at some event that would enhance their political ambitions. Garret was destined in Gregory's grand scheme to be governor of the state as soon as he was old enough. Gregory was doing everything within the law, and his significant influence, wealth, and power to see that it happened.

Kyle and Andrea, the youngest Emerson siblings, were "Irish twins" born a scant eleven months apart. They were enjoying their college experiences to the fullest and were seldom at home longer than was required for them to fulfill their duties to family unity and support. Nicole couldn't remember the last time they stayed overnight in their first floor wing of the house. Both were living on campus in Crystal Springs.

Richard understood her difficulty in adjusting to the Emerson clan. What the family considered close, she found smothering. He always offered her encouragement without causing her to feel disloyal to Cameron. When she arrived so unceremoniously and unexpectedly as Cameron's bride the year before, Richard was the only family member who was not openly suspicious of her.

She was seen as a conniving woman who seduced the heir to the Emerson Empire. Helena and Gregory were unable to completely conceal their alarm at Cameron's impetuous rush to the altar. It had not helped that she stood firm in her determination that there would not be a second marriage ceremony to satisfy her in-laws.

Cameron took the battle in hand but there was open disappointment and concealed resentment that there would be no formal wedding for Cameron. Nicole agreed to a wedding reception and soon discovered why Cameron insisted on them eloping. The lavish affair – spread over three days – was more than she could have imagined in her worst nightmares.

In the months following her arrival at Hawthorne Manor, she believed she gained their respect and acceptance, but the awkwardness of their beginning still hindered their relationships. Gregory and Helena were supportive and affectionate and the other members of the clan were in various stages of acceptance and umbrage.

"You don't look too well," Richard observed as they passed the closed doors of the formal dining hall that could seat one hundred people and moved into the intimate family dining room in the west wing that would only seat twenty-five or thirty, depending on which china was used. "Are you going into town today?" Richard asked, stepping back to allow her to pass in front of him.

"Maybe a little later," she answered, resisting the impulse to unburden herself on him.

Hawthorne Manor was patterned after the stark Scottish castles of the family's ancestral homeland. Built around a large center courtyard, the house had four wings, each with its own turret tower with spiral staircase and private entrance. The master suite was on the first floor of the east wing along with the kitchen, family rooms, and servants' quarters. The first floor of the south wing boasted the large, formal receiving rooms, Gregory's study, library, music room and even included a ballroom that opened onto the vast stone terrace that led to the formal gardens, complete with an orchestra pit. The first floor of the north wing held the nursery suites where the Emerson children spent their years before moving upstairs to the second and third floor suites as they matured.

"I don't think the scampi agreed with me last night," Nicole answered off-handedly as she crossed the dining room and poured herself a glass of juice.

"The sauce was a little heavy," Richard offered, glancing toward the door to the butler's pantry.

Nicole caught the cautious glance and laughed softly, understanding his concern that Riva might come rushing through the door to defend her culinary reputation. She also glanced toward the butler's pantry and shook her head gently. The walls had ears.

Richard lifted the covers from the dishes on the warming trays and inspected the offerings for breakfast. "Is that all you're having?" he asked, spooning an omelet onto his plate and reaching for a piece of buttered toast.

"I had breakfast with Cameron," she said as she sipped at the ice-cold juice.

She stood at the French doors opening onto the conservatory. The spring air was still brisk and chill, but Douglas kept something blooming in the sheltered garden all year long. Three stories above, a cathedral like greenhouse dome sheltered the courtyard from the spring chill.

"Did you know that the glass panels up there were cut and angled to actually bend the light down into this conservatory?" Nicole asked him, studying the glass ceiling overhead.

"I did not know that," Richard admitted with a shake of his head. "And how do you?"

"I did some research," Nicole said off handedly as she turned back toward the buffet. "There are also steam pipes buried along the walks to heat it to greenhouse levels."

"Are you having trouble with your car?" he asked as he settled at the table for breakfast.

"No, just the regular – oil change, tires rotated…" her voice trailed off as the nausea threatened to overwhelm her again, "whatever they do routinely." After studying her glass of juice for a moment, she pushed it away.

"Well," Richard said with his engaging smile, "I'll be leaving in about a half hour if you need a lift into town."

"Thanks," Nicole replied, placing her palms flat on the table and pushing herself to her feet. "I'll let you know," she said as she turned toward the door. "Right now, I'm going back upstairs."

"Can I get you anything?" Richard asked, rising to his feet. "Antacid? Bicarbonate of Soda? Alka Seltzer? Hair of the dog?"

"No," Nicole said with a faint smile, waving him back into his chair absently as she reached the door. "I've not been driven to drink just yet. I thought I would get in a quick trip up to the house this morning to see how things went yesterday. I think I overdid it. You know how it is – you start out at a pace and then think you can do better. Before you know it, you're wiped out."

"I do," Richard agreed with his engaging smile. "How's it going?"

"They seem to be on schedule," she said, heading toward the door.

Nicole heard the phone ringing in her suite from the landing and made a mad dash up the stairs from the mezzanine. She crossed the sun-splattered room to the table near the sofa and picked up the receiver, seeing as she did it was an outside line button was lit.

"Nicole, where's Cam?" Gregory's deep, resonant voice came over the wire without preamble.

"He's there," she said quietly, the nausea rising again, "or he should be. He left more than an hour and a half ago."

"He's not come in," Gregory said and she could hear his irritated sigh. "Just a minute, Nicole," Gregory said curtly. She then heard Ellen's voice and caught the name "Sheriff Clairborne."

"Gregory," Nicole breathed, her hand clenching the receiver tightly. "Is something wrong?"

"No. He's probably had a flat or something on the way in. Jake's checking the Trail. I have to go, Nicole," Gregory said quietly, turning away from the phone as he lowered it into the cradle, but she could hear him talking to someone else before the line went dead.

As the dial tone filled her ear, Nicole stood staring out over the east lawn for a moment and then pressed the intercom button on the phone. Douglas answered immediately.

"Is Mr. Richard still in the dining room?" Nicole asked.

"Yes, ma'am."

"Will you let him know that I will be going into town with him after all? Ask him to buzz me when he's ready."

"Yes, ma'am."

୨୨⋖୨

By the time Jake slowed to turn from the highway onto Sutter Trail, his deputies had set up the roadblock to keep all but emergency personnel off the mountain. Word of an accident involving an Emerson would spread quickly. Cars and trucks of a variety of makes and models were slowing at the check point and being directed to a staging area just on the other side where members of the county's rescue teams were congregating.

Jake heard the squeal of the siren of the county rescue's Range Rover as it careened up the road behind him and he pulled over to allow it to pass. It didn't slow down as it drove through the check point and the siren whined to silence as it pulled into the staging area and the rescue teams unloaded their gear from their personal vehicles and transferred it.

Stafford County's Rescue Team was an alliance of members from his squad, Oak Meadow's Fire Department, and seasoned members of the community; men and women who knew not only the terrain of the mountain, but also its unstable moods and often nasty temperament intimately.

Jake kept his eyes on the road and his mind on his driving as he maneuvered through the check point and took the curves a little faster than he normally would. He was breathing deeply as he spotted Jane's cruiser pulled to the inside shoulder of the road. She moved toward him even as he slowed to a stop and got out.

"There's no sign of a vehicle, Sheriff," she informed him, "I've walked downstream about a half mile and back. I didn't spot anything."

Jake stood at the gaping hole in the guardrail, staring down at the flattened section on the ground. His practiced eye took in details with one sweeping gaze. The mountainside fell away in a steep slope along this part of the Trail and there was no sign the car went down the side of the mountain. No trench freshly cut into the shallow topsoil – no shrubs or underbrush uprooted and dragged downhill – no car on the tiered ledges – no oil shining in the morning sun now climbing above the mountains around them, no twisted metal – no car parts wrenched from where they were supposed to be – nothing.

"The car must have become airborne soon after it left the road," he said, more to himself than to Jane. "If it did, it had nothing to stop it from going into the river."

He heard the sirens of the rescue team coming up the mountain. From his vantage point, he could see three vehicles moving up from below, lights flashing. He glanced back upriver and was relieved to spot the MacIntosh pickup coming down the Trail from the Lodge. As he turned to head back to the road, he was surprised to see Trevor Cantrell emerge from the woods about a hundred feet below and head toward them.

"Trevor," Jake said, turning to offer his ham-like hand to the young man. He was loaded down with his test case and backpack. His rifle was slung over his shoulder and rested on his back with the ease of a man who was used to carrying a weapon.

"Sheriff – Deputy Adler," Trevor nodded in response. "What's going on?"

Jake raised his arm, looking at his watch. They all turned as Emit MacIntosh rounded the curve and pulled to the shoulder of the highway. Jake headed toward him as he swung himself from behind the wheel and stood for a moment surveying the scene; Eric, the oldest MacIntosh son, and his long time crew foreman, Vince Michaels followed.

Almost at the same time, the lead rescue unit arrived, silenced the siren and then threw the vehicle into reverse, maneuvering it precisely in the center of the opening. Sandy Wade, Jake's Deputy Chief pulled up behind the rescue unit and got out. David Haas, Fire Chief and team leader pulled open the storage compartment and began handing out ropes and equipment to George Kaiser, his co-leader. Jake's attention immediately turned to them.

"We have a car in the river," Jane answered Trevor's question.

"Who's?" Trevor asked, moving with her out of the way, running a hand through his dark hair.

"We don't know yet," Jane replied simply.

Trevor watched as the teams, experienced at working with each other, went into action. One team was pulling on safety harnesses, checking their own and double-checking their appointed buddies'. Jake and Emit moved to the side of the road, watching them with a supervisory eye. Within minutes a four-man team connected ropes to the back of the SUV and were rappelling down the cliff to the river.

Jane watched Trevor as he moved about. He seemed removed from the activity around him in some way. He watched the men as they made their way down to the river with an odd expression she could not read. He was a mystery to most of the people in the area. Although many of the females would have loved to have him become a part of the social scene, he kept to the university campus in Crystal Springs and the Estate, wandering through the mountains on whatever mysterious tasks that commanded his undivided attention.

"Trev," Emit called walking toward him, "you on the mountain this morning?"

"Yeah, running samples," Trevor responded.

"You hear anything?"

"I heard gunfire," Trevor said, "but it might have been a tire blowing, now that I think about it. I'd just crossed the bridge and was making my way inland along a stream about a hundred feet from the falls."

Jake turned his attention back to the work at hand, retrieving a roll of yellow caution tape from the trunk of his car to stretch along the mangled guardrail. Jane took one end and they were just tying it off when they heard a car coming from the direction of The Manor. When Richard Weston's BMW came into view, Jake heaved a heavy sigh. When he saw Nicole Emerson leap from the passenger seat, he breathed a curse.

"Jane," he said quietly, glancing at his deputy to make sure she heard him. She watched him with a inconspicuous sideways look. "We have to get Nicole Emerson away from here."

"Yes, sir," Jane said as she moved to intercept the newest Emerson bride.

Nicole leaned against the front fender of the BMW and tried to stave off the nausea that was overwhelming her again. Jake and Richard walked out of earshot and were talking intently under their breath. Nicole strained to hear what they were saying but Jane was doing an excellent job of making sure that didn't happen.

"Let me get you back to The Manor, Mrs. Emerson," Jane said gently, taking Nicole's arm with a gentle but firm grip and guiding her toward her squad car. "The road is closed off and we are keeping it clear for the rescue teams."

"Is it Cameron?"

"We don't know anything," Jane said calmly.

"Who else could it be?" Nicole whispered, not taking her eyes off Richard and the sheriff. "He's not at the Plaza."

"There is just nothing known yet," Jane said softy. "As soon as we know something, we will tell you. Come on, I can see you're not feeling well. Let me take you home."

"I hear the radio," Nicole said, trying to take a step toward the men but unable to escape Jane's grip on her arm. "They've found something…"

"That's just the deputies checking in," Jane answered evenly, easing her into the passenger side of the squad car. She pressed the security latch on the edge of the door to make sure that once it was closed it could not be opened from the inside. She then hurried around to the slide behind the wheel.

Overhead they could hear the sound of a chopper approaching. "That's probably my father-in-law," Nicole said, leaning forward and trying to see through the canopy of thin leaves. "I should wait to see him."

"He can't land around here," Jane evaded, pulling onto the Trail and heading toward The Manor. "You'll see him at the house, I'm sure."

Jake stood with his radio to his ear, listening to the exchange of conversation. He identified Sandy's voice as he asked one of the rescue team members to repeat.

"We've found the car…" a disembodied voice came over a crackling frequency. "It's caught in the whirlpool."

Jake heaved a heavy sigh of dread and turned his attention to photographing the scene so he could get down to the site.

Trevor could hear the radio exchange from where he stood at the edge of the woods. As Jake snapped a few more pictures, he began walking down the Trail toward the place where the river took a sharp turn around the adjacent mountain, creating a whirlpool that was enchanting and mesmerizing on most days… but not today.

༄

Helena Emerson opened the front door of The Manor before Jane cut the engine. She moved gracefully across the deep front porch and down the wide, shallow steps to the squad car. Jane reached down to the panel on her door and pressed the driver's release of Nicole's door lock. As Nicole pulled at the door handle, Helena was swinging it outward to reach for her.

"Deputy Adler," Helena said with a gracious smile as Jane made her way around the squad car to the two women and reached out to gently pat Jane's arm. "We so appreciate your kindness."

Helena Emerson possessed a regal beauty and poise that always struck a chord of disquiet in Jane. She was a stately woman with the rich complexion and dark tresses of her Mediterranean heritage and the manner and grace of one trained in old world society. She moved with a grace and bearing that was born of privilege and the consciousness that the world was always watching. Her eyes were dark hazel with curious flecks of gold and her bone structure strong.

Mae was hovering just inside the door as they entered. She reached for Nicole, pulling her away from the other two women and slipping her arm around her waist.

"Mae," Nicole said with a slow shake of her head, "They can't find Cam and there's been some kind of accident along the Trail." Nicole's large gray eyes seemed to grow larger still as she turned to look from Mae to Jane and then Helena.

"I know," Mae whispered, fighting the tears that threatened. "You need to come upstairs and lie down."

"No," Nicole shook her head. "Jane is going to let us know when they find out what's going on."

"She appears to be suffering from shock," Jane whispered, looking up at Mae. "You might want to call her doctor and have something sent out for her."

"Of course," Helena said, avoiding eye contact with Jane and turning to see Riva waiting in the family room for them.

"I'll call," Mae said quickly. Hawthorne Manor was obviously in crisis mode. Word quickly spread through the community at times like these although no one was actually voicing the unimaginable at the moment.

"Thank you," Helena sighed. "And Riva, would you bring us some coffee... perhaps some pastries?"

The women settled into the deep cushioned sofas in the large Emerson family room. The sun seemed to be dodging the gathering clouds and sent warm shafts of light through the atrium glass ceiling and spilling over into the family room. Helena opened the French doors into the conservatory and then sank into a high-backed chair. Riva returned to set a large silver service on the table between the sofas.

"Thank you, Riva," Helena said as she leaned forward to pour coffee from the silver urn into the delicate china cups. She handed Riva the first cup and Riva turned to carry it to Nicole.

"I don't think I can drink that," Nicole whispered, her hands trembling as she pressed them into her temples.

"Maybe some ice water," Jane suggested, accepting the cup of coffee and leaning forward for the silver creamer.

"I'll get her some tea," Riva replied, hurrying from the room.

"I appreciate the coffee," Jane said, quickly gulping the rich, strong brew as she eased herself from the plush occasional chair back onto her feet. "But I really need to get back to work. Is there anything I can do for you ladies before I go?"

"You will call when you know something?" Nicole asked, reaching out to grip her arm and lifting tortured eyes toward the deputy.

"I will," Jane promised. "Please, Mrs. Emerson, don't get up," she said, lifting her hand as Helena rose gracefully to her feet.

That was a useless comment for as she turned, she saw that Douglas was on duty in the front foyer. His impeccable appearance and countenance a strange comfort in the confusion and chaos that turned all activity of the morning on its head. She nodded slightly toward him as he ushered her to the front door.

His hand brushed her elbow as she paused for him to open the door. She glanced at him and could see the desperate concern in the aging eyes. There was a sheen in them that she knew were the tears that threatened his practiced control. "Everything that can be done is being done," she said softly, reaching out to clap a friendly hand on his arm. He nodded slightly.

"We are at the disposal of the rescue units," Douglas said calmly. "Anything we can do. Anything!"

"Of course," Jane replied as she stepped back out the front door. "Thank you. We'll let you know."

The chopper was on the south lawn as she made her way down the front steps. She caught sight of one of the Emerson's fleet cars moving around the house from the garage. She unclipped her radio from her belt, clicking the button twice. "Gregory's just leaving here. Shall I try to convince him to ride down with me?"

"We're not going to keep him away." Jake's voice came back to her. "We might as well try to get the advantage of controlling his movements. And, we don't need any more cars along here."

"Can you see the western sky from your location?" Jane asked as she cast a concerned eye overhead.

"Yeah," Jake replied. "If we don't raise this Jag before the rains start, this river is going to swallow it whole. You got your gear with you?"

"Yeah," Jane said, slipping behind the wheel of her car and starting the engine, moving along the driveway to intercept the oncoming Emerson car. "I never leave home without it."

CHAPTER FOUR

Gregory Emerson emerged from Jane's squad car and crossed the roadway to where Jake was taking pictures of the guardrail. His heart beat painfully as he saw the gaping hole and twisted metal. He felt an emotion that was not in his nature, helplessness. Most of the rescue team had moved down the Trail to set up for the recovery of the Jag. Jane hung back, watching the patriarch of the Emerson clan survey the scene.

He was an impressive figure, standing just a little over six feet tall with aristocratic features and an almost regal poise and demeanor that – unlike Helena – were more practiced polish than inherited grace. He was tall and wiry, with the rugged, sharp features of his Scottish forefathers along with a charismatic blarney that charmed everyone. There was always a hint of a Scottish accent, carefully subtle and skillfully developed, but completely affected. His hair was beginning to go silver, but his thick brows remained dark and imposing, lending him an authoritative appearance that enhance his bearing.

"Jake," Gregory nodded, shaking the hand the sheriff offered him. "What do you know?"

"We're still sorting things out." Jake answered, taking one more snapshot of the railing and then turning his attention to the new scars on the rock face of the mountain. It seemed the Jaguar made first contact with it – then leveled a section of the railing when it went into the river. He adjusted the settings on his camera and began snapping pictures again.

"It would seem Cameron lost control of the car right about here. There are skid marks starting about a hundred feet up," he said, jerking his head over his shoulder but not taking his eye from the lens.

Gregory said nothing as Jake brought him current with what was known so far, taking in everything he was told without expression or comment. He glanced at the guardrail, swallowing hard as he noticed the bronze paint. He saw the cable still hanging down the mountainside. "Have they located the car?" he asked, not taking his eyes from the gaping hole.

"It's about a mile downstream," Jake said, stepping to the open door of the truck and activating the wench, shifting it into reverse to rewind the cable back onto the spool. The well-oiled crankshaft hummed quietly, but the clanking of the chain as it was dragged back up the side of the slope echoed with a deafening din. "The whirlpool caught it. I'm heading that way."

"The divers are on the scene, Sheriff," Jane called, setting her radio receiver back into place and reaching out to close the open door of her squad car. "I should get down there."

"Go," Jake called, securing the cable and moving around the truck. "We're right behind you." Gregory was already pulling himself into the passenger side of the truck as Jake slid behind the wheel.

The two men fell silent with their own thoughts. Gregory was reminded again of the suddenness of Cameron's marriage and the shock his impulsive behavior was to all who knew him. Nothing had been usual about their lives since Cameron returned from Europe with Nicole as his wife… and now this!

Something about the tone in Jake's voiced turned his thought to his daughter-in-law – so unlike the rest of the choices his other children made for their spouses and completely unlike any of the women Cameron was attracted to before he met Nicole. When he ordered the back ground check, Lee Malcolm found an open book on her life. Her history was uncontroversial and there was nothing to find that would cause alarm. Still…

Until the fateful trip to northern Italy, Cameron dated women in his own social circle; daughters of their friends, colleagues, and business associates. Although none of the many women he escorted to functions, parties, and family events were ever considered serious contenders for his future wife, everyone assume one day he would settle down with someone from their circle. His marriage to Nicole Quinn was a shock.

Not that she was of an inferior social background, quite the contrary. Coming from the scholarly and cosmopolitan world of her parents' art and antiquities acquisitions business, Nicole was used to moving among a much more elite and exclusive international circle than would open their doors to people of commerce and trade such as Emerson International. While EI was building a commerce empire around the world, the Quinns were involved in acquiring treasures of empires of past glories and splendor for the people who could afford to spend fortunes on art and trinkets.

For the same reason, however, Nicole was also quite unprepared for the high profile life and public scrutiny that came with association with the Emersons. Their very public and highly visible lifestyle was a problem from the onset for her. Although she and her family were extremely accomplished, highly respected, and held impeccable credentials in antiques and the arts of the world, Nicole was quite shy and uncomfortable in their very exposed social strata.

While the people she was used to dealing with were usually the powerhouses behind the drawn curtains, never seen by the eye of the public, the Emersons were the front men who were considered the movers and shakers on the evolving world market. There were times he wondered if she was embarrassed by the public attention the Emersons attracted. No, Nicole was nothing like the spouses of his other children.

Gregory was pulled from his thoughts by the sight of the line of vehicles along the Trail. Jake left the truck squarely in the center of the road. Gregory felt strangely out of place as he moved to the edge of the right of way and took in the full scene on the river below. The sight drove all thought of Nicole's differences from his mind.

The divers were suiting up at the back of an Explorer; shrugging into the rubber suits and checking gauges on the tanks and the other equipment they would use. Jane joined them, stepping from her role as deputy to that of one of the diving team. Scattered at intervals between the road and the river, men were using various tools to clear a path. The sound of gas powered chain saws and weed eaters drowned out the softer swooshing sounds of the timed and calculated sweeps of hand held scythes and chopping machetes. It was impossible for the rescuers to talk to each other, but they still moved with coordinated purpose born of experienced teamwork.

Sandy supervised the securing of a rope to trees down the embankment to allow the rescuers a hold grip in their descents and ascents. Andy Hodge sat in his massive wrecker with a crane boom secured in the back well at the side of the Trail, watching the progress and waiting for his cue to join the effort.

Gregory turned to look down the ravine to the swiftly moving water below and felt a cold chill run up his spine as he noticed the sheen of oil that was caught in the center of the whirlpool. The oily circling rainbow shimmered in the eerie, pre-storm light. The sharp bend in the river stopped the car's movement downstream and for the moment was holding it in a rocky underwater grip.

He spotted Emit and his entire crew, including his three sons, among those clearing the vegetation from the mountainside and Trevor was topside assisting the divers who were about to descend toward the river. They moved in a single line toward the rope, holding it with one hand, their fins, tanks, and face masks in the other as they made a cautious descent over the newly cleared path. The odor of freshly cut vegetation joined the distinct smell of rain in the changing air. The chain saws fell silent as the last area was cleared and Gregory could hear the instructions of the team leader as they reached the river's bank and pulled their gear on. Jake was getting an update from his deputies who were huddled around him near the bank of squad cars lining the other side of the road.

"Excuse me, sir," someone said, and Gregory stepped back away from the cleared opening, allowing one of the rescuers to grab hold of the rope and begin the precarious descent. Gregory was used to being in charge and he now found himself oddly out of place and in the way.

The divers entered the water, forming a defined circle around the submerged car before going under. He watched as they disappeared beneath the swirling current and he then moved closer to the edge of the easement. Sick dread was overwhelming him and a dull throb was beginning to pound in his head.

Jake set his deputies to moving vehicles, clearing the area on the Trail at the top of the newly cut path and allowing Andy Hodge to get his wrecker into position.

Time became a distortion as Gregory watched the well-orchestrated retrieval. By the time the divers returned to the surface and crawled out of the river onto the bank, the wrecker's boom was hanging precisely over the submerged car. The team leader took a radio from the deputy at the river's edge and looked up the mountain to Jake.

Jake moved away from Gregory as his radio crackled to life. He turned the volume down and pressed the speaker tightly against his ear. He knew what they were going to say, and there was no reason for Gregory Emerson to have to suffer the torture of hearing it too. He continued walking away from Gregory, but never took his eyes off his deputy and the divers on the river.

"The car's down there, Sheriff," the team leader confirmed, "it's empty, Jake,"

Jake came to an abrupt halt in his casual stroll upriver, "Repeat that," he said, his eyes narrowing as though he could read the lips of his man on the river since he could not believe his ears.

"Repeating ... there's no body. The driver's door is open and the seat belt has been released. There's no damage to the belt."

"Repeat again," Jake breathed glancing back at Gregory Emerson.

"Repeating – there is no body in the car, Sheriff. The driver's door appears to have been open before the car hit the water. The seat belt was released, sir. It's not torn loose or broken. The seat belt catch is intact."

"Copy that," Jake said, more calmly than he felt. He glanced at the sky, reading the signs of the approaching storm and turned to make his way back to the small gathering along the Trail. He was prepared for the retrieval of a car and a body, but now he was looking at a rescue. That was a whole new ball game and his mind was racing as he moved back toward the cleared path to the river.

Word of the divers' discovery spread through the search teams and the attitudes and actions were changing in one focused flow of movement. All but two of the divers were shedding their suits. Gregory saw the change and turned to look around him for an explanation. The men along the mountainside abandoned their power equipment and were heading down toward the river, joining the huddle of divers and deputies and staring first upstream and then downstream while deep in discussion.

Gregory moved purposefully toward Jake. Before he could speak, Jake clutched his arm in a firm grip.

"Jake...?"

"There's no body in the car, Gregory," Jake said without preamble.

"What?"

"The car is empty. He was washed out."

"Washed out?" Gregory breathed, turning to watch the men below. "How... where... what does that mean exactly?"

"Was Cameron in the habit of wearing his seat belt?" Jake asked, shaking Gregory's arm slightly to get his attention.

"I think so," Gregory said, realizing for the first time he had no real clue as to his son's driving habits. Imagines of his son getting in the car with him flashed through his mind. "Yes," he decided, turning a sharp gaze back to Jake. "Why?"

"There was no sign of damage to the seat belt – it was released."

"Meaning...?"

"Meaning he may have managed to get out of the car..."

"... and might still be alive," Gregory completed the thought for him, doing immediately what Jake had done, casting a concerned eye first along the river and then toward the darkening sky.

"I've got to go." Jake placed his radio to his ear once again as he walked across the road to converse with his teams that were already splitting up, some moving upriver and some moving down.

"Take this," Mae insisted, holding out a small pill in the palm of her hand. Nicole took the pill and reached for the glass of water Mae offered to her. Mae watched as Nicole kicked off her shoes and sank onto the side of the bed. The cup of tea sat on the bedside table untouched.

The delicate antique porcelain gleamed in the misty sunlight coming through the window behind it. The brilliance of the morning sun was becoming obscured by the bank of clouds building in the west and moving toward the mountains. The intricate pink and lavender flowers spilled across the side of the cup and spread across the fluted rim of the saucer beneath it. Nicole reached out and ran a finger gently around the cup rim of the carefully executed lift in the handle of the cup. All of this started with this china, she remembered.

She reached for the delicate cup and lifted it so the light would make the porcelain translucent. She studied the hand-painted pattern with practiced skill, seeing the intricate difference from brush stroke to brush stroke. She then raised her eyes across the broad plateau on which The Manor was built to the mountains rising behind the thick grove of trees east of The Manor. Memories flooded her consciousness, sweeping her away from the pain of the present to the moment she first saw the exquisite Royal Albert Lavender Rose china.

She could never have known how her life was dramatically and forever changing at that moment. She had never been on a more routine buying trip for the House of Quinn, spending wonderful days meandering through the familiar provinces of Northern Italy, dropping in on long established dealers and galleries, enjoying the company of old friends and meeting new ones. The northern loop had been her favorite since she was a little girl, accompanying her parents while searching out the treasures people were willing to give up or needed to liquidate.

She had a passion for northwest Italy unequalled to any other area of the world. She always traveled by train from Milan through the beautifully quaint mountain villages, wondering often how long such wondrous places would go unnoticed by the hordes of tourists who arrived in masses to tour other parts of Italy.

On her second evening at her hotel in Milan, while having dinner with a long time friend and gallery owner, she picked up a rumor of a private sale in a surrounding area. After hearing the same rumor again in Le Salle, Morgex, and Dolonne, she decided there was reason enough to make a side trip to check it out. She rented a sturdy little Fiat and headed resolutely higher into the Italian Alps, not at all sure she wasn't on a fool's errand but hopeful she could run the sale to ground.

Once she reached the quaint little village of Aosta – "the rooftop of the world" as it was sometimes called – she planned her inconspicuous search carefully. Clandestine sales were hush-hush for many reasons and hard to verify. Often sellers wanted to prevent news of the liquidation of family heirlooms from becoming public and an embarrassment to the family.

She checked into a rustic old hotel overlooking Sant'Orso and then went hunting for the rumor's scent. Experience taught her that if there was a discrete auction in an area, the curators of the local museums were going to know about it. The trick was to gain enough of their favor to get them to share their secrets.

Nicole was instantly enchanted with the ancient village, finding the layout easy to follow and the people friendly and helpful. Cars were prohibited inside Aosta and strolling through the careful, precise grids designed by the Romans two thousand years before was undemanding and completely relaxing. There was no reason to worry she would get lost or be unable to find her way back to her hotel.

Outdoor markets brought the streets to life with local flair and flavor. Nicole haggled with several of the craftsmen to arrange for consignments of lace and hand woven fabrics. She ferreted out local craftsmen who were open to new opportunities and bought their inventory with the promise of more purchases before calling it a day and settling into a little café to enjoy the local spicy coffee, coppa dell'amicizia.

She quickly discovered the museum offerings of Valle d'Aosta were a stark contrast to those of Florence, Venice, and Rome. Nicole had a talent for languages and a knack for regional dialects. Her raven dark hair and classic bone structure allowed her to blend in with the locals in spite of her alabaster complexion and gray eyes. She wandered about the area, getting used to the thick, colloquial accent and by the end of the first day she picked up enough of the street slang to converse easily with the locals.

When she donned the blouse and skirt she bought in the markets, pulled her hair into a loose bun and slipped on new sandals purchased in the shop next door to the hotel, she was exactly as she wanted to appear, and American on holiday. She joined the locals as they also went to market, greeting merchants in English and nodding to other shoppers with a tentative *"Buon giorno."*

She hit pay dirt when she overheard two farmers who brought their fruits and vegetables to town talking about a local family forced to liquidate family heirlooms because the ancestral villa was draining the dwindling family fortune. After loitering nearby long enough to catch the family name. They fell silent when she approached, but after casually asking them with a giggle if they spoke English and getting a polite but abrupt shake of the head by one of the men, she wandered around their carts inspecting their produce while they fell comfortably back into their Italian gossip.

By the end of the day, she ferreted out the name of the shop owner conducting the unpublished sale and managed to secure an invitation and the privilege of bidding by taking a consignment of his merchandise. The House of Quinn had several New York designers who paid handsomely for unique fabrics and small shops and studios always grateful for original regional art. This was turning into not only a very profitable but also adventurous trip.

The sale was at a family estate between Oasta and Montjovet. Nicole was both awed with the regal castle and saddened by the subtle neglect and decay. She could see that the grounds were untended, the gardens overgrown, and the edifice in sad need of repair. Spreading away from the castle lawns was the remnants of what were once tiered vineyards; destroyed during the two World Wars. Many of the local vineyards never recovered afterwards; hundreds of varieties of grapes were lost forever.

The need of repairs were overwhelming this illustrious but disadvantaged family who were trying to maintain the pretense that their old money was still substantial and their aristocracy still relevant in a modern Italy. The family villa in Roma drained their resources, leaving the country house to this despair.

As she entered the back door of the castle, she was handed a starkly plain catalogue printed with thin ink on course paper. The discovery of the English china in the drab Italian catalogue was a delightful surprise. She wondered why it was not moved to the Villa with the rest of the treasures. One of their clients of the shop had a soft spot for English china and it was a foregone conclusion that if she was able to procure the sale, she had a ready buyer.

The set of Royal Albert was in remarkably good condition. Most of the more than fifty place settings were intact. The House of Quinn's repairwoman could touch up the few chips and cracks of the damaged pieces. She wandered about the other selected offerings set out for inspection, making a note of one or two she might offer initial bids for, but her heart was set on taking the Lavender Rose back with her. She knew their client would purchase it sight unseen and pay the asking price without haggling. If not, a few calls to selected clients would have it sold before she could unpack and inventory it.

As the appointed time of the sale approached, more people quietly arrived, gathering solemnly in the front room of the house. People spoke in hushed tones and averted looking directly at each other. These forced sales of the family treasures were always such embarrassing experiences for the few remaining true aristocrats of northern Italy. Nicole learned to treat the event much as she would if she were attending a family funeral.

About midway through the auction, one five-piece place setting of the china was placed on the auctioneer's table. Nicole scanned the contents of the lot to make sure she had not misunderstood the details. Forty-eight five-piece place settings, six sixteen piece coffee sets, and an assortment of serving pieces and meat platters formed an amazing acquisition. Aside from the commission the shop would make, the points this purchase would score with her parents was exciting to her.

As the bidding began, she stepped clearly into the sight of the auctioneer, making sure he recognized her intention to bid. Once the initial bidding progressed beyond the faint at heart and began in earnest, it was fast paced and non-stop. Nicole knew the resale value of the set and knew how much profit margin she could sacrifice to obtain the collection and still justify the purchase.

The bidding was finally between herself and one other bidder who seemed as determined as she. Her palms were sweating and it was more and more difficult to grasp her bid card because she was gripping it so tightly her hands cramped. She was also aware the card was shaking as she held it up each time. She strained to see the other bidder across the room, but was unable to locate the mysterious competitor in the oddly shaped hall. She struggled to concentrate on the procedures. Her Italian was fluent, but in intense moments like these, she lost concentration as excited Italians became less articulate. She had already exceeded the limit she initially imposed on herself and was anticipating defeat when suddenly the auctioneer was repeating her last bid and looking directly at her, his gavel raised in anticipation of an auction's end.

Nicole's head shot up, her eyes locked onto the auctioneer, and her ears strained to hear anything above the low murmuring of the people surrounding her. The auctioneer was staring deep into the crowd, a question hanging in the air, as he repeated her last bid yet another time. On some cue from the other bidder, he swung his attention back to Nicole and raised his gavel a little higher. As he gave the final three warnings, Nicole felt sweat between her breasts roll from under her bra down to the waistband of her slacks as the gavel fell and the china was hers.

The quick removal of the five-piece setting was anticlimactic as she took the bid confirmation from the auctioneer's assistant and made her way toward the small room at a side entrance where the unseemly financial transactions were kept as far from the family as possible. She would be buying nothing more on this day, she realized, as she calculated in U.S. dollars exactly what she paid for the china.

Nicole fished her papers from her bag and found her letter of credit. The cashier was waiting patiently with the paperwork resting on the antique inlaid table in front of him. He smiled almost indecently at her as she approached. Italian men were neither shy nor easily deterred and Nicole discovered the best response was to pretend they were invisible, totally beneath her notice.

She took the papers that guaranteed the authenticity of the china and inspected them as the cashier verified her letter of credit and inspected the shop's export authorization. The House of Quinn was well known throughout Europe and parts of the orient and Russia. Their standards were high and Nicole caught the change in the cashier's expression as his supervisor whispered in his ear. Since she ignored the cashier's flirtations, she supposed they assumed she could not understand Italian so she ignored the bad manners as well. After making a few clarifications and specifications as to the packing and shipping instructions, she completed the transaction and signed the authorization for the transfer of funds.

"I'm sorry, sir," Nicole heard the shop manager say as she left the cashier and returned to the gallery. Another lot of merchandise was being removed from the table and the auctioneer was winding up another round of bidding. She glanced up to see the auction director and a tall, sandy-haired man standing by the front door. They were watching her curiously as she approached.

"No problem," the younger man replied, and Nicole realized he was an American. His bold stare unnerved her more than the obviously ill mannered come-on of the Italian cashiers and she averted her gaze from his. "I have a feeling it's all going to work out just fine."

The shop owner returned to overseeing his auction and the young American stepped slightly to the side to allow her to pass through the door.

"I think I know you," he said as she stepped into the crisp alpine air. He laughed out loud as he saw her large gray eyes roll before she lowered her dark shades from her head over them. She quickened her step but he had no difficulty falling into step beside her. "No... No really. I'm above such pathetic pickup lines, honest! Aren't you from The House of Quinn?"

Nicole continued her brisk pace, still ignoring him. Knowing she was from the House of Quinn was not something that would get her to drop her guard. The director definitely noted her presence once she produced her papers.

"I've been in your shop on Vermillion in Chrystal Springs. Your parents have your picture in an antique frame over the table that has the guest book on it."

Nicole came to an abrupt halt, stifling her laugh as he outran her a step or two before he realized it. He stopped abruptly; stood still for a moment, and then backed up to her side. She tipped her shades slightly off her nose to actually look at him for the first time. He seemed vaguely familiar but they definitely had never met. There were pictures of the shop in many magazines and brochures published and she did not know if one of that table with her picture was one of them or not. She was not easily persuaded by men coming onto her.

"I'm sure we haven't met," she responded quietly and started walking again.

"No, no we haven't met, but I have a suspicion we were at cross purposes back there," he said matching his pace to hers after catching up with her again and glancing at her sideways with a boyish grin and it was impossible for her not to be charmed. "I was bidding on that china for Helena Emerson, how 'bout you?"

Nicole came to a sudden halt again and turned to face him, studying him directly. It would not have been difficult for him to discover she was a buyer for the House of Quinn or even that she was Nicole Quinn, but she never mentioned anything about her clients. The world had become a dangerous place and business had become highly competitive.

"My mother will die for those dishes," he laughed, "I'm Cameron Emerson."

"You're not!" she gasped, whipping her shades off and looking at him intently. Upon closer scrutiny she realized she had seen the face in the society section in grainy ink of the Crystal Springs Review. "You are! And I did get them for your mother! How bizarre! How in the world did you find out about this sale and get in?"

"We're expanding operations here in Italy," Cameron explained. "Oasta is in the running for a facility. This family is offering some of their holdings for a factory. My contact with the family is a brother – uncle – cousin – once removed – or something. He seemed oddly delighted these guys had to liquidate some of the family heirlooms. Evidently, he's from the wrong branch of the family tree. He mentioned that the grandmother or great aunt or someone had collected china… and you know my mother…"

"I do," Nicole shrugged and looked over her shoulder at the shabby exterior.

"You've got quite a knack for Italian," Cameron changed the subject as they crossed the front drive together. "I thought you were a native until the shop owner told me you were from the States. I usually have an interpreter with me everywhere I go, but they wouldn't hear of me bringing a local interpreter. They take their family secrets very seriously and fortunately, the assistant director speaks English. Would you like to have dinner with a fellow American who hasn't had a whole conversation he could understand in the last two weeks?"

"After what I just paid for that china, I could use a free meal," she laughed shyly. "Where are you staying?" she asked as they approached her little Fiat.

"The Cecchin, Du Pont Roman," he said, reaching to open the door for her. "You?"

She hesitated a moment too long before she answered causing him to flash the disarming grin again.

"Here," he said whipping out his passport and flipping it open for her to see. "I promise I am who I say I am and that I'm harmless," he said holding his hands out palms toward her after putting his passport back in his pocket.

"Somehow I doubt that," she shot back at him, but smiled when she spoke. "The Milleluci is more practical to the IRS," she finally conceded. "and I love it there."

"May I call for you about eight o'clock?"

"Yes, thank you" she smiled, slipping behind the wheel and allowing him to close the door for her. As she maneuvered around the other parked cars, she watched him with quick glances in her rear view mirror. He crossed the front drive to a sleek dark blue Maserati Spyder convertible parked conspicuously beside the other cars. Something told her it wasn't a rental.

They dined at a lovely old place near the Praetorian Gate and Nicole knew she was hopelessly in love with him before the main course of Trenette con sugo di trota was served. They wandered through the walled city late into the night, neither wanting to surrender the day. Finally they were standing in front of her hotel and he leaned down to place a chaste kiss on her cheek.

"May I see you tomorrow?" he asked, as she moved toward the door.

"I have to be in Bergamo by ten o'clock in the morning," she sighed, lifting her arms and letting them fall regretfully. "This was an unscheduled side trip and I've pushed appointments as much as I can and still make my flight home."

"Breakfast!" Cameron said in a rush. "We could meet for breakfast."

"It would have to be very early," Nicole warned with a questioning tilt of her head.

"We can order now," Cameron said taking a step toward the entrance. She laughed out loud as her hand shot out to his arm to stop his advance and push him gently back.

"About seven?" she asked, taking another step toward the door.

"Seven," he agreed, not moving as he watched her enter the rustic old building that belied the elegant appointment of the rooms. "Sleep well."

"How likely is that?" Nicole whispered under her breath as she turned to wave at him with a trembling smile. She had known at that moment that her life was changed forever; she just had no idea how drastically.

The far distant sound of thunder reached her ears and she jumped, pulling herself from the memories. Fear gripped her and she reached to take Cameron's pillow from their bed, smothering her face in it in hopes his scent would calm the rising panic she was feeling.

Charlotte A. Minga

CHAPTER FIVE

Jake watched as Andy Hodge secured his rig into place for the divers to secure the massive chain to the submerged Jag. He lowered the scotches and leveled them to stabilize the vehicle. He then positioned himself behind the wheel to wait for the signal.

The dive team went down again to take a final look at the car to decide the best way to raise it from the whirlpool. As the crew worked to remove the vehicle from the river, the search and rescue team was beginning the extended search for Cameron Emerson, splitting into four groups; two headed upstream and two downstream. Both teams moved in tandem on opposite sides of the river, searching for any indication he managed to get out of the water.

Jake called for state assistance and troopers were dispatched to reinforce the roadblock from the highway and add to the search effort. Reporters and curiosity seekers picked up the news of the search and rescue on scanners and were beginning to converge on the area. Although the roadblock was in place, there were determined people trying to get pictures and stories for the news media.

Trevor descended the mountainside to the riverbank, using the rope hung by the rescue team. He watched – the odd man out – as the clank of the chain rolling down the mountainside echoed around them. He helped the deputies drag the massive chain the last few yards to the riverside and handed it off to the divers waiting in the water.

Emit MacIntosh and Gregory Emerson stood to the side of the road above, speaking softly as they kept a watchful eye on everything that was going on. Everyone on the scene was aware of the change in the air and the darkening southwest sky. All of them lifted their heads as they caught the sound of distant thunder.

"What do you think?" Jake asked, crossing the shoulder to address Emit. "We have what… two – three hours?"

"Just about," Emit agreed, casting a skilled eye toward the western horizon. "Those clouds are building high and fast. It's going to be a mean one." They were interrupted by the sound of the department's flatbed impound truck straining up the steep grade and pulling to the side of the Trail, breaks screeching loudly as the motor fell into a noisy idle and then fell silent.

Jake turned his attention back to his men below. The chain slipped into the water like an enormous metal snake. Trevor and Sandy were keeping it clean of the stumps and residue of the cleared mountainside as the divers pulled it into the river.

The sound of a powerful engine rushing up the mountain road reached them. Jake sighed deeply as he recognized Kyle Emerson's Boxstar gliding to a halt on the road. Kyle and Andrea jumped out. Gregory moved to intercept his youngest children, gathering his daughter in his arms as she burst into tears.

"What's going on?" Kyle demanded, not moving toward the shoulder for fear of what he would see. As the youngest Emerson male, he was just beginning to find his footing in the intimidating dynamics of his own family.

"The dean said there was an emergency at home. He said there was an accident... is Mom....?" Andrea gasped.

"Cam had an accident coming down the mountain this morning. The rescue team is looking for him," Gregory said softly, reaching out to pat his youngest son's shoulder. "He was thrown from the car looks like, so there's still hope."

"Hope?" Kyle breathed, barely above a whisper as he searched the vehicles up and down the roadway. "Where's the car?"

"Oh, no!" Andrea wailed, sobs racking her body as she moved closer to the road's shoulder and spotted the men below. The crane's boom was hanging out over the river and the people on the bank were clearing the area of all the tools and equipment. As Andy engaged the wench, the slack in the chain disappeared off the ground slowly as the chain was pulled taut.

"Kyle," Gregory said firmly, "take your sister home."

"Dad," Kyle almost whined, lifting disbelieving eyes to his father. All his life his younger sister, who was known for her dramatic personality, had been his burden. She was prone to histrionics and over reaction. In times of crisis, too often it was left to him to deal with her.

"Please," Gregory responded, pushing Andrea gently toward her brother. "She doesn't need to be here. Garret is still in Texas and one of us needs to be with your mother, son."

Kyle wrapped his arm around Andrea's shoulder and hesitated only a moment before leading her toward his car. When his father put it like that – acknowledging him as one of the men of the family – he had no choice but to step up. He glanced back at his father, but

Gregory was already making his back above the recovery point.

The Jag was brought up front end first, the distinctive hood ornament of the leaping cat caught the morning sun and the glare flashed from the river. Trevor glanced sideways as Emit approached him, and then drew in a deep, heavy breath. As the crane lifted the car up and out of the water, the front door of the driver's side swung eerily back as water gushed from every cavity of the car's interior. The tortured sound of metal against metal screeched around them as the damage to the door prevented it from swinging closed.

The deputies moved in to maneuver the Jaguar to the river's edge. As they watched, Andy maneuvered the crane to skillfully lift the car straight out of the river. Hodge maneuvered it through the newly cut clearing. As the Jag hung hovering above the road like a grotesque metal fish pulled from the river's depths, Jake made his way toward it. His deputies were also swarming around the car. Trevor eased into the group, making sure not to get in the way, but studying the mangled remains intently.

"Sherriff," Sandy called from where he was standing beneath the passenger side of the car's rear end. "You need to see this." he said as he stood up from where he was kneeling to inspect the tire, mindless of the water pooling beneath the vehicle and creating a new stream down the hill as the water seemed to become a living creature, desperate to return to the river.

By the time Jake reached the tire, Sandy had pulled his flashlight from its belt clip and was shining it on the shredded rubber. He said nothing as Jake followed the beam of light to the tire. Jake took in a deep breath and then held it. Thoughts were flashing through his mind so quickly it left him disoriented for a moment. Then, as he let his breath out, his breathing became heavy.

"What is it?" Emit demanded, moving forward through the opening that appeared as soon as his presence was noticed.

Jake said nothing, but stepped back for Emit to see the circular hole in the remains of the steel belted tire exposed eerily by the beam of Sandy's flashlight.

Thundering silence fell over the three men and then spread over the crowd. The normal noise of the activity at hand fell away into the same silence that captured the three men at the back of the car.

"What is it?" Jane voiced the question that was now paramount in everyone's mind.

"Don't know," someone said as they all began to move toward the Sheriff and Emit. Sandy moved back, allowing Jake to take command.

"There're some tarps in the back of the truck," Jake called to his deputies. "Spread one down and get that tire off the car. Use gloves. Take the whole wheel off and wrap it securely."

One of the deputies pulled the flat bed truck closer and Jake stood to signal to Andy. "When they get that wheel off, take 'er down, Hodge! Jane, get a tarp and make sure this car is as tight as we can get it."

"Sheriff..." Sandy said quietly, glancing around at the State Troopers who were beginning to catch the change in the atmosphere.

"Sandy, get Gregory out of here. Whatever you do, don't let the Troopers speak to him. I need to take another look up the Trail. Emit..."

"We're right behind you," Emit said as he turned and gave a jerk of his head toward Trevor.

◈

Kyle and Andrea Emerson found Helena in the family room, her hands clasped in her lap. She was sitting in a straight-backed chair at the game table, not leaning against the back. Only the sad, tenseness in her eyes and the slight pallor of the skin beneath her carefully applied make-up gave any indication of her fear. The silver coffee set was on the table at her side. Her two youngest children crossed the room to her, each taking a position beside her and leaning down to kiss her soft, smooth cheeks.

"Are you okay, Mother?" Andrea whispered, unable to prevent her fearful tears from spilling over.

"Yes, dear," Helena assured her, reaching up to place her hand against her daughter's wet cheek.

"Where's Nikki?" Andrea asked, taking in the room with a sweeping glance.

"She's upstairs. She isn't feeling well. This has been such a shock. The doctor sent something to help. Mae is with her."

"Dad asked me to bring Andrea home. I'm going back," Kyle said, hesitating a moment to see if his mother would veto the idea. When she merely nodded, he moved toward the door. Riva was bringing in fresh coffee and a tray of sandwiches.

"Kyle, wait," Helena said, turning her gaze slowly from the tray. She heard him suck in an irritated breath and she raised her hand slightly. "Riva, please wrap those sandwiches for Kyle to take with him. I'm sure everyone working on this must be hungry. It's been quite a while now. You'll need to make more."

"Yes, ma'am," Riva replied immediately, turning on her heel to take the tray back to the kitchen. "Mr. Kyle, you can help me," she called over her shoulder. Without hesitation, Kyle followed her into the kitchen.

Kyle Emerson was in his junior year at the university, distinguishing himself more on the tennis courts than in the business courses he was talking. The older Emerson men cast long shadows, and with Gregory grooming Garret for politics and Cameron as his successor, there was no clear direction for the youngest Emerson male. He knew Gregory expected him to take his place in the operations of EI, but so far, he had not shared exactly what that place was to be. So, in the meanwhile, Kyle was enjoying his college years and struggling to carve out his identity in his own mind.

Riva was as much a presence in his life as his mother. Helena was the master designer of their lives and Riva was the overseer who made sure the details were followed through to the master plan's specifications. Holly and Sadie recalled the day she and Douglas arrived to join their family, but none of the others could. It would never occur to Kyle to question her authority in the house.

When they reached the cavernous kitchen, Riva pulled a large roll of wax paper from the pantry and set it on the butcher's block in the middle of the kitchen. While Kyle wrapped the sandwiches from the tray, Riva made more, and then found a box to pack them. She tossed in several bags of chips and then selected the best pieces of fruit she had on hand.

"Mom looks frightened," Kyle said softly as he picked up another sandwich and laid it in the center of a piece of wax paper he tore off the roll.

"Yes," Riva agreed, glancing over her shoulder at the youngest Emerson son. He met her eyes and realized she was frightened too. The normally sparkling eyes masking the playfully loving side of her were shadowed and red rimmed. Riva had been crying! He suddenly realized in all his years, he'd never one time known her to cry.

"I've never seen her frightened like this," he said with a deep sigh.

"Nor have I,' Riva admitted, offering Kyle a gentle hug, only slightly surprised when he dissolve into tears and wrapped his arms tightly around her. She drew in a deep breath to stave off her own threatening tears. She wrapped her strong arms tightly around him and patted the short, spiked hair.

In the family room, Helena sat staring out across the conservatory, trying not to think of the possibility of losing a child. Andrea was on the phone with Lee Malcolm's secretary who was coordinating the travel arrangements for the family. Sadie and Ben would leave Zurich on the next Concord departing. Garret and Vanessa had been at a political fundraiser in Dallas the night before and were already in route home.

"Richard told Lee that Holly's not at their Paris apartment," Andrea said, turning from the phone to speak quietly to her mother. "He's left messages with their friends for her."

"That's all we can do," Helena said as she drew in an imperceptible breath.

Had Holly been born in January when she was due, they would have named her after Gregory's mother and Helena's grandmother, Colleen Margery, but when their first child arrived just hours before Christmas Eve, Holly Noel was an impulsive choice. Helena sighed deeply at the thought of her oldest child. Perhaps had they followed their original plan, she would have a different nature – one more grounded like Gregory's proper, staid, Scots mother or her own gracious and quiet Grandmamma.

Instead, Holly was always a strong-willed child with an irrepressible spirit. From the day she was born she never did what was expected. She was a cheerful and fun loving baby, an irrepressibly happy child, and charismatic young woman. But if Gregory and Helena said up, Holly insisted on down. If they said no, Holly made it her life's mission to circumvent them. Whenever Helena thought of heartache and frustration in her privileged life, Holly was usually a major factor.

She and Gregory hoped that things would change when Richard arrived on the scene. Their sensible, levelheaded son-in-law was a breath of fresh air when Holly brought him home for Christmas seven years ago. Considering the malcontents and avant-garde friends she normally dragged along in her entourage, Richard was a surprising change. Although Holly seemed happy with Richard, she had grown increasingly distant from the rest of the family during their marriage.

Her last trip home was disastrous. She surprised them all when she arrived in September four years ago and announced she was going to stay through the holidays. Within just a few weeks, she took a fancy to one of Emit's interns. When Holly left, she took the young man with her, promising him an internship with a friend of hers in Spain.

The last they heard, she was living with a group of students in an artist colony in Madrid as their patron. There was also a rumor in a gossip column that she was spotted with a group of ex-patriots in Bangladesh, but Gregory's quiet inquiries proved futile. When Holly didn't want to be found, she wasn't going to be found.

She agreed to meet Richard in Paris for their last anniversary. He returned to announce that Holly now had no idea where Nathan was or what he was doing. Richard forgave her as he always forgave her and brought with him the lavish and outlandish gifts she sent to the family along with her apologies and promises to come home more often.

Helena was shaken from her fruitless musing by the sound of new arrivals. As she looked up, her daughter-in-law, Vanessa, came through the back hallway. Helena steeled herself for the wave of renewed emotions as she rushed to her.

Vanessa, the wife of their oldest son, was clearly a driving force in Garrett's political ambitions. She was the perfect match for the one intended for the Beltway someday if not the White House itself. Vanessa was always campaigning in Garret's behalf and was being fine-tuned to the role of first lady. Gregory just needed to settle on Garret's political goal and then secure it for him. Vanessa's life's mission was to be on the right boards, attend the right conferences, be seen in the right circles and make the right political connections. Vanessa was Garret's strongest political asset but drained all the energy Helena possessed when they were in the same room.

"Any news?" Vanessa demanded, as she crossed the room to her mother-in-law. She sank to the floor beside Helena's chair, taking her hand gently in hers.

"None," Helena sighed, tears brimming in her eyes.

"We saw Kyle leaving as we came in. Garret went with him. Where's Nicole? She should be down here with you."

"She's upstairs," Helena answered. "The doctor sent out something to sedate her."

"You're kidding!" Vanessa gasped with an incredulous disapproving shake of her head.

"She's very upset," Helena sighed, realizing there was something insensitive about Vanessa's attack on Nicole at a time like this.

"We're all upset, Helena," Vanessa said getting up and picking up the coffeepot. She pressed her hand on the side to see how warm it still was. "I'll tell Riva to make fresh coffee," she announced, turning on her heel and heading toward the kitchen.

※

Jake waited for Sandy to get Gregory into his squad car and well on the way up the Trail before he followed. He glanced in his rearview mirror to see Emit and Trevor in Emit's truck behind him. There seemed little interest in their departure from the retrieval site. As the two vehicles pulled to a stop on the Trail, Jake heaved a heavy sigh as he left his car and trudged up the road. Emit and Trevor were soon in step with him as they scrutinized the scene.

around him with a new eye. To his left the white scars newly gouged into the rock face seemed more severe in the direct rays of the higher sun. The yellow caution tape fluttered slightly in the rising wind and except for the gentle twittering of the birds in the nearby trees, there was only the muted sound of the deep waters rolling along in the ravine beneath them.

Trevor moved toward the guardrail, glancing over the edge to the river below. The waters were silvery gray in the changing light. Clouds were moving in more quickly and the river was picking up their reflections. Emit and Jake both dropped to one knee and were more closely examining the guardrail. Trevor swung himself over the mangled metal remaining in place, using a nearby tree trunk to scotch his foothold and remain out of the evidence area.

"You need to take a look here," he said quietly. Both Jake and Emit were on their feet in one move and Trevor swung himself back over the rail to allow Jake to take his place.

"There are bolts missing," Jake said as his eyes narrowed. He studied the dirt coated backside of the railing, reaching out to brush away some of the dirt and then giving it a second thought. He pulled his hand back and reached for his radio.

"Jane… come in…"

"Sheriff?" Jane's voice came over the radio barely audible.

"We need the flatbed up here…"

"We've got the car secured."

"Good, we need to take this rail section in with us too. There should be room at the back of the truck."

"I'll see to it…" she answered without hesitation.

"Right now…" Jake said still staring at the guard rail. "Bring another two or three pair of hands with you…"

"Yes sir."

"It should have prevented any car from going through, shouldn't it?" Trevor asked quietly, watching as Emit ran a large, gnarled hand over the metal; and then stood to turn slowly around, inspecting the ground around him.

Emit MacIntosh was a mountain of a man who looked as though he could have arrived on the colonial coast from a pirate ship, liked what he saw and decided to lay claim to it. He had thick, curly black hair and wore a full beard and mustache from which startling blue eyes inherited from his Scots ancestors stared out under shaggy, thick brows. The fact that one eyelid drooped slightly only added to the legendary reputation he had of being a man no one should cross.

"Oh, hell," Jake breathed, running one large hand over his brow and instinctively resting his other on his service revolver as he scanned the surrounding area.

Emit turned back to the mountain, his trained eyes searching the ridge above the Trail. Trevor and Jake turned to follow his gaze. Emit scanned the mountain above him, his practiced eye looking for a vantage point that would overlook this stretch of the road.

"You said you heard gun fire," Emit said to Trevor without looking his way. "Where were you?"

"Just west of the bridge, about a hundred fifty – two hundred feet."

"Could you tell where it came from?"

"Just that it echoed from the east."

"There're only a handful of places where someone would have clear view of the Trail along here," Emit said as he walked up the road, pausing every few strides to look up the mountainside. He spoke almost as though thinking out loud. "Trevor, while Jake's doing what he needs to do here, you and I will take a hike and see if there is anything up there of interest,"

"Take a radio," Jake replied, heading toward his squad car even as he spoke.

"There's a lot of dead air up here," Emit called with a shake of his head. "It might be just useless weight."

"I know, but take it anyway." He pulled a two-way radio from the trunk, tested the battery and frequency and then handed it to Trevor because Emit was already out of sight up the mountain.

Trevor repeated the check out of unconscious habit and then clipped the unit to his belt, hurrying to catch up with Emit. Jake watched as the two men headed out through the dense forest with a natural skill born to them. They moved through the thick growth with an amazing ease.

"It's like they are one with the mountain, isn't it?" Jane commented with an admiring shake of her head. Jake whirled around, he was so preoccupied in thought he did not hear her drive up. Her cruiser was in the middle of the road, the driver's door standing open.

"Yes it is," Jake agreed, turning again to look at the spot where the two men vanished into the woods.

"They had a few more lines to tie down on the tarp and the flatbed will be on up."

"Jane," he said quietly, glancing at his deputy. She watched him with a sideways look. "This is now a crime scene – tape it off."

"Yes, sir," Jane said with raised eyebrows, glancing over her shoulder to see if she could determine what he had seen as she pulled crime scene tape from her trunk. Without question she began taping off the clearing.

Trevor and Emit moved with quick precision through the woods and picked up a trail about two-tenths of a mile from the Trail. Emit stepped onto it, his skilled eye taking in every detail. Trevor waited patiently knowing that Emit would share with him what he chose to share when he chose to share it.

The two men were forming an unusual bond. Emit was an introvert who did not make friends easily, but there was something about the young friend of Cameron Emerson that was gaining not only Emit's respect, but his favor as well. Emit became Trevor's mentor without either one of them consciously realizing it. Trevor was in love with these mountains and wanted to learn all he could about them; Emit was the man who could teach him. Emit was a man who appreciated the love Trevor had for his mountains and was willing to share his wisdom with him.

They intercepted a wildlife trail and Emit came to a stop, stepping slightly to the side to allow Trevor to stand beside him. There was no reason to point out the wildlife tracks and droppings to Trevor, but he waited, casting a squinted gaze at him, "Someone's been traveling this trail recently. You see it?"

"How can you tell?" Trevor asked as he stared along the path as the older man did. Emit paused beside a depression in the soft earth along the edge of the trail and squatted down. "That isn't a track – it's a footprint. A shoe made it," he said, looking back up at Trevor, "not a hiking boot. Can you see the imprint?"

"No," Trevor admitted honestly, squatting beside Emit and looking dutifully at the ground and seeing nothing but dirt and dead leaves from the dying winter.

"I thought you SEAL boys were taught these things," Emit said with only a hint of sarcastic humor.

"No one leaves shoeprints underwater," Trevor said evenly. "We let the Army track the animals. We go after big fish."

"Here," Emit replied with an amused shake of his head. He used his finger to outline the print. Trevor looked closer and thought he might detect something, but wasn't sure. Emit stood up and laughed shortly. "Maybe you'll learn," he said, resuming their pace along the trail. "Maybe you're too waterlogged," he called over his shoulder after a few steps and they regained their steady pace. Trevor could hear the laughter in his voice and smiled comfortably.

Trevor took no offense. He knew Emit's gruff demeanor was not intended to be a slight. They were silent as they moved along the ridge. Emit paused often, getting his bearings and making sure he was traveling the course he plotted while standing on the roadway. He watched the trail closely, stopping and pointing out other prints to Trevor when he spotted them.

"Look at the brush," Emit instructed. "See the broken twigs? There's no fur caught in them, but this looks like lint. And the ground, can you see where the leaves have been trod down?" He paused and was studying the trail curiously. He stared for a long moment into the woods and then turned back to Trevor. "He veered off the trail here. Can you see the new trail through the woods there?" he asked, stepping a little to the side to allow Trevor to stand where he had been. Trevor stared into the woods as he had seen Emit doing, not knowing exactly what he should be looking for.

"I see it," Trevor breathed suddenly in surprise. There was a subtle – but discernable – path emerging from the forest floor.

"Animals don't pack the ground down like that when they move," Emit said, leaving the trail and following the new path. Trevor moved closely behind him. As they reached the boulders, Emit knew what he would see below.

He stepped out of the way, motioning for Trevor to crawl on top of them. Trevor hesitated only a moment before hoisting himself onto the lower ledge and then making his way across to the boulder towering beside it. As he gazed down through the early spring growth, he could see the Trail.

He shifted over as Emit pulled himself up beside him. Trevor felt his breathing growing more rapid as he confronted the ugly truth. Emit caught his arm and pointed down into the rocks below. "Look," he commanded, and the change in the man's tone made the hair on the back of Trevor's neck stand up.

After a moment's scrutiny, Trevor spotted the remnants of the gun stabilizer. Their worst suspicions were confirmed. Someone removed the massive bolts to weaken the guardrail below and then lay in wait on these rocks. Instinctively, he glanced around as though someone might still be lurking about.

"Where were you again when you heard the shot?" Emit asked quietly.

"On the other side of the ravine," Trevor responded, never taking his eyes off the pieces of wood below them. "I had just crossed over the swing bridge and headed downriver."

Emit was silent for a moment then sighed deeply. "You could have heard a shot fired from here if the wind was right."

"It's a clear sight from here. That car was visible from that turn above the tunnel. Who would want to hurt Nicole?" Trevor finally asked.

He could see Emit's head shaking even though he didn't turn around. "Might be that someone has a grudge against the whole family and the Jag happened to be the car that came along. They have made as many enemies as they've made allies," he sighed.

"Gregory's hell bent and determined to see Garret in the governor's mansion and there are a lot of powerfully mean people who take exception to that. And that's just here at home. They've also been doing a lot of messing with people's lives in all the mergers and buy-outs and takeovers all over the world."

"How could someone have found this place?"

"Jake's going to have to sort that one out. I found where… it's his job to find who. Got a rope?" Emit asked and Trevor swung his backpack off, pulled one out and tossed it to him.

Emit caught it and looked for a hold to tie it off. He picked a large tree behind the outcrop, secured the rope to it and then clambered back up beside Trevor. He swung himself over the front face of the rock, tested the rope as well as his footing and then made his way down to the wood fragments as Trevor retrieved his gloves from his pocket and pulled them on in unconscious habit. One thing he learned about Emit was that he was a man of few words and always had a specific purpose for anything he said or did. Emit gathered the pieces of wood and tossed them up to Trevor.

He was about to heave himself back up when he caught sight of the metal pivot farther down. With only a moment's hesitation, he repelled to a small outcrop and eased himself over the edge. Instinctively, Trevor grabbed the rope and tightened a firm grip around it. He realized he was holding his breath as he watched Emit, clinging to the trunk of a sapling as he inched forward to reach the metal piece.

CHAPTER SIX

Lightening split the distant sky as Nicole shrank back from the window, her pulse racing and the nausea overwhelming her again. Mae was instantly at her side, leading her toward the bed and insisting she lie down. Nicole stared for a moment at the picture on her bedside table. The owners of the Milleluci Hotel had snapped it that morning in Aosta when she and Cameron met for breakfast.

The sedative she was given along with the photo allowed her the mental portal to escape the horrors of the present reality and revisit another time when the world was a warm, sunny, and more friendly place. She and Cameron had a splendid view of Sant'Orso as they dined on the generous selection of meats, cheeses, and cakes that made the Milleluci a choice place for a substantial breakfast. They lingered over their meal, too aware of the engineers waiting for Cameron's approval of the renovations of the newly acquired complex and her need to be at the auction in Lombardy later that day.

Nicole's luggage was brought from her room and loaded into the Fiat by the hotel staff. It stood ready for the journey across the Alps as Cameron walked her from the lobby. She was not surprised when he leaned down and kissed her quickly, but she was unprepared for the response she felt. Without thinking, she reached for him to kiss her again, which he did with prolonged pleasure.

"Do your parents know you're running around Italy alone like this?" he asked as he handed her into her car.

She laughed softly, reaching backwards for the seat belt and securing it in the clasp. "It's the nineties," she laughed. "They are letting me cut my teeth in Italy. I'm still not allowed to travel in the Orient or Russia alone."

"Good," Cameron said, leaning into the car to kiss her again. "We'll do that together one day."

The comment took her off guard and she leaned away from him for a moment, studying the intensity in his eyes then sighed deeply. She had no idea what would come of this pleasant interlude in her trip, but they would see. She put the car into gear and eased away from the hotel and him, heading out of the village and onto the mountain road taking her out of the valley and eastward.

For two days the kiss haunted her. As she made her rounds of their suppliers in Bergamo and drove back to Milan to supervise the packing and shipping of the items she had purchased in Lombardy, her mind never strayed far from the hours she spent with Cameron Emerson. She found herself reliving the moments they shared, the words spoken, and wondering if she would ever see him again.

On Friday, Nicole turned in her rented Fiat and boarded the train to cross the Dolomite Mountains, leisurely traveling through the Trentino Alto Adige region to the medieval Tyrolean town of Trento for another private auction to which The House of Quinn was cordially invited. After another successful buying spree and careful attention to the transferring of funds and supervising the packing and shipping of her treasures, she boarded the train to continue on to Bolzano.

Nicole always stayed at Schloss Korb, an eleventh century fairy tale-like castle in the heart of vineyard country that could fulfill any woman's need for fantasy when she was in Bolzano. She was looking forward to the softly lit and beautifully decorated rooms, the heated pool and sauna and hoping to pick up a tennis game as she left the train station and hired a local cab. She was exhausted from the hard week of rushing between auctions of art and antiques. Schloss Korb was the perfect place to rest, relax and take a few days off to revisit the La Via Del Vino. Of all the provinces of Italy, Trentino Alto Adige was her favorite and she always stole a few days for herself while she was there.

Nicole took a long, luxurious bath and then headed down to the lobby to pick up a brochure of the regional activities. There was always some kind of festival, fair, costumed event, or pageant going on. No matter what month of the year Nicole found herself on the "gateway to the Dolomites," she never lacked opportunities to savor the local flavor.

She caught a shuttle into the center of town, and was settling into a quiet corner of a restaurant with her collection of tourist brochures and a glass of local wine when a shadow fell across the table. She seemed to know he was there before she looked up. Her heart was pounding and her pulse racing as she met Cameron's twinkling eyes.

"Hi," he said, pulling a chair out and plopping into it as though running into her at a hotel in the Italian Alps was the most natural thing in the world. "I'm in desperate need of help," he confessed, patting his jacket pockets. She didn't ask him how he knew where she was because she was speechless. The pale mountain sunlight caught the highlights in his hair, bringing out the deep red tones.

"Here we go," he said, finally pulling a folded piece of paper from his pocket and laying it on the table, opening it up, and smoothing it down with his hands. "Can you teach me how to say these phrases in Italian?"

Nicole took the paper, unable to suppress her laughter as she read down the list. *Your estimate is too high. These are not the specs we approved. I don't care if he is your uncle, his bid is too high. Do you think I'm crazy or just had too much vino? We aren't rebuilding Rome here!*

"Having trouble with contractors?"

"They smile and pretend not to understand my translator," Cameron complained, his eyes narrowing with suspicion. "I don't believe it for a minute."

"Where is the translator from?"

"The Zurich office. My sister, Sadie sent him down."

"There could be a problem with the dialect," Nicole offered.

"I think they know exactly what I'm saying. It wouldn't surprise me if they all speak English," he said with a deep sigh, sinking back in the chair and looking around for the waiter. "I'll have two of whatever she's drinking," he called with his boyish grin, pointing at her glass and then holding up two fingers. "They do understand English here, right?" he whispered out of the side of his mouth, still smiling at the waiter.

"Yes," Nicole laughed with the waiter, neither able to resist his charm.

"Would you like a job as an interpreter?" he asked, leaning back for the waiter to set two glasses of sparkling red wine from the local winery in front of them. "I was really hoping this would be hard liqueur," he admitted as he lifted one glass and sniffed at the aroma.

"Lesson number one," she said glancing toward the waiter for his agreement, "The local wine the finest in the world."

He glanced at the waiter who seemed to be waiting for him to taste the wine. He drew in a deep breath and smiled, taking a sip and nodding passionately and then taking another few sips.

They lingered at the table through dinner, Cameron venting his frustration and aggravation over the difficulties of getting the remodeling at the Aosta complex underway. Between the local authorities and craftsmen, they were meeting obstacle after obstacle. They were already facing serious cost overruns and delays.

After dinner, they wandered through the winding, narrow streets that were lined with brilliantly colored houses. They crossed the arched bridges and passed the arcades as they strolled by the cloisters and chapel of St. John, pausing to enjoy the frescos that adorned the walls. She could sense the tension draining from him as they walked.

"Where are you staying?" she asked as they made their way back to the restaurant.

"Oh," he said, the impish gleam leaping back into the light brown eyes, flecked with gold, "this great place a little ways out of town. The Schloss Korb."

"Really?" Nicole asked, somehow not terribly surprised. She felt as though she had known and loved him all her life; it had just taken her twenty-four years to find him. She knew she was setting herself up for a broken heart, but was unable to regain reason or logic.

"You?" he asked, not able to pull off the innocent charm as smoothly as he wanted.

"Schloss Korb," she admitted.

"Then, maybe you would like a ride back?" he suggested, not reacting to the accusing light in her eyes.

"Maybe," she said, falling into step with him as he led her to the Maserati that was parked in the lot of the Hotel Elefante.

Nicole was never able to completely recall every detail about the days that followed. She felt as though when they stepped back into the fairy tale castle of Scholss Korb, she stepped into a dream. They spent the weekend exploring the many magical hamlets and villages of the region, daring the challenges of the saw-toothed ridges of the Austrian Alps, and discovering snow-capped peaks, alpine meadows, and breathtaking waterfalls along the well-marked trails.

She called her parents on Tuesday, assuring them she was fine and that she was simply taking a few days R&R with a fellow American. Cameron informed his Zurich office he was researching the area for expansion of the European territory. Nicole taught Cameron snatches of Italian, pithy phrases and expressions that would completely convey his contempt and disapproval of the contractors and architects at the Aosta facility without truly offending them.

They visited the castles, toured the cathedrals and churches, indulged in the local cuisine and haunted the quaint little shops that offered everything from costumes to masterpieces of art. They ignored the reality that would interrupt their fairy tale for almost a week before surrendering to the responsibilities of their lives. They traveled the steep, cliff-hanging roads of the area, arriving at Trentino's southern border and the Mediterranean charm of Lake

Garda.

It was in Riva del Garda that Nicole discovered the delicate antique dress in a shop in the town that encompassed the atmosphere of a seaport and the shadows of the local castle, the Rocco. She laughed when Cameron told her it was the reason they had come to Italy, and was appalled when he insisted on buying it for her. She refused, but decided to buy it for the shop. She was never sure why she didn't add the dress to the inventory shipped out that week. Perhaps in her heart of hearts, she knew it was never meant for the shop. Instead, she carefully packed it among her clothes to keep it close.

When they returned to Schloss Korb, their mood changed, knowing duty was calling them back to their separate worlds. Cameron had a meeting scheduled with his contractors for the Aosta facility and her parents called to insist she catch several private sales they learned were taking place in Tuscany.

The next morning, Cameron put her on a train to Pesaro e Urbino and kissed her goodbye. Although they talked about seeing each other when they got home, Nicole had a sick feeling things would be far different once they left the magic of Italy.

As the train sped through the Emilia Romagna province, she considered the many obstacles they would face in Stafford County. They not only lived in very different worlds, but also came from starkly different backgrounds. The Emersons were counted among the most elite and wealthy American families, often referred to as the closest class to royalty descending from the colonists.

She recognized the sad truth that for all his promises, her respite with the heir to the Emerson throne in the hidden valleys and out-of-the-way places of Italy would be something she could always remember as being as surreal as the morning mist that collected in the recesses of the mountains, but would only be memories to revisit once she returned home. She and Cameron were not only from separate worlds, but they belonged on different planets. He could never fit into her small, contained world, and she was certain there was no place for her in his.

She returned to the rigorous demands of work, plowing through the seemingly endless lots of other people's memories and family history, making notes on the catalogues she was handed as she arrived at the auctions and securing many of the specific items her parents wanted. As her days were consumed with the cataloguing of her purchases and the endless paperwork required for the transactions, the mystical hours she and Cameron spent together became little more than faded memories consigned to the recesses of her mind.

A week after saying goodbye to Cameron in Trento, she returned to the restored country villa on Carciano di Cotignola in Revenna that was her usual place to stay when in the area and phoned her parents to share news of her latest acquisitions for the shop. They were pleased enough to not mention the week lost to her frivolous side trip. She changed from the jeans and over blouse she was wearing in her searches through the combined lots of the sale into a light weight sun dress, and then retreated from the confines of her room to the terrace overlooking the pool.

Now that her obligations to the shop and her parents were fulfilled, she turned her attention to the chance to revisit some of her favorite sites of Ravenna, another well-kept secret of the region. Its location allowed it a unique heritage, indulging the influence of Constantinople more than that of the Roman invasion. Before she returned to Milan, she would visit the church of San Vitale and the other churches that offered a step back into the most interesting shadows of the Dark Ages, she decided. She picked up rumors of an unpublished sale in Forli, but it was nothing more than a blind hunt. She was unable to glean the slightest hint as to who was holding it so gave up.

Emilia Romagna and the Marches were not her favorite part of Italy. She was not as comfortable getting off the beaten tracks and exploring the walled cities and Byzantine remains. The specters of the marauding barbarians who invaded the area seemed to cling to the ancient sites. As the solitude closed in, she was looking forward to returning to her more familiar haunts.

She found a chaise lounge on the far end of the terrace, settled in with her glass of wine as the shadows lengthened across the terrace in front of her. She was deep in thought when she sensed she was not alone and was jerked from her absorption with a start. As was his habit, Cameron left her speechless. Her mouth gaped open slightly as she watched him patting his jacket pockets again. This time he pulled out a stack of index cards, tapping them into perfect alignment before handing them to her.

"I need some more lessons," he said without preamble as though he had just left her minutes before.

She glanced at the card on top and saw *I give up, build it any damn way you want* written in his loose, careless hand. She laughed out loud, tears threatening to slip from behind her sunshades. She translated the phrase, leaving out the profanity and repeated it several times as he learned the inflections. She slipped the top card to the bottom of the stack and read the second one. *How much is the bribe... excuse me... the permit again?* The third card read *Forgive me, I thought you said your uncle... I didn't hear you say godfather.*

"Cameron!" she laughed, shaking her head.

"I'm learning the tricks of the trade," he boasted, holding his hand up like an oath. "You were right. It was all in the dialect. It's just a matter of getting to know the local thugs."

"You're shameless," she declared.

"I'm realistic," he countered. "The local authorities are shameless." He was watching her intently. "What about that last one?"

She looked down at the stack of cards and shuffled through them again. "What last one?" she asked fanning them out in her hand to check a third time.

Cameron snatched them from her hands as though he didn't believe her and then began patting his pockets again. "Aha!" he cried, pulling a single card from the inside breast pocket of his jacket and handing it to her.

"*I love you; will you marry me*" she read, feeling the breath rush from her lungs and not sure she could inhale again. She finally caught her breath, not believing what she was reading. When she lifted her head, tears blurred her vision, and he was standing up, reaching for her hand. He pulled her to her feet, leading her off the terrace into the privacy of the walled garden to the rear of the villa. Once away from the other guests, he brought a velvet box from his pants pocket and ceremoniously dropped to one knee.

"Cameron," she whispered, shaking her head and remembering all the complications she had pondered after he left the last time, "you can't be serious."

"I've never been more serious about anything in my life," he said solemnly, pulling her face down to kiss her tenderly. "These last few days without you have been agony."

"We hardly know each other," she sighed.

"We've always known each," he said, reaching up to push a stray strand of hair from her face. "You know it's true."

"Cameron," she said, shaking her head. She knew there were hundreds of reasons why the idea was ludicrous, but she was having trouble thinking of any one of them.

"Tell me you don't love me," he challenged, "and I'll go away."

She sucked in her breath, the idea of saying such a thing abhorrent to her. "I can't," she admitted.

With that, Cameron pulled the delicate diamond ring from the case and slipped it onto her left hand, then stood up to pull her into his arms.

"This idea is insane, Cameron!" she whispered between his kisses.

"We can marry in the church in Aosta. We can get a license through the consulate. I've already checked into it and paid the bribe," he added, unable to check his sense of humor for long. "I mean fee."

"What will our families say?" she whispered, shaking her head and trying to imagine how her parents would react to their only daughter marrying a man they had never met half way around the globe. Then she tried to image the reaction of Gregory and Helena Emerson to the news that the heir to the helm of Emerson International had married an antiques buyer from a tiny shop in the historic district of Crystal Springs. The thought made her shiver.

"They'll come to understand how deeply we've fallen in love," he said with a shrug of his shoulders.

"How can you be so sure?" she asked, moving into his embrace.

"Because for the last week I've felt completely lost without you – I kept turning around expecting you to be there, realizing you were supposed to be there; knowing we belong together. I don't want to go on like that. I don't want us to be apart."

"Neither do I," Nicole admitted.

"So, let's get married," he said, taking a step back to look into her eyes.

"This is terrifying," she admitted, thinking about either direction her life was about to take. "I can't imagine what life with you would be like, but at the same time, I can't imagine life without you now, either."

"That sounds rather like I win by default," he said as though they had just decided where to have dinner, "but, I'll take it."

"Take what?" she gasped.

"The 'yes' and we'll go back to Aosta and get married."

"Oh, Cameron..." she whispered, shaking her head again, "I just don't know that that's the way to go about this. My parents – your parents!"

"Look, if we go home and tell our families we want to get married, we're going to get caught up in the Emerson way. My mother and father will make our wedding a circus and what few doubts we have now will look like nothing compared to what will happen once they get involved. If we go home before we are married, we'll be looking at six – eight months, maybe even a year before it can be done their way."

"I don't know what my parents will say," Nicole sighed.

"We can have a formal ceremony when we get back if you like, but let's get married here," Cameron insisted. "You don't know my family."

"Don't you think that's the pertinent point here?" Nicole responded, reason still trying to catch hold of her sanity.

"No!" he answered quickly. "I mean you don't know how they take the simplest thing and make it into this enormous, out of control event. They never do anything by halves – they don't really do things by wholes – they take things and double and triple them! We really need to marry before we go home or we could lose each other in the fallout. Trust me. Everything will be okay."

Nicole felt the tears spilling from her eyes as she saw the lightening split the sky again. She was pulled from her escape of memory in the Italian countryside and slammed back to the brutal reality of the moment. She lay back on the bed, remembering his promise. "Don't lie to me, Cam," she whispered, covering her eyes with her arms. "Everything has to be okay. You promised me everything would be okay!"

※

By the time Kyle and Garret arrived at the recovery site, the mangled Jaguar was loaded on the flatbed behind the pickup. Jake and Sandy were wrapping a severely damaged section of the guardrail in plastic and securing it in the well of the wrecker with strong twine. Confused, Kyle grabbed the grocery bag of sandwiches from Garret and crossed the roadway, handing the bag to one of the deputies. "Mom sent these," he said off-handedly.

"What's going on?" Garret demanded, moving toward the trailer. He walked around the flatbed, his face paling as he saw the damage done to the car. "Dad? …have they found…?"

"No," Gregory said, anticipating the question. The ambulance called to the scene was parked with the driver sitting in the front seat, listening to the radio chatter between the search teams coming in from the river.

"Why is the door twisted back like that? How did that happen?" Kyle asked, staring at the bent door panel still swinging in the gusting winds. Every move caused metal to screech against metal, sending a piercing grating scream into the air. "Can they stop that noise…?"

Jake glanced over his shoulder and saw that Sandy and Jane were searching the cruisers for something to tie the door against the car's frame to hold it. Jane pulled a bungee cord from her trunk and called to Sandy. They swung themselves onto the flatbed and began the task.

"Where's the back tire?" Garret asked, looking around. "Did he lose a wheel? Is that why he left the road? What happened? Isn't anyone going to tell us anything?"

"Boys, please," Gregory intoned softly, turning his attention to Jake as he was approaching.

Trevor listened to the exchange going on among the Emerson men. He stared into the boiling sky, watching the approaching clouds with a curious gaze. The skipping radio chatter from the rescue team was filling the airways, giving those left at the scene an idea of their progress but also putting nerves on edge. This was the worst possible place to have to depend on two-way radios. There were always pockets of dead air where the mountainous terrain blocked the signals. A flash of lightening split the sky to the west with thunder following after several seconds on its heels. Every eye solemnly scanned the darkening sky.

"Should they keep searching in this weather...?" Trevor asked, turning to look at Emit and Jake who were standing not far behind him as a search helicopter flew overhead, drowning out the end of Trevor's comment.

"No," Jake replied quietly, dread clearly evident in his voice. "We'll have to suspend the search until the storm blows over. They're bringing the teams out at Corey Bend. I'd imagine that's the best place, don't you think, Emit?"

"Yeah," Emit agreed, turning his brilliant blue eyes toward the river. The deputies were setting reflective barricades into place across the Trail. "Better make sure you secure those in some way. That isn't a spring shower moving in."

"We will," Jake assured him as he ordered his search teams off the river. They were disciplined enough not to question his orders. They were deep into the ravine and trusted him to keep them apprised of any changes in conditions. They all heard the message relaying from radio to radio down on the river. Unconsciously, Jake counted eight responses from the teams and knew they had all gotten word that the search was being suspended.

"They can set up a command post at The Manor if they want," Gregory offered hesitantly. He was suddenly out of his element. "What would be best?"

"We can't do anything until this storm passes, sir" Jake said, raising his voice to be heard over the chopper that was making another pass overhead. "I need to get back to Oak Meadow with these," he went on, jerking his head at the car and evidence he collected from the scene. His deputies were checking again to make sure the bungee cords were secured.

"Just let me know what we can do to help," Gregory finally said, reaching out to squeeze the huge upper arm. "Anything... everything I have is at your disposal. You know that goes without saying."

Gregory headed toward the 4X4 Garret and Kyle drove down and Kyle moved out of the way of the truck and trailer headed down the Trail. Andy reversed action and the hoist was retracting into the housing. The Troopers were sitting in their cruisers, waiting for the last of the deputies to clear out on their way to pick up the rescue teams. They would man the roadblocks to The Manor at the foot of the Trail to keep everyone off the mountain until the Emerson private security arrived with reinforcements. In a matter of minutes, Jake, Emit, and Trevor stood alone on the side of the road.

"This wasn't a spur of the moment thing," Emit said as he helped Jake gather up the last of the gear and stow it in the trunk of his cruiser.

"Definitely not a crime of opportunity," Jake agreed. "This was carefully planned and skillfully executed. It took a very keen mind… a clever mind… a devious mind." He paused a moment and glanced around the forest, wondering.

"How long do you think it took to determine where to strike and then find that spot?"

Emit followed his gaze back up the mountain, drawing in a deep breath and holding it a moment before loudly exhaling. He shook his head and then sighed again. "It wasn't all that hard a spot to get to," Emit finally answered. "It wasn't rough terrain."

"But you know, it took some calculating to figure it all out. You say it's not hard to reach?"

"No," Emit confirmed. "It was just a hundred feet or so off a wildlife trail.

"So it didn't take any physical strength… just a head for calculations and a good aim." Jake stood staring out over the ravine, listening to the final radio chatter coming off the river as the rescue teams reached the Trail and checked in.

"And no conscience," Emit added, following Jake's stare down to the river.

"You see anyone out and about up there lately?" Jake asked, turning a steely gaze toward Trevor.

"No," Trevor said simply, shaking his head and feeling an uncomfortable flush beginning at the nape of his neck.

"You got a set pattern you follow every day on those tests?"

"Pretty much," Trevor answering, lifting his eyes to return Jake's steady stare. "I hit different sector in different days, but usually the same route."

"Ever come across anybody while you were going about your business?"

"Occasionally I see Emit and his crews in the higher sectors, but never in this region along the river."

"It was definitely murderous intent," Jake murmured.

"It was that," Emit said heaving a weary sigh.

"Somebody laid up there waiting for that car – picked up a rifle… took aim and shot!"

"Like you said," Emit responded, "Murderous intent."

"You need a ride anywhere?" Jake asked, turning to speak to Trevor, but he was nowhere to be seen.

"He's gone," Emit said opening the door of his truck and turning to look back at Jake.

"Where'd he go?"

Emit made a quick jerk of his head toward the river. They spotted the young man as he made his way upstream. "Image he's getting to shelter before the storm breaks." Emit stooped over to pick up the thick rope that still dangled over the side of the embankment. Without saying anything else, he began looping it easily over his shoulder and around his elbow as he pulled it in and then handed it to Jake.

"He'll be okay?" Jake asked, tossing the coil of rope into the trunk and slamming the lid.

"He's a mountain man at heart," Emit said, dismissing Jake's concern. "He knows more about this area around here than I do now."

"Is that so?" Jake asked, squinting his eyes to follow the diminishing form of Cameron's new best friend until he disappeared around a bend in the river. "I'm going to need you to take me to that sniper's nest in the next day or so."

"Just let me know when," Emit said, turning and heading toward his truck.

☙❧

Like her given name, Sadie Marguerite Emerson Faraday was a unique blend of her mother's poise and grace and her father's keen mind and business acumen. She inherited her mother's dark hair and eyes along with her father's clear, Scot's complexion. Unlike her more petite sisters, she stood almost six feet tall and shoulder-to-shoulder with her brothers and husband. She spoke six languages fluently and was the powerhouse behind the successful Emerson International European expansion of the last five years.

Her husband, Ben Faraday, was Gregory Emerson's handpicked choice for not only the International Project but also his son-in-law as well. Together, Sadie and Ben carried EI to an international presence no one could have imagined when the expansion first began. The Faradays were based in Zurich, but commuted continually from the company's offices in Paris, Munich, Madrid, and London. The Emersons had homes or apartments in just about every European country and Sadie and Ben were very much involved in the day-to-day operations of all the European facilities.

Sadie paced from one end of the elegantly appointed VIP lounge at the Charles DeGaulle Airport in Paris to the other, unable to hide her agitation at the delayed boarding of the Concord. They were in route to Zurich when the call about Cameron came and would have missed the connection from there had they continued on so they turned back to Paris to make the next flight. On the table beside the cream and hunter green striped silk covered sofa, the ice was melting in her drink. Ben scanned the latest emails on his new IBM Think Pad that was resting on the small desk in the corner.

"I feel so helpless," she sighed, pausing at the huge picture window that looked out over the tarmac of the airport.

"We are helpless," Ben mused, closing an email from the Frankfort agent and looking up at his wife. "But I'm sure everything is being handled at home."

"There's something Dad's not telling me," she said as she turned to level her gaze on him. "I know him and I know he's not being completely honest about this accident." She talked to her father as soon as they landed again in Paris. All he would tell them was that Cameron had been in an accident that morning on the Trail and he needed them to come home.

"More than likely," Ben admitted, "but, what good would it do to burden you with all the details when you have hours on a plane ahead of you?"

"I always prefer to know what I'm walking into," Sadie said, reaching down to retrieve and then stare into the diluted drink. "Where is that steward?"

"That might not be the case when it comes to your family, Sadie," he said, closing the laptop and getting up to cross the room and gather her into his arms. He was almost six foot four, a striking compliment to her height. He had an athletic look about him although he'd never been drawn to sports. He reached for the glass and carried it to the wet bar in the corner of the room to pour the contents out, and then opened the small refrigerator built into the cabinet below.

"How could Cameron have missed a turn on the Trail, Ben?" she sighed, pressing a well-manicured hand into her forehead. "We all know that road like we know the driveway at Hawthorne. We don't miss turns on that road."

Ben selected a club soda and twisted the cap off. The last thing Sadie needed at the moment was anything that would dull her instincts or aggravate her mood. He poured the soda over fresh ice, selected a wedge of lime from a crystal bowl on the counter and then carried the glass to her. As she took her first sip, the door opened and the uniformed airline associate announced that the Concord was ready to board. She began immediately to gather their carry-on bags as Ben returned to his computer to pack it away.

Sadie carried the crystal glass with her to the gate, sipping at the soda as they watched the assistant expedite their check-in and speak to the gate agent. He preceded them through the jet way and into the plane, stowing their bags in the compartment for them as they settled into their seats. As the assistant passed by on his way off the plane, Sadie handed him the glass. The young man took it without the faintest display of surprise or emotion.

As the second oldest of the Emerson children, Sadie learned her lessons in manners and decorum from Helena but her attitude of superiority from her father with the earnest intent of excelling in her true passion, seeing that at any hour of the day, an Emerson International entity would be open for business somewhere in the world. She spearheaded the expansion in Europe with a skill and cunning she learned at her father's side. She was now being tutored in Japanese and Mandarin with her sights on expanding into the Orient.

"Dad sounded so strange," Sadie sighed as she leaned her head back against the seat and glanced sideways at Ben. He was already positioning the tray to hold his laptop.

"Cameron's been in an accident, Sadie, how do you expect him to sound?"

"It's more than that, Ben," Sadie said barely above a whisper, very aware of the closeness of the plane and mindful of listening ears. "There's something he hasn't told us."

"We'll know soon enough, my dear," Ben said softly, reaching over to pat her hand that was clenching the armrest as the plane was pushed away from the terminal by the tug. She was a nervous flyer under the best of circumstances. Ben folded his laptop down and eased it carefully under his seat, glancing out the window as they reached the runway. His eyes narrowed and a dark shadow passed across them.

He agreed with Sadie. This was more than merely an accident. Something monumental was happening at The Manor. He had been in the family long enough to recognize the call to arms and the raising of the castle gate when he heard it. He took a deep breath and slowly let it out, wondering if his brother-in-law was still alive and if not, why not.

He inhaled deeply and patted Sadie's hand. "I'm going to the men's room before takeoff."

"Goodness," Sadie sighed. "We were in the lounge for hours. Why didn't you do that then?"

"I'll only be gone a minute," he said completely unruffled by her sharp response.

He headed to the lavatory toward the back of the jet. He glanced curiously at the passengers on the plane, nodding to those who looked at him with his calm ease. Just as he reached the lavatory, a man on the aisle caught and kept his glance. Ben raised a questioning brow at him and smiled curiously. Almost imperceptivity, the man shifted in his seat and Ben saw the familiar EI monogram on the cuff of his long sleeved dress shirt.

After stepping into the lavatory a moment and splashing cold water on his face, he grabbed a towel and buried his face in it. He wasn't sure if the presence of EI security on the plane brought him comfort or more alarm. This was not a call to arms, this was an all out security alert.

CHAPTER SEVEN

Cameron Emerson never knew it was humanly possible to endure such pain and survive. He was caught in a blinding abyss of agony and unable to determine the exact origin of any of it. Pain racked his body from every cell; every movement carried him to a deeper level of suffering. Consciousness was his greatest enemy but the misery would not allow him the mercy of unconsciousness. He was unable to open his eyes or move his arms and legs.

He lay on hard stone but there was a cover over him and thin cushion under him that seemed to provide some level or heat but no comfort. He could feel something supporting his neck, but it was also cold and hard. He quickly learned to stay limp, because any movement sent intense anguish exploding through his body; but he was unable to avoid the involuntary muscle spasm that sent the pain rushing from head to toe.

Unable to see, he turned his mind to identifying what he could hear. He thought he heard the distant sound of thunder. At times, he thought he might feel air moving over his face and he could hear the sound of the river. He heard the unmistakable sound of helicopters but was unable to determine from what distance or direction. Sometimes they seemed to be overhead and others they sounded as if they were only the buzz of a bee in a field of clover in the summertime. He didn't know which was real

He had no idea how long he had been wherever he was. Nor could he remember how he got there. As the fog of pain ebbed in and out of his mind, he realized at some point that he must be in an underground cavern. There was no light filtering through the blindfold. He could smell the distinctive odors of mineral waters, fungus, and damp rock. Occasionally, he heard the scampering of creatures along with their curious noises.

The last memory he could conjure up was walking across the glade with Nicole. He could remember the uncertainty in her eyes as they discussed the exact location of the house. He wanted it closer to the river. She wanted it in the shelter of the back grove of trees. Trotter McGee warned them they might have some drainage problems that far back, but Nicole wanted a larger front lawn. He finally agreed, a large front lawn was as a safer buffer between the house and the river's edge.

He had no idea how long ago that had been. He knew there were days if not weeks between that moment and this nightmare. He remembered a meeting at the Plaza with his father and a teleconference with his sister, Sadie. He also remembered a meeting with a man who was speaking first in a foreign tongue and then speaking in English but not what was said.

The effort to remember brought only a deeper, more intense headache and he moaned, listening as his moan was shortstopped not far over his head and then silenced. He heard thunder again, this time louder than before. He wasn't sure if that was because his mind was clearing or a storm was coming down on top of him. He tried to take a deep breath and it seemed as though a knife plunged into his side. He gasped and the shooting pain only radiated throughout his chest, causing an involuntary jerking of his arms and legs which brought fiery pain enveloping his body.

As the shuddering pain began to subside, he thought for a moment he caught another sound. He grew still, straining to hear anything around him and it was at that moment he knew he was no longer alone.

"Who's there?" he called, unable to prevent the tensing in his body and unable to muffle a sharp cry. The pain brought a drop into a semiconscious surrender.

"Listen!" Cameron was pulled from his muddled thought by the intense voice above him and then felt a mouth close to his ear. The sound he heard was hissing coming through closed teeth. "If you understand me – then do that once for yes, twice for no. Got it?"

Cameron discovered he could move his tongue in his closed mouth without sending excruciating pain shooting through his body. He forced a breath through his clenched teeth over his chapped and cracking lips one time. He tried to take a deep breath and the pain brought him to a sudden spasm, sending his moan bouncing off the walls around him.

"You can't do that again," the voice growled into his ear. He heard the distinctive hiss again. "Do you want to live through this?"

Cameron concentrated on hissing through his teeth. After a prolonged hiss that took all of his strength and breath, he slowly inhaled again, and then gave the short, distinctive hiss as instructed.

"Just to make sure we are communicating, do you want to live?"

Cameron took a shallow breath and then hissed once.

"Okay then. I have some water for you, just open your lips and let me pour it down the back of your throat. Don't try to swallow. Think you can do that?"

Cameron hissed once. He steeled himself for the pain as the cloth wrapped around his head was loosened. He moaned loudly when his jaw was grasped. After the initial shock of pain shuddered through him, he went limp.

"Just stay like that and lie still. Can you do that?"

Cameron shifted his eyes sideways to look into eyes that were hard and steely. He had never seen this man before and it was difficult to put thoughts together. Cameron held his breath as the pain began to ebb. "Learn to do what I say if you don't want to die. Understand?"

Cameron went limp, unable to fight the pain wracking his body. He felt a rough cloth on his lips and realized there was some kind of soothing balm spread on then. Then a thin blade was slipped through his teeth. "Just rest your tongue under that," he was commanded. He realized a slight trickle of water was moving over the blade and his parched tongue and down the back of his throat. "Don't try to swallow. You could strangle if you do. I promise you don't want to cough or get strangled." As the water slowly trickled into his throat he relaxed and felt relief from his thirst.

"I've got to move you out of here," the strangely unfamiliar voice said in his ear. "Make any noise and you can wind up dead," Cameron tried to speak, but only guttural noises came out. He heard the hissing in his ear as a reminder and fell silent. "Do you want to live?"

Cameron hissed once.

"Okay. No noises then. Got it?"

Cameron hissed once. He felt a thin piece of wood slipped between his teeth and positioned against the sides of his mouth. "When you want to scream, bite down on that instead. It won't prevent the pain, but it will lessen it."

Cameron felt the rough cloth going back around his head. The pain from his leg was so intense he moaned deeply. As he was pulled from his position and felt something being wrapped around him a blessed darkness rose up in his mind and pulled him completely into it.

When he came to again, he was strapped to some kind of board and was being dragged through dark woods along painfully unlevel ground. He moaned and bit the wood between his teeth, triggering a shooting, blinding pain up the left side of his face and then down the side of his body. There was a hood over his head but he could see slightly out of his right eye through the loose weave.

The sky was boiling with dark clouds. The smell of rain was heavy in the air and thunder moved around them in a continuing roll. He could hear running water not far from them and realized they were following a mountain stream. He had no idea where he was. He had no idea where they were going. And most alarming of all, he had never before seen the man who was dragging him determinedly through the woods and deeper into the mountains.

He heard the sound of a helicopter in the distance and as it grew closer, was pulled abruptly sideways into thick brush, triggering the searing pain through his body. He felt burning tears in his eyes but as the man hunkered down over him, he bit hard on the thin wood, repressing the scream that wanted to escape for fear of what would happen if he did.

"We don't have much farther but if you want to live, you will do nothing to cause attention to us. Understand?"

Cameron tried to take a deep breath, felt the stabbing pain in his chest and exhaled quickly. After a moment, he managed to hiss once.

"Good," he heard as the chopper swept overhead so low the dust and winter debris was caught in the draft and swirled mercilessly around them.

As the chopper flew away, Cameron moaned slightly as the bindings holding him in the mummy-like wrappings were grasped and he knew he was about to be pulled again over the unforgiving terrain of the mountain forest.

"We don't have much farther to go," he heard spoken in his ear. "Then you can scream all you want. No one will be able to hear you."

※

From his office window, Jake watched as his deputies moved the evidence from the various vehicles into the motor pool garage. The heavy clouds moving in threw Oak Meadow into dusky shadows, giving the scene an eerie sepia look and strange feel. Sandy called hurried instructions to the others as rain began to fall.

Jane loosened the straps securing the Jag's wheel and hefted it off the truck bed onto a work cart. She then transferred it to a cleared workbench and removed the plastic tarp. The metal from the guardrail lay already uncovered on the floor, a large piece of black plastic underneath it. Every gust of wind that rushed through the open doors caused the railing to move in a macabre rhythm and an eerie tattoo as it rocked against the concrete floor. She heaved a sigh of relief as all the evidence and equipment was brought from the trucks and the doors were lowered.

Sandy grabbed a push broom and began sweeping the puddling water toward the floor drain as Jane turned her attention to the railing. The growing intensity of the rain made itself known on the roof overhead as it increased to a nerve-racking din between the flashing bolts of lightning and the thunder that came chasing after it. A fingerprint kit and the department camera waited on the floor beside the rail.

Jake headed toward the break room, filled the insert for the big urn with coffee grounds, thought for just a moment and then spooned an extra measure of coffee grounds in and pressed the lighted red button. He heard the water rush through the connecting pipe into the reservoir. Almost instantly, water began seeping through the filter and depositing an aromatic black brew into the carafe.

Satisfied they would soon have a sufficient supply of caffeine for the long task ahead he returned to his office and turned on the weather radio to follow NOAA's tracking of the storm. Thunder was now rolling across the mountains like repeating oceans waves crashing on a shore. Once the warm air in the valley rose into the higher altitude of the mountains, there the clouds thickened and the storm's intensity increased.

He glanced out the window across the street. The rescue teams were unloading their gear from their cars and scurrying into the firehouse. Against the light pouring out of the station into the storm's gloom, they were more silhouettes than recognizable individuals. There was a resigned exhaustion to them, unable to tap into the adrenaline rush that a successful rescue could bring.

One outer door stood open and he saw that some of the men and women were already repacking their gear, readying their Go Bags to resume the search as soon as conditions allowed. Others were making their way toward the scattered vehicles parked along the street. He knew what they were thinking, because every bolt of lightning splitting the sky and every crash of thunder vibrating his windows, brought a mental image of a badly injured Cameron out there somewhere along a merciless stretch of the river and a desperate need to do something – anything was overwhelming.

He poured a cup of coffee and crossed the squad room to his office. He pulled the plastic bag containing the splintered pieces of wood and metal swivel bolt from his pocket before shrugging out of his jacket and sinking into his well-worn chair that fit him as only a chair could after years of use by the same body. As he sipped at the coffee, he studied the fragments of the hand-made stabilizer.

When the storm moved out he would have Emit take him to the sniper's nest. Coming from the coastal land of Florida, he never enjoyed the deep, demanding sports of the mountain. Those men across the street traveled through the many valleys and across the dangerous mountainsides and called it entertainment. Jake preferred a safer form of recreation. He enjoyed the trout fishing of the high country and the hunting of the lowlands, but scaling the sheer rock faces of the mountain or battling the rolling whitewater of the river rapids was not for him.

"Sheriff," Jane called from the open door, pulling him from his thoughts. He looked up at her, not moving a muscle as she stepped into his office, holding out her gloved hand with the one thing that confirmed this could not possibly be a tragic accident. "We're not going to get anything from ballistics. It must have hit the hub."

"Someone tried to kill an Emerson, Jane," Jake breathed bleakly, watching the small piece of squashed metal wobble about against the steel blue of the rubber glove on her hand. "Right here on this mountain... in broad daylight... in cold blood!"

"Yes, sir," Jane nodded simply.

"What is your gut instinct?" he asked as Sandy joined them in the sheriff's office.

"First one?" Jane asked, looking across the short distance between them with candid intensity. "Honestly?"

"First one," Jake repeated with a slow nod. "Honestly."

"The obvious – a very rich man comes home from a business trip with a new – relatively unknown bride and within months, someone tries to kill him," Sandy jumped into the conversation from the door, answering the question in a robotic monotone while Jane decided how tactful she should be. "We've got to look at Nicole, Jake."

"Homicide 101," Jane said with a shrug of her shoulders, "look at the spouse first and then make your way through the family and friends to any known enemies."

"Rule number one," Jake agreed reluctantly with a nod.

"Although, the Emersons have made a lot of enemies lately," Jane countered, deciding to play devil's advocate since she'd lost her place as chief accuser. "Every time I turn on the news or pick up a paper these days there's something about another takeover or buy-out by EI. The press is painting them like the barbarians at the gate most of the time. I saw an exposé the other night about the European expansion. They are not exactly welcome in a lot of those places but the locals can't afford to refuse their money."

"If they are too poor to say no to them," Jake mused, "they certainly couldn't have the money to send an assassin halfway around the world."

"They could have family already in the country," Jane offered.

"We *have* to look at Nicole for this," Sandy insisted with a shake of his head. "You said it yourself – first the spouse – then the rest of the family – then friends – and then move on to more obscure possibilities."

"We'll need background on her," Jake sighed, swiveling around in his chair to stare into the mountains. "She's from Crystal Springs, it shouldn't be difficult."

"Born and raised in the same town and they just *happened* to run into each other on the other side of the world?" Sandy cocked his head meaningfully, drawing in a deep breath as the questions that surrounded Cameron Emerson's sudden marriage began to take on new shades of sinister shadows. He shook his head gravely to underline his suspicions.

"There's also Trevor Cantrell," Jane said studying the mangled bullet in her hand. "What does anyone really know about him? Everyone just accepted both of them because Cameron brought them into the family circle."

"Go carefully," Jake warned, looking at Sandy pointedly. "Use only the sources in Crystal Springs you know you can trust."

"EI's been moving pretty fast since Cameron moved into the penthouse beside his dad," Jane continued as she leaned back against the bookcase behind her. She chose this rural area for her own reasons and brought a greater understanding of corporate America than any of them would suspect. "Something about this seems to have the kind of style and flavor of a professional hit, don't you think? I mean, the guys at that level play a hardball that can be ruthless."

"Ruthless, but not usually deadly," Sandy countered with a slow shake of his head.

"I'm not so sure…" Jane replied.

"Check it all out," Jake said, swiveling back around to his desk and reaching for a pad and making notes as he spoke. "The press is going to converge on us. For the record ~ we have no comment for the media. For the moment, this is a terrible accident and we were pulled off the rescue search because of the storm and as soon as it moves through, we will resume the effort," Jake ticked off his bullet points on his pad. "Be very careful to use the term *rescue* and not *recovery*; no sense in upsetting the family more before it's absolutely necessary."

"Yes sir," both of his deputies said in unison.

"Do you really think he could have survived?" Jane whispered, tears filling her eyes.

"Until we find him," Sandy said, unwilling to entertain the idea of giving up, "we won't know."

"Nothing can get out about a sniper. We don't need panic, we don't need vigilantes roaming all over the mountain, and we certainly don't want our perp to know we know it was not an accident. Sandy," Jake continued, his mind beginning to process thoughts faster than he could coordinate the orders. "Call Rosemary MacIntosh and ask her to prepare us a list of all employees and the guests who have been at the lodge for the last few weeks. See if there are any new faces…"

"Should we ask them not to take any new reservations?" Jane asked.

"Emit will know how to best handle this. He'll also keep his parties out of that sector and trustworthy eyes on it until we've concluded the search. He'll know we'll need to keep the accident scene and the rescue grid free of traffic, both on the road and the river. Anyone other than the Emerson and MacIntosh families will need to be escorted on and off the mountain. When all is said and done, the mountain is private property. They have that right."

"But we don't have that kind of resources," Jane said with a sigh.

"No, but Emerson International does. Call Lee Malcolm and tell him we need some help up here. He's probably just waiting for an official request as a courtesy to the department anyway."

"Gotcha," Sandy said, heading for his desk in the squad room.

"If anyone asks about the guardrail being gone, tell them we want to test the integrity of the metal. Under normal circumstances it shouldn't have given way like it did. Let's play the game as long as we can. Jane, get back up to the Manor and see if you can talk to the newest Mrs. Emerson. Be very sensitive and subtle, but see if you can get a handle on why she wasn't in her own car this morning."

Jake pulled himself from the chair, swept the plastic bag from the desk and headed toward the garage with Jane following close behind. Stu Curtis was the newest addition to the Stafford County Sheriff's office as crime scene specialist. He was dusting the metal guardrail with graphite on the off chance this very meticulous killer had been careless. The Jag had already been covered with clear plastic.

⁂

Jake was relieved to see the Emerson International car swing into the back lot shortly after the noon hour and pull to a stop just outside the bay door, breathing a sigh of relief as Lee Malcolm stepped in out of the driving rain, carrying a large satchel and leaving watery footprints with every step.

"Lee," Jake said, crossing the bay to offer the younger man his hand.

"Sheriff," Lee Malcolm said, shaking Jake's hand with a strong grip. He looked much younger than he was. Although he served several tours with the Army Rangers, he somehow managed to keep his All American athletic build and boyish charm. He could as easily have just left the University practice field as EI corporate offices. He walked with an unconscious swagger and confidence that prevented most people from challenging him or questioning his authority.

With no further comment, Jake turned and headed back to his office. Lee stopped in the break room for a cup of coffee and then joined Jake, closing the door behind him.

"It goes without saying that everything at EI is at your disposal," Lee said as he settled into a chair and set the coffee mug on the edge of Jake's desk. "The choppers are on standby and will be in the air again as soon as the weather permits. I've selected fifteen of my best men who have mountain rescue experience. They are in route. Gregory is making the Manor available as their command post since it's closer to the search area and that will prevent us from getting in your way around here. It will also be more discreet keeping them on the Estate."

Without saying a word, Jake picked up the evidence bag containing the splintered wood and metal pivot and tossed it across to him. Lee snatched the bag out of the air, inspecting the graphite stained pieces through the clear plastic. He felt the hairs on the nape of his neck stand on end.

"As you can see, there are no prints. I've got a guardrail section in the bay with missing bolts and no fingerprints on it either," Jake said, clearing his throat as he leaned forward. "I've got a sniper's site located. I've got a steel-belted tire that was all but shredded by this," he said, tossing the second evidence bag containing the mangled bullet onto his desk.

Lee reached across and picked it up, his eyelids dropping like the hoods over a snake's eyes, shielding his emotions. "I don't guess this leaves any doubt, does it?" Lee breathed, a strange, gnawing bile began to churn in his stomach.

"You telling me this didn't already occur to you?" Jake asked quietly, leveling clear, almost accusing eyes on Lee. "I assumed you went on alert when you heard Cameron was missing."

"We did," Lee acknowledged without resentment, "but merely as precaution. At a time like this, the movement of family members is more predictable and we take precautions to protect them from the press and paparazzi. I always add extra security when any of the family travels, but when word of the accident gets out – and I assume you are still reporting it as an accident – there will be more interest in their movements."

"Lee, my team and I are good at what we do. We're good at keeping the peace. We keep our eyes on the summer residences and respond to domestic fights around town. We know the mean drunks and most of the thieves and petty drug dealers. We don't do this kind of thing. I am out of my league before I even start."

"If we can help, you only have to ask," Lee said without hesitation. "I have a file of all the threats against the Emersons, covert and suspected. I can get those to you but the origins of most of those threats would suggest this is much closer to home."

"Sandy is in charge of the investigation," Jake said, leaning back in his chair and reaching for his coffee. "He's already convinced it's Nicole so I assigned Jane to take the personal approach with her. Jane's more objective at the moment. She's gone up to the Manor to see if she can interview Nicole."

Jake took a long swig of his cooling coffee and sighed deeply before leaning forward in his chair. "Sandy!" Jake called, raising his voice so that it would carry out into the squad room. "Mr. Malcolm is going to assist in the investigation. You two can use my office," he concluded, getting up as Sandy reached the door and nodded silently as he closed the door behind him.

"Did you bring the file on Nicole?" Sandy asked, dropping into Jake's chair and moving the half filled cup of coffee to the table behind him. "I bet an in-depth investigation of the new bride was done before the newlyweds stepped back on American soil. Did I lose my money?"

"Only child of Janet and Drake Quinn," Lee said, flipping open the file and turning it around before laying it on the desk in front of the deputy. "Usual childhood illnesses; graduated from high school two years ahead of her class and earned a liberal arts degree and a master's in art history at the U," Lee recited. "She was popular and active on both campuses. She has been working in her parents' antique shop since she was just a kid. She's good at it and loves it. If she has any secrets she's better at concealing them than we are at rooting them out," Lee said with a shrug. "Maybe in view of this latest development, you will see all the information with a different eye."

"The trip to Europe?" Sandy asked, flipping through the neatly typed report.

"An annual buying trip with standing reservations for most of the trip in establishments the family has used for years. Identical to just about every one she's ever taken, with one exception."

"And that was?"

"A side trip to Aosta, Italy. That's where she ran into Cameron."

"And her reason for that side trip?"

"She got wind of a private sale, ran it to ground and the rest is history. It's become a family legend already. They love to tell it."

"And it just happened to be while Cameron was there?"

"Yes. He heard about the estate sale from one of the contractors they were using. The matriarch of the family was known for her obsession with collecting antique British china. Cam wrangled an invitation. It was all coincidental."

"Like the one morning she doesn't go into the office with Cameron the tire on her Jag is blown out by a sniper?" Sandy sighed, rubbing his hand over his upper lip. "I don't like coincidences."

"Neither do I, but sometimes chance is just as dangerous," Lee said with another shrug. "And she doesn't always drive in."

"What do you know about Cantrell?" Sandy asked suddenly changing the subject, leveling his gaze back on Lee, "ever check him out?"

"Trevor?" Lee asked, unable to hide his surprise at the sideways skid in the conversation and unwilling to give him a direct answer. "He's closer to Cam than his own brothers and has been since they were in college. Why do you ask?"

"I don't know," Sandy said, shaking his head slowly and lifting his gaze to stare out the window into the driving rain. "It just seems he's acted real odd through all this. Or, maybe because he's been haunting the mountain for the last few months and nobody really knows what he's doing or why. Ever found any connection between him and Nicole?"

"Never looked for one," Lee admitted, "There was no reason to. There may be some overlap when they were at the U. She was there at least part of the time he was working on his undergraduate degree. His study is in chemistry and biology – hers in fine arts. I don't see them wandering into each other given the layout of the campus. What makes you suspicious?"

"Gut instinct," Sandy said, shaking his head as though to clear cob webs. "There was just something about him today – I don't know – something I just can't quite put my finger on, but he's acting odd for a man whose best friend just went off a cliff. Instead of being down there with the rescue team, he was coming and going. No one really knows where or why."

"Did anyone ask for his help or suggest he join the search?" Lee said with a shrug. "Sandy. I know I wouldn't just insert myself into a trained team."

"Can I make a copy of your file on Nicole?" Sandy asked, not answering Lee's question, his attention focusing on the evidence bags on Jake's desk.

"Of course," Lee said, draining the last of the coffee. "I'll make a few calls and see what I can find out about Cantrell if it will make you feel better."

"It will," Sandy sighed softly and hesitated only a moment before heading for the copier.

An hour later, Lee Malcolm stood at the door of his office staring through the inner glass wall that looked down over the atrium below. Workers were moving around, in and out of their offices and meetings; they were seeing to their responsibilities with no idea of the drama going on involving Cameron. He sighed deeply as he turned away from the scene.

As soon as he returned to the office, he put the call into his top investigator to compile a comprehensive file on Trevor Cantrell. He expected it to be on his desk by the start of business tomorrow. With that task off his list, he turned his mind to the more pressing issue of the safety of the family members.

Only a few hundred of his most trusted lieutenants knew that an extreme alert had been issued worldwide at every EI holding. With as little notice as possible, tight security measures that were already standard policy for their many facilities would now be enforced more intensely.

In the varied entities around the world, their employees would hardly notice the enhanced measures. A few would wonder why the sudden stickler for detail in the standing security policies, but they would merely fish their security badges out of their wallets, from their purses, out of the glove compartments of their cars or line up to get duplicates made because they had no idea where theirs were. They would then go on about their business as usual.

The report of the accident produced the natural blind for the Emerson family to reach the protective walls of Hawthorne Manor. No one would question the assembling of the family in the wake of the tragedy. By the time the press got wind of the fact it wasn't an accident, the family would be safely ensconced at the Estate or at the Plaza... except for Holly, he thought as he heaved a heavy sigh and turned back to his desk.

Holly was his recurring nightmare. – the sliver of glass in his foot he felt excruciatingly with every step he took but could never actually locate – the ripple in the carpet that always caused him to stub his toe and fall flat on his face. Holly Noel Emerson Weston was the rattle in the car he couldn't find – the static on his television he couldn't clear up – the intermittent glitch in his computer he couldn't even define – the bane of his existence as EI security chief.

In his entire duration at EI, Holly was the variable that he could always depend on to throw the entire equation out of order. She was the offbeat that threw the rhythm out of sync. She was the rebel who felt it her God given duty to devote herself to breaking the rules, making it her life's work to not only be unconventional but also disdainful of everything expected of her. She was the child who refused to grow up with a personal trust large enough to indulge her every whim; and they were varied and many.

Lee could not deny that Holly was an engaging young woman with an enchanting personality. Most people who knew her described her as a charmingly free spirited, avant-garde, quirky, and eccentric. She could behave in the most outrageous ways and still have people excusing her antics and defending her conduct because she was doing nothing more than being herself. It was a phenomenon he long since stopped trying to understand and simply coped with as an ongoing irritation.

The last time she was home was four years ago when she took a fancy to a young intern at the MacIntosh Lodge. Suddenly she was consumed with fly fishing, rock climbing, and whitewater rafting. She spent most of her days at the Lodge and no one knew where she was spending her nights.

When she left, unceremoniously and without telling anyone good-bye as was her habit, she took the intern with her. The last anyone heard, they were with all the beautiful people at Cannes for the film festival. An item appeared in the gossip columns about them, but by the time Lee alerted his French manager, they had disappeared into the Swiss Alps for skiing. Word came from Rio they were in Brazil for Carnival, but he was never able to verify either.

She had enough friends among the ultra rich and reclusive that she could remain a perpetual houseguest of one or the other, avoiding hotels and commercial transportation. The only thing Lee was sure about where Holly was concerned was that she would only be found if and when she wanted to be. The one comfort he had was in knowing that she was as adept at avoiding the press as she was her family. They too seem to chase her shadow more than her activities. Rumor in the press was that a shot of Holly Emerson brought big bucks to any photographer who happened across her.

He sank back into his chair and pulled his pad in front of him, going over each task listed and making sure every conceivable circumstance in this crisis was covered. He gathered up the files he pulled from inside the vault off of Gregory's office and slid them into his attaché case, thus completing phase one.

He nodded silently to the team of guards on duty in the executive lobby. "I'll be in my apartment," Lee said, sighing at the thought of the days ahead of him. "Can you get someone to go out to my house and secure it for me?"

"I'll see to it on my way home."

"What makes you think you are going home?" Lee called, fishing his house keys from his pocket and tossing them to his aide. "Send one of the newbies."

As the team leader headed toward the garage, Lee pressed the elevator button. The stainless steel doors reflected a distorted image of himself but Lee could still see the deep creases of concern that were wrinkling his forehead. After stopping by his efficiency apartment on the twenty-second floor, he grabbed his gym bag and headed back out for the exercise room. This was one night he wouldn't be able to rest or sleep. He might as well get in a few laps and maybe find someone to spar with him.

※※

Nicole blanched as a bolt of lightning split the sky, snaking its way from a menacing dark cloud and striking somewhere behind the back of the garden. Right on its heels, the thunder washed over the Manor and rattled the windows. She shivered as she was pulled from the safe haven of her memories of the Italian countryside to the horrors of her reality. The images of peaceful Italian villages were splintered by the memory of the flashing lights and squad cars at the scene of Cameron's accident, and the waking nightmare of Cameron injured and clinging to fragile life somewhere along the river in this terrible storm.

Mae hovered, trying to get her to lie down, but Nicole thought if she did, the nausea would overwhelm her again. Mae pressed another antacids into her hand and held out a glass of tepid water from the bathroom.

"Take them," she ordered.

"I can't sleep, Mae," Nicole said, dropping the pill back into Mae's hand. 'They are only making me feel worse."

"They will help you rest," Mae insisted, pushing the water toward her.

Nicole was distracted by the sound of a car barreling up the front drive. She knew by the sound of the engine and speed that it was one of EI's fleet cars. EI's teams were patrolling the Manor grounds. Security was being tightened around them and the walls were closing in even more.

Nicole allowed Mae to lead her across the room and she sank into the deep, soft cushions of the love seat. She covered her eyes with her arm as she rested her head on the back, realizing as soon as she did that she would not be able to escape into sleep. In spite of the tranquilizer, her mind was racing. She heard Mae slip from the bedroom and the distinctive creak of the ancient floor as she crossed the sitting room to the door and eased out.

Nicole sighed deeply as she got up and crossed to the massive walk-in closet. She moved toward the back, sliding the often worn garments across the clothes' rod until she spotted the heavy canvas garment bag at the very end against the wall. She pulled if from the closet and then carried it to the bed and carefully tugged at the zipper. As she eased the bag open, sight of the antique dress she was married in brought tears to her eyes.

She lifted the ivory Chantilly lace dress from the bag and spread it across the bed. Her hands smoothed over the beaded bodice, feeling the tiny seed pearls that were sewn on one by one by some long dead seamstress. She fingered the fine ivory silk and turned her head away to prevent her tears from staining it.

She pushed the dress to the side, crawling onto the massive king-sized bed and lowering herself onto the pillows. She closed her eyes, willing herself back to that moment when they returned to Valle d'Aosta. The local officials were so intent on pleasing the new president of Emerson International that they cut through their own red tape and issued the legal documents required for Nicole Elizabeth Quinn and Cameron Thayer Emerson to become husband and wife.

In the shadows of the Matterhorn, in the quaint Italian village where Hannibal invaded with his elephants and Napoleon came through on his way to Marengo, they were married. Monumental historic events laid claim to the region, but to her, it would always be the place where the enchanted fairy tale began with their marriage in the eleventh century Sant Orso chapel on a sunny July afternoon.

They were able to steal three days, hidden away in the seclusion of a mountain villa offered to them by one of the men who was negotiating with Cameron on the expansion before the Italian media got wind of the marriage. After that, it was more of a run for their lives as they made their way back to the states.

Cameron was right. She would never regret the impulsiveness of their elopement. Returning to Crystal Springs was a rude awakening. Nicole had never experienced the scrutiny and critical attitudes she encountered as the newest Mrs. Emerson. For weeks she was stalked by the press. There were daily reports of her activities and commentaries on everything she wore, her hair, and the speculations as to why one of the world's most eligible bachelors would have succumbed to the charms of this studious home town girl.

The exposure was brutal, and the ambivalent atmosphere of Hawthorne Manor only compounded the stress. There was nowhere Nicole could find to get away from the continual scrutiny but the massive gardens and surrounding grounds. If she wasn't reading about her shortcomings in the papers, she was hearing it from sometimes well meaning but other times catty and insensitive family members. The only thing that made life at the Manor tolerable was their love for each other and Cameron's determination to protect her through the ordeal.

She was getting used to the attention of the curious press, but she was having a harder time with the rivalries she encountered behind the Manor walls. Cameron took her to the glade soon after they returned, sharing with her the childhood memories of their excursions. The Emerson children would trek through the back gardens, to picnic in the quiet cove of the river.

Although she was taking the brunt of the blame for their bolt from family tradition, it was Cameron who first began talking of building there. He was the one to order the surveys, hire the architects, then contract the roadwork.

Nicole felt the sedatives finally dragging her into an exhausted sleep. She heard the thunder as it rolled once more across the mountains and over the Manor. As she drifted into a deep, dream filled sleep, she found herself trying to swim upstream in a torrent of water. As hard as she tried, she was unable to reach the broken and battered body of Cameron who lay helpless on the banks of her nightmare.

CHAPTER EIGHT

The front door of the Manor opened before Jane was half way across the deep stone terrace. Douglas moved back to usher her in as she stepped into the front entrance hall, nodding hesitantly to the Emerson's houseman as he bowed slightly at the waist. In her four years on the Oak Meadow force, she had never been inside the Manor before this morning. Now she was making her second visit within hours.

Douglas held his hands out for her raincoat as she shrugged out of it, giving no indication he even noticed the rainwater dripping onto the highly polished marble floor. She removed her cap and handed that to him as well, shaking her short, dark blonde hair with unconscious habit. There was an atmosphere of quiet busyness about the house as he led her through the front hall toward the family room.

Helena was still sitting in front of the fireplace where a fire burned fiercely. Lamps bathed the room in a golden light as the shadows grew deeper under the darkening clouds. Andrea was sitting in the chair beside her mother; eyes red-rimmed from the emotions that periodically became overwhelming. Gregory, Garret, and Richard stood just outside of the doors opening onto the conservatory in quiet conversation. High overhead the increasingly heavy rain made an annoying tattoo on the glass roof.

As Jane entered the room Helena gracefully rose to greet her. Jane saw the alarm leap into the older woman's eyes. "I have no news," Jane said to quickly calm the room of their worst fears. "I stopped by to see if there is anything I can do. The teams are all safely back in Oak Meadow, gearing up to get back to the search as soon as conditions permit. How is Nicole?"

"Sedated," Vanessa interrupted abrasively as she entered the room from the far corner. "She's the family's designated shrinking violet."

Jane did not miss the exchange of looks between the other family members. Helena's shock was evident only in that she blinked a fraction of a second too long. Gregory's lips pursed slightly and a small furrow appeared between the dark, shaggy brows before he turned his back on the scene and crossed to the chair beside Helena's. Kyle and Andrea glanced at each other and then their parents in turn. Richard remained apart from the others at the door to the conservatory, lowered his head, and studied the pattern of cobblestones in the pathway.

"Vanessa," Garret said pointedly, stepping into the room and moving purposefully toward his wife.

"I only meant that she's the delicate one among us Emerson wives," Vanessa said with a nervous laugh and less than warm smile; moving out of her husband's approaching path. She was quite adept at saying the words expected of her but leaving no doubt with anyone listening what her true feelings were. In the circle of her own friends and supporters, she was known as a witty, cosmopolitan woman. Those who were not as captivated by her sharp tongue were less enamored with her.

"Is she feeling any better?" Jane continued, taking mental note of the subtle family dynamics emerging.

"Not much," Vanessa informed her, retaining control of the conversation as she crossed the room to stand beside Garret once he stopped advancing toward her. They were a striking couple. Garret inherited the rugged handsomeness and powerful charisma of Gregory with prominent features that conveyed strength and confidence but also a boyish charm that most found endearing. His mind was sharp, his wit was keen, and he possessed the sensitivity and personal appeal that did not come naturally to his wife. He was definitely the right Emerson for politics.

Vanessa was a sleek woman whose hair was honey blond at the moment. That was subject to change with her whim and the next trip to her hairdresser. Presently, she was wearing it short. It gave her soft-featured face an edge that matched her personality. Both see and Garret were being carefully groomed for a life in the public forum but it was evident that while all the traits needed were inherited by Garret, they were only affected by Vanessa. She was the less attentive pupil even as she took her husband's arm with practiced skill more than affection. Had a camera been present, it would have been the perfectly appropriate somber reaction to the mention of the present circumstance.

"I could tell she wasn't feeling well when I brought her back to the house. I was hoping to speak to her very briefly if I could, though" Jane said.

"Douglas," Helena spoke up, graciously taking control of the awkwardness that now possessed the room, "will you show Deputy Adler to the east wing?"

"Yes, ma'am," Douglas said as he stepped to the doorway behind Jane. "This way please ma'am."

She was led back through the front entrance hall and up the wide staircase. The floor was bone dry. There was no hint of the puddle she left just moments before. Nor were her cap or raincoat anywhere in sight. At the landing where the stairs divided, he took the right staircase. Jane slowed her pace slightly, star struck for a moment by the gallery of ancestral portraits. She could not imagine calling this place home.

Mae answered the soft knock on the sitting room door almost as though she was waiting on the other side. She paled when she saw Jane and stepped back, looking over her shoulder toward the open door between the sitting room and the master suite. Douglas bowed slightly again, and returned the way he had come.

"Is she sleeping?" Jane asked softly, reaching out to gently touch Mae's wrist. "I just wanted to check in a minute and see how she's doing. I was called away so quickly this morning..."

"Oh," Mae said, the breath she was holding escaping in a quick gasp, "I thought you were here to tell us..."

"We are still locked down because of the storm," Jane sighed. "How is Mrs. Emerson? I believe she said she had eaten something that disagreed with her?"

"Her stomach is settling," Mae said glancing over her shoulder to the open door. "The doctor ordered a tranquilizer but I don't think it's helping."

"Who is it, Mae?" Nicole mumbled, easing herself into a sitting position and trying to peer through the open door. The sedatives were now slowing her reflexes.

"It's Jane here, Mrs. Emerson," Jane called, easing herself nimbly around Mae. Jane crossed the sitting room, stepping into the inner sanctum of Nicole and Cameron Emerson's bedroom. With one practiced glance she swept the scene, her photographic memory taking mental note of every detail.

The bedroom was boldly decorated, filled with a collection of antiques and art that Jane guessed would impress any curator and challenge any insurance adjustor. The collection was a curious blend of masculine and feminine, giving testimony to the careful thought and consideration to both Cameron's and her tastes and interests. The basic color scheme was a deep burgundy, incorporating a bold Scots' plaid in the valances over the floor-to-ceiling windows and the bed skirt under the comforter.

A deep navy silk robe was thrown carelessly across a chair on the far side of the bed. The items on the night table indicated that was Cameron's side of the room. The massive wardrobe that rose almost to the fourteen-foot ceiling was standing slightly open, a rack of ties visible from where she was standing.

Nicole was on the king-sized bed, bracing herself with one arm on the bed and the other hand pressing against her forehead. Her knees were curled under her. She was still dressed, having removed nothing but her shoes. She wobbled slightly in her drugged state.

She was pale and what makeup she might have put on was no longer evident, but her eyes were what caught Jane up short. There was a deep dread and sorrow that caused deep circles under the large gray pools, but curiously, there were no tears. Her dark hair was pulled to the side and moved like a shimmering length of cloth when she sat up and swung her feet to the floor. At the foot of the bed, a garment bag was gaping open, an ivory silk and lace dress was bunched up in a heap on the opposite side of the bed.

"Have they found him?" Nicole breathed, swaying slightly as she gripped the edge of the mattress to steady herself. Mae moved silently around them. She took the dress, shook it out gently and then put it back on the hanger and the hanger into the bag, zipped it closed and carried it away.

"No," Jane said softly, shaking her head. "I wonder if you are up to answering a few questions for me."

"I am," Nicole whispered, looking toward the night table for the glass of water.

"Good," Jane said, easing herself toward the small wing back chair near the bed. "I was worried about you this morning."

"I must have eaten something last night," Nicole answered vaguely, turning toward Mae again. "Will you ask Riva to bring us something to drink? Would you like something to eat, Deputy Adler?" Nicole asked looking back at the deputy.

"No, thank you – and, please, call me Jane," Jane said quickly, "but you go ahead. Don't you think it might be a good idea to get something on her stomach?" she asked, trying to both distract Mae and get rid of her for a moment.

"I don't think it would stay down," Nicole muttered, easing herself to a standing position and waiting a moment to allow her head to clear a bit before walking into the sitting room.

"Perhaps some dry toast or some crackers?" Jane suggested and got the wanted reaction from Mae. "A little chicken broth might help?"

As Mae called the kitchen, Jane sidled over to the night table where several prescription bottles were standing. As inconspicuously as she could she checked the labels, committing the information to her photographic memory.

"Is the car still in the river?" Nicole asked, sinking into the love seat and turning around. She frowned slightly as she stared back into the bedroom. "Jane?"

"No," Jane said, moving quickly to join Nicole. "We were able to raise it before the storm hit. It's been carried to the station. We need to know if he was in the habit of wearing his seat belt."

"Always," Nicole said without hesitation. "Why?"

"Because the driver's seat belt was released – not broken. We are just trying to piece together what happened this morning."

"Cameron's very strong," Nicole said, lifting haunted eyes to Jane's. "He knows these mountains. The river would have taken him downstream really fast. It would take him a long time in this storm to hike out… but he and Trevor know the mountain…!"

Jane sighed softly, not sure how to proceed with her interview. After a moment's thought, she decided to save it for another time. As she talked with Nicole, she realized how much the drugs were affecting her. There were many ways through an investigation.

"Well," she said crossing the room toward the door, "I know that's going to be a great advantage to him. May I come back and check on you later?"

"That is kind of you," Nicole murmured, already giving in to the drugged fog that clouded her mind.

Jane made her way back down the front stairs. Douglas appeared as she reached the bottom of the stairs. She started to ask him where he learned to materialize and dematerialize as he did but decided it wasn't the appropriate time for humor.

"Would you ask Mr. Weston if I might have a few minutes of his time?" she asked instead.

"Of course," Douglas said with a gentle smile. "Would you like to wait in the study?"

"Yes, Thank you," Jane replied, following him down a side hallway she did not noticed before as she crossed the front foyer. He led her to Gregory's study and closed the door when he left.

Jane stood in the middle of the massive room trying to grasp the idea of living like these people did. The room was chilly because there was no fire in the massive fireplace on the inside wall. The room was paneled in a deep red cherry, polished to a high sheen and glowing softly in the clouded light coming through the deep-set windows of the outer wall. There was floor to ceiling shelving everywhere except for the fireplace and the wet bar beside it.

Soft leather sofas faced each other in front of the fireplace and two matching armchairs created a circle at the open end. A chess table sat between the chairs and a game was in progress on the inlaid marble chessboard with intricately carved ivory pieces. Jane was studying the game when the door opened and Richard Weston joined her.

"Do you play?" he asked, crossing the room and extending her his hand.

"A bit," she allowed, stepping back from the table and shaking his hand. "Someone is about three moves away from check," she noted.

"Really?" Richard asked, glancing curiously at the board. She sank to the edge of one of the chairs when he indicated she should and shifted her nightstick and weapon a bit before sitting.

"We have discovered," she said, taking a deep breath and letting it slowly out as she pulled her notepad from her pocket, "the event this morning on the Trail wasn't an accident."

"Oh?" he asked, a deep furrow appearing between the pale blue eyes. "What did you discover?"

"Evidence of foul play," Jane said quietly.

"There's no doubt in your mind it wasn't an accident?" he asked, obviously stunned by the news. "What makes you think that?" Richard asked as he leaned forward slightly. "What have you discovered?"

"We are still sorting things out," Jane evaded. "We will need your cooperation in the coming days. Lee Malcolm is working with Deputy Wade on threats that have been made but we may need to look further into less obvious motives."

"I don't understand," Richard said as he reached behind him to pull a pad from the desk and then fished a pen from his pocket. "What should I be doing?"

"Just giving some thought to helping a forensic accountant take a look a recent activity that might have produced a different type of threat. I understand there have been some incidents in the EI holdings because of the takeovers and mergers. We have some time but I wanted to give you a heads up."

"Of course," Richard said, tossing the pad on the table in front of them and then rising. "I see what you mean," he said as he turned his attention absently toward the chess board. "I will get a finance team working on the prep for that."

He crossed the room to open the door for her.

When Connie responded to her check in, she was told to hold for Jake. She was back on patrol and on the far side of Oak Meadow when she heard Jake's voice.

"Malcolm just left here," Jake's voice joined her in the squad car. "He's going to have someone bring us what information he has. Come on back to base. We need to strategize a bit."

"Copy that," Jane said into her radio, looking for the first place to turn around. The mention of Lee Malcolm caused a flutter in the pit of her stomach and a slight blush to her cheeks and she was glad she was alone.

※

Lee Malcolm set the original files on his disk, quickly flipping through them until he came to the one he was looking for and read the contents with renewed interest. When Trevor Cantrell appeared in Cameron's life, there was a background check. He had not been overly concerned at the time when he was unable to collect much information about Trevor time in the Navy or the time he appeared on campus. There were no red flags with skimpy military records, especially when Special Forces were involved. Trying to look deeper would not have been a good idea for anyone.

Trevor distinguished himself quickly, finding his niche in the SEALs. Lee expected large gaps in Trevor's file after he became one of the very few to make it through BUDS training. Now those gaps were coming back to haunt him and he stared at the file open in front of him. With a deep sigh, he picked up the phone and started to punch in numbers. Halfway through the first ring on the other end, he dropped the receiver in the cradle, closed the folder as he picked it up and headed out of his office. He always felt better on the move. He wasn't one to sit in the office and wait for others to return his calls.

He nodded to his man on the door at the executive parking garage exit, noticing it was no longer a lower level guard but one of his top men. He made his way to his car and maneuvered through the mid-morning traffic into the center of town, past the courthouse to a high-rise that rose on the other side. He pulled into the attached parking garage and found an empty slot.

As he rode the elevator to the twelfth floor, he tapped the file folder against his leg in an unconscious nervous habit. He should have called first, but something about the events of the morning made him hesitant to leave a detectable trail behind him with this task. He stepped off the elevator and pushed through the double doors that had "Driscoll and Associates" in neat block letters painted on the frosted glass of the old doors.

"Well, hello stranger," the young woman behind the reception desk said with a smile as she saw Lee walking in.

"Hello, beautiful," Lee smiled at Enid Abernathy, Chet Driscoll's secretary, moving quickly to shake her hand. "How have you been?" he asked casually.

"Doing good," she said with a quick smile as she pressed a button on the panel of her phone. "Chet, Lee Malcolm is here to see you."

"Tell him to leave his gun with you," Chet's voice joined them in the room.

Lee shook his head, laughing out loud as he pulled his weapon from his shoulder harness. Enid produced a plastic shoe box for it. He turned toward the closed door leading to the offices and heard the tell-tale buzz as the lock on the door was released from some remote location. He glanced up at the security camera hanging over his head in the inner hallway and gave a slight salute. Chet Driscoll was waiting for him about half way down the hall to his corner office.

"Lee! Good to see you," Chet said as the two men shook hands. "I thought you might be by."

Chet Driscoll was an average looking man, standing about five foot eleven. He had dark brown hair and light brown eyes that were piercing. He was fit and walked with an easy gate that belied his physical strength and agility. Lee had sparred with him too many times to underestimate him.

"Oh?" Lee replied as he followed Chet into his office. Chet motioned toward one of the chairs positioned in front of his desk and then headed for a Mr. Coffee pot on the small wet bar in the corner of the office.

"We heard what happened on the mountain this morning."

"Oh?" Lee said again, watching his mentor as he poured them both mugs of strong, black coffee. "How?"

"Oh, those mountains have eyes and ears of their own," Chet said with a dismissive shrug. "What can I do for you?"

"Well," Lee said as he set his file folder on the edge of the table beside his chair and took the steaming mug from Chet's hand, "I need some help filling in the gaps in one of our background checks." He knew there was no use in pressing Chet on his sources so he dropped it.

"Who?" Chet asked, lowering himself in his chair and sipping carefully at the dark brew. It had been steeping in the pot for a couple of hours and was just about to become bitter tasting. He watched Lee carefully.

Chet was an enigma in Crystal Springs. Many suspected he once worked for some government agency but no one knew for sure. He was on the cutting edge of all things and always had the newest and most exciting toys. His professional profile identified him as a venture capitalist and that was a provable fact. But there were other profiles that indicated he was not as retired from his alternative careers as he claimed. No one was sure if the "securities" in his company profile referred to protection or commodities. Lee concluded in his dealings with Chet that he was involved in both and a few other things.

"Trevor Cantrell."

"Trevor!" Chet repeated, allowing his surprise to show openly. "Trevor Cantrell? Really?"

"You know him?" Lee asked expressing his own surprise in his tone.

"He took several of my classes at the Universality," Chet answered. "What has sparked your interest in him?"

"He's been making powerful friends and is in a lot of places these days," Lee answered, lifting the folder he had with. "After what happened," he said, setting his mug of coffee on the desk in front of him, "I have some concern about the gaps in this report. I certainly don't want to be caught flat footed if it turns out he's not what he claims."

Chet took the report and scanned it briefly. He read the brief descriptions of Trevor's Navy record a second time, knowing that what wasn't there was more telling than what was. He also realized the reason for Lee's unannounced appearance in his office.

"I take it there are some unanswered questions about the accident this morning," he finally said, leaning back in his chair and meeting Lee's gaze.

"It wasn't an accident, Chet" Lee said quietly and was immediately aware of the impact of speaking the words out loud.

The men fell silent as Chet lowered his gaze back to the report on Trevor Cantrell. Lee watched as he scanned the words again, wishing he was better at reading this man. He took little comfort in the fact that Chet Driscoll was a man that no one was ever completely able to read. He waited for Chet to speak.

"What can I do for you, Lee?" he finally asked.

"I need more information on Cantrell," Lee said without hesitation. "He seems to be a wild card here. Everyone will just feel better when we can eliminate him as a concern."

Chet pursed his lips and continued to study the report in front of him. He chose his words carefully as he considered the request of one of his protégés. He stared at the code beside Cantrell's discharge.

He knew it to be both medical and of a highly classified nature. He sighed deeply and then looked back up at Lee.

"I will do this," he said with a finality of someone who is used to taking charge of situations. "I can check with a few people and then I'll let you know if there is any reason to be concerned. I can't fill in these blanks for you, Lee. Do you realize this young man was not just a Navy SEAL?"

"Huh?" Lee asked as his head straightened up. The conversation had taken a turn he was not expecting and he was caught more than a little off guard.

"When you get a response like this one," Chet said picking up his file folder, closing it and handing it back to him, "there is more told by what the Navy doesn't release than what it does. I will tell you right here and right now that Trevor Cantrell is not who you are looking for if there was foul play. If he were involved in trying to harm anyone, you would never know he existed and you would never know he was anywhere near that mountain."

Lee inhaled deeply, hearing but not completely absorbing the information. "Chet, someone took a sniper shot from an overlook on the mountain and put a bullet in the tire of Nicole Emerson's Jaguar with Cameron behind the wheel, doing about forty – forty-five miles an hour along a winding mountain road."

"I see," Chet said, taking another sip of his coffee. He was quiet for a moment, processing the additional information. "Lee, this was a clever scheme and obviously it took considerable skill. It was devious but you seem to overlook the fact that it wasn't successful."

"It wasn't successful?" Lee repeated slowly, considering the thought Chet offered him. "So, then what was it?"

"You need to make sure you ask the right question," Chet said. "Remember your training with us. What questions are being asked?"

"Who would want to harm the Emersons?" Lee responded immediately.

"The Emersons?" Chet repeated. "But, you just said it is Nicole's car."

"*It is Nicole's car,*" Lee repeated.

"Was Nicole supposed to be in the car?" Chet asked solemnly.

"Yeah," Lee answered quietly, reaching for the notebook he carried in his shirt pocket. He shook his head slowly, as if he was clearing his mind more than disagreeing with Chet. "We have to assume there is a possible danger for all of them."

"Granted," Chet agreed as he watched Lee begin to mentally connect dots he had missed.

"Are you sure you are looking at all possibilities?"

"How can I be sure of that?" Lee asked, lifting his eyes toward his mentor.

"I don't know that you can," Chet said quietly. "Just leave your mind open and don't make assumptions or dismiss any possibility."

"Except that Cantrell isn't involved?" Lee asked, unable to completely mask his sarcasm.

"Except that Cantrell isn't your shooter," Chet replied softly.

"How do you know that?" Lee demanded, his frustration with the responsibility of the Emerson safety was weighing heavily on him.

"Because if Cantrell wanted anyone dead, he would not make the mistakes this unknown did." Chet said with a lifting of one eyebrow.

"What mistakes did this unknown make?" Lee asked.

"Now *that*...," Chet said with a professor's approving nod of his head, "is your question."

༄

Within an hour of Lee leaving the station, one of his aides arrived in Jake's office. The aide said very little as he handed off the expandable file that was about six inches thick. Jake pulled the elastic band over the edge of the file folder and the top sprang open revealing several manila file folders inside. Each was labeled with a numbered file code.

"This is the code key," the aide said, pulling a separate envelope from his inside pocket and handing it to Jake. Jake unfolded it, glancing down the spreadsheet at the description of the files beside the number. There was a file on threats deemed to be serious and reported to the appropriate government agencies around the globe. He suppressed an ironic smile as he read the list of internationally renowned bodies: Interpol, the FBI, the CIA, Scotland Yard, Israel's elite Mossad, the French Interior Ministry, and others he would have to look up to know who they were.

"Thank Mr. Malcolm for me," Jake said as a dismissal and turned his attention to the reports in hand. It was one containing threats not taken too seriously but logged and researched nonetheless. It was a thick file informally labeled "crackpots" with casual notations made along the margins. The last item in the file was the background information compiled when Cameron married Nicole so suddenly and unexpectedly. The remaining file was a list of recent activity in Emerson's acquisitions and the disgruntled people who voiced more than the cursory opposition to the mergers, takeovers, and buy-outs.

Jake sighed as he reached for the radio on his desk. He pressed the activate button and summoned Sandy. He flipped through the file folders until he found the number that corresponded to the list of serious threats. "Got some homework for you," he said, handing Sandy the file.

"What's this?" Sandy asked, leaning against the desk and holding the file on his outstretched hand as he opened it.

"Some threats against the Emersons that might not be idle talk," Jake said, sinking wearily into his chair and leaning back. "Look through it and see if anything jumps out as a possible motive for what happened this morning."

"Okay," Sandy said, heaving a heavy sigh as he allowed the file folder to close and turned toward the door, "but you don't think I have the number to MI6 in my Rolodex, do you?"

"I didn't know you have a Rolodex," Jake commented, allowing a slight smile to curl his lips. "Did I authorize that purchase?" he jabbed, shaking his head slowly. "Just look through it and see what seems interesting or a possible lead. If you see something you want to know more about, call Malcolm."

Sandy Wade had been with the Stafford County Sheriff's Department for almost a decade. He was in his mid-forties and came from Miami when he was caught up in the firestorm of the corruption investigation of the eighties. He was suffering from not only burnout but also disillusionment when he answered a disturbance call at a West Palm Beach marina and met Gregory Emerson who was leaving a meeting at the club house..

Gregory saw not only the desperation in the young officer, but also the potential. He offered him a spot on the Emerson security detail with a recommendation to the Oak Meadow sheriff's department. Sandy moved to Crystal Springs and worked for Gregory until there was a spot open in the Oak Meadow department. He accepted Jake's offer to join the deputy force. He gained respect quickly and was the expected replacement for sheriff when Jake retired.

Sandy set the file on his desk and grabbed his mug up in one movement. There was dark sludge in the bottom of the cup where the morning's dregs had settled into a gummy sediment. He ran hot water into the mug and spilled it out until it was relatively clean and then poured fresh coffee in. He sipped it slowly, rubbed the grit from his tired eyes, and then opened the file and began reading.

He was surprised at the number of threats against the Emersons individually as well as corporately. Jane could be right. Cameron and Gregory had been expanding quickly and in some areas ruthlessly – taking advantage of unstable markets to move in and make offers the owners couldn't refuse or they were buying up shares of bailing investors in hostile takeovers. After paging through the reports once, he settled back to read them more thoroughly and then divided them into stacks depending on how likely each one was to be a legitimate danger.

"How's it going?" Jake asked as he stopped by Sandy's desk an hour later. He scanned the separate piles of reports and glanced inquisitively at his deputy.

"Some of these aren't even in English," Sandy said, dropping his pen and leaning back in his chair, stretching his back as the chair tilted backwards. "I think it's safe to assume that if there were any international terrorists passing through town, someone might have noticed," Sandy sighed wearily, thumping the tops of two stacks of files.

"You think?" Jake commented with a wry smile, lowering his large frame into the wooden chair at the side of the desk. The protesting creak seemed to echo through the almost deserted squad room.

"You know, Jake," Sandy said, leaning forward and inspecting the remains of coffee in his mug and deciding not to chance it was still drinkable, "I know we are used to living with Emerson International around here, but somehow it doesn't always register just how massive the company is. Gregory and Helena are just rich neighbors to us, it seems just like a home town store until something like this reminds me of how big EI has become."

"I know," Jake nodded. "When you are at the hub of the wheel, you don't always know how far out the spokes go."

"Why, that's very profound, Sheriff," Sandy said with an affected awestruck look and weak laugh. The chance to take a breath and relieve tension was a welcome relief.

"I thought so too," Jake countered with a comical shake of his head.

"There are threats here from all over the world! Arabs... Russians... Colombians... the Chinese!" Sandy commented with an amazed shake of his head, "not to mention the Constantines in Crystal Springs."

"The Constantines are in that file?" Jake asked, his interest peaked.

"Yeah," Sandy nodded. "Seems like one of the sons made a comment about Garret's possible run for office. Something to the effect that politics could be unhealthy."

"They see Garret's political interest as a rising threat for them in this area for sure," Jake sighed. "If someone had taken a shot at Garret we might have this solved."

"You would think when they were run off the East Coast they could've found a better place to go than Crystal Springs," Sandy mused. "Miami – or Vegas – are so much friendlier to their ilk."

"Too much competition," Jake commented. "They are looking for a place to lay low after what happened on the Coast. I hear CSPD has expanded their organized crime unit since they moved to town and formed a task force with the FBI."

"You know, I have a new respect for Lee Malcolm," Sandy admitted with a sigh. "I always thought he was little more than a rent-a-cop, but he has to deal with some serious menace here." Sandy flipped the file folder closed and let it sail to his desk with a backhanded toss. "It's beginning to really remind me of Miami around here."

"Lee Malcolm controls a sizable private army," Jake said with a solemn nod of his head. "Security is no small issue for Emerson International, both on the corporate side and the family's personal safety."

"Well, since we haven't seen any foreigners in these parts lately, this makes this picture even more disturbing. Absent a militant Arab terrorist fanatic or a Russian Mafioso – a Columbian drug lord – we're coming back uncomfortably close to home, Jake."

The two men fell silent, staring intently at each other as the words were finally said out loud. They hung in the air, almost a visible entity – just one without a face at the moment. "We would have spotted someone around here who didn't belong, Jake. If we didn't notice them coming through town, Cantrell or the MacIntoshes would have spotted them on the mountain. I'm afraid this killer may have a face all too familiar. I think you need to take a look at personnel files at The Lodge, sir. That's the most logical access point. Emit uses a lot of college kids up there."

Jake made no comment. He had already traveled the investigative journey that Sandy was taking and come to the same disturbing conclusion. "Malcolm is on that," he informed his deputy. "He has more resources to check them all out than we do. But, I'm going to pick them up for him. When I do, you can look through them before we pass them on."

"This isn't the kind of random shooting that happens elsewhere. Someone went about this with a frightening cunning," Sandy sighed.

"I know," Jake answered, pushing himself up out of the chair. He knew Sandy's investigative technique. He threw every possible theory and suspect onto the pile and then determined motives and opportunity and worked through a process of elimination. "Keep those files in your possession at all times and under no circumstances let anyone else get a look at them."

"What about this one?" Sandy asked, tapping the last file on the desk.

"That's the one on Nicole," Jake answered, getting up and carrying it to Jane's desk. "Since Nicole's your first pick for this, Jane needs to take that piece. She'll have a more objective eye."

CHAPTER NINE

"I'm just asking," Vanessa said to Garret's reflection in the mirror hanging over the wet bar in the library. "What do we really know about either one of them?"

"Van," Garret said with a warning shake of his head, glancing quickly at Richard.

"Richard knows what I mean," Vanessa hissed, turning to enlist her brother-in-law's agreement. Richard was pulling crystal glasses from the cabinet and setting them on a large tray on the bar counter. He made no comment. "Do you know what Lee has in his file on either one of them?"

"No," Richard replied evenly. "Security is not in my job description," he continued in his easy going, jocular way. "Let me know if you decide to ask Lee about the way he's been doing his job. I'd pay good money to see that."

Garret laughed out loud and Vanessa finally laughed as well. The idea of any one of them approaching Lee Malcolm and demanding to know if he was doing what he should be doing as security chief for Emerson International was ludicrous. Lee Malcolm was a formidable character. As Vanessa regrouped her thoughts and decided on her next step, she sighed heavily. It was ridiculous that Lee would not have thoroughly checked out both Nicole and Trevor when they appeared on the scene.

"First Trevor and then Nicole... you know Cameron has a history of rash behavior when it comes to making fast friends," she finally said looking from Garret to Richard. "He runs into Trevor in a dorm lounge the night before Thanksgiving, discovers he's alone for the holidays, and then drags him home! Before you know it, they are closer than brothers... two limbs on the same branch... thick as thieves; does that really make a lot of sense to either one of you?"

Richard concentrated on arranging the glasses on the tray and made no comment. Garret avoided eye contact with her, having learned that when his wife was in this mood it was not wise to give her the smallest action she could consider to be encouragement. It made no difference that they both ignored her.

"Then he meets Nicole at an Italian auction and discovers she's bidding on a set of ugly china to sell to your mother and the next thing we know he's bringing her and the china home to stay. You have to admit, that's strange, Garret. It shows what I think is a dangerous impulsiveness that may have now caused very serious consequences."

She was rewarded by the shadow of uncertainty that flashed across her husband's eyes before he blinked and turned away from her. The relationship between them had always been a power dance. As Garret's star rose in the political sky, she was more tenacious about staking her own claim for her piece of the power pie.

Garret stared at the bar counter for a moment and then glanced at Richard. "What do you think, Rich?" he asked, not looking at his brother-in-law directly as he voiced his doubts.

"I don't think the china is all that ugly," Richard said offhandedly, eliciting the smile from Garret he was seeking and the consternation of Vanessa he enjoyed.

"You've spent more time with Nicole than the rest of us. What impressions do you have?" Garret pressed.

"I've not spent all that much time with her," Richard countered with a shrug. He leaned back against the wall and folded his arms across his chest. "But I don't see the menace in her that you do, Vanessa. She's just a very young woman who is caught up in a large, close family. It's not what she is used to."

"You spend more time with her than anyone else outside of Cameron – and of course Trevor – but we won't go there for sure," Vanessa said, watching him curiously. "You two seemed to bond fairly quickly, too."

"Well," he said, turning a clear gaze toward Vanessa. "We both enjoy jogging but that doesn't lend itself to long conversation," he laughed shortly and shook his head. "And – I do have to admit I relate to a lot of what she's going through. Not all of us melded into the family as quickly as you, Vanessa."

"What does that mean?" she asked, turning to level her intense gaze on him. Garret glanced quickly at Richard, offering what support he could with a sympathetic shake of his head. Richard pursed his lips and took a deep breath that was so slow and so deliberate that no one saw him take it.

There were several less than flattering articles in the press lately about Vanessa and she was now overly sensitive about her image. She earned a reputation for being ambitious and more than once on the fund raising trail Garret's handlers warned her that she wasn't born of the Emerson cloth. The organizer of one of the meet and greets in Austin actually asked her if she realized that the trouble everyone was going to wasn't about her. Unfortunately, the comment appeared as a blind item in the local gossip column and was still a sore subject with Vanessa.

"I just mean not all of us are as adept at taking on this clan as you have been," Richard said in his charmingly appeasing manner, relieved to hear Garret's supportive laugh.

The truth was that Nicole was much more intriguing to the press and whether she realized it yet or not, Vanessa saw her as a formidable opponent instead of a sister-in-law. Her marriage to Cameron was the story that reporters' dreams were made of and Nicole's reticence with the press and very private tendencies only fueled their obsession with her.

Without intent and completely oblivious to what she was doing, Nicole remained the mysterious beauty in their eyes. Her refusal to grant interviews, her natural grace, poise, and desire to remain out of the public eye was genuine and not the publicity maneuver Vanessa often employed. It didn't help that Vanessa was constantly striving to achieve the allusion of the mystery that was a part of Nicole's natural personality.

"I think you're jealous," Garret teased as he turned to face her.

"That's ridiculous," Vanessa hissed, but she wasn't as convincing or as confident as she was when the conversation began. "There's nothing about her I even admire. She's a quiet mouse of a shop keeper who faints if someone says boo to her. Why would I be jealous of her?"

Garret knew better than to offer an answer. He glanced at Richard who was tactfully concentrating on the tray of glasses and avoiding eye contact with either one of them.

"She'll never fit in, you know. From the moment Cam showed up with her, it's been one problem after another. First it was the wedding. I can't imagine insulting your mother by refusing such a generous offer. What normal woman wouldn't have jumped at the chance of having a dream wedding like Helena offered them?"

"Maybe a married one," Garret answered, amused by his own witty response. He didn't often take sides in the family disagreements, but he did in that one. "A second ceremony was not at all appropriate. It suggested the first one somehow wasn't authentic."

"You have to admit a second wedding was a bit extreme, Van," Richard spoke up, casting a sideways glance to catch his brother-in-law's agreeing nod. "Nicole's idea of a reception was definitely more sensible."

"And," Garret said, scooping ice from the icemaker hidden ingeniously behind the hand carved concealing panel into the leather-tooled bucket, "I can see why Nicole was offended. For anyone to suggest a second wedding was an inappropriate one from the off set. I agree with Richard, Mother meant well but she was out of line there."

"Now there's the family dinner thing," Vanessa said, changing her tactics when she realized she was getting no support whatsoever over the elopement. "Weekend dinners at the Manor have always been a whole family event as long as anyone around here can remember. I don't blame Helena for being offended by Nicole's demand that Cameron have dinner alone with her in their suite."

"Mother isn't offended, Vanessa... you are. Besides, that was Cameron's idea," Garret said, pouring in the last scoop of ice. "He told me so himself. Neither one of them is at home during the week for dinner more often than not. With Cam at the office and Nicole working at the shop – they need time to just be together."

"And they are still newlyweds," Richard commented, not looking at either Vanessa or Garret. "They need some space. I can tell you from personal experience that this family isn't exactly underwhelming."

"And, as Richard said, they are newlyweds," Garret reminded her.

"Are you insinuating that we weren't?" Vanessa asked, turning a look toward her husband that caused him to shake his head slowly and sigh deeply. "And now, this house isn't good enough for her," Vanessa continued, not waiting for comments.

"How insulting can it be to your parents that she doesn't want to live here? Not to even mention the mess that they are making on the other side of the Estate. Have you seen that road construction? And the *glade*! Where did she get the audacity to bulldoze the glade? It's practically a family sanctuary."

"She never indicated the Manor wasn't good enough," Richard spoke up.

"And the glade was Cameron's idea as well. It was a childhood haunt for us... Mom and Dad never went there. They are fine with it all. They are scheduled to start the footings today, aren't they?"

"They are," Richard said as he placed the top on the ice bucket, "come to think of it."

"Garrett!" Vanessa hissed.

"Their own daughter doesn't want to live here, either," Garret said with a laugh. He glanced at Richard, "Have you been able to run down my wayward sister?"

"I've left messages around," Richard said, sighing heavily. "If she's traveling, it could take a few days to connect with her. But, if she doesn't want to be found, then she won't be."

"You mean it might not matter to her that Cameron is missing?" Vanessa asked disapprovingly, her focus momentarily diverted from her newest sister-in-law to her first target of disdain.

Holly had always given her quite a bull's eye for criticism and scorn. Vanessa was a passionate Emerson who planned and plotted diligently to become Garret's bride. No slip of etiquette or antic could ever be close to what consternation Holly brought to the household. Vanessa took the family's position in the community much more seriously than the family did. Holly's contemptuous amusement in the face of Vanessa's disapproval only fueled Vanessa's umbrage.

"How can she just ignore her parents the way she does?" she asked, shaking her head in disapproval.

"The last time I heard from her she was in Istanbul," Richard answered Garret's question, tactfully changing the conversation back to the original focus.

"This time of year?" Vanessa asked with surprise. "It's beastly cold!"

"He said the last time he heard from her, Van," Garret commented. "He didn't say it had been recently."

"When did Holly ever do anything conventionally?" Richard asked with a quiet laugh. For all the confusion and unorthodox ways she brought to his life, no one could question that he was madly in love with her. "That is part of her charm, isn't it?"

Vanessa sighed, disturbed that she wasn't being taken seriously in anything she said. She shrugged, and then heaved another heavy sigh. "I don't care what you say; I'm telling you that something's not right here. Cameron was a fool to marry someone he hardly knows and it could very well have cost him his life."

Vanessa caught Garret's furious glare and fell silent. She selected a bottle of wine and then pulled the corkscrew from the small drawer beside the sink and slipped it over her thumb as she headed across the library to return to the den. Garret watched her a moment and then opened another concealed panel and grabbed a decanter of hard liquor from it before following her.

Holly was a heartache to which his parents would never really grow accustomed. As long as he could remember she was determined to do the exact opposite of whatever was expected of her. More than once she was dismissed from boarding schools and sent home in disgrace. He could not count the times she was escorted home by the Crystal Springs police or the Oak Meadow deputies without once showing the least concern that their parents were disapproving and brokenhearted. She was never happier than when she could stir up the family. He would never forget the uncomfortable holidays she dominated and ruined with her motley crews.

With a sigh, Garrett picked up the ice bucket and tightened his grip on the liquor. Richard carefully lifted the tray of empty glasses to follow him. A sudden hush fell over the group as they walked into the hall and saw Nicole and Mae standing just outside in the hallway.

Vanessa gasped, realizing Nicole heard every word she said. She had the good grace to blush, lower her gaze and then slowly shake her head in embarrassment. Nicole was deathly pale, Mae's eyes were flashing a fury that would have shocked Vanessa has she been able to look either one of them eye to eye.

"Nicole," Richard said softly, moving forward with his effortless charm and grace to take Nicole's icy hand a moment before she wrenched herself free and backed away from them. She turned on her heel, mindful of Mae's quick movement to the side as she moved out of her path.

"Nikki," Garret called, but she was already halfway up the stairs. Mae was following closely on her heels.

"Great, Van," Garret hissed, turning to make his way into the den. "Great!"

༺༻

Jane shrugged out of her department issue parka as she reached the protection of the bay. The wind blowing at her back as she crossed the parking lot was icy, causing her to shiver. She paused only briefly as she passed Stu examining the guardrail. She hung the fleece-lined parka on a hook on the wall and then entered the squad room, making her way through the back hall toward her desk.

She saw the file with the Post-It note on the front and Sandy's instructions scrawled across it. After several false starts, she was able to decipher the scribbling: *"Take a look and see what you see here…"* She heaved a deep sigh, picking up the file, setting it off to the side. Sometimes she wondered about the inbred relationships in Stafford County. What was Jake doing with a confidential file from Emerson International's chief of security and what had he offered in exchange?

She discovered early in her career to document her impressions of interviews and interrogations separate from the official record. Those moments of intuition and insight that could seem irrelevant at the time of questioning could later prove to be key points once all the evidence was in and the truth emerged.

She recorded her audio notes on her meeting with the young Mrs. Emerson before she lost the essence of what she saw and heard while driving down Sutter Trail. Later, when the urgency of the moment passed, she would transcribe the contents of the tape, but at the moment, there were other matters that required her attention. She opened the file and took a deep breath, first shuffling through the collection of information and then stacking it carefully back in the original order before settling in to study it.

Inside the manila folder was the life of Nicole Emerson. As she unclipped papers that contained copies of her high school and college transcripts as well as a copy of her college application, she felt a twinge of unease at the extent of the invasion into Nicole's private life.

She glanced through Nicole's medical records, noting she suffered the normal childhood ailments; common ear infections and viruses. At the end of the section on her medical history she realized why the investigator was so interested as she unclipped the next section and began reading the short introductory paragraph. Here was a history and summary of the boys and men Nicole was known to have dated.

"D'you get the file?" Sandy asked, pausing on his way through the squad room to the bay.

"Yeah," she said and was unable to hide her disgust.

"Problems?" he asked, detouring slightly to walk by her desk and glance over her shoulder.

"Did you look through this?" Jane asked, lifting the folder from the desk and holding it up.

"Some," he answered with a shrug. "Why?"

"They have no right..." Jane said with a shake of her head.

"They are Emersons," Sandy said after hesitating a moment. "She married the heir. They are different."

"Above the law?" Jane almost spat.

"No," Sandy said looking into his almost empty coffee mug and then glancing toward the break room. "It wasn't illegal I'm sure. They don't see things like we do."

"So you mean Nicole knows they put together all this information?"

"Cameron Emerson is the golden child chosen to take over Emerson International. Nicole must understand the concern when he just up and married an unknown. They did the same on Vanessa and Richard and Ben. She couldn't expect anything else."

"I feel like a peeping Tom," Jane admitted, glancing down at the section of the report documenting Nicole's romantic history. "This just isn't right."

"They are different, Jane," Sandy explained yet again. "Gregory certainly is going to safeguard his family against everything he possibly can."

"Seems as though he should have been investigating his own enemies instead of his family, though," Jane said as she drew in a long breath and exhaled it quickly.

"Sometimes, unfortunately, one can be the other," Sandy replied with a slow shake of his head. "You can't blame a man for doing what he has to do to protect his own."

"He certainly wasn't able to safeguard his family against this sniper, was he?" Jane asked with an ironic frown as she set the section involving Nicole's past romances to the side. It wasn't completely inconceivable that some disappointed former boyfriend wanted Cameron out of the picture.

Jane thumbed through the legal documents obviously pertaining to the marriage since they were in Italian and realized there was something not in the file. There was nothing here about the doctor whose name was on the prescription bottles she had seen in Nicole's bedroom. She shuffled through the last few pieces of paper in the file and discovered that except for a traffic report there was nothing in the file dated any later than last summer.

"I suppose they did their deep background and found her acceptable, you think?" she asked herself as she lifted the traffic report from the file and scanned it. She had to start over and read it more carefully to discover the relevance and why it was in the file at all.

Nicole was listed as a witness to a hit and run accident. In the margin of the report she scrutinized the tidy notes made by Lee Malcolm. It appeared to be the name and number of an investigator from the Crystal Springs traffic division. She glanced at the date – just three weeks ago.

She pulled the report from the folder and crossed the room to make a copy of it. She wasn't sure why, but there was something incongruous about the report being in Nicole's background file. More than likely it had been misfiled. Malcolm must have intended to drop that into a file that was an altogether different invasion of Nicole's privacy, the current one that picked up where this one left off.

She slipped the copy of the traffic report in her own file,folder and turned her attention back to her former train of thought. She pulled her notebook closer and flipped through a few pages to where she had written down the names of the drugs Nicole was taking. She drew a square around the list and across the top added the name of the doctor who dispensed them to her and the drug store where they were filled.

※

Nicole paced from the window in her dressing room overlooking the side lawn to the window in the sitting room overlooking the front drive. The thunder was almost nonstop now as the storm rolled across the plateau toward the Manor. There were only seconds between the flashing lightning and the crashing thunder. Mae stood quietly, watching the agitation as it grew in intensity with every moment.

"That woman is vile," Nicole said with a heavy puffing of breath formed a circle of condensation on the front window. As an afterthought, she wrote "vile" in the condensation with her finger.

"She is that," Mae agreed.

"I don't understand her, Mae," Nicole said, turning to sink into the deep cushions of the sofa. "What have I ever done to warrant her attitude towards me?"

"She doesn't need a reason to be the way she is," Mae said reaching for the throw on the back of the sofa to spread over Nicole's lap and stopped as Nicole waved her away.

"I need to get out of here for a while, Mae," she said, standing up and heading for her dressing room again. "I need to see Mom and Dad."

"Nikki!" Mae said as she followed her through the bedroom, "that's not a good idea. The storm…"

"I can't stand it, Mae," Nicole turned on her heel and took a quick step backwards to prevent Mae from rushing into her.

"There are bound to be news crews everywhere," Mae said after a moment's thought. She knew Nicole and she knew when she could be reasoned with and when her mind was made up. There was no deterring her now.

"I'll take your car. With my rain hood and sunshades, I should be able to slip out of this fishbowl. I can't just sit here and I can't be around Vanessa."

Mae sighed deeply, knowing there was no changing Nicole's mind once it was made up, so she left the suite and returned with an old floral scarf.

"If you wear this," she said lifting her knee slightly to fold it into a triangle as she wore it over her own head," they will probably think you are me if you are moving fast enough and don't look at them."

"I love you, Mae. You'll call me if there is any word… any word at all."

"Of course," Mae muttered, not trying to conceal her disapproval. "And you will be home for dinner, right?"

"I'm not making any promises," Nicole replied as she pulled a jogging suit from her dresser and quickly donned it. She took the scarf from Mae, gathered her purse and the keys Mae hesitantly handed her and headed toward the back stairs.

Just inside the turret doorway was an ancient hall tree with her trench coat hanging from a two pronged brass hook and her umbrella in a large metal urn beside it. She grabbed her raincoat and pushed the heavy door open, pausing long enough to prevent it from sounding when it closed behind her.

She was cautious as she descended the stairs, pausing at the first floor doorway to listen a moment. She could hear the voices of Kyle and Andrea but did not stop long enough to try to eavesdrop. She tiptoed past the slightly opened door and headed down the half flight of steps leading to the back courtyard. She stopped at the back door, surveying the rain that seemed to be falling at an almost horizontal slant. She pulled on her trench coat, belting it snugly around her waist and pushed Mae's scarf deep into one of the pockets.

She pulled the hood of her coat over her head, put her sunshades on as protection against the wind and rain and stepped out of the basement. It was cold and stinging as she lowered her head and made a quick dash toward the old carriage house that had been converted into a combination game house and garage. She jumped puddles on the flag stone path and then dodged a torrent of rain water flowing off the garage roof into a stone lined drain to reach the back side where Mae's little Ford Escort was housed.

As she felt the relief of the garage's shelter, she pushed the hood off her head and pulled the scarf from her pocket. Smoothing the damp tresses from her forehead, she tied the scarf around her head. Once she settled behind the wheel and adjusted the seat to her longer legs, she flipped the visor down to inspect herself in the vanity mirror. She dropped her sunshades on the seat beside her and took Mae's from the dash and slipped them on. She laughed as she saw her reflection and turned the key in the ignition.

The guards at the front gatehouse merely glanced at her as she drove by. She watched them in the rearview mirror in case they had second thoughts until she came to the first curve. The rain was relentless and it took so much of her concentration to follow the steep descent down the mountain that she reached the end of the Trail before she realized she had passed the accident site.

The officers manning the roadblock were hunkered down in their SUV, facing the traffic approaching from Oak Meadow. They barely glanced at her as she eased passed them with a slight wave of her hand to hide her profile. The going was easier with the four lanes through Oak Meadow to the highway. With the storm raging around her, she kept a steady speed. Half an hour later, she was pulling into the outskirts of Crystal Springs. It seemed the storm had followed close on her heels.

The sight of the warehouse in the flashes of lightning was strangely comforting as she pulled into the alley between the warehouse and the shop. The side door opened as she slid out of the car and she looked up to see her father waiting for her. She ducked under the arm that was holding the heavy metal door open and heaved a heavy sigh of relief as she stepped into the familiar receiving area. Wooden crates were lined up along the walls with various foreign shipping labels.

Drake Quinn was an imposing former athlete with broad shoulders, trim waist and was aging extremely well. He wrapped a strong arm around her and pulled her close.

"Mae called you," Nicole said as she pulled the scarf from her head and pushed it deep into her coat pocket. She shrugged out of the coat as Drake reached for it. He shook the rain from it and then tossed it on one of the wooden crates.

"I was here anyway," Drake said, waiting for her to move toward the office where a space heater was beginning to take the chill from the small enclosure built into the center of the warehouse.

"What are you working on?" she asked, standing in front of the heater trying to shake off the chill she was feeling.

"A consignment from the Philippines," Drake said, picking up an unlit pipe from his desk and setting it between his teeth. "How are you, daughter?"

"Terrified, Dad," Nicole admitted, convulsing into tears and falling into his arms. "I can't wrap my mind around a world without him now."

❧

"What'd you find?" Jake asked, standing over Jane's shoulder and trying to read the notes she had scribbled on her pad. He could tell she had uncovered something. There was a city map of Crystal Springs spread across part of her desk and hanging off the end of it, caught and held in place by the trash can below.

"Well," she said with a sigh as she leaned back in her chair and pushed her pencil over her ear into her hair, "a couple of curious things."

"Such as?"

"Did you see this police report in the back of the file?"

"No," Jake said, propping his foot on the edge of the printer table and leaning back against the file cabinet. "I really didn't look at the file."

"Most of the file is background," Jane said, absently stacking the bulk of the papers and reports in as neat a pile as she could. "Information about Nicole before she married Cameron - a lot of information and I would question the legality of how some of it was gathered…"

"What did you find?" Jake repeated, shortstopping the direction her thoughts were taking. "Did it ever occur to you that Nicole made her life an open book? Most likely she is completely aware of the file and everything in it. Did that possibility ever occur to you?"

"No," Jane readily admitted. "The Emersons compiled a background on Nicole up until the marriage and that's where *this* file ends."

"*This* file?" Jake pressed.

"I'm betting there is another file… a later file."

"Oh? And why would you risk your money?"

"Because of this," Jane said, waving the recent traffic report in his face. "There's a gap of more than a year, and then this."

"You've got them wrong, Janie," Jake said with an unapologetic shake of his head. "Gregory isn't the overbearing ogre you think."

"I'll bet money there is a second file," Jane shrugged.

"And you'd lose your money. You don't know how their world is," Jake said softly, realizing he didn't really need to defend the Emersons.

"I know," Jane laughed softly, "they're *different* from the rest of us mere mortals," she said, raising two fingers of each hand in the air to put "quotes" to her words.

"That's not what I meant," Jake protested. "They have different concerns than the rest of us. They can be the target of people who don't look twice at you and me but see any Emerson as a deep pocket and bull's eye. What do you or I have that would catch the attention of anything more than a petty thief?"

"Point taken," Jane allowed. "Which is why I think this is odd. Assuming this is the only file they have on the newest Mrs. Emerson and that last item didn't just get misfiled, it's odd that it would be here at all."

Jake turned his attention back to the report. "Who's Oscar Caprini?"

"He's a man who ran a red light on Butler at Paulson about three weeks ago and broad-sided another car."

"What does he have to do with Nicole?"

"Take a look at the names of the witnesses." She waited as he scrutinized the almost indecipherable handwriting and knew immediately when he spotted Nicole's name.

"So she witnessed a car accident…"

"The second driver is listed as unknown, Jake. Oscar Caprini is the only one listed on the report because the other car left the scene." Jane continued. "Oscar Caprini ran a red light and slammed into the other car! How many times have you known a victim in an accident to flee the scene?"

Jake fell silent, taking a greater interest in the report. He started over, reading the details with a more critical eye. Jane leaned back in her chair, giving him time to digest the new information.

"Have they identified the other driver?"

Jane picked up the empty file and flapped it at him a couple of times. "There's nothing else about the accident in this file, but I thought it was worth suffering a little condescension so I called CSPD."

"And?" Jake asked, handing her the report back and standing up straight.

"Larry Daniels," Jane said, reaching for her pad, "know him?"

Jake shook his head and leaned back against the filing cabinet, folding his arms across his massive chest.

"She was supposed to be driving that car, Jake," Jane said with pursed lips. "We can't ignore that fact just because Cameron is the more logical target."

"Where was that accident?" Jake asked, pointing toward the map.

"On the lower west side."

"That isn't close to the Quinn's shop or warehouse, is it?" he asked, obviously unable to identify the exact area. "And I know it's nowhere close to the Plaza."

"Not close to either one," Jane said, shaking her head slowly. "It *is* a block north of the medical center, though. I spotted some medicine bottles on Nicole's night table. The scripts were written by a doctor not listed in her medical history here but who has an office in the building two blocks from that intersection."

"What are you going to do now?" Jake finally asked her.

"Go to Crystal Springs for a face-to-face with Larry Daniels and Oscar Caprini, and check on a few more details. But not officially."

"I don't want to know," Jake laughed, knowing that look. He had learned that Jane was a good investigator and employed some interesting techniques at times. The Oak Meadow department was considered jokes to the CSPD but they had yet to meet Deputy Adler.

Jane closed the files and stood up, heading toward the bay before she heard him call from the hallway. "Besides, if you are going to invade Nicole's privacy, I'd prefer it not be in uniform."

She stopped in mid-step, glancing over her shoulder and heard the telltale laughter as he went into his office and closed the door.

CHAPTER TEN

"Officer Daniels?" Jane asked, coming to a stop in front of the cluttered cubicle desk where the middle-aged officer was napping while bent over the stack of folders in front of him. He was very experienced at what he did because he lifted his head without the slightest surprised reaction to her sudden appearance.

"Yeah," he responded without any indication that she startled him.

His quick, dismissive glance at Jane, now dressed in a blouse, skirt and low heels was the exact reaction she wanted. She pulled a manila file folder from an old attaché case she kept in her trunk just for such occasions and held it up.

Obviously Larry Daniels was a man resigned to the fact that he had reached his highest rung on the department's ladder. His raises were now guaranteed by his years of service and the cost of living adjustment Crystal Springs initiated several years back. He would receive no more promotions and he was only a few years from the gold plated watch and retirement. His weary apathy was apparent.

"I'm Jane Adler and I wondered if I could ask you a few questions."

"About...?"

"The traffic call you caught on Paulson and Butler a couple of weeks ago," Jane answered, opening her folder and fishing her copy of the report out and handing it to him. She watched as he scanned the paper and then memory kicked in.

"Yeah," he said with a laugh and shake of his head, "One crazy call, huh? You representing the insurance company?"

"I just need to fill in a few of the gaps in our report," Jane said, elated by but not correcting his false assumption. "Did you ever find the SUV or identify the driver?"

"We found the vehicle," Daniels said, leaning back in his chair and dangling his long arm over the side. "...abandoned behind an abandoned warehouse out near the airport. It was stolen the day before the accident but not on the hot sheet because the owner was out of town… didn't know it was gone 'til he got back."

"I see," Jane said, pointing toward the chair beside his desk, "May I?"

"Sure," Daniels said, kicking it toward her slightly with his foot. "Take a load off."

"You've listed three witnesses here and they all state that Mr. Caprini ran the red light?" Jane said, pulling a steno pad from her attaché along with a ball point pen and flipping the pad open.

"Yeah," he said, picking up her copy again and squinting to read his own scrawled handwriting.

"Were any of them able to give a description of the other driver?"

"Nah. All of them were focusing on Caprini. He was the one at fault. One of the witnesses…" he paused as he looked again at her report, "Lockwood… Ed Lockwood. He headed toward the car to see if the driver was hurt and had to jump out of the way because the guy almost ran him over getting out of there."

"And this other witness, Shipman… Meghan Shipman?"

"That gal's crazy," Daniels said, leaning forward and shaking his head.

"What makes you say that?"

"She was quite the drama queen."

"Drama queen?"

"Yeah – just trying to make a mountain out of a molehill and get attention."

"Oh? How," Jane asked quietly.

"Trying to make a big deal out of a simple car accident,"

"How?"

"Listen," Daniels said looking at her with squinted eyes and his impatience taking his tone up an octave, "I've got a shift starting and have to get out of here. The gal was a nut."

"Ok. Is this the entire report filed?" Jane asked, waving the copy at him.

"That was all there was to it," Daniels retorted snatching the copy from her hand and slapping it down on his desk.

"What about the other woman," Jane asked as casually as she could. "Nicole Emerson?"

"She didn't see anything either. She said she heard it but was looking the other way when the cars crashed. She had nothing."

"Did you pull any prints from the car when you recovered it?"

"There weren't going to be any prints we could use on that car," Daniels said with a dismissive laugh. "It was in the warehouse lot and was released to a garage owned by the lot attendant's brother. There were so many prints, we weren't going to get anything of value from it."

"So auto theft didn't print it?" Jane pressed.

"Look," he said leaning forward and assuming a more aggressive tone, "There was no suspect and we don't take prints unless we have a suspect."

"I see," Jane said, reaching for her copy of the report. For a moment, she thought he wasn't going to give it back to her but after a moment's thought, he handed it across the desk.

"What company did you say you were from?" Daniels asked, suddenly aware he was missing something.

"I didn't," Jane said, plucking the report out from under his hand and getting up. "Thanks for your time, Officer Daniels."

She stopped by the clerk's office and obtained the follow up report detailing the stolen vehicle recovery. It was as uninformative as the accident report. With a resigned huff, she headed back into the pouring rain.

◆◆◆

"Good afternoon, sir," Douglas said as he checked the contents of the warming tray on the buffet of the family dining room.

"Good afternoon, Douglas," Gregory said evenly, not about to allow the fatigue and fear he was feeling to show. "I saw the kids downstairs, except Nicole. Do you know where she is?"

"I believe she's resting in her suite, sir," Douglas said, and tried to execute a hasty retreat through the butler's pantry.

"Douglas," Gregory called, picking up a small biscuit and spreading a thin layer of fresh butter over the golden crust, "I know that tone. What is it?"

"There was another unfortunate scene, sir" Douglas responded immediately to the opening he expertly orchestrated. Gregory and Helena had long depended on Douglas and Riva to keep them informed of what their children were doing, especially when the behavior was undesirable. "Miss Nicole overheard a conversation and was quite offended, I understand."

"And should she have been, Douglas?" Gregory asked.

"I would think so, sir," Douglas said with a slight nod. "It was a regrettable lapse of judgment on Miss Vanessa's part to be sure."

"Thank you, Douglas," Gregory replied, lowering his gaze to hide the darkening of his eyes and the tense lines that appeared on his brow. He was going to have to do something about his elder daughter-in-law. What once would have been labeled 'feisty' when she was younger and less in the public spotlight was quickly becoming a personality flaw for her as well as a political liability for Garret.

"May I get you anything else, sir?" Douglas asked, turning again toward the door.

"Nothing, Douglas," Gregory said, popping the buttered bread into his mouth and shaking his head slightly. "I'm just going to go up and check on Nicole."

"Yes, sir," Douglas said with approval that was more evident in his voice than he realized. Douglas liked the gentle, refined Nicole. Even though she was often the odd one out in the boisterous and gregarious Emerson clan, there was a calm dignity about her that appealed to him and Riva. They agreed that Vanessa could take a page from her book and be a better woman for it.

Gregory left the room and made his way to the back turret. As he climbed the smooth stone steps, the lingering chill from the storm seeped into his bones, making him feel old and tired.

With the apartments available to the family in the Plaza, there was no reason to continue the commute between the drafty old house and the office. He and Helena talked often about closing the house, leaving Douglas and Riva to oversee it and open it only for family holidays. But now, with Cameron missing and perhaps dead, he didn't know what he was going to do. It was a new and unpleasant feeling for Gregory. It would be years before Kyle could obtain his education and be readied to step up. He couldn't remember another time in his life when he didn't know what to do. In the last few hours, he found himself contemplating shutting down the expansion and bringing Sadie home to take Cameron's place. The fact his thoughts were carrying him to such a dark place was alarming, indeed.

On the second floor, he breathed a sigh of relief as the warmth of the hall engulfed him and the door to the staircase slammed slightly behind him. His footsteps fell silently on the thick, plush carpet and he hesitated only a moment outside the suite before tapping soundly on the thick, solid door. He waited, listening for any indication she was going to open the door and then knocked again, this time a little louder.

He turned and made his way down the stairs again to the hallway outside of the master suite and then on toward the dining room. Helena had arrived and was checking the warming dishes to see what was on the lunch menu. She turned a weary gaze in his direction and he nodded his head toward her in encouragement.

"Douglas," Gregory said as he poured a cup of coffee from the silver urn on the side table, "Nicole must be sleeping. Would you ask Mae to check on her and tell her I would like to see her?"

"Yes, sir," Douglas said as he picked up an empty coffee cup. He glanced briefly at Vanessa as the Emerson siblings began to file into the room. He was glad to see that she was nervously avoiding his gaze.

Richard moved to stand at the fireplace, leaning against the shoulder high mantle. Vanessa stood unusually subdued beside Garret, studying the luncheon selections. Andrea and Kyle settled themselves at the far end of the long table, watching the scene in quiet intensity.

"Excuse me, sir," Douglas said, stepping into the room and approaching Gregory. "Mae tells me that Miss Nicole left the Manor."

"What?" Gregory breathed, turning his piercing stare toward Douglas. "When?"

"About an hour or so ago, as I understand it."

Gregory swept the room with one glance, taking in the reaction of Douglas' words on those present. Helena, Andrea, and Kyle were obviously hearing news. Garret, Richard, and Vanessa were not so surprised and were not looking at each other or anyone else, which was more telling than anything they could have said.

Gregory handed his coffee cup to Douglas as he crossed the room. "I'll speak to Mae, please," he said quietly.

"She's in the kitchen, sir," Douglas said, resisting the impulse to look at Vanessa but was rewarded by the rising blush in her face he could see from the corner of his eye.

֎

It was shortly after noon by the time Jane reached the older neighborhood that had seen better days and pulled to a stop in front of a house that was badly in need of attention. She was developing a nagging headache that wasn't helped by the frequent vibrating thunder around her.

"Ms Shipman?" Jane asked, peering through the heavy wrought iron and thick glass of the security door to the older woman behind it, "I'm Deputy Jane Adler and I'm doing some follow-up on the accident you witnessed about three weeks ago on Paulson. May I ask you a few questions?" She pulled her badge out of her pocket and held it against the glass.

After only a moment's hesitation, Meghan reached down and turned the lock and then pushed the door outward, pausing to give Jane time to move out of the way. Jane pulled off her raincoat and left it dripping on the porch chair before she stepped into the overly warm house and smiled amenably at Meghan, divorced and an accountant.

"You'll have to forgive the mess," she said with a shallow sigh. "It's hard to keep things clean this time of year… tax season coming on, you know."

"Don't worry about it," Jane said quickly, scooting a pile of old newspapers from one of the sofa sections and easing down on the cushion covered in cat hair. "I won't take but a minute of your time. Could you tell me what you saw that day?"

"Well," Meghan said, settling herself into her worn and comfortable Lazyboy, "I'd gone to the doctor and it was almost an hour before I could see him. I was waiting for my daughter to pick me up. We were going to grab a quick dinner before I had to get back to work."

She waved a hand toward her dining room that was now her working office. Jane could see parts of the dining table legs between and behind cardboard file boxes. Stacks of papers completely covered the table top except for a small work space in front of the only window.

Jane smiled knowingly with a gentle nod. She felt something nudge her foot and moved her pad enough to catch sight of the little calico cat that was easing out from under the sofa to rub against her shoe. It stared up at her with wide, curious green eyes. She reached down and scratched the top of the cat's head and was rewarded with a bright smile across Meghan's face as she clicked her tongue and the kitten pounced towards her.

"I was waiting for the light to change so I could cross Paulson," she said, leaning over to scoop the cat up in her lap. Jane could hear the loud purr across the room and smiled. "She's a sweetheart," Meghan announced, scratching behind the cat's ears.

"The others were waiting to cross Butler. All four lights were red," she said, leaning back and glancing involuntarily to the right as she began to recall the moment. Then the light on Butler turned green. The 'walk' signal was flashing and the others began across the street. There was a blue Chevy waiting to turn right and no other traffic on Paulson. He motioned for me to go on and cross and waited for me to clear the turn lane. When I did, he pulled out and the white van ran the red light and slammed right into him."

Jane began making notes. She drew a rough sketch of the intersection, jotting down Paulson on one of the lines and Butler on the other. She made two male stick figures on the northwest corner that Meghan had indicated where the men were standing to cross Butler and a female figure for where Meghan had been standing diagonally across the intersection. Meghan leaned over the arm of the LazyBoy to see what she was doing.

"The other woman was on this corner," she supplied, pointing at the corner between herself and the two men.

"Okay," Jane said, adding another stick woman. "So she and the men were crossing the street with each other?"

"Well, they were and they weren't. She was pretty far behind them. They had already gotten across the street before she actually reached the corner. She was about halfway across the eastbound lane."

"Okay," Jane said, making an "X" on Butler in the middle of the crosswalk and two "X"s on the edge of the left lane.

"That's it."

"And where were you when the accident happened?" Jane asked, holding her pad out to her.

"About there," Meghan pointed to the middle of the south bound lane of Paulson, watching as Jane added her "X".

Jane studied her sketch a moment and then took and released a light breath. "So," she said, looking up at Meghan, "where they crossing with the light?"

"Yeah," she answered readily. They were crossing with the light and I was jaywalking."

"I see," Jane smiled.

"That's why I tried to tell that cop that if the Chevy hadn't slowed down to let me cross, that van would have run right over that woman."

Jane was so stunned by Meghan's words it took a few seconds for them to sink in. She sat staring at her sketch, trying to absorb the words without allowing any visible reaction to them.

"I'm sorry," she finally said, clicking her pen in and out a time or two and gripping it between her fingers. "What did you say?"

"I said, I really think that the white van would have hit that woman crossing Butler if it hadn't been hit by the Chevy. I tried to tell the cop that, but he didn't seem to care. The car sped up."

"Sped up?" Jane repeated; she felt foolish that this information was catching her so mentally flatfooted.

"It did. Since I was crossing against the light, when I heard the car rev up, I wanted to make sure where it was."

"It was moving which way on Butler?"

"East."

"And the Chevy was heading…"

"North on Paulson," Meghan finished her sentence.

"So the Chevy was blocking your view…"

"A little," Meghan admitted. "But they were both moving. I heard the car rev up about the time the Chevy driver must have seen the car coming through the red light. I think he couldn't decide whether to speed up or slow down. I saw his break lights flash a second before he sped up and then the van slammed right into him. I just think that woman was really lucky. If the Chevy had pulled off when his light turned green, I think that van would have hit her."

"And then what happened?" Jane asked quietly, watching Meghan intently.

"The men took off running the other way," she said with a slight laugh and then an embarrassed shake of her head. "If they had been hurt it would have been awful," she said, shaking her head again. "But when I think back on it now, it was funny. The look on their faces…"

"I understand," Jane said with a nod.

"The woman just froze in the middle of the street and it's a good thing. The van hit the Chevy about square in the back door and it spun around twice before hitting the mail box and street sign right here…" she said, leaning forward to drop her finger on the notepad sketch. The kitten leaped from her lap onto the back of the lounge chair.

"And the van?"

"It went this way," she said, using her finger to show a one hundred eighty degree turn, "and landed about here." She moved her finger to the opposite corner. "It wound up facing the way it had come – up on the curb."

"The men," she continued, tapping the two male symbols, "headed toward the Chevy and by that time others had heard the crash and were coming around. Several people headed toward the van and the driver sounded like he was going to strip some gears when he threw it into reverse and stomped on the gas. He bounced off the curb, threw it into drive and took off like a bat out of hell."

"So - there was a man driving the SUV?" Jane asked studying Meghan's face as she settled back in her LazyBoy and the kitten crawled back into her lap.

"Oh, I just meant the generic he," Meghan said with a slight shrug. "I couldn't see the driver."

"I see," Jane said with a sigh.

"Sorry," Meghan said with another shrug of her shoulders. "It was just seconds. It seemed like it was all in slow motion, but it happened so fast."

"I understand," Jane repeated, flipping her notebook closed and returning it to her pocket. "I appreciate your time." She stood up and waved a hand as Meghan made a move to get up. "Please, don't bother the kitty."

Lee Malcolm stood at the door of his office peering through the glass wall onto the Atrium below where the approaching storm was beginning to distort the light coming through the glass roof. Around him the normal events of the day for Emerson International continued. People went about their work unaware of the family drama playing out in the Emerson household. He was pulled from his thoughts by the ringing of his phone. He glanced at the clock on his desk as he lifted the receiver from the cradle.

"We've had no success in locating Holly Weston," a female voice came over the line. "We've checked all her known haunts in Europe and have a friend trying to check any visa requests and passenger manifests at the airlines. I've even reached out to some paparazzi I know."

"Broaden the search," Lee commanded. "Check with the smaller airports in Europe and see if they have seen her with any of their clientele."

"Affirmative."

"Report again before 1700 my time," Lee said, pressing the hook switch to disconnect the call and then pressing in a speed dial code. Every operative under his command or he could beg, borrow or steal was on this assignment. He even resorted to asking Chet Driscoll for recommendations for reinforcement operatives. He didn't know all the names of the people he was dealing with, he just knew he could trust anyone who Driscoll recommended.

"Gene," he said into the mouthpiece, turning his back toward the door out of a primeval habit to control the action. "We're expanding the search. You're probably going to have to take this one personally."

"I've already got my bags packed. Any suggestions?"

"Finding Holly Emerson?" Lee almost snorted. "Yeah, pray for divine revelation…"

Lee looked up to see his secretary coming through the door. She crossed the room silently and handed him a note. Lee read the words, "Gregory Emerson holding for you."

"Thanks, Gene,' Lee said, disconnecting the call. "What line, Lisa?"

"One," she said, turning on her heel and leaving his office.

"Yes, sir," Lee said as he answered the call.

"Lee, my daughter-in-law has left the Manor."

"Vanessa?" Lee asked, unable to disguise his irritation. He was too busy at this moment to deal with Vanessa Emerson's temperamental tantrums.

"No. Not Vanessa," Gregory breathed, "Nicole."

"Gregory…"

"I know. Mae says she went to her parents. You've got to get over there and get her back here."

"Yes sir," Lee sighed, hearing the desperation in Gregory's voice.

Lee pulled his suit jacket off the hanger on the back of his door and shrugged into it as the private elevator descended the twenty-two floors to the garage. He merely waved to the guard on duty as he sprinted to his car. He left the Plaza and breathed a curse as someone cut in front of him, causing him to slam on his brakes.

What should have been a fifteen-minute drive from the downtown business district into the historic section took him almost half an hour because of the increasing rain and lunch hour traffic. He drove first past The House of Quinn, a quaint old mansion restored to its original glory and a stark contrast to the encroaching modern buildings around it that were considered to be "progress." He made the block and then pulled up in front of the Quinn home behind the Escort.

Janet Quinn answered his ringing of the bell. She was a handsome woman and it was obvious where Nicole had gotten her beauty. She had the alabaster complexion and dark hair of her Italian ancestry, thick, dark hair, not quite as dark as Nicole's but every bit as sleek. Her eyes took on the color of whatever she was wearing. Today they were amber tinted, picking up the gold of her sweater.

"Mrs. Quinn, I'm Lee Malcolm, Mr. Emerson's security chief. Is your daughter here?"

"Yes, she is," Janet said with the quiet dignity that always charmed and sometimes intimidated those in her presence. "Please, come in."

Lee was too aware of the inclination to rub his shoes on the backs of his pant legs lest he disturb the impeccably decorated and appointed house. He had no knowledge of antiques or art, but he knew when he entered a museum. As he waited in the front hall, Drake Quinn was coming down the steep, starkly simple stairs. A rich colored Oriental runner made the stairs seem as though they wore a regal train.

"Drake," Janet said quietly, turning toward her husband with an unique intimacy that was almost embarrassing to Lee, "this is Mr. Malcolm, security chief for Gregory." She was so close to his ear she could have been whispering her love for him.

"Mr. Malcolm," Drake said, extending his hand. Drake Quinn was as impressive in his bearing as his wife. They had the serene poise that came with the traveling they did, the people they associated with, the prestigious clients they had and the elite circles in which they moved. "How may I help you?"

"May I see Nicole?"

"Of course," Janet said, extending her hand with a grace that should have seemed exaggerated but fit her comfortably. Ironically, the Emersons had little cause to be alarmed by Cameron's marriage to Nicole. Although the Quinns were not in the same financial bracket, they were definitely social equals and academic superiors. They had the grace and charm that could walk as calmly with European and Oriental royalty as with the grocer and beautician down the street. For all their sophistication and refinement, they were completely gracious and approachable, a trait they either instilled in their daughter or she inherited it.

Lee followed her lead and stepped from the hall into the living room, spotting Nicole on the sofa. Without a trace of make-up and curled into the deep cushions, she was very much the child of the household. As he moved further into the room, he realized someone was sitting in the high-back chair facing the sofa and was unable to hide his surprise when he realized it was Jane Adler.

"Mrs. Emerson," Lee said nodding deferentially toward Nicole, "Deputy Adler," he said, turning to raise his eyebrows toward Jane.

"Lee," Jane responded with a curt nod.

"I wasn't expecting to see you here," he commented, trying to sound casual but heard the edge to his own voice ringing in his ears.

"Nor I you," Jane countered with a slight upward defiant tilt of her chin.

"Mr. Emerson asked me to come," Lee said, turning his attention toward Nicole. "He's very distressed that you left the Manor and would like for you to return with me."

"Why?" Nicole asked quietly, actually sinking deeper into the sofa's cushions as though they could provide her with some kind of protection. "What difference could it possibly make to them whether I'm there or here?"

Lee turned slightly and met Jane's knowing look, sending her a silent appeal for help. He didn't know why Jane was here, but he hoped she would persuade Nicole to return to the safety of the Manor without raising undue alarm in her parents.

"Nicole," Jane said quietly, getting out of the chair and indicating that Lee could and should sit down. She crossed the room to sit beside Nicole and reached out and took her hands, holding them gently. "You probably should think about going back. The Manor is completely protected and we don't know yet exactly what's behind all this. Don't you think that's where Cameron would want you to be right now?"

Lee slipped into the chair Jane vacated, watching the two women. Obviously there was a bond forming. Nicole stared at Jane for a moment and then sighed, nodding her head. She then closed her eyes and leaned her head against the sofa back. Lee could see the tears glistening beneath the thick, dark lashes and felt a strange sorrow looking at the pale and drawn face of a young woman who should not be suffering this tragedy. She was a curious blend of her parents and even in her present state, breathtakingly lovely.

Jane glanced at Janet who sank down on her haunches in front of her daughter. She reached up and smoothed the hair away from the waxen face and then caressed it gently. "Do what you want to do, baby," she whispered with the same intensity that seemed so intimate with her husband and yet so nurturing with her child.

Lee remained silent, not sure what he would do if she refused. The alarm was a silent one, but the alert was of the highest degree. No Emerson was to be left vulnerable or unprotected. His present priority was to get every Emerson family member into the protective sanctuary the Manor provided. Nicole's impulsive bolt from the clan was a danger he was not yet prepared to explain. Only a handful of people knew that Cameron's plunge over the cliff was no accident. That was the way it must remain until the investigation was complete.

"You are both invited to the Manor as well if you would like to be with her," he spoke quietly.

"Would you feel better if we were there?" Drake asked, coming to stand behind Janet.

"No," Nicole said after a slight pause and then a shake of her head. "You've got to inventory and check the consignment and it's bad enough that I'm not there to help you. I really wanted to see the pieces you got." Tears welled into her eyes again, a sign of the confusing emotions that were overwhelming her.

"You will," Janet assured her as she straightened up to allow Nicole to stand.

"I'll make sure she gets safely onto Sutter Trail," Jane offered, looking at Lee for his consent as they stood on the front porch waiting for Nicole. She could detect his relief.

"I'll arrange to have one of my men to meet her at the roadblock and escort her up the trail," Lee said, more to himself than to her.

"Good idea," Jane agreed.

"You are in Crystal Springs out of uniform and here because...?" Lee asked as they waited on the front porch for Nicole to collect her things and tell her parents goodbye. The rain had only increased and there was little chance of them being overheard.

"I was interviewing a witness to a traffic accident," Jane said evasively. "CSPD isn't exactly cooperative with us. There is an oaf of a detective over there who thinks I'm with an insurance company if it should come up, by the way. Jake asked that I come by and see if Nicole were here and if I could get her home. Gregory called him too."

"A traffic accident..." Lee said shaking his head slightly. With all that was going on around Oak Meadow, Lee was mystified as to why Jane would be working a traffic accident in Crystal Springs. He fell silent. Jane watched as his mind began to connect the dots.

"Was that the accident that Nicole witnessed?" he asked, turning to look at her directly. He was intuitive enough to realize when there was something he was missing, and he was definitely missing something here.

"The hit and run?" he asked.

"Yeah. A hit and run with a twist."

"Oh?"

"Yeah. One guy was broadsided by another guy who ran a red light and the guy who was hit ran."

"Yeah?" Lee replied, knowing there was more to the story and wondering when Jane would get to the point.

"They found the car later. It had been stolen."

"Then it would make sense the driver would flee the scene."

"It would," Jane agreed. "But that's not the whole story."

"Okay," Lee said, unable to completely hide his irritation with the guessing game.

"Officer Daniels mentioned that one of the witnesses was a kook. I decided to find out why. She kept trying to tell him that the hit car would have run over one of the other witnesses if it hadn't been stopped by the car that ran the red light."

She watched as the light dawned in Lee's mind. She saw the widening of his eyes and then almost imperceptible drop of his jaw. He blinked twice and then turned his gaze from her. Lee swallowed hard, almost choking because his throat had gone suddenly dry.

"Ask the right question," he muttered as he stared beyond the images in front of him. "What mistakes were made?"

"What?" Jane asked, moving a step closer to him to hear over the driving rain. "What did you say?"

They were interrupted by the front door opening and Nicole stepping between them. Jane moved toward the steps in front of her and Lee stepped behind her, following her to the curb.

"I can drive myself back," Nicole said quietly as she opened the car door and slipped behind the wheel.

"No problem," Jane said with a smile, patting her shoulder as she leaned over her. "I'm headed back to the station. I'll follow you back in case some reporter is watching and wants to get a statement."

"I hadn't thought of them," Nicole admitted. "Thanks, Jane."

"No problem," Jane said, closing the door and heading toward her car parked across the street.

"I need to talk to you," Lee said as he followed her across the quiet residential street.

"I know," Jane answered simply.

"Can you meet me for drinks later?"

"Where and when?" Jane asked as she opened her car door.

"I'll call you," Lee said as she closed the door and she nodded.

൙൭

"I can't for the life of me understand Holly or Richard," Sadie said as she shrugged out of her clothes and crossed the room to the bath in their Plaza apartment. Ben was standing at the window looking out at the raging storm.

The Concord flight was uneventful but the three and a half hours seemed like a lifetime of wondering what was happening at home. For a while, Sadie thought it was going to take them longer to get through the New York traffic between JFK and Teterboro than it had for them to get from Paris to New York. The Emerson jet was there when they arrived and they flew into the capital where a driver waited for the last leg into Crystal Springs.

Sadie insisted there needed to be an EI officer at the Plaza when the truth hit the news. Gregory only offered cursory argument because she pointed out the Plaza was as secure as the Manor. There was nothing she could do at home and the office offered her the opportunity to monitor communications. She was removed from the family drama for a reason and this wasn't a day when she could deal easily with the family dynamics graciously.

"How's that?" Ben asked, setting his suitcase on the luggage rack in the master bedroom and turning toward his wife.

"I don't know how she can distance herself from the family the way she does and I don't understand why he stays married to her."

"How long has it been since she was in touch?"

"With me?" Sadie asked, pausing in her unpacking to open the heavy drapes and allow what little light offered to creep into the room.

"Or him?" Ben shrugged.

"It's been three – three and a half years since that summer she came home and carried Emit's young guide off with her when she left, hasn't it? What was his name?"

"Neal something or other, wasn't it? And Richard? When did he last see her?"

"Well, they met in Paris for their last wedding anniversary," Sadie said as she fished her brush from her cosmetic bag. "They were married in January… but if I recall, it February when he took leave. Just a few months ago, anyway."

"I thought she called you at the office not too long ago."

"She called the office," Sadie said, returning to her task. "She left a message with the receptionist that she wanted to see me when she was in Zurich and she'd let me know where she would be staying. I was in Munich. She said she was with a friend and they were traveling she didn't leave a number and never called back."

"That's our Holly," Ben said with a tolerant smile.

"How can you think she is amusing?" Sadie asked, unable to appreciate his unperturbed attitude about Holly's total lack of consideration for anyone else.

"I really don't" Ben said, laughing out loud, "but you have to admit, there isn't anyone else like Holly. She's completely self-consumed and narcissistic, but she's also completely engaging. She can charm the wallpaper right off the wall, Sadie… you know she can!"

"No one would blame Richard if he divorced her," Sadie returned to her original thought. "Not even Daddy."

Sadie had lived her entire life under the shadow of her gregarious and charismatic older sister and was not at all immune to the stark differences between them. Holly's presence always generated an energy and excitement that would captivate anyone in attendance. She could walk into a room and have everyone enthralled by her allure before her second step.

"He has certainly proved his worth to EI over and over again. Daddy wouldn't lose him because of Holly's behavior. You know he wouldn't. He depends on Richard too much. He's been Daddy's right hand for years and will especially be in the next days if…"

"He loves her, Sadie," Ben said shortstopping the direction his wife's thoughts were leading her with a shrug of his shoulders. "She's his wife."

"But how can he keep loving her? She humiliates him any time they are in the same room and parties her way around the globe like she's single and available. She flaunts her boy toys under his nose like they were stray pets she picked up. I just don't know why he puts up with it, that's all."

"Who can explain love?" Ben asked, crossing the room to slip his arms around her. "I have to admit, the bigger mystery to me is why you love me."

"You're sweet, but you aren't going to take my mind off my family right now. It's only a matter of hours before I have to return to the belly of the beast."

"Vanessa?" Ben guessed.

"She gets witchy when she's stressed," Sadie said, sighing deeply. "She's ambitious and has her heart set on being the First Lady someday. She's probably afraid Daddy will insist Garret return to the company if…"

"Don't cross bridges before they appear," Ben said, changing her thought's direction again as he lowered himself to the bed and kicked off his shoes. The jet lag was catching up with both of them.

"You're right," Sadie agreed, sitting on the edge of the bed beside him. "I don't know how Nicole is going to cope. I think she's lost weight since we were home for the holidays. She's not adjusting at all well to the family from what I hear."

"From whom have you heard this?"

"Everyone in one way or the other. Mum… Daddy… Riva… Douglas…"

"It's not easy," Ben said, poking gently at her. "You Emersons can be a tough crowd."

"Not Cameron," she said, stretching out beside him and allowing the fatigue that was toying with her mind to overcome her. "Cameron is different. I can't bear to think of him out there somewhere, hurt and no one looking for him."

"Don't go there, Sadie," Ben said quickly, rolling over on his side to drape a protective arm over her. "You know they will be searching again as soon as they can get back on the river."

"He can't be dead, Ben," she moaned, the fatigue allowing fear to overwhelm her. "Please God, he can't be dead!"

"Rest, Sadie," Ben said softly, stroking her cheek with the back of his hand. "You need to try to get some sleep. Richard is coming in this afternoon as soon as the storm breaks and he can handle anything that comes up. You know he can."

CHAPTER ELEVEN

Jane watched as the Escort in front of her stopped at the roadblock where Sutter Trail met the highway. She laughed out loud at the reaction of the State Trooper when Nicole lowered the driver window and he realized who she was. One of the familiar EI vehicles was waiting. As Nicole started the long climb up the Trail toward the Manor, Jane maneuvered a U-turn.

She headed toward the station house, the interview with Meghan Shipman beginning to play through her mind. Instead of turning toward Oak Meadow, impulsively, she headed into Crystal Springs again. There was just something nagging at her that she could not ignore. As she picked up speed on the highway, the windshield wipers were an annoying interruption to her thought processes.

Her drive back to town was slowed by the storm. In several locations there were signs that the torrent of water was going to breech the drainage system and flood the highway. Lightning flashed around her and thunder followed immediately. She heaved a heavy sigh as she slowed for the heavier traffic going into Crystal Springs.

She fished her cell phone from the console between the front seats and set it in her lap. Once in town, she pulled off the road and called the station. Connie answered on the first ring before she could pull the traffic report from the folder in the passenger seat.

"Connie," Jane spoke into the cell phone, still uncomfortable with the contraption. "Look up an address for Ed Lockwood in Crystal Springs for me, would you?"

"Who's he?" Connie asked, her voice crackling through the interference of the cell signal.

"Not sure yet," Jane replied. She pulled her notepad from her pocket and reached for the magnetic pen that was attached to an adhesive base stuck to her dash. She paged through her notebook to the first clean sheet. When Connie read off the address, she jotted it down quickly. "Thanks," she called over the line and then pressed the end button on the phone.

With cars splashing by, she pulled a map book from her glove box and looked up the address. She sighed as she discovered that it was across town. With a resentful glance into the dark sky, she pulled away from the lot and back into traffic.

Ed Lockwood was an elderly man who answered the door only after her knock turned into pounding on the front door. He stared at her through ill-fitting bifocals and only removed the chain latch when she showed him her badge twice. She lips thinned with her impatience under steel control as he fumbled with the chain and the door swung inward.

"My daughter says I'm too careless about answering the door," he explained as Jane dropped her raincoat on the front porch before entering. "She wants me to move into a home."

"We can't be too careful these days," Jane commented as she stepped into the living room. It was neat and clean and she could hear a yapping dog somewhere in the house. There was also a huge yellow tabby staring at her menacingly from the back of the sofa.

"What can I do for you, officer?"

"Deputy," Jane clarified, showing him her badge again. "Deputy Adler. I'm from the Oak Meadow Sheriff's Department and I'd like to ask you a few questions about an accident you witnessed several weeks ago."

"Uptown. That was more exciting than most of my doctor appointments," he said with a laugh.

"Can you tell me what you remember, Mr. Lockwood?" Jane asked, accepting the flapping of his hand as an invitation to take a seat. She settled herself on the sofa, looking apprehensively at the cat. "I hope it is friendly," she said, staring into the large, unblinking yellow eyes.

"Oh, he's a pussy cat," Ed said, laughing at his own joke. He sat on the opposite end of the sofa and reached up to stroke the cat. The cat never took his eyes off her. What was it with old people and cats?

"Well," Jane said, heaving a heavy sigh and reaching for her notebook. "About the accident, Mr. Lockwood..."

"I really didn't see much," he said, shaking his head and frowning regretfully. "Everything happened so quickly."

"So, you had been to the doctor," Jane prodded, hoping to jog his memory, not knowing exactly what she was looking for.

"Yes," he said with a nervous laugh.

"And you were with another man?" Jane asked. "One of the witnesses said you were walking with someone."

"There was another man," Ed said with a nod, but we were not together. We were just crossing the street at the same time."

"Did you notice anything unusual or out of the ordinary before the accident?" Jane tried.

"Not a thing," Ed answered, shaking his head vigorously. Jane flinched as the cat got up and jumped from the back of the sofa and settled himself between them. "I did see the young lady," he went on as he began stroking the cat again.

"Which young lady?" Jane asked, not sure if Meghan Shipman would be considered young to him.

"The one crossing the street with me," Ed said with a smile. "I heard the young man with her say he was going to go get the car. Such a nice young couple. We rode down on the elevator together."

"Couple?" Jane said, making a cursory note in her pad. "The accident report didn't mention a couple," she said, tilting her head questioningly at him.

"Probably because he was going to get the car for her," Ed surmised, then smiled at her. "Such a polite young man."

Jane inhaled deeply, then slowly exhaled, more to give herself a moment to think than in exasperation with the circular conversation She glanced at Ed Lockwood and smiled slightly.

"One of the witnesses said she was jaywalking," Jane said with a soft laugh. "And she said there was another woman crossing with the light."

"Yes," Ed confirmed. "I rode down the elevator with the lady crossing with the light and the nice young man who was getting the car. He was so careful with her."

"So," Jane said, sorting through the confusing thoughts that were spinning in her head. "So, this... couple... can you describe them?"

"Well," he said, looking beyond her to his recall. "She was probably in her mid-twenties. She had long dark hair and pretty eyes. I remember her eyes. You just don't see gray eyes like that very often."

No, you don't, Jane thought as a mental image of Nicole flashed into her mind, glad to know they were both talking about Nicole Emerson. "And the man?"

"Well, he was rather average," Ed recalled. "He was tall. I don't really remember a lot about him.

"Do you remember what color eyes or hair?"

"I never saw his eyes. He wore dark shades, even inside."

"What about his hair?" Jane asked.

"It was not as dark as hers, but it was dark."

Jane realized she was holding her breath. She cleared her throat and exhaled slowly. "Mr. Lockwood, do you mind telling me the name of your doctor?"

"Dr. Goldman," he answered readily. "He's on the fifth floor of the medical building."

Did they get on the elevator with you… were they already on the elevator… or did they get on from another floor?"

"No, they got on with me on the fifth floor."

Jane nodded as she jotted the name in her notebook and stood up. She put the pad in her pocket and reached out to help him get up from the sofa.

"Thank you for your time," she said as she backed toward the door and held her hand out to shake his at the same time. There was no way she was going to turn her back on that cat.

"You're welcome," he said with a smile as he pushed his glasses higher on his nose.

As she shrugged her damp raincoat back on, she heard the chain slipped back into place. She made a dash to her car and slid behind the wheel. She backed out of the drive and headed toward the medical center.

Twenty minutes later, she pulled into the underground garage of the medical building several block from Mercy Hospital. She reached to turn off her wipers as they began to screech against the drying glass. The rain had not lessened the activity in the building and she wound her way to the top of the garage and headed back down before she found a parking place.

She made her way to the elevator and made note of the parking level. She nodded to the man who stepped back to allow her to exit first as they reached the lobby. There was a janitor busy mopping up the water being tracked in by the people hurrying in from the storm. She crossed the lobby, dodging several "wet floor" caution signs to the building directory hanging on the side wall.

She concentrated on the floors rather than the names. There were only three occupants listed for the fifth floor, a urologist group including Dr. Goldman, the Kauffman Group, plastic surgeons, and the Kenworthy Clinic. Within the Kenworthy clinic, she spotted the name Paul Geldman, the name on the prescriptions she had seen on the prescription bottle on Nicole's bedside table. Jane stood staring at the directory as the pieces fell into a picture she didn't like.

Nicole was seen by Ed Lockwood on the elevator coming from the floor of the Kenworthy Women's Clinic with a man who was definitely not Cameron Emerson. By the description Ed Lockwood gave, there was no way the man was Cameron. Jane crossed the lobby to the elevator and pressed the button for the basement, trying to figure out what she was going to do next.

※

Gregory Emerson stood at the top of the stairs hesitating a moment before making his way to the closed door. Nicole arrived at the Manor less than a half hour before. He leaned in toward the door, trying to hear any activity that might be detectable from the other side, even though he knew the door was thick and solid. He tapped lightly, straightening up as he heard the knob turn and Nicole opened the door. She was pale and the gray of her eyes seemed to have spilled out into the dark circles underneath.

She was dressed in a plush velvet robe, dark emerald green in color and a Christmas gift from Cameron. She pulled it closely around her neck and moved back for him to enter. Gregory stepped into the brightly decorated sitting room, taking in the careful neatness that was an indication of her extreme stress. He learned early in his relationship with his daughter-in-law that when she was upset, she resorted to straightening and cleaning.

"We missed you at lunch," he said, lowering his lean frame down on the love seat that was set in front of the fireplace. In a few weeks, if Nicole followed her habit, she would rearrange the room so that the seating would look out over the gardens as the grounds men started their turning of the beds and spring planting.

"There is a new shipment at the warehouse," she said quietly, easing herself into the Queen Anne chair beside the sofa. She pulled a small throw pillow into her lap and fingered the age-darkened fringe around it.

"Vanessa is hoping to see you. She would like to apologize."

"There's no need," Nicole said with a sigh, dropping her gaze from her father-in-law's intense scrutiny. Although Gregory Emerson intimidated most people, Nicole quickly discovered his softer side. In spite of the shock of Cameron's sudden marriage, he liked Nicole and was soon convinced the two were deeply in love. "She was just saying aloud what everyone thinks."

"No, she wasn't, dear" Gregory countered. "In spite of what you may think, Helena and I understand. We realize how difficult it is for any young couple not to be alone in their own place."

"Thank you" Nicole responded. "I've never meant any offense..."

"I'm well aware of the fact that a little of us Emersons goes a very long way," he said with the smile that was known worldwide. "It's just hard for Helena and me to realize our brood is grown and should be wanting to fly the coop, so to speak. That wasn't the case in our generation. We didn't have the resources and opportunities yours has."

"I'm glad to know you understand," Nicole said honestly. "Cam said you did, but I wasn't sure myself. It's not that this isn't a beautiful home and you have done nothing but make me feel welcome..."

"You don't have to explain anything," Gregory said gently. "And you certainly owe no explanations to Vanessa. She and Garret have the townhouse in the capital and Sadie and Ben live on a separate continent. They have the distance you don't and Van has certainly not been fair. I think she understands that now and is anxious to apologize."

"The rain is getting worse," Nicole said in alarm, glancing over his shoulder and out of the windows into the darkness of the stormy afternoon. "I thought when I was driving back that it was passing over, but it just doesn't stop."

"I know," Gregory responded, following her gaze. "The teams are on standby at the firehouse and Lee has assembled some of our men to assist. We'll find him, Nicole. I promise you that. We *will* find him..."

Neither one of them added the thought that was unavoidable: dead or alive, Cameron Emerson would be brought home. He saw the gray eyes go darker and the tears threaten again. He stood quickly, reaching down to take her hand. "I know you're tired, but please, humor your mother-in-law and me. Join us for a little while. You don't need to be alone right now and neither do we."

Nicole hesitated but saw the genuine concern in his steel blue eyes and glanced down at the carpet. The last thing she felt like was being around others now. She nodded slightly and stood up. "I'll change and be down in a minute or so."

She heard the door close behind Gregory and drew in a deep breath and sighed. Regardless of what the next few days brought, her life was irrevocably tied to Cameron's family. She slipped out of her robe and stood in front of the closet wondering what she should put on. Cameron's clothes hung on one side, awaiting his return. For a moment, her mind turned to the horrible reality that might be awaiting her within the next few hours and she turned from the closet, moving into the bathroom because she was sick again.

When she descended the stairs half an hour later she was even more pale and drawn. She would have crawled into bed if she weren't afraid of offending Helena and Gregory. They were trying so hard to help her feel included in the family. As she reached the bottom of the stairs, she heard voices coming from the study so she turned at the first hallway and made her way toward it. She learned very early to move soundlessly about the house. That way, if she did not want to join a group of the family she could ease away and no one ever knew she was there.

She paused outside the door and listened. She could hear Helena's soft, melodious voice and Gregory's, deep and resonant. As she waited before entering the room, she caught the presence of a third person, but wasn't sure who it was. She heard the click of the butler's pantry door behind her and stepped awkwardly into the room before Douglas could catch her trying to eavesdrop. She was relieved to see Richard standing at the bar on the far side of the room.

"Nicole," he said, his face brightening into a smile as he spotted her. "I hope you're feeling better."

"Thank you," Nicole replied without answering his question.

"Would you like something to drink?" he asked, pausing a moment before resuming his place opposite Helena.

"No, I'm fine," Nicole answered, reacting to Helena's welcoming motion by crossing the room to sink onto the sofa beside her.

"We were just talking about the construction on the house," Richard said, sipping at a glass of Scotch. "They've gotten the road cut to the site."

"I know," Nicole said dully. "They are going to start digging the footing tomorrow."

"I talked to Lyle Johnson this afternoon. I told him to wait," Richard said, pulling one ankle up on his knee and leveling a gentle look on her.

"Our general contractor? Why?" Nicole asked, a chill going through her and causing her heart to thud in her chest. "Why would you do that?"

"To prevent any kind of problems with traffic while the rescue continues," Richard said evenly, realizing he had upset her.

"They come and go from the old highway, how could that cause problems with the rescue?" she asked, shaking her head in confusion.

"I just thought it might be better to wait a few days."

"Cameron scheduled the footings to be dug before the spring rains," Nicole said, glancing from Helena to Gregory. "He's going to be upset if we change those plans without consulting him. If we are to have the house finished by fall, they have to stay on schedule."

The silence that engulfed the room was deafening but Nicole seemed completely unaware of it. Gregory looked quickly at Richard and imperceptibly shook his head. Richard concealed his initial surprise with the smooth grace that was so much a part of his nature. They watched in stunned alarm as Nicole jumped from the sofa and hurried from the room.

She reached the sitting room and closed the door behind her, leaning against it and fighting the unidentified terror that was threatening to overwhelm her. She was almost blinded by the tears that pooled in her eyes as she reached the desk, hunting for the card of the general contractor overseeing the house and wiped her eyes so she could read his phone number. Whatever else happened, the construction on the house must continue. To stop construction was to concede that Cameron wasn't coming back alive and the house would never be built. She wasn't about to do that. She couldn't!

She dialed the contractor's number, swallowing several times and taking deep breaths to calm herself. No matter what else was happening, the construction on the house would go forward. That was what Cameron would expect. That was what was going to happen.

༄༅

"I don't care what your parents say," Vanessa said, her voice unusually low as she smoothed her cleanser over her face and watched Garret in the mirror, "Nicole is snobbish, condescending, and arrogant."

"Vanessa," Garret said warningly, "you really don't want to keep this going."

"I don't appreciate your father taking the tone he did with me," she said as she buried her face in a washcloth and removed her makeup.

"You were out of line, Van," Garret said. He never understood the hostility Vanessa felt toward Nicole.

At first, everyone was suspicious of Nicole. Rumor ran rampant. Everyone in their circle of friends had a theory of what happened and how Nicole managed to lure him to the altar. But, as time passed and the family got to know her, there was no doubt that Cameron and Nicole were crazy in love and she wasn't the opportunist everyone assumed her to be. When the initial shock of Cameron's impetuous behavior began to wane and they settled into a routine, Garret understood why the reserved Nicole captured his brother's heart.

"I was just saying out loud what everyone else has been thinking for the past year and a half," she countered, unwilling to concede anything. "You will never convince me that your parents haven't been offended by her attitude. The idea that the Manor isn't good enough for her is just disgusting."

"She's never said that," Garret said, shaking his head. "All she's ever said was that she wanted her own home. The one they are building is nice enough, but certainly not anything compared to the Manor."

"Look what it's costing to build that road at the back of the estate," Vanessa said, glancing at the door as though someone might walk in at any moment. She jerked a brush from the vanity drawer and began dragging it through her hair. "There are any number of other places that wouldn't be as expensive. There's certainly plenty of spots between here and Oak Meadow right on the Trail where they could build. But no, she has to have the site that has to have a special road built!"

"I'll say it again," Garret said with a weary sigh, "Cameron decided on the glade, Van," "Why is it you only hear what you want to hear? How many times do you have to be told? Nicole had nothing to do with choosing the site."

"Why are you so determined to defend her?" Vanessa snapped. "What is it about that creature that makes everyone seem to just simper when she walks in a room? Helena and Gregory are bending over backwards to please her... Cameron is completely besotted by her... Richard thinks she's the best thing since the World Bank... but I can tell you, he's not at all pleased with the money they are spending on that house."

Garret stopped in mid stride to the closet and turned to stare at her. He was used to his wife's volatile personality and the tangents she often took, but he was completely unprepared for this one.

"In the first place," he said, pulling a hanger from the clothes bar and draping his shirt over it, "what money Cam does or doesn't spend certainly isn't a matter for either you or Richard to be discussing."

"Right," Vanessa almost screeched, "that's for the *real* Emersons to decide, isn't it? No one says a word about the money Richard funnels to Holly for her world-wide jaunts and no one says a word about this showplace Nicole is erecting for herself in the glade."

"Vanessa," he said calmly, "listen to yourself! Holly is entitled to spend her money any way she chooses. And, what is it about Nicole that brings out such venom in you? What has she ever done to you? You are always getting so indignant for other people, but she's never been anything but courteous and gracious to you and everyone else."

"Gracious," Vanessa repeated, a short laugh becoming a snort before she could prevent it. "Elegant... graceful... dignified... everyone thinks she's so wonderful. Every time her name appears anywhere, there is an exaggerated adjective preceding it. You can't buy press like she and Cameron get. We have the best PR firm in the country on retainer and Nicole gets great reviews just walking out of the house and showing up at that ridiculous little shop of her parents."

Garret drew in a deep breath and slowly let it out. Suddenly he recognized his wife's emotion for what it was. All these months he chalked off her acerbic comments as just nothing more than her dry sense of humor, but it was much deeper and darker than that. Vanessa was jealous of Nicole. She craved attention and admiration. She wanted a life in the political realm more than he did. She dreamed of being the mother of the Emerson political dynasty. She and Gregory were the driving force behind his aspirations and he suddenly realized from where her anger was sprouting.

She was right. Cameron and Nicole were quickly becoming the darlings of the Crystal Springs' social scene. When they showed up at any affair, the cameras began to flash and everyone took notice. Nicole could walk into a room and her very presence created interest. There was something mysteriously alluring about her and the irony was that she avoided public appearances as much as she could. She was as unassuming and genuine as she appeared.

"You know, if someone does a poll," Vanessa said, unable to restrain the need to have the last word, "your father might decide he's backing the wrong son for the governor's office."

Garret stared at her for a moment realizing there was truth to what she was saying but knowing that Vanessa's concern was unwarranted. Cameron naturally possessed the public presence and image that he had to carefully cultivate. Although Garret was the rising star in the political scene, Cameron could probably step into the race and walk off with any election he wanted.

"It's something you'll start thinking about if you are as smart as I know you are," Vanessa hissed, tossing the brush back in the drawer. "And if your father expects me to apologize to Nicole because she heard something she didn't like while she was eavesdropping outside the den, he's going to be very disappointed."

"Vanessa," Garret said, crossing the room to link his arms around her shoulders and meet her flashing glare in the mirror. "Cameron doesn't want a political career. Nicole doesn't want what you want. They are not our enemy."

"Garret... what if Cam..."

"Don't go there until we have answers, Van," Garret replied quietly. "Don't do that to yourself and don't do it to me."

She grabbed hold of Garret, sobs beginning to wrack her body. When her distracting rage was taken from her, she had nothing left but to face the horror that might be coming to engulf her family and it was more than she could bear.

☙❧

Cameron Emerson fought his way through the fog that consumed his consciousness and tried not to move. He knew that any movement would send the excruciating agony radiating through every fiber of his being. He tried to remember anything, but the effort only caused the throbbing in his head to intensify and the darkness flirting with the edges of his mind.

Muscle spasms would hit him occasionally, causing an intense flash of pain to streak across his chest and then radiate out into his arms and legs, forcing him to go completely limp. For a moment, he was unable to catch his breath as the suffering increased in intensity, thrusting through his chest like a knife plunged into it. His breathing became shallow and eventually the pain began to subside to the dull consuming throb rather than the fiery explosion.

Distant lightening shot a flash of light around him and was gone as instantly as it came creating shades of light and dark to his surroundings. Turning his head triggered nausea so he kept still, surrendering to the exhaustion that overwhelmed him.

With extreme trepidation, he raised his right hand slightly. He felt a biting grab in his ribcage and caught his breath, causing the crescendo to shoot through him again. He dropped his hand to his side and heard his whimper echo around him. His arms and legs were chilled, but his torso and head were warm.

"Hello?" he called softly, trying to see into the darkness without turning his head. "Hello!" he called louder. There was no response.

He stared through the slits of his swollen eyes into the darkness above him and tried to formulate a rational thought. His memories of traveling down the Trail and heading into the office were becoming clearer. He remembered the sudden loss of control of the Jag. He remembered careening sideways into the rock face. He remembered what seemed to be a disembodied voice threatened him with death if he did not do what he was told. Did any of it happen or was it all a terrible dream?

Moving his head with extreme care, he strained to see around him. He caught a flash of light and jerked away against the stabbing pain that shot through his head. Then he heard the distant thunder as it rolled across the mountains. He resisted the urge to take a deep breath, recalling the man's warning him to stay still and stay quiet or he was going to die.

He felt a tear of frustration roll from the corner of his eye and its stinging path across his chaffed cheek. He was unable to determine what was real and what wasn't. Which memory was true? Which was not? Was he hallucinating or was this nightmare real? Where was he? Trying to think at all brought confusion over him like a dense fog and he fell into a restless sleep, interrupted by the excruciating pain that followed every twitch and involuntary jerk.

CHAPTER TWELVE

Lannagin's was a bar and grill on the outskirts of Crystal Springs. Lee Malcolm arrived first, arranging for an out of the way table where lovers found discreet intimacy and he and Jane could talk without fear someone would overhear. He thought about ordering a drink but decided against it. He didn't know what else the Emerson tragedy would require of him, but he knew for certain that this day would not be over for him any time soon.

He spotted Jane as she walked through the outer doors. She was just slightly over average height with delicate features and what appeared to be a fragile frame. Lee had seen her in action and knew that the slight build camouflaged her strength and abilities. She had dark blonde hair that she kept highlighted with golden streaks and stylishly cut to a short length, dark hazel eyes, and the healthy complexion of someone who not only was born with good skin, but knew the importance of taking care of it.

The subtle spark that ignited between them at their first meeting had at some point developed into a strange friendly antagonism. Lee tried to recruit her out of the academy for Emerson International's security force but she opted for the Sheriff's department instead. He took no professional offense, but on a personal level, the decline rankled at him in a way he didn't fully understand.

She was a rising star on Jake's team. She was not only up to the physical demands of the job but she had an intuitive intelligence that seemed to tell her when there was more to an investigation than was being detected.

Like that traffic report in the file. It was gnawing at him to think he missed something she spotted. He lifted his hand slightly as her gaze swept the restaurant. He noticed the heads that turned as she walked through the bar into the dining area. As she made her way around the tables and chairs, he signaled a waiter. They both arrived at the same time.

"Drink?" he asked her as she shrugged out of her raincoat and tossed it onto the chair beside him and then dropped into the one across the table.

"Ah," she said staring a moment at the waiter as though for inspiration then met his gaze evenly. "What are you drinking?"

"Club soda," Lee said, unable to mask his disappointment.

"I'd like a daiquiri please," Jane said with a smile for the waiter. "I'm off duty."

"Thanks for meeting me," Lee said quietly.

"No problem. Your princess is back behind the castle walls. You want to tell me what caused her to bolt?"

Lee let the question pass and Jane didn't press. She learned that she could usually determine what she wanted to know if she kept her eyes open, her mind alert and her intuition honed. They waited until the daiquiri was set in front of her and she tasted it before continuing their conversation.

"Would you like anything else?" the waiter asked Lee.

"Are you hungry?"

"Starving," she admitted, picking up the menu on the table. "I've not eaten since breakfast. Who could know the day would turn into this?"

"Ain't that the truth?" Lee breathed, the extent of his exhaustion beginning to catch up with him. "Okay, now tell me what triggered your interest in that report."

"What do you mean?" Jane asked, scanning the offerings of the menu.

"I've read it several times. What do you see that I missed?"

"Nothing," Jane said, closing the menu and setting it to the side. "It was just the fact that it was there."

"And...?" Lee prompted, wondering if he was going to have to grovel before she satisfied his curiosity.

"At first I thought you had just misfiled the report."

"What?"

"Your file was background material on Nicole up until she married Cameron."

"And..." he repeated, fighting to maintain patience.

"And..." she said drawing the word out into several syllables, "nothing for more than a year and then that silly little traffic report. I thought you meant it to go into the 'other' file," she said, lifting her hands to make her quote signs in the air.

Lee could not help the ironic laugh that escaped. "So it was blind luck," he accused, feeling some measure of vindication.

"It was good investigation," she countered unfazed by his intended condescension because she knew he was impressed. She didn't question her satisfaction on that level because she wasn't ready to admit she wanted to impress Lee Malcolm. She looked up as the waiter returned. "You buying?" she asked, casting a look at Lee over the menu.

"Order what you want," Lee said, suddenly remembering her considerable appetite. It took a lot of fuel to compensate for her metabolism.

"I'll have the steak and lobster," she said without hesitation. "House salad, blue cheese dressing on the side, loaded baked potato and ice tea."

"I'll take the sixteen ounce T-bone," Lee said without picking up the menu, "roasted potatoes, Caesar salad and your sautéed mushrooms."

"Did you ever talk to her about that accident?" Jane asked, carefully mentioning no names and leaning back for the waiter to set a basket of steaming yeast rolls between them.

"No," Lee said, not elaborating. "I assume you have?"

"Well… actually, I haven't," Jane admitted, enjoying the upper hand and not fooling herself into believing it was going to last long. "But I have talked to the other witnesses."

She spent a considerable amount of time selecting one of the large rolls, carefully tearing it into pieces and then smearing real butter over the steaming insides. Lee ducked his chin slightly, a sure sign he was in deep thought.

"Did you know," Jane asked, handing the buttered bread to him with a devilish twinkle in her eye, "it was a hit and run accident?"

He took the bread, never taking his eyes off hers. "Yes, I did. It was a stolen vehicle. I'd take off too if I'd just stolen a car and then someone broadsided me."

"So would I," Jane agreed. "But, Meghan Shipman is under the impression that had Mr. Caprini not run the red light and slammed into the stolen car, it would have run over Nicole."

"What?" Lee whispered, inhaling so sharply he almost choked.

"Did you have one of your men with her that day?"

"The day of this accident?"

"Yeah?"

"If I'd had a man with her that day, do you think you would be telling me anything I didn't already know?"

"Am I?" she pressed, unable to resist the subtle needling. When she saw the dark shadow cross the deep brown eyes and the creases from his nose to the corners of his mouth deepen, she took a breath and slowly let it out. "Guess so," she whispered, buttering a small piece of bread and popping it into her mouth. "There was a man with her and it wasn't Cameron."

"This Meghan Shipman saw a man with her?" Lee asked, finally putting the bread into his mouth.

"No, she didn't," Jane said with a shake of her head. "But," she continued, leaning across the table, "another witness, Ed Lockwood, rode down in the elevator with her and a man."

"How do you know it wasn't Cameron? Did he recognize her? Did he say it wasn't Cam?"

"When you describe Cameron Emerson, what's the first thing you always think of?"

"His hair," Lee said without hesitation.

"Right," Jane agreed, smiling broadly and nodding her head in admiration. "That Robert Redford auburn hair!"

"So, who was with her?" Lee asked, trying to reclaim some of his dignity.

"Well," Jane said, leaning back in her chair and releasing a sigh, "I don't know... yet. But he had very dark hair. It wasn't any shade of red" she shrugged. "Now, you have to admit... two weeks ago that accident was just an odd little occurrence in Nicole's life. But yesterday morning, someone went to some serious effort to blow her Jag right off the side of the mountain. That raises some serious questions about whether or not one thing has something to do with the other, don't you think?"

"You think she's the target," Lee said.

"I think the possibility certainly needs to be investigated. Everyone is assuming Cameron was the intended victim. That's the logical presumption, given who he is and what he is up to in that mega-conglomerate they have mutated several times over. But, if you have a scope strong enough to take a bead on a tire, Lee, it's strong enough to be able to tell the difference between a Jag and a Mercedes even if you can't see the driver."

"Not to mention one is a deep bronze and the other a metallic blue."

"Exactly! Another thing," Jane said casually. "Ed Lockwood seemed to think Nicole and whoever she was with were a couple. There was no mention of the man in the police report because he left her to go get the car from wherever they parked."

"Okay," Lee said, watching her with an intense fascination.

"Don't you think it's strange that she would witness an accident, stay to speak to the police and this guy never reappeared? He was considerate enough to go get the car for her, but stayed out of sight once there was attention drawn to her there?"

She could see the wheels turning in Lee's mind and smiled impishly. "There's more," she said, lifting her shoulders in exaggerated excitement.

"When I tried to interview Nicole this morning, I was in her bedroom. She had prescription bottles by her bed. I made a note of the doctor and the meds. The doctor who wrote the scripts for her has an office on the fifth floor of the old medical building where Mr. Lockwood sees his urologist."

"Really?" Lee asked, watching her closely. He knew there was something else, but he wasn't prepared for what Jane said next.

"I think Nicole is pregnant. Why do you think there was someone – not her husband – who was with her at the OB/GYN that day?"

✌✍

"I'm telling you something's going on," Vanessa hissed as she grabbed Andrea's arm and pulled her sister-in-law into the morning room. She glanced over her shoulder to make sure Douglas wasn't close enough to hear.

"Like what?" Andrea whispered, following Vanessa's furtive glance toward Douglas and Riva in the family dining room. They were busy getting the room ready for supper.

"I don't think Nicole was here last night," Vanessa said as she eased the door closed and moved toward the sofa.

"Of course she was," Andrea said, laughing at Vanessa's insinuation. "She came back yesterday afternoon. I saw her go directly up to her room."

"She sneaked out after that," Vanessa stated, pushing Andrea onto the sofa and sinking into the other corner.

"In the middle of that storm?" Andrea asked incredulously. "Where would she go?" Andrea demanded, her voice rising enough to cause Vanessa to jab her with her elbow. Andrea shot a quick look across the room to the door and sighed heavily.

"Maybe a little secluded cabin somewhere in the back woods?"

"Van!" Andrea exclaimed, her face going pink as she dropped her gaze from her sister-in-law. A few words of rebuke about her unseemly behavior from Helena the afternoon before caused Andrea to try to keep her distance from Vanessa, but she had been hunted down in her mother's morning room. She wasn't sure how to escape Vanessa without incurring her wrath.

"Remember how Holly used to slip off to meet that guide that worked at the Lodge? What was his name? Coffler? Colter?"

"Caulder," Andrea said with the blush growing deeper. She spent the same summer so infatuated with the young guide herself that Holly's departure with him was still mortifying to her.

"Caulder! That was it! Caulder!"

"Vanessa!" Andrea whispered, casting another furtive glance at Douglas and Riva. "Someone might hear you!"

"Oh, like everyone in the family doesn't know they took off together? You don't think Holly actually discovered a new passion for hiking that summer, do you?"

Van saw the look in Andrea's eyes and sighed. She was little more than a kid the last time Holly swooped in.

"Grow up, Andrea," Vanessa said, reaching out and placing a hand over hers. "You can't not know the truth about Holly. She gives a whole new meaning to slut. I don't know how Richard tolerates her."

"Holly's not a slut," Andrea cried defensively, her family loyalty bringing a fire to her not normally seen in the shyest of the Emersons. "And Nicole isn't either."

Cameron was her favorite brother although she was closer to Kyle. She loved Nicole and she'd had a crush on Trevor since Cameron brought him home. The idea they would betray Cameron was more than she could bear to think about.

"Nicole loves Cam. And Holly's not a slut; she's just free-spirited. Nate took an internship in Spain at the end of that summer. He called his advisor and told him. Richard understands Holly and loves her very much."

"Nate! That's his name!" Vanessa said, causing Andrea to shoot a quick glance at Gregory and Garret who were approaching and then shake her head at Vanessa. "You're very naïve, Andrea," Vanessa continued, patting her youngest sister-in-law's hand. "There's no doubt that Richard loves Holly, but he also loves his position at EI and his position in this family."

Andrea was surprised that she wanted to retort, *like you don't, too?* but she controlled the impulse. Instead, she sighed and shrugged her shoulders. "I know Nicole and Trevor. They're just friends."

"Everyone knows there is no such thing as 'just friends' between men and women," Vanessa said, shaking her head and tightening her grip on Andrea.

"No, I don't know that." Andrea said vehemently. "I know a lot of men and I am just friends with them."

"You may consider them friends, but I guarantee you, they don't see you as just a friend."

"I don't care what you say," Andrea muttered, growing weary of the debate. "Cam and Trev are like brothers and Nicole loves Cam.

Cam has complete trust in Nikki and so do I."

"That's the same thing Richard always says about Holly," Vanessa reminded her with a wicked snicker. She made her face seem longer and lowered her voice in imitation of Richard, "Holly is just a free spirit and a nonconformist. We can't expect her to behave in conventional ways. She wouldn't be Holly if she did."

"Well, Holly *is* different," Andrea said with a sigh. "She always has been. It's not like she wasn't the way she is when she and Richard married. He knew that. And you're wrong about Nicole and Trevor."

"I'm telling you, Jane thinks Nicole had something to do with Cameron's accident or she wouldn't keep coming back here!"

"Vanessa," Andrea breathed, no longer finding Vanessa's wicked sense of humor tolerable. "This is Cam – my brother – and Nicole you're talking about!"

"I'm not joking, Andrea," Vanessa said turning to stare into Andrea's horrified eyes. "They don't think this was an accident. They believe Nicole and Trevor planned this and plotted to kill Cameron. There's no other conclusion they could be coming to."

Andrea was so horrified she was unable to catch her breath. She jumped from the sofa and ran from the room afraid she was going to be sick. She rushed into the back hallway, pushing through the door that led to her room and barreled into Kyle's across the hall. He was just pulling on his shirt and he stopped in mid-thrust of his arm into the sleeve when he heard her coming.

"Andi!" he said, alarmed by the sight of her, "what in the world?"

"Do you think Nicole and Trevor killed Cameron?"

"What the devil?"

"Van says the police think Nicole and Trevor are behind the accident. Why would they want to kill Cameron?"

"Andrea!" Kyle almost shouted, reaching for her and shaking her roughly to get her to stop talking. "Think about what you're saying! You can't take Vanessa seriously! You know how she is!"

"...but to suggest something like that!" Andrea gasped.

"Exactly," Kyle agreed. "Nicole isn't the villain here! Trevor isn't the villain!"

"Then there is a villain?" Andrea breathed, the horror overwhelming her again as she sank onto the edge of his bed. "It wasn't an accident?"

"No," Kyle admitted, lowering himself onto the bed beside her and draping his arm over her shoulders. "Nobody knows who or why yet, Andi. But I do know that it isn't Nicole and it isn't Trevor."

"Then who?"

"Nobody knows. There are countries where Daddy has holdings that he can't ever go to because there is such a danger of kidnappings and assassinations. There are some places where there is a bounty on any Emerson head because people don't like the company."

"I know we've laughed about OM standing for Outer Mongolia, Kyle, but this isn't Outer Mongolia! This is Oak Meadow! This is Hawthorn Manor! This is home! How did this happen to us here?" she whispered, tears filling her eyes and spilling down her face. "Nothing makes sense anymore."

"No," Kyle agreed, getting up and pulling her to her feet. "There's no sense to this, Andrea. There has to be some explanation, but I don't know what it is. Maybe it was some hunter and it was all just horribly coincidental. Bullets land somewhere after they are fired. You read sometimes where a stray bullet from a hunter goes miles and miles and through some window and kills a baby sleeping in a crib or a guy just minding his own business watching a ballgame. Crazy stuff like that happens."

"But who would be hunting in our woods this time of year?" she asked, putting the cold hand of logic to the theory.

Kyle remained silent. It seemed for everything he offered as comfort, she zeroed in on the obvious flaw. He had no explanations to offer. He sighed deeply, the germ of suspicion wiggling into the back of his mind beginning to grow into a monstrous creature. Nicole and Trevor had become extremely close as soon as she arrived at the Manor. No one ever thought anything about it before because she and Cam seemed so in love.

Of course Trevor would welcome anyone who made Cameron as happy as he seemed to be with Nicole. Seemed to be, Kyle thought, wondering if Cameron and Nicole had been putting on a front to prevent anyone from seeing trouble in their sudden marriage. That would be in Cameron's nature. He was never one to let his concerns show. Kyle thought back over incidents of the past few months.

Nicole was never really comfortable at the Manor and always seemed to resent the closeness of the Emersons. When his mom dismissed Nicole's elusiveness as her need for newlywed seclusion, it seemed perfectly logical. Then the talk started about building the house. His parents seemed okay with the idea, but Vanessa had been keeping her resentment front and center.

A bolt of lightning crashed close to the Manor, shifting Kyle's attention from his sister to the storm. Thunder rolled over the house, bathing it in a reverberating shutter. He looked at Andrea and then tightened his arm around her shoulders. They both fell silent, each in their own dark thoughts.

～～

"I thought you needed to be apprised of what's developing," Lee said, settling himself behind his desk. The Plaza was all but deserted, with the night lighting in the atrium outside his office turning his glass wall into a mirror, reflecting his image back to him. The storm seemed to be subsiding as he drove from the restaurant back downtown. There were distant flashes of lightning occasionally that sent eerie shadows from the glass roof.

"The deputy really thinks Trevor may have something to do with this?" Gregory asked, his voice booming through the speaker phone and filling the office.

"He's the primary suspect at the moment, sir," Lee confirmed. "I think at this point we would all like to think someone flew halfway across the world to exact some personal revenge against Emerson International, but all evidence points to someone closer to home."

Lee could hear the heavy silence as Gregory absorbed this conclusion. Trevor Cantrell came into Cameron's life as unexpectedly as Nicole Quinn, he remembered. Until Cameron met Trevor, he had no interest whatsoever in the treacherous treks into the higher elevations of the mountains. Trevor was the one who introduced the perilous hobbies into Cam's life. Until then, Cameron was more than content with the annual fly-fishing excursions, white water rafting and hunting parties with the seasoned and trained guides of Emit MacIntosh – family events – not wild, solitary excursions.

"Are you looking further into his background?" Gregory's voice filled the room again.

"I am," Lee said evenly. "I wanted to talk with you first, Gregory. This is getting messy. We're going to start stepping on toes pretty soon. I didn't want to take action you would not approve of… and there is more."

"What else?" Gregory asked, Lee could hear him bracing for the next disturbing revelation.

"A couple of weeks ago, there was a hit and run accident in Crystal Springs. I got a copy of the accident report when it went across the traffic desk because Nicole was listed as a witness."

"And?"

"I didn't think there was anything to it because she didn't see the actual collision."

"I sense a 'but' coming," Gregory sighed.

"But," Lee admitted with a nod of his head, "Jane Adler looked deeper into it and uncovered some strange twists. The car that left the scene was not the car at fault. Turns out it was stolen – CSPD found it a couple of days later abandoned in the industrial park out near the airport. Jane interviewed the other witnesses and one reported it looked like the driver of the stolen car was deliberately heading toward the crosswalk when the other car struck it. She is convinced the driver would have run down Nicole but for the accident."

Lee heard the dead silence over the phone line. He could imagine the look of Gregory's face. He waited, allowing Gregory time to react and respond.

"What is going on here, Lee?" Gregory asked.

"I don't know, sir," Lee admitted candidly.

"Do you think my daughter-in-law is in danger?"

"I think she could be," Lee admitted. "Jane thinks she may have been the intended target all along. It was her car this morning."

"What could be the motive?"

"I don't know that either, sir.

"This wasn't a crime of opportunity, Lee," Gregory said hoarsely and Lee heard a distinctive change in his voice. The normal regal stance failed him, causing Gregory to sound like a feeble old man for the first time in Lee's experience with him; the usual confidence that exuded from every pore of his being evaporated into the chilly air. "Keep me apprised of any development… no matter how insignificant it may seem. Get to the bottom of this… wherever that is."

"Yes sir," Lee replied before he heard the dial tone.

⁂

Nicole stood at the window watching as the stormy light of day was overcome by the darkness of nightfall. The rain was beginning to stop, but she could still hear distant rumbling of thunder from every direction. Storms often circled the mountains before moving on. She pulled the drapes closed and heaved a heavy sigh glancing at the clock on her bedside table and sinking onto the side of the bed and hanging her head.

"Are you sick again?" Mae asked quietly from where she was sitting on the love seat reading by the glow of an antique lamp.

"No" Nicole sighed raising dark rimmed eyes to her. "He's out there Mae" she whispered, lowering her head into her hands and giving way to the tears again. "It's such a horrid night and he's out there somewhere."

Mae placed a bookmark in her book and set it aside. "I know," she said simply. Sometimes there were just no words. She watched helplessly as Nicole fell backwards, covering her face with her hands and surrendering to the heart wrenching sobs.

Downstairs the family was beginning to gather in the den before dinner. The news was spreading and as Garret turned on the television the first words they heard were the teaser about the accident on Sutter Trail, which was synonymous with the Emersons and Macintoshes. Helena sat in her customary chair before the fire, her back straight and her demeanor quiet. She turned slightly to see the screen as Garret adjusted the sound.

Andrea and Kyle sat together in reading chairs at the back of the room. There was a curious tension between them and Vanessa that went unnoticed except by the three of them. Vanessa, from her perch on the sofa directly in front of the TV cast resentful glances at Andrea. Richard stood at the table, setting out glasses and checking the ice bucket.

Gregory entered from his office, his face pale and drawn. As he sank in the companion chair beside Helena, she reached for his hand. She caught the deep concern in his eyes and lifted her brows slightly. Gregory merely shook his head and then lifted the brandy he brought from his study to his lips.

The room fell silent as Sadie's image appeared on the screen. She was standing in the lobby of the Plaza and Gregory grunted in satisfaction. She had not allowed the news crews onto the Emerson executive floors. She was dressed in an Armani suit with a pale yellow silk blouse and a glimpse of Ben could be seen behind her. Microphones were swaying in front of her as the news anchors lead-in drowned out whatever was being said by Sadie.

The press conference going on at the Plaza was joined in progress.

"All that is known at the moment," Sadie said in a voice that was raised in an uncommon tone, "is that there has been an accident on Sutter Trail. After a tire blew out, the car my brother was driving went into the river. The rescue effort was suspended because of the storm and will resume at the earliest possible opportunity. For safety reasons, access to the Trail is closed. We ask that you be patient and leave the Oak Meadow Sheriff's Office with the help of the State Troopers to do their jobs."

"Good girl," Gregory muttered, listening to his daughter with pride. "Sadie always knows what to say and how to say it."

Vanessa's face flushed bright red in spite of her efforts to prevent it and she bit her lower lip, feeling as though Gregory's words were directed towards her.

"Look at her," Kyle whispered into Andrea's ear, glaring at Vanessa.

He'd spent more time than he wanted trying to calm his sister after her conversation with Vanessa and he didn't appreciate the perpetual troublemaking. He gained some sense of satisfaction watching her squirm under the gaze of his father.

"That was well handled," Richard remarked as he set filled wine glasses on a tray and began to make his way around the room.

"Very well handled," Garret agreed, ignoring the glare of Vanessa.

Douglas appeared at the door to announce dinner. With a quiet not at all the customary for the family, they left the den for the dining room.

"It's going to be a long night," Gregory comment, running a hand over his face and shaking his head.

"Miss Nicole has sent her apologies," Douglas said to Helena as the family headed for their places at the table. "She's not feeling well enough to join the family for dinner."

"As if that's news," Vanessa spoke before thinking. She was brought up short as Garret stopped in front of her and whirled around.

"Enough," he said so quietly it was more startling than it would have been if he had shouted.

"Indeed," Helena commented, bringing gasps from all of the Emerson children. Never had any of them known Helena to openly correct anyone. Normally, a call to her morning room signaled there was an issue she wished to address.

Vanessa felt sick to her stomach as she slipped into her chair, glancing furtively at Garret. She knew she was blushing deeply and the fact that everyone at the table was avoiding looking at her only made matters worse. Garret's neck was flushed and the anger was climbing into his cheeks as a rigid jaw line. Gregory took the chair at the head of the table, bowed his head and prayed.

✥

"Well," Jake said, scanning the front-page of the Crystal Springs Gazette, "Now we know why we have a glut of calls flooding the dispatcher."

"We've had a couple of calls that are threatening. We better get some more cars on patrol," Sandy mused, getting out of his chair and heading for the coffeepot.

"I've got that covered," Jake sighed. He had been in the office most of the night coordinating the effort with Lee's security teams and the Highway Patrol. Working in a collaborative effort, they should be able to keep the curiosity seekers and crackpots off the

Estate if not out of Oak Meadow. "Malcolm's got his force covering all access to the Manor. The Highway Patrol has closed Sutter's Trail so the area can be cleared for the rescue teams. I've got the squad on full alert to just keep things quiet in town."

Jane picked up the paper Jake dropped on the chair and began reading the article. The picture used had been taken at the reception held in the newlyweds' honor at the Manor the year before. Beside Cameron, Nicole was radiant in a silk dress that was probably the one she caught a glimpse of in her bedroom the day before. Friends and family surrounded them and everyone was toasting the couple's happiness.

In a perfect world, the couple would be safely going about their business, planning their future and happily in love. Even in a less than perfect world, she and her colleagues should be left to carry on their rescue or recovery operations without the press getting in the way. But this was not a perfect world she mused, looking at the handsome face of Cameron Emerson smiling out of the photo. Theirs had become a world of betrayal.

She was doing her best to get her notes organized and her file updated. She spent much of the night trying to tape record her thoughts and impressions of the witnesses she interviewed and was compiling them into some kind of usable order. Jane dropped her chin into the palm of her hand and sighed, closing her eyes to ease the strain and weariness that was overtaking her. She could have used another couple of hours of sleep. She had been with Lee later than she intended and had more alcohol than was wise.

"Officer Adler."

Jane opened her eyes and turned in her chair to see Ed Lockwood approaching her desk. The desk sergeant was just behind him, watching her reaction to his appearance at the station. She stood up, extending her hand to him and motioned to the chair beside her desk as the sergeant returned to his sentinel duties. "Mr. Lockwood, what brings you to Oak Meadow this morning? Can I get you some coffee?"

"Oh…ah… thank you, no. I was looking at the paper this morning," Lockwood said, waving off her offer. "That's when I realized that one of the men in the picture is the man who was with Mrs. Emerson the day of the accident."

"What?" Jane asked, her mind clearing itself of everything else but this man's words and focusing intently on what he was saying.

"When I was looking at the picture in the paper," Ed Lockwood said as though she should know what he was talking about. "When I saw him, I remembered. He was there that day."

Jane reached across the span between her desk and the conference table and jerked the morning paper up, laying it on her desk in front of Lockwood. She studied the photo, as Lockwood took his reading glasses from his pocket and cleaned them on the inside of his windbreaker. He put them on and studied the photo much as Jane had.

"Him," he said, putting his finger on the photo. Jane leaned forward, and had to reach over and move his hand before she could look into the grainy face of Trevor Cantrell.

"He was with Nicole that day?" Jane asked quietly. "The day of the hit and run?"

"Yes. It was he."

"You're certain?" Jane pressed, her professionalism masking the incredulous racing of her thoughts.

"Oh yes, quite."

"I see," Jane nodded. "So, when the accident happened, what did he do?"

"I don't remember him doing anything really," Ed Lockwood said with a slow shake of his head. "Neither did she for that matter. When the cops got there, she spoke to them a minute and then left. It was obvious she wasn't feeling well. They took her statement first – as a courtesy, you know. But, as I think back, there was a car waiting for her just a little ways down the block."

"Did you get a look at that car?" she asked hopefully.

"As a matter of fact, I did," he smiled. "I don't know much about cars these days, but I still recognize a Jeep when I see one. That little girl almost had to crawl up in it like a jungle gym. This fellow didn't even have time to get around to help her she moved so fast."

"Well, Mr. Lockwood," Jane said, standing up to indicate she would walk him out. "Thank you for coming. If you think of anything else, please let us know."

"I tried to call," Lockwood said as he got out of the chair, "but I kept getting a busy signal."

"The article in the paper is generating a number of calls," Jane said, reaching into her drawer and getting one of her cards for him. "My direct number is on the card and by-passes the switchboard if you think of anything else. I'll walk you out."

As she walked back into the squad room, Sandy was leaning back in his chair watching her and Jake was standing at the door of his office. She glanced at them both knowing they had overheard Lockwood as she lowered herself into her chair and picked up the paper.

"Why would Trevor Cantrell be with Cameron Emerson's wife for a doctor's appointment?" Sandy asked the question out loud that all of them were thinking.

"I've got a better question than that," Jane said with a quick shake of her head. "Why was Cameron's best friend taking Nicole to an appointment with an obstetrician?"

"What?" Jake and Sandy said in unison.

"I suppose that's something we should ask Nicole about," Jake said with a slow shake of his head, "and Cantrell, too. Sandy," he continued, turning back toward his office, "get over to the Plaza and see what else Lee Malcolm might have found out about that young man. Jane, get back up to the Manor. This time, you talk to Nicole. Don't let her put you off any longer."

Charlotte A. Minga

CHAPTER THIRTEEN

Long before the morning sun began to tinge the eastern sky, Nicole sat beside her window, wrapped in not only her thick velour robe, but also a blanket she pulled from the linen closet. She watched the changing face of the night, not allowing the haunting memories of her life with Cameron to obscure the brutal reality of this day.

Although she allowed Mae to help her to bed the night before without objection, she was unable to sleep. Somehow, Richard's well meaning cancellation of the work at the house unnerved her. She reached the builder at home, insisting that he continue as Cameron directed, He explained it would be too wet, but promised to have the site checked in the morning. She then left a message on Lee's voice mail that they were to be allowed access to the glade. She was concerned her instructions would be countermanded by someone along the way.

As the sky deepened into the strange surreal denseness before the dawn, she left her sentry watch of the night and pulled a warm jogging suit, thick socks, and her heavy walking shoes from her dressing room and hurriedly dressed. When the light of the new day grew strong enough for her to see the path, she slipped down the back stairs and out of the house. The rising sun seemed to be spitting coral colored clouds of cotton into the sky to herald the new morning.

She could hear Riva and Douglas in their apartment preparing for the day as she eased her way through the service area and out the door. The sounds of their casual intimate banter touched a chord of longing deep within her. She drove the images of her cherished mornings with Cameron out of her mind and held her breath as she turned the lock and took care to prevent the door from slamming behind her. She drew her fleece jacket on over her sweats. She pulled the hood over her head as she made her way around the carriage house to the path that would take her through the gardens, out the back gate of the Manor grounds and across the mountain to the glade above the river.

The carriage house once housed quarters for almost twenty servants on the third floor with common areas on the second; a stable for the horses on the ground floor. There was still a fine carriage in one of the few remaining stalls in the back. It was brought out for the Emerson's annual summer picnic and occasionally for spontaneous family jaunts. When Cameron and his brothers and sisters were small, part of the servant quarters were converted to a playroom, complete with soda fountain, juke box, dance floor and game machines.

Any time the Emerson children were home, there would always be a nostalgic trip to the game room where their competitive streaks would overcome any maturity they had achieved in adulthood. Cameron and Sadie still enjoyed pinball marathons. Garret was the proverbial hustler not only at the pool table, but at Ping-Pong as well. The required video equipment and games had been added to the collection in the last few years and Kyle and Andrea ruled in that domain.

Usually, one of the first items of business when the Emerson clan began to congregate at the Manor was a journey to the carriage house, where old challenges were resumed and championships defended; but not this time. In the predawn kiss of morning, Nicole paused outside the carriage house, wanting to hear the carefree laughter and good-natured teasing that always filled the room when the family was at home but all she could hear was the birds awakening in the trees.

Normally, the trek through the gardens, across the back acres of the estate and through the stretch of woods to the glade was not taxing, but she was weak from her inability to keep anything on her stomach these last few days and exhausted from lack of sleep. The muddy spots along the trail sucked at her plodding feet and she was breathing heavily as she neared the end of the formal garden.

The sky was a lovely shade of pink, turning the morning clouds to fluffy lace as she caught her breath and thought of the many times she and Cameron had come this way together. As the fears began to swell in her and the tears threatened, she heard the distinct sound of someone coming along the other path that formed the oval walk through the garden.

Nicole stopped and watched the curve of the opposing pathway, knowing before he appeared between the evergreens it would be Richard. She moved toward him and met him at the far end of the gardens.

"You should have waited for me," Richard said, slowing his pace and falling into step beside her.

"I didn't feel like jogging," Nicole answered simply.

"Than what brings you out so early this morning?"

"I'm headed to the glade," Nicole replied.

"After that storm!" Richard exclaimed, motioning toward the concrete bench behind them. "What possible reason would you have to do that?"

"To make sure the workers show up," she said, sinking onto the bench and instantly feeling the damp of the cold concrete soaking through her jogging pants.

"If they don't show up, Nicole," Richard said, looping his arm across the back of the bench and her shoulders, "it's because it's too wet to dig trenches."

"Footings," Nicole said quickly, as though she needed to defend the house.

"Okay," he said with a gentle pat on her shoulder, "footings. I know you were disturbed when I cancelled the work today, I apologize. It was quite thoughtless of me."

Without her realizing it, tears welled in her eyes and began to run over her cheeks, dripping off into her lap. There was still something that bothered her about Richard assuming the task of the construction schedule she couldn't quite identify. If it was too wet to work, the general contractor would be experienced enough to make that decision.

"Come on back to the house," Richard said, standing up and holding his hand out to her. After a moment's hesitation, she allowed him to take her hand and pull her from the bench. She was very quiet as they headed back to the house. A dread that was like nothing she had ever known flooded through her.

༻✷༺

Trevor heaved a heavy sigh as he shifted the test case on his shoulder and began the final push through the upper quadrant of his test area. Deep in the woods the fragile dawn was making slow headway in dispelling the gloom left behind by the storm or the dense surreal mist that hovered just above the ground. There was still a threat of rain in the air and a gusty wind stayed in the upper branches of the trees for the most part, but occasionally rushed downward, sending the sodden winter leaves scattering about in muddy clumps and chasing the mist into deeper recesses of the mountain.

He topped the last crest above the Manor and sighed deeply as he contemplated being back at the cabin soon. He slept very little the night before, trying to deal with everything that happened in the last twenty-four hours. He set out before dawn, knowing the trails so well he could use the faint pre-dawn light to find his way so that he could maintain his testing schedule. If he didn't, his research would be compromised and his thesis in jeopardy. If the rescue teams got back on the river today, he would have today's samples tested and recorded before hand at least.

Movement below caught his attention and he instinctively reached for the rifle slung over his shoulder to ready position. He swung the test case to the opposite shoulder and gripped the rifle just behind the trigger, his index finger curled around the guard. He paused, searching for movement through the thin spring growth. He had a bird's eye view of the back gardens and caught sight of a flash of color through the tender leaves and stepped closer to a tree trunk to conceal his presence.

Nicole Emerson, clad in a bright umber jogging suit walked briskly along the path. He could tell by the swinging of her arms she was struggling with the mud. He watched as she made her way past the fishpond and headed into the wide loop through the apple orchard. Then he caught another flash of color from the opposite direction.

Richard Weston was jogging at a respectable pace toward her. They met at the farthest point of the back gardens, just before the path forked, one leg circling back to the Manor and the other heading into the backwoods. Trevor stepped a little closer to the edge of the path, pulling back the long tendrils of one of the wild hawthorn bushes that gave the Manor its name.

"What have we here?" he muttered out loud, letting his test case slide from his shoulder to the ground. Trying to keep Nicole and Richard in his sight, he fumbled with the clasps to open it, then carefully felt for the pair of binoculars he carried with him. He pulled them from the case, pushing the cover off the lens as he raised them to his eyes. "Chance encounter or planned meeting?" he muttered as he brought the pair into focus

Trevor was as stunned as anyone when Cameron returned from the now infamous trip to Italy married to Nicole. Once he met her, however, he understood how the raven-haired beauty captured Cameron's interest and then his heart. For all her shy reticence, there was an elegant mystery to her that would appeal to Cameron. For all her respect for Gregory and Helena, she was not overly impressed with the rising Emerson brood although they certainly overwhelmed her.

Nicole had an innate flare and refinement that trumped class and celebrity that was both intriguing and infuriating to the Emerson women and alluring to the Emerson men. She found herself in the midst of an Emerson storm of competitiveness and envy that left her confused and uncertain how to react to her new family since she had never experienced sibling rivalry and did not have a competitive nature.

Nicole moved off the path to a concrete bench that was spidered by blackened cracks and weathered to a deep gray by the elements. She lowered herself to it while Richard stood in the path, moving back and forth in cooling down strides. Her back was now to the mountain. Trevor locked onto Richard's face trying to read his lips or his facial expression to determine the nature of the conversation, but he was too far away.

After a moment, Richard joined Nicole on the bench and Trevor tensed as he saw his arm go around her shoulders. Nicole fell slightly sideways, resting against Richard's chest briefly. After a few minutes, the pair rose from the bench and headed back the way Richard had come, side by side. He matched his pace to her slower stride. Trevor followed their progress along the path through the sparse spring foliage of the trees, keeping them in the tunnel vision of the binoculars until they disappeared through the gate separating the formal Manor gardens from the back grounds.

Trevor drew in a deep breath and slowly exhaled as he lowered the binoculars and reached for his test case. He rearranged the contents to allow room for the field glasses to fit back inside among his test samples and equipment. As he snapped the clasps back into place, he glanced down the mountain. Richard and Nicole had long since moved out of his line of view.

He grabbed the case and slung it back over his shoulder, then picked up the rifle and continued on his way. There was a malevolent smell to the very air. As the new dawn claimed the eastern sky, he realized that it was suspicion and a distrust that was taking hold of everyone. He first caught wind of it while he stood with Jake on the road yesterday. Now it was spreading with an unstoppable pace. As he reached the glade and veered deeper into the mountain, he felt it breathing down his neck.

He headed through the woods, plunging through the dry underbrush left by the winter and followed trails when he came across them and then cut through the raw forest when it was the most expedient straight line between himself and his destination. He was breathing deeply by the time he intercepted the trail above Sutter Trail and he made his way along the new trail he and Emit discovered the afternoon before.

He pushed through the woods to the rock formation, scrambled up and across the massive boulders until he reached the place where the sniper lay in wait. He was breathing heavily as he stood and surveyed the river below. He could see the yellow caution tape, suffering from the abuse of yesterday's storm as it sagged raggedly across the gaping void.

He pulled his canteen from his belt and slowly removed the top, studying the scene below. He glanced at his watch. It was almost the same time Cameron must have traveled the Trail the day before. He cast a practiced eye toward the rising sun, just beginning to clear the crests of the mountains. He sipped at the water in his canteen, pulled from a mountain spring that was as pure as any he ever tasted. The water was still almost freezing cold as he swished it around in his mouth and then swallowed it.

He settled onto the top of the boulder, using his backpack and test case as a back rest of sorts. Within minutes the bone chilling cold of the rock seeped through his jeans but his training allowed him to ignore it. He waited, checking the position of the sun and his watch in random interims. Finally, after about half an hour, he caught sight of movement high on the Trail. He struggled up from his position and bounced up and down on the balls of his feet to get the blood flowing.

He kept his eyes on the black car rushing towards him as he reached down and picked up his rifle. From his backpack he pulled a scope out and attached it to the barrel. He adjusted the sight and locked it on the oncoming car. It was one of the fleet of cars used by EI security. He fixed the car in his crosshairs, following its descent.

As it rounded the curves with easy speed, he locked his gaze on the front windshield. It disappeared as the Trail looped back on itself. Trevor's pulse quickened as it neared. He glanced quickly up to relocate the car as it emerged from the tunnel and then back through the scope. He could feel the pulse pounding against the cold steel of the rifle scope against his face.

The car took the last curve before reaching the site where the Jaguar went into the river and Trevor followed it as it passed below him, realizing as it did the angle of the sun probably made it impossible for the shooter to see who was behind the wheel. All he could see through his scope was the reflection of the tree branches and sky overhead.

He lowered the rifle as he watched the car continue on its way. He now had more information but no answers to the questions that were whirling through his mind. With a deep inhale of breath, he pulled his backpack on, positioning it carefully before tightening the straps. He secured his test case over his shoulder and slung his rifle between the two as he made his careful descent off the rocks.

Jane swung off the Trail and paused briefly to speak to the guard on duty at the Manor gate. He was one she didn't recognize and she found herself wondering what reinforcements Lee called in from the vast pool of security that EI had around the world. This one looked a little Arabian or slightly Oriental. She could believe that at the drop of a threat, he could spin himself into a martial arts torpedo.

She watched him pull a two-way radio from his pocket and begin speaking into it. He waved her on and by the time she made the mile drive through the grounds to the house, another EI security guard was waiting on the front terrace. He, too, was not someone she recognized and had a foreign look about him. There was something about the cut of his hair and his complexion that hinted he was not on home turf. It was obvious Gregory was thinking of international terrorism, but she was now convinced the threat was terrifyingly closer to home.

"Officer Adler," he said, touching the brim of his hat and stepping back to escort her to the front door. She caught a touch of an accent, but was unable to identify it.

Douglas was waiting just inside the front door, his eyes betraying not only his exhaustion, but his confused sorrow as well. At some point, the family had unconsciously come to accept that Cameron was dead and they were now waiting for the river to surrender his corpse. As cold as the water was, that could take some time. The rain in the upper elevations the night before had so swollen the river, resuming the search today was impossible.

"Good morning, Officer Adler," Douglas said, closing the door behind her. There was a stoop to his shoulders she had not seen before.

"Good morning, Douglas."

"The family is in the dining room," he said, extending his hand in that direction. "Is there any news?" he was unable to resist asking.

"No," she said quietly, "I just need to speak to Nicole again if she's up to it this morning."

"I'll let her know," he said, showing her into the den. "There's coffee and breakfast in the dining room if you would like…"

"I'm fine," she said with an absent wave of her hand. She could hear the low murmur of conversation going on in the dining room across the hall. She drew in a deep breath, practicing her questions for Nicole in her mind as she had all the way up the mountain.

This was a very delicate situation and she needed to make sure she handled the interview well. There were several conclusions that could be drawn from the information they had. There were a number of explanations as to why Trevor Cantrell would escort his best friend's wife to an appointment with an obstetrician; some benignly innocent and others perversely suspect.

She pulled her notebook and pen from her breast pocket and began jotting down prompts. First she would ask Nicole what she remembered of the accident on Paulson Street. When Nicole asked why she was interested in that, she would mention the possibility Nicole was also in danger. She would offer the witness' contention the driver seemed to be heading directly toward her.

"Miss Nicole will see you in her rooms," Douglas announced as he returned to the room.

"Have they resumed the rescue?" Nicole asked, crossing the room to take Jane's hand. When she did, Jane could feel her trembling. She stared deeply into the wide gray eyes as she shook her head, looking for insights into this mystifying young woman. Who was she? What was she? What was she capable of?

"No," Jane said quickly, watching as the pain flooded into Nicole's eyes and her knees went weak. Again, was it relief or grief? She couldn't tell. "The winds are still too high to resume the search on the river," she explained.

"I know," Nicole sighed, sinking into the deep cushions of the sofa and covering her face with her still shaking hands.

Jane closed the door and then settled herself in the chair so that she could look directly at Nicole. She glanced at her notebook and scanned the reminders she jotted down preparing for this moment.

"Nicole," she said smiling encouragingly at the young woman, "I need to get a little more information about the accident you witnessed a few weeks ago."

"What?" Nicole gasped, losing her fragile hold on her self-control. Cameron was lost along the river and this woman was asking about a car accident in Crystal Springs?

"I understand you witnessed an accident on Paulson and Butler."

"Well," she said, running a thin hand through her hair and staring absently at the carpet at her feet. "Not really."

"You're listed on the accident report," Jane said evenly. "Can you tell me what you do remember?"

"What does that matter?"

"You told the officer that you saw Mr. Caprini's car run the red light," Jane prompted, trying to divert her attention away from her confusion. "He was driving the blue Chevy at the scene."

"I did," she confirmed. "And I heard the squeal of the other car's brakes behind me, but I really didn't see the accident. I told all of this to the officer who responded to the call."

"You were coming out of the medical building after your appointment, correct?"

"Yes," Nicole answered without thinking. Immediately she realized what Jane had asked and she actually shrank away from her. "How do you know that?"

"Did Trevor wait at the doctor's with you or come back after you?"

"He waited with me," Nicole said slowly, lifting knowing eyes to stare directly into Jane's gaze. Jane saw the honest change of expression as Nicole's eyes narrowed and she sat straighter against the cushion.

"Did he take you into Crystal Springs?"

"Yes," Nicole said, not blinking. Her gaze was direct and challenging. Gone was the confusion caused by her concern for her husband and present was the clear, sharp instincts of an offended woman. "Cameron was out of town. I was so nauseated I was becoming dehydrated. I had an appointment later this month so that Cam could go with me, but I was so sick Dr. Geldman suggested I stop by so he could make sure everything was okay and he could write a prescription for something to help with the nausea."

"And so you asked Trevor to take you in?" Jane continued, finding it more difficult than it should have been not to flinch under Nicole's now indignant stare.

"Yes."

Jane hesitated a moment, giving Nicole the opportunity to expand on her answer if she was inclined to offer an explanation, but Nicole made her ask the next question. "Why?"

"I was too nauseated to drive myself."

"Why Trevor?" Jane repeated. She couldn't tell if Nicole was distracted or being evasive.

"Because I wanted to be the one to tell Cameron he is going to be a father and that was the only way I could be sure that would happen in this house," she said without the bitterness the comment could have carried.

"And did you?"

"Did I what?" Nicole asked dully, obviously growing weary.

"Were you the one to tell Cameron he is going to be a father?"

"Yes," Nicole replied, a smile and slight blush tingeing her face with the first color Jane had seen in her alabaster face.

"And the rest of the family – have you told them?"

"No," Nicole admitted. "Not yet."

"May I ask why?"

"You've seen them, Deputy Adler," Nicole said with a weary sigh. "They are very…" she paused, searching for how to express her thought, "…involved… in everything about each other's lives. Cameron and I just agreed to wait a while before we shared the news. This is a very private matter and the Emersons don't always appreciate the concept of boundaries. This is the first grandchild. It is probably the only time we will ever have our baby to ourselves."

"So is the prescription helping with the morning sickness?"

"Sometimes," Nicole sighed. She had felt so ill for so long that she wasn't sure she was ever going to feel better.

"I don't mean to offend," Jane said softly, glancing around her as she began to experience the overwhelming presence of the Emersons, "but has no one become suspicious of your morning sickness?"

"Well," she said with a smile playing at the corners of her mouth, "I guess I've earned a reputation of being delicate and difficult around here. And, some days are just worse than others."

"Like yesterday?"

"Yes," Nicole sighed. "I'm supposed to taper off the medicine as I get farther along. I tried to eliminate the evening pill night before last. It wasn't a good idea."

"You normally go into Crystal Springs with Cameron each morning, right?"

"Sometimes, but I wouldn't say 'normally.'"

"Oh?"

"Often Cameron flies in early with Gregory. Sometimes Richard rides into town with me. Sometimes I ride in with Richard. Sometimes I go in alone. It just all depends on what the day's agenda is for each of us. I don't like being in the helicopter and don't mind the drive."

"And yesterday?"

"My car was due for service and I'd rescheduled twice already. Cameron said putting it off any longer might affect the service warranty, so he took it in for me."

"So," Jane said, turning her attention again to her notebook, "tell me everything you remember about the accident on Paulson."

༄༅

Nicole stood at the window of her suite, staring out into the gardens brushing her hair. She could see Douglas and Kyle in the orchard just beyond the side yard. They appeared to be inspecting the storm's damage to the trees, but they were deep in conversation. Everyone was searching for mundane, ordinary activity to assuage the terror of their reality. The sun was climbing into the morning sky, chasing away the remnants of yesterday's clouds and giving a false brightness to one of the darkest days the Manor had ever known.

Movement below her caught Nicole's eye and she saw Helena emerge from her bedroom into the walled garden below. Unaware Nicole was watching, her shoulders were sagging and her face was drawn and pale. On Helena's face, Nicole saw the emotion she felt. The morning sickness was not as bad this morning, but Nicole's stomach was now cramping with the anxiety she was suffering.

Nicole turned from the window, unable to watch Helena's grief and deal with her own. The chopper arrived earlier, whisking Garret and Gregory away. Nicole crossed the room and dropped to her knees in front of the fireplace. She turned the regulator, allowing more gas to escape and the flames shot higher around the artificial logs and the heat rushed her.

She continued to brush her hair, feeling the heat in the tresses as they dried, trying to feel the warmth of the fire in her body, but she was colder than she had ever been. She was feeling a chill that was permeating from somewhere deep within her. It seemed to be radiating from her soul, numbing her to the reality that she might have to face a life without Cameron. In the light of the new day, the cold, cruel reality was taking hold of the family. Cameron wasn't coming out of the river alive.

She closed her eyes, tried to pray and discovered she was too afraid to. She was raised to accept God's will as best. This morning, the idea that God's will would take Cameron from her and their child was more than she could absorb. She tried to imagine a lifetime without him. To never see his smile, never feel his lips on hers, his caress in the middle of the night as he instinctively reached for her in his sleep, or never hear his laughter again. The thought was more than she could endure.

She inched back toward the loveseat before the fireplace, pulling her legs up and wrapping her arms around them. She lowered her chin onto her knees and stared at the dancing flames. Somehow she thought she would know if Cameron had died the day before. Something in her would have died at the same instant. She was certain. They were so in tune, so much one in so many ways, how could he die and she not feel him gone? How could he die and she go on breathing?

A cramp shooting across her belly caused her to moan softly as her hand moved to ease the tightness. Somewhere in the recesses of her mind, the thought of forever being tied to the Emersons because of Cameron's child without him was terrifying. She was discovering how much her life was now consumed and controlled by them.

Outside of Cameron and her parents, the only people she felt close to were Mae, Richard, and Trevor. They were her confidantes and friends. She could always depend on them as buffers during the first days at the Manor.

Mae was her connection to herself and her individual identity. When her parents realized how difficult she found life at the Manor, they suggested Mae come to be with her. Mae had been Janet Quinn's housekeeper before Nicole was born. During her parents' many travels away from home over the years, Mae was the constant in Nicole's life. Mae was the one who carried her back and forth to school, took her to her voice and dance lessons, made sure she practiced her music and was there when she woke in the night with a fever

Nicole had been stunned at the subtle change in Cameron when he was around his family. It wasn't something obvious or overt. Rather, it was a subtle veiling of the man she knew him to be. Only when they were alone or with Trevor did she see all the safeguards fall away and the man she fell in love with in Italy emerge. Whenever he was around any member of his family, there was a very subtle but distinct reticence and reserve that took hold.

Richard was her compatriot within the Manor walls. He understood the intentional and unintentional slights the Emerson clan could inflict on anyone not born to their realm. He, too, suffered the sibling jealousy that was inevitable when someone was injected into the family. Richard was the friend who helped her cope with the day-to-day challenges of being assimilated into the Emerson tribe.

Nicole felt a wave of nausea and moaned. She got to her feet and headed to the bedroom where her medicine stood on her bedside table. Cameron's baby was causing her as much aggravation as his siblings, she thought with a rueful laugh. They both turned her stomach on occasion. She popped the top off the bottle, poured one of the pills into her hand and reached for the glass of water on the table.

Dropping onto the side of the bed, she crawled into it, pulling the blanket over her and curling into a fetal position. She just could not imagine having to raise Cameron's child by herself. The night she told Cameron she was pregnant, they talked about the pressure she would endure as the mother of the first Emerson grandchild.

Helena and Gregory both held an Old World sense of family and a definite perception of dynastic birthright. Their child would be the heir apparent of the next generation and as such, would hold a place of dubious and ambiguous honor. Cameron warned her that the pressure she felt as the wife of an Emerson was nothing compared to the burden she would experience as the mother of one.

They talked about what they wanted for their child. They talked about the difficulties they would have to face when what they wanted was not in line with the expectations of the elder Emersons. The prospect was formidable when she thought Cameron would be at her side. The idea of facing the Emerson clan alone was overwhelming. How was she ever going to raise their child the way they planned without Cameron's strength?

Before she realized it, the pillow was wet with her tears and she was unable to breathe. She sat up, threw the covers back and got out of bed. She couldn't stay cooped up in the house with her fears and anxiety. She had to get out of the house or she was going to go mad. She knew there was no way she would be able to leave the Estate again. After her mad dash home, she was sure the security team at the gate would be instructed to discourage her leaving the Manor.

She left the suite and made her way downstairs, using the front staircase, as was her custom. As she reached the front hall, she could hear Vanessa and Andrea. They were in the morning room and chatting easily. Sometimes Nicole envied their comfortable relationship. Nicole was about to step into the room and join them when their words brought her to halt.

"You don't really believe she and Trevor are having an affair!" Andrea's voice floated into the hall.

"I do," Vanessa's followed. "Not that I blame her. He's drop dead gorgeous."

"You think?" Andrea asked, then convulsed in giggles at Vanessa's look.

"It will be interesting to see what happens now that Cameron is gone…" Vanessa said, getting off the sofa and crossing the room to where Riva left the silver coffee carafe.

"Vanessa!" Andrea whispered in horror. "They'll find Cameron when the waters recede. Kyle says he's probably found a cave to hole up in until he can hike to the road."

"I'm sorry, Andi," Vanessa said quickly, suddenly realizing how callous her words must seem to Cameron's little sister. She glanced up at herself in the mirror over the coffee service and when she did, she saw Nicole standing in the hall.

Vanessa breathed a low curse as she watched Nicole take a step backwards, the look of abhorrence on her face shocking Vanessa with its intensity. She turned to see Andrea's tears flooding her eyes and streaming down her face. "How can you think such things, let alone say them out loud?" she gasped, getting off the sofa and leaving Vanessa alone in the room.

Vanessa stood stirring her coffee, staring unseeingly into the cup. She had already suffered Garret's fury and Gregory's warning displeasure over her comments about Nicole. If her husband and father-in-law heard about this, she was in serious trouble.

With a sigh, she set her cup on the table and headed down the hall after Andrea. By the time she reached the back hallway, she could see Nicole running across the terrace, pulling her fleece jacket on as she went. Vanessa watched as she reached the end of the garden and headed into the back woods.

"Wonder where she's headed," she breathed, her eyes narrowing. For all the family's fuss, she wasn't convinced there wasn't something very suspect about Trevor Cantrell and Nicole Emerson.

CHAPTER FOURTEEN

The trip from Oak Meadow to Journey's End Lodge was not an easy or quick one. The road into the high country was two-lane until it wound past the Manor, following the mountainside at the point of easiest construction once the state highway gave way to the old county road.

Beyond the Manor, however, it narrowed to barely one lane with upcoming traffic having the right of way since those coming from the Lodge could see straight down the mountainside. There were pullout spots along the way for descending vehicles to move to the widened area and allow the traffic coming up to pass.

Jake sighed deeply as he slowed for the final hairpin curve and braced himself for the resistance he knew he would feel as the squad car drew every ounce of power from the engine for the final steep grade.

Only a crazy stubborn Scot would opt to remain at the top of the mountain like this, he mused, exhaling the breath as the car topped the mountain where it leveled off onto the high plateau and the entrance to the Lodge came into view. Once a trading post on the northern pass through the mountains, The Lodge now required an invitation or recommendation from an existing guest to visit.

Over the generations since its establishment, The Lodge spread from the original stone homestead which was now used as a root cellar by Rosemary MacIntosh across the high valley and into the high country. The Lower Lodge was a rustic building a half-mile further up, almost at the peak of the mountain. It was built on the edge of a breathtaking lake and used for overnight excursions for hardier, more adventuresome clients.

Even further up the mountain was the Upper Lodge that was reserved for the most experienced and demanding clientele. From there the most adventurous guests could do some serious rock and mountain climbing, and it was accessible only by foot or horseback.

This early in the spring, the Lodge was not officially open. Jake and his sons would be scouring the area looking for the damage the fading winter had caused and taking appropriate action. Jake made his way around the Lodge to the back, spotting Emit's Ranger parked just outside the back door. Several other off-road vehicles were pulled behind the maintenance shed.

Rosemary MacIntosh opened the door before Jake could get out of the cruiser. She held a paring knife in one hand and a bowl of apples in the other as she stood back to allow him entrance to her kitchen. Although she had a full staff, she still liked to keep her hands in the preparation of the meals served.

She was more than a foot shorter than her husband and could be described as stout and sturdy. Standing just barely five feet tall, her Native American heritage was quite evident in her strong angled features and dark, coarse hair that she wore pulled back in a loose bun at the nape of her neck. Her hands showed the scars and calluses her passion for her work produced. Her nails were cut short and her hands were weathered like fine, creased leather by constant use of them both in and out of doors.

"We having apple pie for dinner?" Jake asked with a broad grin as he sucked in a deep breath of the aroma of apples and pungent spices simmering on the huge stove.

"Nope," she said, shaking her head and laughing. "Dumplings."

"As good," Jake pronounced, crossing the kitchen to the commercial coffee pots steeping on the warmers. "Emit here?"

"He's on his way down from the Upper Lodge," she said, setting the bowl on the center table and picking an apple out of the bunch. She inspected it expertly, cutting out little spots and blemishes with an expertise born of years of doing what she loved.

Jake lowered his massive frame onto a work stool that was seldom used in Rosemary's busy kitchen and cast a hungry eye toward the first batch of dumplings that had come from the cavernous ovens. "You checked to make sure those are any good?" he asked, jerking his head toward them.

"Of course," Rosemary said, not lifting her gaze from the apple she was peeling.

Jake drew in a deep breath, glancing again at the pastries. They were golden brown, the sprinkled sugar on top sparkling in the sunlight streaming through the windows as it began to crystallize, lined up across the cooling racks, the thick amber colored filling peeking teasingly at him through the openings between the folds of dough. He sipped at his coffee, keeping a careful eye on the Rosemary. "Need a second opinion?" he asked, grinning broadly at her.

She was unable to restrain her laughter, and cast a quick glance across the kitchen to her cook and nodded. He laughed aloud as he grabbed a turner from the counter and in one fluid move, swept one of the dumplings from the cooling rack and onto a plate, setting it in front of Jake.

"How's the season shaping up?" Jake asked, taking the fork Rosemary handed him and spinning the plate to find the perfect place to cut into the crust.

"It's been quiet, so far," she said, returning to coring and peeling her apples. "We have three parties due in at the end of the month, but the weather's not been the best for this time of year. Too wet."

"That storm yesterday was brutal."

"That's what I mean," Rosemary said as she placed the apple in the center of a circle of dough and expertly folded the crust around it. "The storms are doing a lot of damage in the high country. Emit's got a number of trees he's going to have to move out of the river before there can be any rafting. It's already causing some strange flooding, he says. Streams are backing up, overflowing their banks, and the runoff makes getting in and out for clean up really hard."

"How many he got helping him this year?" Jake asked, putting the last of the apple into his mouth and casting a hungry eye across the room where her assistant was pulling another batch from the oven.

"About a dozen or so. They come and they go, depending on their classes."

Emit had a working alliance with the forestry department of the university to man his crews. He provided the internship required for the major and could depend on the students to be to be both motivated and already know something about the mountains.

"Any new faces?"

"Always new faces," Rosemary said, looking at him candidly as she carried the large pan and slid it into the huge oven. "Emit set copies of his personnel files out on his desk for you. He knew you'd be along for them."

Jake sighed deeply and then brightened as she used the turner to slide another dumpling onto his plate. "I'll bring you some more coffee," she said as he picked up the plate and headed down the back hallway toward the family quarters.

The files were stacked on the corner of an otherwise neat and tidy desk that gave clear evidence of the disciplined and ordered nature of Emit MacIntosh and his staid Scots heritage. He set the plate to the side and lowered himself into the chair. He pulled his notebook and pen from his shirt pocket and found a clean page before reaching for the files. He shuffled through them, reading the names neatly typed on labels that were affixed to the tabs.

There were eight part time employees who were hired for seasonal work. Seven of them were interns assigned through the school. One was a name completely unknown to him and he jotted it down on the pad, opening the folder and scanning the application that was the first document in the file. He was reading the application a second time when Emit arrived.

"So, who's Peter Lenox?"

"A friend of Ethan's," Emit said, lowering his massive frame into the chair across from his desk and linking his hands behind his head.

"Know him well?"

Ethan was the youngest MacIntosh son.

"Don't know him at all," Emit said, shaking his shaggy head. "Ethan met him at school this semester and he needed some work. We needed an extra pair of hands so he brought him home."

"He's not working through the intern program?"

"He's not a forestry student… just loves the outdoors. His old man has moved him all over the place. They lived in Seattle a while and then his family moved to Houston then Oklahoma."

"You checked his references?"

"More or less," Emit shrugged. "He's a new friend of Ethan's, he is a steady worker and we haven't given him keys to the place. He's never here without one of us."

"Never gone missing while he's been on the job?"

"Never."

"How 'bout the others?"

"They all work with a buddy," Emit said as he unlinked his hands and sat forward. "None of us go wandering about the high country alone. That's not smart… no matter how well you know the mountain."

"Just Cantrell," Jake said quietly, watching Emit's expression carefully.

"He's not in the high country, Jake," Emit said, not taking offense to the comment. "It's not as dangerous down on the Estate as it is at this elevation. When Trevor comes this way, he respects the buddy system too."

"So," Jake said, closing Peter Lenox's file and setting it aside, "who's his buddy around here?"

"Me," Emit said in a tone that brought a smile to Jake's lips. There was a very clear warning in the word.

"You know Cantrell about as well as anybody then," Jake continued, taking a deep breath and plunging into the area he knew might offend Emit. "You think there's any reason he'd want to harm Cameron or Nicole?"

"Nope." Emit said so quietly it was more unnerving than his roaring bellow when he was angry.

"You know it looks odd, him being so close to Nicole like he is."

"He's close to Cameron and Cameron is close to Nicole. Trevor loves Nicole because Cameron loves her. There's nothing odd about that because there's nothing he wouldn't do for Cameron and following that line, nothing he wouldn't do for her."

"So, you don't think Cantrell is capable of something like this?"

"We're all capable of something like this, Jake," Emit said evenly, watching the slightly younger man with an intentness that was unnerving, "given the right circumstances. What I said was that Trevor would never do anything to hurt Cameron."

"You think he could hurt Nicole?"

"That would hurt Cameron," Emit said, tilting his head sideways to indicate there was a foregone conclusion there. "Those are copies if you need to take them on with you," he said, nodding toward the file folder in Jake's hands. No need to remind you that they are confidential, I know."

"A second thing," Jake said as he closed his notebook and shoved it into his shirt pocket. "I need to see the Sniper's nest."

"A good idea since you are heading up this investigation," Emit said evenly.

"Can you take me to it?"

"I have a better idea," Emit said, rising from the chair as though there was an invisible lift beneath him. For all his massiveness, Emit was amazingly agile. "I'll have Trevor take you to see it. That will give you a chance to ask him about the bees you have under your bonnet."

୨୦୧

Cameron felt consciousness playing again at the edges of his mind. He moaned deeply in protest. The pain was excruciating and he was unable to put the confusing pieces of memory together to create a picture that made any sense to him. He was colder than he had ever been and the blindfold over his eyes, normally icy cold, was now warmed by the fever he felt raging through him.

He could not tell reality from the images of the nightmares that haunted the semiconscious state masking itself as fitful sleep. He had been in the river but he didn't know why. He was pulled from the river but he didn't recall how. He had flashes of memory of the woods in the middle of the night. None of it made sense.

The pain was washing over him in throbbing waves. He was unable to tell where it was originating. It was just a constant agony.

He heard the dreaded squeak of the door and knew that he was back. He tried to repress the moans shuttering through him, but was unable to. He felt the cloth pulled from his eyes and tried to open them but couldn't.

He felt a strangely gentle touch to his battered face then moving to his forehead. He again tried to open his eyes before he felt the icy cold of the new cloth. He recoiled and felt the blinding pain flash through him like lightening would split the sky over the mountains during the storm; then the darkness washed over him with the next wave of pain.

When he came to again, he could hear the voice in his ear telling him of the torture that he was about to endure. He felt the hot tears seep from between his swollen eyes into the icy blindfold as the splint was taken from his broken leg and the pain only increased when the leg was grasped and twisted. The scream escaped from his chapped lips without him even realizing it was his. He tried to defend himself but discovered a new wave of pain when he pulled against the restraints and the blindfold fell from his eyes.

He could barely see through the swelling, but what he did see caused him to scream again. A knife flashed in the sunlight from the window as it was plunged into his calf. His scream filled the room and echoed through the blackness that overwhelmed him again.

಄

Dennis (Trotter) McGee smiled and waved at the Emerson's guards as they stepped out of the portable gatehouse at the back entrance of the Emerson Estate. The guardhouse was brought in by one of his own haulers a few weeks ago and set into place at the insistence of Gregory Emerson. He was a man who wanted his possessions protected at all times.

"Morning, sir," the Emerson Security detail said as he glanced into the backseat of the king cab and then noticed a second guard emerge from the gate house to inspect his tools and equipment in the truck bed.

"How's it going?" Trotter asked, the hairs on the back of his neck standing up.

"Okay," the man at his window said with a wave of his palm. "The new roadbed is a little unstable after that rain, but we don't have to tell you that, do we?"

"Nope," Trotter said amicably, wondering what was going on. He refrained from stating the obvious… that he had excavated the new roadbed and knew it better than anyone. "Anything else I should be careful of?" he asked as he watched the second guard return to the gatehouse and then glanced back out his window to the one at his side.

"Nothing other than the obvious when you are in the mountains."

"See you in a bit," Trotter said, taking his foot off the break and easing forward. "I promised Mrs. Cameron I would check on the conditions, but I won't be long."

He alternated his attention on the road in front of him and the gatehouse in his rear view mirror until he made the first curve. Nothing else my butt, he thought. Something was definitely going on. First he gets a call from Lyle telling him to stop construction until further notice and then he gets another call from him telling him to check and see if he could excavate to footings.

He thought Lyle was joking at first, but then realized that he wasn't. For whatever reason, Trotter was here to check on the site conditions when he already knew what they would be. He'd seen the news about the accident Cameron Emerson had yesterday but all this was really weird.

As expected, the storm the day before turned the new roadbed into a river of sludge and he was concerned he would not be able to reach the site and return without serious trouble. He came across some areas while they were excavating that would need specific attention to drainage. Fortunately he was aware of exactly where those spots were as he maneuvered through the still loose gravel. They had graded up to the cove that would end at the house.

He reached the first trouble spot and slowed considerably. There was a rut washed out across the road about a foot wide but not as deep as he would have expected. He geared down and drove on, reaching the second area to realize they were spot on in their evaluation of the drainage efforts required there.

At the end of the graded road, he pulled to a stop behind his half-filled dump truck. Trotter got out of the cab and felt the gravel sink beneath his weight and held onto the truck door until he felt solid ground under his feet. He closed the door and watched his step as he made his way around the newly excavated area and the mounds of gravel still waiting to be spread. The grass in the grade was soggy and the newly turned earth dangerously slick.

His equipment was where he left it. His dozer was pulled to the edge of the excavation, its massive scoop sunk about a foot into the ground during the rains. His ditch digger and Bobcat were parked to the side of the glade. The flat bed trailer used to bring the equipment to the site was parked back away from the excavation, its large tongue propped on an upended wheel of timber from one of the trees they had felled.

Lyle was appeasing Nicole Emerson. He was able to see for himself how the glade would drain and he made his way around the gravel mounds and the piles of turned earth toward the river. As he moved across the glade, he took mental note of the conditions. The natural basin of the glade was an excellent drain and the glade was actually in better shape than he would have expected. He shaded his eyes and looked into the morning sun toward the rock formation at the top of the basin. They weren't going to know how it was going to affect the drainage until the house was built but he bet it was going to be a problem.

He made his way down to the riverbank, surveying the small cove where he would build a dock and boathouse once the house was completed. The river was raging below him, still white-capping in the gusting winds. The backwash was crashing against the riverbank below him and he decided he should raise the pilings of the boathouse. He would not have expected the river rise to be so stark in such a short period of time.

He turned and made his way back toward his truck, deciding the trip up had been worth the trouble. There would be no footings poured today, but at least Lyle could call Mrs. Emerson to assure her they had been to the site to check on the conditions. He reached the excavation of the cove area and came to an abrupt halt.

Something in the mound of turned earth caught his attention. He moved closer, curiosity overriding his desire to get back to his shop. The rains had pounded the turned dirt into muddy mounds. What had been large chunks of dirt, rocks, and roots were now molten mud. The sun was topping the trees on the east side of the glade, and something uncovered in the dirt caught his attention. He stepped cautiously toward the mud and sunk ankle deep, mystified at what his backhoe had unearthed and the rains exposed.

He made his way back to his truck, grabbing a plank and a shovel from the bed and then went back across the glade. He set the plank over the thick mud and made his cautious way across it. It sank below the surface of the mud about four inches then gave him a sure footing.

He reached across the distance between himself and the mound and pulled at the object with the edge of the shovel then breathed a curse, catching his breath and losing his balance, stepping into shin deep mud as the object was pulled free of the surrounding mud and landed on top of the mud in front of him.

༄

Connie stood in the break room doorway as Jake topped off his coffee and then headed out the other door.

"Give me about two minutes and then show Cantrell to my office," he called over his shoulder to her.

"Yes sir," Connie said, turning to look at Jane. "He's gorgeous!" she mouthed, eliciting a disgusted groan from Sandy and a laugh from Jane.

"Give me a break," Sandy said, shaking his head and moving toward his own office.

"He can't help it, Sandy," Connie whispered, causing Jane to laugh out loud.

Connie rolled her eyes and patted her chest as she returned to her task. Jane rose from her chair, moving so she could watch as Connie led Trevor to Jake's office without being noticed.

Although she caught glimpses of Trevor the day before, she was too busy with her tasks to really get a close look at him. She could tell that he was taller than six feet when he passed under the doorway. He had rugged good looks, weather tanned with dark, curly hair. He moved with a grace and confidence that was seldom inherent. She had the feeling he could handle himself in most circumstances and was as comfortable with the preppy university crowd as he was the MacIntoshes and that was no small accomplishment.

She waited for the sound of Jake's door clicking closed and then headed toward Sandy's office for his file. Sandy might not be interested in anything going on this afternoon at the station, but she certainly was. As she passed Jake's closed door, she could clearly hear the soft resonance of Trevor's voice. Catching sight of Connie hovering at the fax machine in the hallway, she swallowed a laugh that would bust her for lingering outside Jake's door if it slipped out.

Trevor settled himself in the chair beside Jake's desk and watched as Jake moved items around absentmindedly. Jake's office surprised him. On the wall behind him was a bookcase that held a fairly impressive collection of law books. A credenza behind Jake held his phone, a police scanner, and his CB radio.

"I appreciate you coming by," Jake said, looking for his steno pad for notes.

"No problem," Trevor said, crossing his ankle on his knee.

"Can I get you some coffee?"

"I'm good," Trevor answered with a wave of his hand.

"Emit suggested you might be able to take us to that sniper nest," Jake said, setting his pen on his pad and leveling his gaze on the young man in front of him. He caught the surprise in Trevor's eyes and sensed a flash of uncertainty before he met his gaze.

"I'm able to do that," Trevor said after a moment's thought, his gaze shifting to the window behind Jake toward the mountains. "I have a meeting with my advisors next week – but I have time."

"Emit said it wasn't difficult to reach," Jake continued, reaching for his cup and sipping the coffee.

"Not if you're Emit MacIntosh and read the mountain like others read a morning paper," Trevor commented with a sheepish laugh.

"Well, I can understand that," Jake laughed. I've been here almost twenty years and I don't like going beyond the city limits if I can help it. I'm grateful for a great team who will go for me. So, you think you can get me in there?" Jake pressed.

He watched as Trevor again shifted his gaze beyond him through the window. He saw him heave a deep sigh and tilt his head, his lips pursing slightly. "There might be an easier way into the place, but it's a good bit longer. I can take you the way Emit and I went, but it's not an easy climb from the highway."

The word "climb" was discouraging. Jake glanced down at this desk and then back up. "So, who do you think would do something like this?" he asked, watching Trevor closely.

Trevor's lips formed a thin line and his eyes narrowed. He met Jake's gaze with a steely calm, shrugging his shoulders slightly. "I don't know," he said quietly shaking his head. "I don't know."

Jake broke the intense gaze between them, glancing away from the look in Trevor's eyes. There was something that disturbed him, but he was unable to read him. With Cameron missing and threat hanging over people he cared about, it was natural for him to be upset and resent Jake's questions. There was something else, though, Jake decided as he shuffled through papers on his desk; something deeper than concern.

"When would be a good time for you to take us to that nest?" he asked, letting the papers fall to his desk in a scattered pile and leveling his gaze on Trevor again.

"Now would be as good a time as any," he said quietly. "How are you at a little rock climbing?"

"Not good," Jake said honestly.

"Then getting there from the highway is going to be a problem. It's the quickest way in, but the trickiest."

"So then, where?"

I would say use the logging roads off the new road they've cut into the glade and then go from there. It's a longer trek, but not as rough."

"Am I okay like this?" Jake asked, standing up and moving from behind his desk so that Trevor could see him.

Trevor's hazel eyes looked him over and he shrugged. You might want to get a little heavier coat," he said standing up. "The wind is biting this morning."

"Good idea," Jake said, opening the door and standing back for Trevor to leave his office. "You've been in that sector this morning?" he continued as he stepped into the hallway behind Trevor. He saw the tightening of Trevor's shoulders.

"My test sites are higher up," he answered.

"Just a minute," Jake said, tapping Trevor's elbow slightly and seeing the instant reaction in him, followed by the subtle but distinctive control. "I need to get David in on this. You know him, don't you? He's the fire chief and head of our rescue team."

"Why don't I wait for you both at the back gatehouse?" Trevor asked, not even turning around as he crossed the station and left through the front door.

"Good idea," Jake called as the front door swung closed behind him.

൞

Jane got up from her desk and took a deep breath and let it out in a loud rush. She was carefully transcribing her notes from the interview with Nicole and was saturated with the information she gathered. She stood up, stretched and walked down the hallway. Trevor Cantrell had left the station about half an hour before. Jake and David had their heads together across the street and now there were definite signs they were both going somewhere. She figured they were heading into the mountains to the sniper nest and she wanted to go with them, but since Jake hadn't asked her, she didn't feel comfortable suggesting it. She decided to see what Sandy had accomplished. He was just hanging up the phone when she reached his desk.

"What's this?" she asked, flipping open the folder on the edge of his desk curiously.

"Malcolm's file on Cantrell."

"Anything jump out?" she asked.

"About what you would expect," Sandy said with a slight shrug. "Varsity basketball… swim team… lettered in track… manager of the football team. Guess he's a little on the wiry side to play, huh?"

Jane opened the file and began thumbing through the report and then shuffling through the documents at the back. As she pulled Cantrell's military service history to the top, she scanned the information. As she lifted the first page and scanned the second, her eyes fell on Cantrell's training records.

"What?" Sandy asked, hearing her catch her breath and looking at her to see the look on her face.

"BUDS." Jane mumbled, reading from the file.

"Buds?" Sandy repeated. "What kind of buds?" he asked, shrugging. 'Best buds… beer buds…

"Basic Underwater Demolition SEAL training," Jane said, glancing back at the file.

"Cantrell is a Navy SEAL!" Sandy scoffed, reaching for the file, "you're kidding!".

Jane stepped backwards and moved the file out of his reach, scanning further into the report. There was little actual information in the report, but the fact he passed BUDS was telling enough. He transferred to HAZ-MAT training after the third year and resigned his commission at the end of his tour of duty. "Did you read his service record?"

"I scanned the file," Sandy said, a defensive tone creeping into his voice.

"He's a SEAL," Jane repeated quietly. "The print date at the bottom of this report is three years ago," she said, handing him the report.

"He's a former SEAL?" Sandy asked, unable to hide that he was impressed.

"No," Jane said, retrieving the report and looking at him with a shake of her head. "There are no former SEALS. It's like a Marine… once one always one…"

"Meaning…" Sandy asked, unable to control his sarcastic bent.

"I don't know," Jane admitted, turning on her heel and heading toward her desk. "But it means something."

"Great," Sandy muttered, heaving a heavy sigh of frustration. "Just great…"

Jane returned to her desk, dropping the report back into Trevor's file folder.

"Where are you going?" Jake called as he paused in the squad room, casting an eye out of the window toward the fire station across the street. He saw David Haas checking the gear in his truck.

"To interview the rest of the family the way you said," she said over her shoulder, grabbing her badge and clipping it to her belt before retrieving her weapon from the gun safe in the top drawer.

"Where are you going?" she called after Jake as she followed him through the squad room to the front door, hoping he would invite her along.

"Cantrell is going to take David and me to the sniper nest," he said with obvious trepidation.

"I'll trade you" she said with a bright smile.

"I wish I could," Jake sighed, "but I need to see the spot myself."

She was shrugging into her parka when she was caught short by Connie's voice calling from the dispatch office.

"Lee Malcolm is on his way. He wants to make sure you're here when he gets here."

"Hang around," Jake called as he turned and left the room.

Jane paused for a moment to overcome the feeling that formed in the pit of her stomach. She was aware of Jake turning his back and was glad there was no one else in the squad room to see the blush rising from her collar into her face. Somehow, she had to get over this reaction every time Lee's name was mentioned.

She sank into her chair, straightening the pages in the Cantrell file, trying to regain her composure. David's truck was still across the street, but he was nowhere in sight.

Jane pulled her weapon from her holster, replacing it in the drawer safe, listening for the tell-tale click of the lock. She pulled her badge from her belt and tossed it in as well, resisting the nervous urge to slam it closed.

Lee Malcolm came through the front door and simply waved at the desk sergeant before coming through the squad room and heading toward Jake's office. He waved a hand at her in a silent command to follow him. Squelching the hint of resentment at his arrogance, she grabbed a pen, her pad and headed into the hallway.

"The Feds are moving in on us with the assumption that Cameron has been abducted," she heard the agitation in Lee's voice coming from Jake's office.

Sandy rushed from his office. "You've got to be kidding!" he breathed with a half-hearted attempt at a laugh. The smile fell from his face as Jake cleared his things from the chairs around the conference table. "He's not kidding, is he?" he turned to Jane.

"Doesn't look like it." Jane said as she was the last to enter Jake's office. She closed the door behind her.

"The Feds tagged a call they deem credible," Jake explained as they entered.

"What call? From where?"

"Our tip line."

"Seriously?" Sandy asked angrily. "How?"

"That's crazy," Jane said, as she lowered herself into the only empty chair remaining around the small conference table in the corner.

"The FBI swarmed the Plaza about an hour ago. We sent them packing. They didn't have a warrant and arrived with an offer to help. But this is more than an offer to help. It's only a matter of time before they hit Oak Meadow," Lee said, unbuttoning his jacket and loosening his tie.

"What... how?" Jane found herself babbling as she tried to process the latest development.

"Evidently because of the international assets of EI they've been monitoring your lines.," Lee said with a deep exhale of breath.

"Well," Sandy said, leaning his elbows on the table and propping his chin in his hand, "what about the bullet we found in the tire? The car wasn't stopped. It was forced off the road!"

"They do know about the bullet, right?" Jane asked, looking first at Jake and then toward Lee. She saw the shield drop into place over Lee's dark eyes before he lowered them. "They know, right?"

"It's all in the report," Lee said, but Jane kept her eyes locked onto him.

"You didn't tell them it would be impossible for anyone to have orchestrated this from the outside and not been seen coming and going up here?" she pressed.

"What is impossible," Lee said, his gaze returning to hers, completely devoid of any emotion, "is trying to tell the FBI anything. They're trying to take over the investigation. It's as simple as that. I don't know why but I've seen them jump like this before. Having a kidnapping in this tri-state area gives them an excuse."

"What kidnapping?" Jane almost shouted, unable to believe Lee and Jake were allowing the absurdity to continue.

"They have a call they have categorized as a ransom call," Jake said, not as eager to get his deputy as stirred up as Lee was. "They are working that aspect of this case."

"Jake," Jane said, barely above a whisper, "what call!"

"That call from Crazy Cotton," Sandy spoke as the answer dawned on him. "He's been calling here all morning."

"Cotton Prater? They can't be serious! He claims to have the Lindbergh baby, know where Jimmy Hoffa is and where the second shooter from the grassy knoll is hiding out. He started calling yesterday right after the alert for the rescue squad went out! Do they know who Cotton Prater is?"

She was taken off guard by the laugh that her words elicited from Lee. She turned her glare on him and he held up an apologetic hand and shook his head and inhaled deeply.

"Sorry," he muttered. "I am just off kilter today..." He inhaled deeply and exhaled slowly before continuing. "It was an anonymous caller," he informed them. "They don't know who it was or where it originated. I think that is what triggered this knee jerk reaction. They really can't afford to just ignore it, though."

"Jake," Jane breathed, gaining control over her initial reactions and trying to clear the fog of confusion. "We know that call is a hoax!"

"We know that," Jake said casting a sideways glance at Lee and then back at Jane, "but the FBI doesn't seem to care."

"You told them about Crazy Cotton?" she asked, swinging her incredulous gaze back toward Jake.

"I've told them that they are way off base with this, but they have decided it should be deemed a viable tip and they are insisting on getting involved."

"They know, Jane," Jake said, the disgust obvious in his words. "It's out of our hands now, and I think that was the point."

"That's just insane!" Jane continued. "We know that whoever blew out that tire has to be so familiar to us all that no one notices him or her coming and going. We know we're not dealing with outsiders, here."

"Well," Lee said, inhaling deeply, "the FBI will figure that out later rather than sooner. In the meantime, we continue our own investigation."

Jane sat back in her chair, almost feeling as though she had sustained a body blow. She glanced around the room and noticed that no one was looking anyone else in the eye. She took a deep breath, wondering how she was going to feel at the end of the day when someone from their inner circle was charged with the murder of Cameron Emerson.

"We all know the odds of us ever recovering Cameron's body," she said so softly it was almost a whisper. "Someone on this mountain lay in wait and sent him over that cliff. Is this laying groundwork to protect whoever that is?" she asked, watching the three men around the table. "Is that how this is going to play? If so, tell me now and I won't break a sweat."

CHAPTER FIFTEEN

Trevor glanced in his rear view mirror as he pulled out of the Oak Meadow Sherriff's office and headed toward Sutter Trail. He raised his hand to shield his eyes from the sun that was now climbing to a mid-morning vantage point in the aquamarine sky. He pulled his sunshades from the well between the front seats and slipped them on.

He figured at best he had about half an hour before Jake and David showed up at the back gate to the estate. He had to hurry. He needed to get to the cabin and then back to the gate before they arrived. Given the reticence Jake obviously felt about trekking through the mountains, Trevor was banking on him not getting in any hurry. He unconsciously reached behind his seat and touched the smooth leather of his test case. He needed to get to the cabin before he led Jake and David to the ambush site.

He was familiar with the drive and was able to handle a speed others would be uncomfortable with on the winding old highway. As he neared the back gate, he was able to again see the storm damage to the construction of the new road. What had been huge clumps of dirt that had fallen from the deep treads of the workers massive vehicles along the road were reduced to puddles of sludge by yesterday's rain. He pulled to a stop at the gate house and waited as one of the guards came to the side of the Jeep. Trevor removed his shades and shook the man's hand.

"Sherriff Clairborne is on his way," he said with a slight smile. "If I'm not back when he gets here, will you tell him I'm on my way? I need to get these samples back to the cabin."

"Absolutely, sir," the unfamiliar guard said with a nod.

Trevor shifted and pulled away, discouraged at the state of the new roadwork. The storm had taken quite a toll. He inhaled deeply, wondering how he came to be in the situation he was in now. Everyone looked at him with what his grandfather would call a jaundiced eye. He wondered how he became so involved in the lives of these people. Somehow, things just happened, and at the time, nothing seemed strange or out of line. Now, after the fact, he realized he made some serious mistakes.

He knew everyone was suspicious of him. He could see it in their faces. If Jake Clairborne wasn't suspicious, it was only a matter of time. Trevor wondered what they were all going to think and what would happen to him when if truth came out. He couldn't dwell on the laws he had broken, the sins he had committed or the consequences he would face. He had done what he had done. Perhaps he could someday justify and explain his actions, but he seriously doubted it.

※

Richard watched the large red square on the roof of the Emerson tower seem to grow as the chopper hovered momentarily over the helipad before dropping down in a less than easy bump. The winds were still high. He reached to the floor for his briefcase, turning to nod his thanks to their pilot as he swung himself from the cockpit and bent at the waist to move clear of the downdraft.

As he reached the elevator shaft, the chopper lifted off, circling the rooftop once and then banking sharply to the right as it headed back to the hangar. Richard stepped into the elevator and the doors slid shut. The quiet interlude between the roof and the inner sanctum of the Emerson penthouse was a short one. The doors slid open quickly, disgorging him into the hallway that led to Gregory and Cameron's offices.

He stopped dead in his tracks as he saw Joan standing in the middle of the hallway, her face drained of all color and her hands shaking. She was just coming from her office and he moved quickly to her.

"What's going on?" Richard asked. "What's happened?"

"A man just called on line two who claims to have Cameron."

"What?" Richard gasped, taking three strides across Gregory's office and reaching for the phone.

"He hung up," Joan said in desperation, the tears of frightened frustration creeping into her eyes.

"Call Lee Malcolm," Richard whispered barely above a whisper.

"I did," she said, unable to speak above a whisper. "He's not in the building, but he's on his way."

"Come sit down," Richard said, reaching for her arm and leading her to the sofa. "Tell me what happened."

Joan sank gratefully onto the firm cushions of the plush corduroy sofa that could have easily passed for velvet and ran a trembling hand across her chin and down her throat.

She was so relieved it was Richard Weston she saw first after the harrowing experience of the phone call. He was such a kind, gentle man and she was glad he was there to take over and make decisions. He stepped to the wet bar in the corner, grabbing a bottle of water from the small refrigerator and twisted off the cap. He handed it to her and took several deep breaths to still his pounding heart while she took a few sips.

"What happened?" he asked again, lowering himself to the arm of one of the leather chairs that flanked the sofa.

Joan was interrupted before she even began by the arrival of Sadie and Ben. Shortly afterwards Gregory strode into the room and closed the door behind him. His very presence seemed to bring color to Joan's face as she jumped from the sofa and met him half way across the room.

"Someone called to say they have Cameron," she said hoarsely, moving easily into the crook of the protective arm that Gregory instinctively offered her. Richard might be the sensitive one, but Gregory was the patriarch of the Emerson family, including his employees.

"Calm down, Joanie," he said evenly, taking charge of the room with one sentence. Joan had been with Gregory Emerson for more than two decades. She was the cornerstone of the efficiency and professionalism of the executive suites. She was levelheaded and not easily rattled, but she was obviously on the verge of hysteria now. "Tell me what happened. Tell me everything."

Gregory guided her back to the sofa and eased her down into the cushions. He stooped down in front of her, taking her trembling hands in his and looking intently into her eyes. "Tell me what happened"

"There were all kinds of voice mails on the service," she said with a sigh and shook her head again. "I had Lisa clearing them."

Gregory nodded slightly to encourage her careful attention to detail. "We'll have those calls diverted to the operator and take that burden off you today. Go on."

"Then line two rang."

"You're sure it was line two?" Sadie asked softly, leaning forward toward Joan from where she had lowered herself onto the sofa beside her. Line two was an encrypted secure line used only by the family. The number was protected as much as the combination to the vault tucked invisibly away between Gregory and Cameron's offices.

"I'm positive," Joan cried, the stress of the situation overwhelming her. "That's the only reason I answered it," she admitted, looking back at Gregory for understanding. "The phones are ringing constantly. I was just letting them go to voicemail, but this was line two!"

"We understand," Gregory said, squeezing her hands gently and nodding encouragingly. "Tell us about the call."

"I think it was a man, but it was a strange voice. He sounded like he was trying to disguise it or maybe he was just really nervous."

"And he said…?" Richard spoke from behind her. Joan visibly jumped in surprise and then laughed self-consciously.

"Sorry," he muttered quickly, shaking his head and lowering himself back into his chair.

"He said, 'Don't look for Cameron in the river because he's not there. I have him and I'll call back.'"

The room was eerily silent as they all stood staring at Joan. She looked from Gregory to Richard behind him, and then cast a quick sideways glance at Sadie and Ben.

Emotion was overcoming her and she was unable to stem the tears that were beginning to slip from her eyes and down her cheeks. "Maybe he *is* alive…!" she cried in a whisper that broke the silence with as much force as a scream would have, then she lost control and convulsed into unrestrained tears.

Sadie glanced at Ben, tears filling her own eyes. She drew in a deep breath, swinging her telling gaze toward Richard. The only thing that might be worse than Cameron stranded along the river after being injured in an accident was the idea of him being at the mercy of a kidnapper.

"Call Lee," she said, turning as Richard straightened up and headed for his office. "I'll call the FBI and get them back here."

༜

Jane was at her desk, gathering all the files and notes she had collected in the matter of Cameron Emerson's case and dropping them into a cardboard file box on the floor. She ignored Jake when he approached her desk, knowing she was unable to speak calmly about the way this investigation was being hijacked. He was silent as she continued to clear her desk and then reached into the top drawer and pressed in the code to release the gun safe. She pulled her weapon from it and grabbed her badge with the other hand. She was aware that Lee, Sandy, and Connie were watching from the hallway. None of them had ever seen this side of her.

"Jane," Jake said quietly, reaching out to place his ham of a hand on her shoulder and then dropping it to his side when she recoiled. "It's not what you think."

"And what is that, Jake?" Jane demanded, snapping her badge to her belt and holstering her weapon. "What do I think?"

"We are just a small town department," Jake continued, lowering himself onto the corner of her now cleared desk. "We don't have the resources to take on an investigation like this one by ourselves. We have to cooperate with other agencies."

"Is that what this is?" she asked, not looking at him as she pulled her parka from the back of the chair. "Is this what you call cooperation? We have a known kook who confesses to every crime that airs on Dateline, 20/20 or the local news and we just step aside when the FBI decides to use him as a convenient patsy?"

She was aware of the buzz sounding from the hallway and she threw a resentful glare in that direction, seeing Connie shrink out of sight and then Lee reach for the pager clipped to his belt.

"Where are you going?" Jake asked, moving out of her way as she shrugged into the parka.

"You told me to interview the rest of the family, didn't you?" she asked reaching for the keys to her cruiser in a shallow dish on her desk. "He said we are to carry on with our own investigation, didn't he?" She asked as she jerked her head toward Lee. He moved to one of the empty desks across the room and was dialing the phone.

"Who are you going to see?" Jake asked her as she leaned against the desk behind her own.

"Anyone who will talk to me," she said with a shrug of her shoulders.

"It's a good idea to have an appointment before you head out," Jake reasoned. "We don't know for sure where everyone is. Who do you plan to interview first?"

His strategy worked as he turned her focus back on the investigation and away from the intrusion by the FBI.

"I don't know," she admitted, dropping into her chair and leaning backwards. Suddenly the fatigue and frustration was all too evident as she leaned her head back in the chair and sighed deeply.

"There's been another call," Lee said as he moved toward them.

"Another call?" Sandy echoed, close on his heels.

"Someone really needs to make sure Cotton is taking his meds," Jane muttered, swiveling her chair back toward her desk and reaching out to grasp the edge and pull herself to it.

"This wasn't Cotton," Lee said as he met Jake's gaze. "This one looks like it's legit. We need you in Crystal Springs, Sherriff."

"I'll be right behind you," Jake said, turning to Sandy. "You and Jane go with Haas to meet Cantrell. The two of you should be able to get back to the nest once he shows you were it is and you can show me later."

Jane pushed herself back from her desk and sprung to her feet with a quick movement. Her excitement over the change of assignment was obvious and the look of humor on Lee's face was enough to cause the flush to start creeping out of her collar again. She turned away from him to follow Sandy toward the back door.

◈

"Any indication the car was stopped on the road before it went over the cliff?"

Jake Clairborne looked from Special Agent in Charge Terrance McNatt, to Special Agent Jack Stanley and shook his head emphatically, "None whatsoever."

The FBI team had descended on the Plaza by the time Lee returned. Terrance McNatt, Special Agent in Charge and Jack Stanley were now in the conference room grilling Jake and the EI security crew chiefs. Lee was downstairs with the team's technicians watching as they tapped into the phone system to pick up any incoming call to the executive offices. A female agent had relieved the receptionist at the lobby desk and another was questioning Joan.

"If it is a kidnapping, that would explain why the front door was open and the seat belt released," Stanley said with a lifting of his eyebrows.

"It's impossible. Strangers on the mountain don't go unnoticed," Jake reminded them.

"This may be a crank call," McNatt said, turning to take a mug of coffee from the cart wheeled into the room by Richard.

"If they stopped the car and kidnapped him," Ben said, following the scenario of the call, "why make it look like an accident?"

"It's bought them time, hasn't it?" Stanley offered.

"Then why call to keep the rescue teams out of the area?"

"To keep people out of the area," McNatt stated as though the conclusion was obvious.

"It has that," Jake agreed. The idea that while he and his deputies were searching the river for Cameron some unknown kidnapper might have taken off through his county with Cam in the trunk made Jake sick to his stomach.

In a corner of the room, Special Agent Cheryl Coolidge was talking quietly to Joan. "This phone system has caller ID. Did you notice the incoming number?"

"Not really," Joan whispered, raising tortured eyes to the agent. "I thought it was one of the family. And, I thought it was from the

Manor because I did know it wasn't an internal call. It crossed my mind it might be Holly but it wasn't an international call."

"Holly Emerson?"

"Yes," Joan said, snuffling and reaching for another tissue in the box beside her. "Well, Holly Weston, now."

"How did you know it wasn't an international call?"

"Overseas calls all read some kind of trunk line code coming through the system rather than the originating number even over that line. Calls from Mr. and Mrs. Faraday never show the overseas office number – just that code."

"I see," Cheryl said, making a note on her pad. "Could the operator have transferred the call to you?"

"No, Line two is an independent line. Calls can't be transferred to Line two. If it had come through the switchboard, it would have had to come to my extension."

"So, you're sure it was a state side call, but you didn't notice the incoming number?"

"No," Joan almost whimpered. "I just assumed it was Mr. Gregory or Garret. There have been so many calls back and forth… I didn't pay the attention I should have."

"Don't start kicking yourself," Agent Coolidge assured her. "You haven't done anything wrong here. Tell me what the caller said, word for word, as best you can remember." Cheryl said as she placed a small tape recorder on the table between them and turned it on. "Close your eyes and think a moment, then walk me through what happened this morning when you got to your office, step by step."

Joan nodded and opened her mouth and inhaled sharply. She closed her eyes, let the breath out and then inhaled again. "I'd been clearing the calls from the service when line two rang. I picked up the phone and a man said, 'I have Cameron Emerson and they should stop looking for him in the river.' And then he said, 'Tell Gregory I'll call back later.'"

"He indicated that Cameron is alive?" Cheryl asked.

"Yes," Joan said excitedly, opening her eyes and looking at Cheryl.

"Okay," Cheryl said, jotting the words down in her tight shorthand, "go on."

"That was it."

"That's all? Did he ask for money?"

"No."

"Did he mention getting money together?" Jake asked from behind Cheryl. He had gravitated toward them.

"No. He didn't mention money. No money."

"He said Gregory? He called him by his first name?" Cheryl asked, retaking the interview with a quick glance of annoyance at Jake.

"Yes."

"Not Mr. Emerson?" she pressed.

"No! No, he called him Gregory!"

"Okay, Joan," Cheryl said, "you didn't recognize the voice?"

"No."

"Was there anything notable about it? An accent? Was it deep or high pitched?"

"Neither," Joan sighed with a shake of her head. "It was average."

"You mentioned before that the voice sounded distorted. How?"

"Well," Joan said, closing her eyes and taking a minute to remember, "there was a strange tone to it, kind of like there might have been another line open – like someone was on an extension. It sounded distant or hollow."

"Could it have been interference on the line? Like you said, you talk to a lot of people from all over the world, Joan. Think about accents. Did you hear a regional or foreign accent?"

"None," Joan answered. Her eyes were closed again, concentrating on Cheryl's words.

"What about background noises?"

"Background noises," Joan repeated, opening her eyes and looking at Cheryl as confusion rose in her mind.

"Hear *any* noises?"

"No!" Joan said, suddenly realizing how odd that was.

"Nothing? No other voices?"

"No."

"Office noises? Phones ringing... copier copying... printer printing... intercom voices in the background?"

"No," Joan said, shaking her head.

"House noises? TV? Radio? Kids? Dogs? Cats? Pots? Pans? Washing machines? Vacuum cleaner?"

"No."

"Traffic noises? Cars? Trucks? Horns honking? Planes overhead? Trains.... boats.... anything? Any sound other than his voice?" Cheryl asked, smiling encouragingly at Joan. "You're doing great. Just think back on the call and tell me everything you can remember."

"There was just an open line noise," Joan said again, opening her eyes and looking at Cheryl. "You know how you can kind of hear an open line or that strange hollow sound on some cell phones?"

"I do," Cheryl assured her, reaching out to pat her hand.

"Sounds bogus, don't you think?" Richard asked, shaking his head and looking from agent to agent.

"Do you think it is a hoax?" Joan whispered, casting a self-conscious look at Lee and Richard. "I've caused all this fuss over a hoax?"

"You've not caused any of this," Cheryl was quick to tell her. "We don't know at this time what this is," she answered, trying to comfort the distraught woman. "A lot of crank calls come in when something like this happens. This is probably only the first one."

"How sick is that?" Joan gasped, "but how did he know the number?"

"It's very sick," Cheryl agreed, turning her attention toward the door as the techs entered Joan's office across the hall.

"But how would he know the number for Line two?" Joan repeated. "Do you think Cameron gave it to him? That kind of makes sense."

The FBI technical chief crossed to Joan's phone and attached his recording device to it. "The lines for these four offices are independent of the main trunk number," he said quietly, glancing first at Terrance and then Jack. "The switchboard can transfer all other numbers in, but this entire bank is secured and has unpublished numbers. That number two line is independent of the others and encryption protected."

"That's what I told you," Joan said glancing from one to the other of the new arrivals.

The agents exchanged glances and then looked around for family members. "This caller had an unlisted number into this office. So it might be legit," Jack whispered to Lee Malcolm.

"Joan's right," Lee agreed. "If someone has Cameron, it could be his way of letting us know he's alive. He might have told them to use this number to get our attention."

"Well, he's done that," Gregory sighed, rubbing his temples as he sank into a chair.

❧❦

"There he is," Jane said as Sandy maneuvered the department's 4X4 along the now deeply rutted roadbed. Trevor's Jeep was parked on a wide spot on the shoulder. When he saw them approaching, he headed across the loose, wet gravel, watching as they got out of the car and looked around at their surroundings.

"This is beautiful," Jane said, turning in full circle as she took in the panoramic view.

"It is," Trevor agreed, "We'll be taking the old logging roads so you need to follow me closely. Some of them have gotten really unstable. If I veer right, stay right behind me."

"Great!" Sandy muttered as they returned to their vehicle and then sped up to catch up with Trevor's Jeep.

They traveled along the road bed another tenth of a mile or so and then followed Trevor as he pulled off the new road onto a barren logging road. It was slightly muddy, but the decades of heavy traffic of first wagons and later large haulers carrying logs from the mountain to the mills had packed the dirt so firmly, water ran off the road too fast to allow it to soak in very far.

The logging roads were rough and the forest growth encroached on both sides. Sandy cursed every time he heard the side of their vehicle scratched by limbs and brush as they bumped along the road. Jane was exhilarated. Twice they drove through creeks that washed over the road then traveled along three different logging roads before Trevor pulled to a stop and got out of his Jeep with his rifle in hand, shrugging it onto his shoulder.

Jane and Sandy emerged from the 4X4 and Jane removed two rifles from the gun rack, handing one to Sandy as he rounded the car and pulling ammunition from the metal box under the passenger seat. She spilled several into Sandy's outstretched hand and Trevor waited patiently in the middle of the road while they loaded and checked the rifles.

The sun was climbing higher into the sky and shone with a brilliance that can only come after a fierce storm and the sky has been cleansed. Jane pulled a cap from her parka pocket and positioned it on her head.

"How far from here?" Sandy asked as he gripped the rifle and headed toward Trevor.

"Not far," Trevor called over his shoulder, barely looking back.

Jane paused for a moment, orienting herself and getting her bearing. She reached for the radio on her belt and unclipped it. As they made their way along the increasingly difficult path of the long abandoned logging road, she pressed her radio button three times.

"Come in, Dave," she spoke directly into the microphone. Blessedly there was little wind today and she did not have to fight to be heard as she had the day before.

"I'm here," Dave's voice floated from her radio.

"I think we are about a quarter of a mile above you," she said, noticing Trevor's quick backwards glance toward her. She waited to see if he were going to correct her but he merely plunged on through the woods.

In less than another tenth of a mile, Trevor left the logging road and picked up an animal trail. The going got more difficult and their pace slowed. As he moved, Trevor called over his shoulder.

"Emit believes he followed this trail."

"The same way we came?" Jane asked. They were now single file and she was between the two men but she knew they were on the Oak Meadow side of the crime site.

"No way to know," Trevor said with a shake of his head. "We didn't have time to back track before the storm hit."

As they moved along the trail, Trevor hesitated and then came to a stop. He looked around him, studying his surroundings. He inhaled deeply, as he stared into the woods, moving slowly, almost pace by pace along the trail. Finally he spotted something and left the trail to move along the forest bed directly into the woods.

As they moved, they could hear the sound of the river growing louder. The downward terrain became more difficult to traverse and more rocky. Hugh boulders were exposed as they neared the river. Trevor veered to the north and came to a large outcropping of boulders rising in front of them like the walls for a fortress.

"Up there," Trevor said, standing aside.

Jane slung her rifle onto her back and started the climb up. She seemed completely comfortable on the rocks. He watched as she examined the boulders and then made her way up, finding her handholds and toeholds with practiced skill. She reached the top and turned to see Trevor not far behind. Once on top of the boulders, Jane took in the view.

"You coming?" she called down, looking back at Sandy and grinning. He caught himself grinning back and glanced away quickly.

"I swear you're part antelope," Sandy shouted, pulling up his right pants leg and reaching for the first hand hold. He struggled to reach the top of the boulder and paused a moment to look around.

Jane stepped to the edge of the outcrop and peered over. Sutter Trail wound along the mountainside below her, the engorged river rolled along, the banks flooding downriver near the narrows. David Haas' Dodge Ram was sitting in the middle of the Trail, just beside the drooping caution tape across the gaping hole left by the missing guardrail. Dave was leaning against the front of the truck; his head drooped slightly against his chest.

She pulled her radio from the clip on her belt and pressed the button twice. She heard three squawks in response and held the radio to her mouth. "Heads up, Dave."

They all watched as his head shot up and he made a wide sweeping search of the mountainside. He reached for his radio. "Where are you guys?" he asked, shading his eyes from the midday sun.

"You're eleven o'clock, about thirty-five – forty feet up," Jane replied, twisting her wrist and allowing the sun to catch the dial of her watch, sending flashes out.

Dave again searched the mountain but it was obvious he could not see them from the Trail. He shook his head, gave an exaggerated shrug of his shoulders and gave up. He headed toward his truck. As planned, he headed up the Trail.

"How far up do you want me to go?" his voice came over the radio.

"Until we tell you to stop," Jane spoke. As she watched the truck maneuvering the twists and turns of the Trail, she inhaled deeply and let it out slowly. "Wow," she breathed, glancing over her shoulder to Sandy right behind her. Trevor had stepped out of the way to allow them to work. "He sure found *the* spot, didn't he?"

"Jane?" Dave's voice came over the radio again.

"Keep going," Jane instructed. "I want to see exactly where he picked up the Jag."

They watched in silence as Dave drove up the Trail, they would lose sight of him briefly when he took a sharp curve, but caught him again until he reached an elevation almost level with their own.

"That's it," Jane said, watching as the truck disappeared around the curve of the mountain and did not reappear. "Find a turn around and come back."

They waited in silence. The birds began their cheerful call to each other again. The rushing of the river continued as a background noise. Jane and Sandy both checked the safety on their rifles and then took up positions side by side on the boulder, watching the Trail.

"There he is," Sandy said, moving closer to Jane as they watched Dave reappear along Sutter Trail at about the same speed anyone would normally travel the curving mountain road. Jane pulled her rifle from her shoulder and lifted it to eye level.

"It's a clear shot," Jane commented, shaking her head. Trevor watched as the highlights in her hair were caught in the overhead sunlight. She and Sandy followed the progress of the truck along the Trail through the scopes on their weapons.

"I can't see who's driving," Sandy said, lowering his rifle and shading his eyes with his hand.

"We need to check about the same time Cameron was coming along here," Jane sighed, turning to look at Trevor. "The conditions aren't right. Where did you find the mount?"

"Emit spotted it down there," Trevor answered as he stooped and pointed through the crevice in the rock formation. It was about ten feet or so down."

Jane dropped to her haunches beside him, following the line of his pointing finger, studying the ground. "You think he dropped it or he tossed it?" she asked, turning to address both men.

"I think he dropped it," Trevor answered.

They were interrupted by the squawk of Jane's radio and Dave's voice came over the air. She moved away from the edge of the boulder. "Thanks Dave," She said into the radio. "We'll need to come back up here in the morning about the same time of the attack. We'll see you in town."

The Dodge Ram glided on past them below, and the three of them watched as it passed and were silent as they followed Dave's progress until he was out of sight.

"Why dropped it?" Sandy resumed their conversation.

"Because tossing it would be a stupid thing to do, and this guy isn't stupid," Trevor replied, settling back on his haunches. "I think he used that V in the rocks as a stabilizer because there isn't room for a tripod there and when he tried to pull the mount free, it splintered on him."

"Makes sense," Sandy agreed.

"And I think he is well trained," Trevor commented hesitantly, "but I don't think he is highly skilled."

"Why?" Jane asked, turning her full attention to him.

"Because he needed a stabilizer," Sandy interjected.

"Exactly," Trevor said, meeting the deputy's gaze evenly.

Jane knew she was missing something but didn't want to interrupt this moment. Sandy was uncharacteristically antagonistic towards Trevor and she sensed there was some kind of meeting of the minds occurring.

Jane moved across the rocks again, heading down. Sandy seemed surprised and shrugged his shoulders, following her. Trevor stood for a moment staring down at the highway. He shook his head sharply before scrambling off of the boulders.

"Can you show us where you and Emit came up from the highway?" Jane asked Trevor once they were all three back on the ground and headed back to the trail.

"Sure," Trevor answered as they fell into a synchronized pace.

"What brought you to this neck of the woods," Jane called to Trevor as they reached an animal trail and followed it.

"School," Trevor answered simply.

"And your major?"

"Environmental science."

"What sparked your interest in that?" Jane asked, closing the space between them so they could better hear each other.

"The Navy. I was assigned to HAZMAT and decided it was as good a career as any."

"The Navy..." Jane repeated. "Where were you stationed?"

"Norfolk."

"And you chose the university because...?"

"Because they accepted me," Trevor said with a glance over his shoulder.

"It's not known for its science department," Jane said with a slight laugh.

"I met Professor Richards once and was really impressed. I wanted to study with him."

"In biology," Jane mused. "...you met him?" Jane asked in surprise. "...before you applied to the U?"

"Yeah."

"Really! Where?"

"He works with the Navy from time to time," Trevor said offhandedly and picked up his pace. As Jane matched her pace to his she realized it would be next to impossible to continue their conversation.

Trevor came to such a sudden halt that Jane almost walked into him. She was pondering the information about Ellery Richards. In Crystal Springs he was a local celebrity and known eccentric; renowned for his work in the emerging science of criminal forensics but she had no idea he had connections with the Defense Department.

"Here," Trevor said, turning to look at her and waving at the access point where he and Emit climbed from the Trail. Jane followed his wave and saw the Trail below.

Jane and Sandy were debating which one of them would go back and get the 4X4 and which one was going to climb down the steep incline when both of their radios came to life. There were two quick squawks.

"Sheriff wants you to meet him at the construction site of the new Emerson house as soon as you can get there," Connie's voice filled the air.

"Roger," Sandy said, meeting Jane's incredulous gaze. They turned to say something to Trevor, but he was out of sight.

CHAPTER SIXTEEN

Gregory Emerson stood at the window of the penthouse staring out over the city as it sprawled from the downtown area and out over the valley to the mountains beyond. The FBI was clearly in charge now. The minutes were ticking away and the tension in the office was increasing with every moment. Garret was slouched across the leather sofa, his casual demeanor masking his extreme anxiety.

Of all of Gregory's children, Garret was always the most difficult to read. That was why Gregory knew he was perfect for politics. Garret possessed the amazing ability to connect with all people without truly revealing himself to anyone. In spite of his outward calm, Gregory knew Garret was raging because he was so helpless at the moment.

Gregory was psyching himself up to negotiate for the life of his son. Every financial institution used by them around the globe was on alert for a possible transfer of funds and was waiting for his direction. There was nothing he owned he would not give, nothing within his power he would not do, but for the second time in two days he felt powerless. In the cold light of facing the probability that Cameron was dead, he wanted with all his heart to believe someone managed to snatch his son from the side of the mountain and wanted only money for his return.

He wanted to believe Cameron was not in the car when it crashed through the guardrail and plunged into the river, but to do that he must ignore the fact that a bullet tore through the tire. He would like to forget the mental image that tormented him every waking moment and in every sweat-producing nightmare of that door swinging grotesquely in the wind. As he tuned out the quiet noise around him he tried to focus on the reality at hand.

As terrifying as the thought of Cameron having been in the twisted Jag when it hit the river, the alternative was far more ominous. Jake was right. No one came and went on the mountain unseen – not often and long enough to orchestrate this. Although the Estate was secluded, Sutter Trail was well traversed by both families as well as Emit's crews and guests of the Lodge. They hunted in the forests, fished in the lower streams and rafted in the upper ones.

No matter how much he wished he could avoid the truth, whoever was behind this was someone they knew and trusted. Someone so close to them that he moved along the trails causing no surprise or concern. If Cameron were kidnapped, whoever had him was so close to the family, that there was no way he could allow Cameron to live.

The image of Trevor Cantrell floated before Gregory's eyes. It seemed superimposed on the tinted glass. As much as the thought brought a guilty shame, it was the only logical conclusion that made sense. No one could argue that Cameron was closer to Trevor than to any of his own brothers. They connected the moment they met. Trevor became like another child of the household, coming and going at will; always welcomed, always at ease around them, very often completely unnoticed.

The ringing of the phone on Joan's desk interrupted his troubled thoughts, sending his heart racing. Joan cried out in alarm, shrinking back from it as though it was a serpent that appeared before her. Gregory stepped from his office into hers and Garret rose from the sofa in one move to follow him.

The huddle of agents broke immediately from their quiet conversing in the outer office and moved into position much as players would take a mark on a theater stage. The tech moved to his equipment and fit the headphones to his ears. Cheryl moved to stand behind Joan, placing her hand protectively on her shoulder as though somehow just answering the phone could put her in danger. Jack Stanley and Terrance McNatt stood back like coaches watching their team taking command of the field.

"It's not line two!" Joan whispered as the phone rang a second time and she stared at the display.

"It's okay," Cheryl said quietly as the phone shrilled the third ring, "answer it."

"Emerson International," Joan said, her voice sounding strained and unnatural. "Gregory Emerson's office, this is Joan."

"I need to speak to Gregory," a voice came abruptly over the line. As instructed, Joan handed the phone to Gregory. As instructed, he counted slowly to five before raising the receiver to his ear, watching the technician who monitored the tracing device. He saw the technician look up and nod.

"Gregory Emerson," he said with more calm than he imagined possible.

"Mr. Emerson, this is Bill Galloway on the back gate at the Manor."

"Bill, I need this line clear," Gregory said abruptly, his held breath rushing out of his lungs with the words. He steeled himself against the initial reaction to lash out at his security supervisor.

"Sorry sir, but you need to get someone up here. Trotter McGee has unearthed a body in the glade."

❧

"You still think he's involved in this?" Jane called over her shoulder as she and Sandy settled into a steady pace.

"I still think he's in this up to his neck."

They were silent as they moved through the woods. They retraced their path back to the logging roads and finally reached their 4X4. There was no sign of Trevor's Jeep.

"You don't think he's playing us?" Sandy demanded angrily, sliding in behind the wheel and reaching for the bottle of water he left in the console cup holder.

"How?" Jane asked, reaching for the seat belt and turning to shake her head at him in consternation.

"There was obviously a short cut back here," Sandy said as he turned the ignition and the motor growled to life. "His Jeep is long gone."

"He had a head start, Sandy. He's more familiar with this area and moves faster than we do. You really need to back off him."

"I don't care what you think," Sandy said, maneuvering the vehicle backwards along the logging road until he reached a place to turn around. "He's hiding something."

By the time they reached the glade it was already teeming with activity. Jake's squad car was parked in the newly graveled cove along with several vehicles from the Emerson security fleet. Jake sat behind the wheel of his cruiser and four men in the signature Emerson navy pinstriped suits were leaning against the fenders of their cars.

"Is it Cameron?" Jane asked as she expelled a huge sigh.

"Can't be," Jake said, getting out of his car and leading the way across the roadbed to a mound of earth. "It's skeletal remains. The contractor freaked out when he saw bones and said 'body' to the guard on the back gate."

"A skeleton!" Jane repeated.

"It happens," Sandy said, looking over the area with an experienced eye.

"What does?" Jane asked, but was brought to silence as they approached the huge mound of earth. She gasped slightly as she caught sight of the dark brown bones washed clean of all mud that were protruding from the newly turned ground. There were several human bones exposed and some were away from the mound with a shovel nearby.

"I came up to check on the site conditions," Trotter said from behind her and she jump in alarm. "Sorry," he whispered as she turned to glare at him.

"Sorry," he repeated, shaking his head. "We didn't get much of the dirt loaded into the dump truck before the rain started. A lot of it washed back into our excavation. And then I spotted those."

"It happens," Sandy said again with a shrug.

"*It happens,*" Jane mimicked in a low, almost menacing voice as she grabbed his hand and pulled him away from the group gathering around the bone riddled earth mound. "What happens?"

Sandy laughed and started walking off the excavated area into the meadow, knowing she was close on his heels. "With the natural cove here on the river, it has been a safety harbor for river traffic for hundreds of years, Jane. It's not at all uncommon to come across skeletal remains – especially along the rivers. It happens. It's probably some poor sap who thought he was going to make it to the gold strike in California a hundred years ago. He died and was buried here."

"Oh," Jane replied more calmly. "When you explain it that way it makes sense. But, when Connie said 'body'…" she muttered.

"Connie just repeated what Trotter told the guards at the gatehouse," Sandy answered, shaking his head slightly.

"So what now?" she asked, turning to walk back toward the mound."

"Usually we get someone from the U to assist in the removal. There is a high sensitivity about unearthing old burial sites."

"And in the meantime?" she asked as they joined Jake and the Emerson security team.

"In the meantime," Jake said, turning towards them as they approached him, "You need to head back to the station and get your gear. Grab evidence bags, tarps, and your waders."

"Right," Sandy said, turning on his heel and heading back toward the 4X4.

"Does that take both of us?" Jane asked tentatively but merely nodded at the look on Jake's face and followed quickly behind Sandy.

෴

Nicole paused for a moment and watched the work going on in the glade. She stayed hidden from the group by pushing through the underbrush of the surrounding area, never really leaving the shelter of the woods. The group was congregating around one section of the excavation, inspecting something very closely. She moved slowly, watching where she stepped and carefully noting the ground beneath her feet. The tree roots soaked up rainwater quickly on the mountainside, but the sodden leaves carpeting the forest floor were slick and dangerous.

She had never been to the cabin but she knew where the trail to get there started. As she reached the far edge of the glade she glanced back at the commotion going on. There was an eerie silence in the forest as she moved along the well defined trail. She considered returning to the Manor but the memory of Vanessa stopped her. She needed to see a friendly face and hear a kind word and Richard was at the Plaza. Trevor was the only other friend close by.

She walked a few yards into the woods, stopped and looked around her, and then realized that once she was in them, they were not nearly so dark and foreboding as they seemed from the sun-washed glade.

She continued on, fighting the fatigue as well as the nausea that was so much a part of her these days. Both reappeared without warning whether there was anything on her stomach or not. The path was dry enough deep in the woods that she didn't have to watch every step she took, but it also covered some rugged terrain. It climbed steeply beyond the glade and Nicole quickly became winded.

She stopped for a moment at a fallen tree just off the trail, sinking gratefully onto the rough bark and leaned her cheek gingerly against a thick branch that stretched upward. The woods were quiet around her; her presence sending any living creature into a watchful silence.

As she sat staring back toward the way she had come she could hear the sound of car motors bouncing around the mountain and echoing across the sky. She drew in a deep breath and let it out. How strange her life had become.

As she stared through the woods sloping back the way she had come, she realized she could see a sliver of the river through the trees as it snaked its way through the mountains. In her mind's eye she could see Cameron surfacing after the car went over the cliff. He was gasping for air but strong enough to keep his head above the strong current of the water. What she could not imagine was him disappearing beneath the whitecaps, never to surface again.

The current of the river would carry him fast and far, she realized, but he had to have grasped hold of something and found some way of pulling himself from the rushing waters onto the bank somewhere. With the roadways far from the river in some places it could take him quite a while to hike out. If he was injured, it would take him even longer. If he were seriously injured, she needed to believe he found shelter and was waiting to be rescued. He was fit and familiar with these mountains. He would find his way out. Nicole had to believe that. She had to.

She got off the tree trunk and brushed the bits and pieces of clinging bark from her sweat pants, taking a deep breath and heading deeper into the woods. She came to a fork in the path and stopped dead in her tracks. She studied both. The left was less traveled and seemed to angle back toward the newly cut roadway. To the right she could hear a rushing stream and saw that it was more worn. She knew the cabin was deep in the heart of the mountains, so she veered right, moving away from the river and the newly cut road.

The sound of the rushing waters grew louder as she wound her way through the woods. Soon the path veered to the right again and ran alongside a mountain stream. Rocks were scattered along the creek bed, creating a gauntlet of obstacles for the determined tributary. The cold spring water rolled over some, careened around others, and seemed to leap through the air to make its way to the river. The new spring growth reached out from the banks, sending green arms stretching into the sky to form a canopy overhead.

The cabin appeared suddenly, taking her by surprise when she rounded a bend and it seemed to materialize from the side of the mountain. Made of massive logs felled more than a century ago from the surrounding woods, it was aged and seasoned. The roof was of cedar shakes that were weathered for the most part to a deep, dry gray. They lay in thick tiers over the steeply rising roof and sporadic repairs gave an almost comical patchwork look to it. A porch wrapped from the front around to the right side where the stream scampered by.

Stone steps led up to the porch; the door had only a latch to hold it closed. Newly split firewood was stacked under a lean-to shed on the left – an impressive amount of seasoned wood was on the far end of the porch. A thin curl of smoke snaked its way upward toward the distant sky. The ancient trees stood as sentries on guard, creating a clearing around the cabin, as though holding the rest of the forest at bay. As she stood looking at the cabin, she could believe she had stepped back into another era.

She climbed the stone steps, worn uneven by ages of trampling feet and paused a moment on the porch. There were two rather new repairs that looked like white scars in the aged wood and a slightly more weathered section of the railing that had been replaced at an earlier time. She reached the door and studied the old latch curiously, never having seen anything like it before. She knocked on the door, feeling the rough, dry wood scratching her knuckles and leaned her head toward the thick door, listening intently. There was no sound from inside.

She turned and stared back down the path she had traveled and then swept her gaze around the clearing. She tested the latch, finding that it toggled easily beneath her slight tug. She knocked again and pushed the door open with her shoulder. The door swung inward with a telltale creak that rankled her nerves. The interior of the cabin was dim and more unnerving than the deeply shaded porch. The fire in the fireplace had burned down to nothing more than red glowing embers, offering no help at illuminating the cabin's interior.

"Trevor?" she called quietly, pushing the door back and hearing another creek in the top hinge jangled her already frayed nerves and set her heart pounding harder. "Trev?" she called again, her breath getting more rapid and shallow as she stepped into the main room of the centuries old structure. The floor gave slightly beneath her weight as she sucked in a deep breath, holding it to try to quell the sound of her own heartbeat in her ears.

She advanced into the room, moving toward the fireplace and glancing over her shoulder to make sure the door would not swing closed and latch behind her. Not completely comfortable without the means of a quick exit, she stepped closer to the fire and reached for a log from the pile that rested on the knee high hearth. She propped it in the doorway and then laid another one gently on top of the black charred wood. She watched as the embers began to glow as they welcomed the fresh wood and then burst into new life as tiny fingers of flame seemed to stroke the seasoned wood.

After making sure the log was not going to smother the dying embers, she carefully placed another one on top. She straightened up and turned to take in the rest of the cabin. An old cracked vinyl sofa was in front of the fireplace with several Afghans spread across it as a makeshift slipcover. The wool yarn had balled up, giving them an almost knotted look. She reached down and pulled some of the tiny fuzz balls off like cockleburs stuck to a dog's coat and tossed them into the fireplace.

The flames were devouring the newly added logs, the resin exploding like tiny mines planted deep inside the wood. She glanced across the room to the rickety table in what had to be the kitchen behind the adjacent wall. Trevor's test equipment was spread over it and one of his heavy parkas was hanging on a rough peg behind the door, assuring her she was in the right place. She was crossing the room to see what the kitchen offered when she thought she caught an odd sound.

She looked sharply toward the back wall and saw a door she had not notice before. Had the door moved slightly? Had she heard some sound from the back room or had it been the burning logs shifting? She glanced toward the front door to make sure it still stood open should she need to make a hasty retreat and then turned to stare at the inner door.

"Trevor?" she called again and then fell silent, listening for any sound. She could hear birds in the tops of the trees outside and the sound of the stream as it splashed past the side porch beyond the chimney wall. The fire crackled merrily behind her. Then her straining ears caught a distinct sound from the back room and a cold chill ran down her spine causing her to shudder.

"Trev?"

She backed away from the door, her fear and concern fueling dual emotions. There was no doubt there was danger on the mountain. Someone shot at her Jag and sent it plunging off the Trail into the river. She stepped closer to the door and distinctly caught a sound on the other side. "Trev?" she called a little louder, visions of him laying on the floor, victim of whatever killer was roaming the mountain alternating with visions of a hulking unknown threat waiting to lunge at her if she opened the door or turned her back to run.

She eased into the kitchen, spotted a sheathed hunting knife beside the test case on the battered length of board that resembled a chest high bench more than a kitchen counter and wrapped her hand slowly around the hilt. She felt the weight of the knife in her hand and positioned it carefully in a defensive hold.

She did not notice the shadow behind her on the porch as she eased herself noiselessly across the wooden floor, carefully testing each board before taking a step. She did not see the face in the window as she pulled the knife from the sheath and let the leather case drop to the floor as her hand reached out to unlatch the closed door. As the door swung inward, she leaned sideways, peering into the deep shadows. She clutched the knife tightly and raised it to readiness, clutching it to her chest.

She heard the rush of noise and felt the movement behind her but was unable to react quickly enough to defend herself. As the light from the front room finally illuminated the bedroom she opened her mouth to scream but an arm wrapped around her neck in a choke hold. She gasped for breath, dropping the knife and reaching up to uselessly grab at the arm that was squeezing the breath out of her.

As the darkness played first at the edges of her mind and then engulfed her, she had the distinct impression of being lifted slowly from the floor as the choke hold served the intended purpose and she sank into the darkness of unconsciousness.

୨୧

Kyle stood in the kitchen and paced back and forth, stepping out of Riva's way as she moved around the room preparing the evening meal. She came to an abrupt halt as she turned from the massive restaurant size refrigerator and found him gazing into it over her shoulder.

"Kyle, please!" she almost shouted, setting the colander filled with raspberries on the center table and reaching toward him. He playfully jumped out of the way and then retreated toward the snack bar to perch himself against one of the stools. "Why don't you take some of those cookies up to the glade? Douglas said they've called Dr. Richmond in to remove some old bones. I'm sure they would appreciate something to eat about now!"

"A skeleton!" Kyle said, standing up and turning toward the table where the cooling cookies were scattered across several racks. "Really! Remember when they found that old Indian burial ground on the other side of Oak Meadow?"

Riva disappeared into the pantry and returned with a large wicker basket. She pulled a clean dishtowel from the drawer, flapped it open and laid it out as a liner. She handed it to him and then pointed toward the cookies. "There's a cooler just inside the cellar door downstairs and some sodas in the fridge in the playroom."

"I'll get those for you, Kyle," Douglas said, having entered the room in time to realize that Kyle was about the set Riva off. Kyle needed to be gotten out of her way or she would quickly become irritated.

Everyone in the house was feeling the confinement. Andrea and Vanessa were barely speaking and Nicole hadn't been seen for quite some time. Helena retreated to her suite shortly after lunch and asked them to disturb her only if there was news of Cameron. They all knew something was going on what with Gregory and Garrett being called to the Plaza the way they were and the strain was getting unbearable.

Within fifteen minutes, Douglas was setting the cooler filled with ice and canned drinks in the back of the Tracker. Just as he was handing Kyle the keys Andrea stepped out of the playroom and crossed the patio toward them.

"What's going on?" she asked, separating the towel around the cookies and pulling one out to take a bite.

"Riva thought it would be a good idea for me to take a snack up to Dr. Richmond. They've found another skeleton!"

"I want to go!" Andrea said, her voice almost resorting to a whine.

Douglas resisted the urge to caution the two to stay out of the way in the exhumation of the remains. Sometimes Riva and Douglas didn't realize how grown the Emerson children were. Perhaps, he thought as he watched the Tracker take a corner a little too fast and heard the squeal of the brakes – that was because they often acted as though they were still children.

∽∾

Ellery Richmond's appearance defied all attempts to pinpoint an exact age or ethnicity. Years in the sun of many archeological digs had tanned his already dark skin like smooth leather and his youthful bright blue eyes twinkled from deep creases and wrinkles. He was spry and agile, excited about the discovery of the ancient remains and eager to get to work. He wore an old pair of khaki pants and a faded flannel shirt over the crisply starched white dress shirt he always wore to class as well as the scholarly sweater vest in the still chilly spring air. Strong, high top boots were seasoned by his many digs around the globe.

Jane and Sandy had followed the anthropology professor through Oak Meadow and were immediately at the side of his car to help him with his equipment and across the uneven ground. He greeted them cheerily and motioned to the trunk of his car from which he pulled an old leather bag and handed it to Sandy. He inhaled deeply, taking in the astounding view of the river and then turned toward the less appealing site of the construction.

Jake stood talking to Trotter as the newly arrived trio joined the group at the edge of the excavation. He was sketching quickly in his pad as Trotter's arms flayed in descriptive arcs.

"So, you don't know exactly where this mound of dirt came from," Jake asked, lowering his notepad and raising his gaze to Trotter.

"Not exactly," Trotter admitted, shaking his head slowly. "Maybe when the entire crew gets back…"

"We don't have the professor that long," Jake sighed. "He's a busy man."

Jane, Sandy, and Ellery reached the earthen mound where the men were congregated around the bones protruding. Ellery set his case on the ground and nodded his approval of what had already been done.

A large sheet of black plastic was spread out across the ground, ready for collection of bones. While Jake was talking to Trotter, the

Emerson security team followed Emit's direction and spread black plastic over the line of planks that covered the ankle deep mud around the base of the mound. This wasn't Emit's first time to this kind of rodeo.

Ellery pulled on a pair of old leather work-gloves, worn smooth and supple from years of use. He picked a careful way across the plastic, and then squatted beside the mound of earth and reached into his bag, pulling out a small pointed spade. He began to ease the mud away from the bones until he could pull the first splintered fragment from the earthen mass, then turned and handed it to a very surprised Jane.

"Can we get some water to wash these off?" Ellery called over his shoulder as he turned back to the mound.

Immediately, one of the Emerson guards was on the radio in search of jugs of water.

"Put it on this end of the tarp," Ellery said with an encouraging nod to Jane, smiling gently at her hesitation. "I think it's part of a thigh bone and we'll just build our specimen from there once we clean off each piece."

Jane resisted the shudder that wanted to run through her as she took the bone, surprised at its weight and feeling the damp coolness through her blue plastic gloves. She carried it to the tarp, laying it in the approximate position of a thigh if someone were to lie down on the plastic. As she straightened up, she turned to discover Sandy and Jake behind her, each with another piece of their macabre jigsaw puzzle.

As Jane returned to the mound Ellery glanced up and nodded toward his bag. "There's another spade in there if you would help me," he said, repressing the smile at her shocked expression. "If you want to work over there in the trench under the trees, I suspect you will find the grave."

"Where?" Jane asked, standing up to look around her.

"Over there," Ellery said, raising his arm to shade his eyes and pointing to the area closest to the grove. "I'm seeing tree roots in here too."

Jane glanced at Jake, waiting for him to rescue her from the detail only to see him nod in agreement. She stooped over the bag, peering into the depths with a revulsion she had never experienced on a crime scene. There was something strangely unsettling about the remains found here in a glade that was so quiet and peaceful. She spotted two small spades and lifted them both out, holding the second one out in front of Jake and Sandy. After only a moment's hesitation, Sandy took one and followed her. As they approached the grove they spotted bones protruding out of the caving walls of the

219

turned trench among the severed tree roots. They were washed clean by the rain, leaving them a eerie shade of dark beige.

"Think you'll be through with the excavation today?" Trotter asked Jake, watching the activity around him.

"Once we get past the bones broken by the backhoe it should go faster," Jake assured him, "but call my office later and we'll let you know."

Jake watched as the contractor headed toward his pickup and pulled several empty five gallon paint buckets from the bed and a roll of rope and brought them back to the group of men watching the professor supervise the extraction of the remains.

"We've pulled water from the river when we needed it," Trotter said, shrugging slightly. "Just leave these here somewhere. I'll get them later." He returned to his truck, climbed behind the wheel and began backing away from the site.

Emit moved across the meadow and scooped up the buckets by the handles and looped the rope over his shoulder before heading across the glade to the riverbank. His movement caught Jane's eye and she stood up, watching him as he tied the rope to the first bucket and then lowered it into the river's current, capturing water with an ease that amazed her.

"This still seems to be an odd place to bury a body," Jane commented, pausing a moment to stare at the open glade around them before beginning the gruesome task at hand. There was just something that was bothering her. Her gut instinct was screaming in her ears that this picture was not right.

"Probably not when it was buried," Sandy said, following her sweeping glance around the glade. "There was a great deal of river traffic years ago. It wouldn't have been unusual for that natural harbor to cause this to be a regular stop."

Jane shook her head slowly, watching as Sandy used the small spade much like a pickax.

"But with this large meadow, you'd think digging through these tree roots was a job. Why not just bury someone in the meadow? There are plenty of stones along the river to protect a grave."

The trees shielded the area to some extent and the trench drained the water away from the grove. Once they were past the initial mud left from the rains they were able to pull clods of almost dry dirt away from the exposed broken bones and then deposit chunks from the footing wall onto the ground. Sandy tamped the dirt gently, allowing it to fall away and breaking up the clods between his fingers.

"You want some gloves?" Jane asked softly with a sigh.

"They're just old bones, Jane," Sandy laughed, careful to keep his voice low.

"I know," she said, barely above a whisper. "There's something to be said for being able to call in the crime techs and turn a scene over to them. I've just never seen anything like this. Have you?" she asked, after hesitating a moment.

"Not really," Sandy admitted. "I've caught some calls on decomposing bodies, but not to this extent."

"We have a male," Ellery called, inspecting two broken pelvic bone pieces that Jake carried and laid on the tarp.

Jane inhaled deeply, holding it a moment and then slowly letting it out. She jabbed half-heartedly at the wall of the trench and then began pulling clumps of dirt free as she followed Sandy's lead. As they worked, the task grew easier. They collected the broken fragments and were soon unearthing whole bones.

Jane was getting the hang of the process when she thrust the spade into a new section of earth and eased it out. As she did, she screamed and jumped out of the trench as a skull dislodged itself from the clump of earth and rolled toward her, the two back sections of the skull were missing, which stopped the motion of it and caused the skull to come to a halt with the vacant eye sockets impacted with dirt staring unseeingly up at her. Her reaction elicited some subtle chuckles and she sucked in a quick breath, regaining her composure as best she could.

"I'm sorry, Professor," Jane gasped, staring at the splintered skull.

"Don't let them tease you, Jane," he said glancing back at her as he scampered toward his bag. "There is something about a skeleton that seems to touch a primeval fear in us all."

He selected several new tools, a piece of plastic, and then returned across the glade to her. After spreading the plastic beside the skull, he lay prone on the ground as he cleared the dirt from around the skull before lifting it out. Jake joined him, squatting on the other side of the trench and watching the process.

Ellery carried the skull to the tarp and began the process of cleaning it. As the dirt and debris fell away, he turned the skull over, gently shaking the last of the crust from the surface, exposing a distinctive hole between the eyes. He looked at Jake who paled at the sight of the bullet hole that had torn off the back of the head as it exited.

"Whoever this fellow was," Ellery said, shaking his head sadly, "he didn't die a natural death."

"I've got some kind of cloth here," Jane called, tugging at exposed material protruding from the dirt. Sandy removed another large bone and carried it to the tarp. He stood staring down at the collection, trying to determine where the latest bone fit. As he stared at the body in front of him, he sighed heavily.

"Professor?" he called, moving back from the plastic a step and feeling a sick feeling boiling in his stomach.

"Yes?" Ellery said, hearing the tone of distress from the deputy. He crossed the small distance between them and looked inquiringly at Sandy. At the sight of the look on Sandy's face, he looked down at what he was holding in his hands. Ellery stared down at the skeleton that was taking shape on the plastic sheeting and then sighed much as Sandy had.

"Oh my!" Ellery said, a clicking sound coming from his throat as he shook his head. "Oh dear!"

"What?" Jake demanded, taking long strides to reach them. He stared for a moment at the plastic as both Sandy and Ellery did and then turned to peer intently across the glade to the trench. "That's another thigh bone!" he said after a moment. "We've got two bodies in that grave!"

CHAPTER SEVENTEEN

Jane stood up and turned toward the road at the sound of a vehicle making its way toward them. She paused only a moment as she saw the Emerson Tracker wheel in beside Emit's pickup and returned to the task at hand. After some discussion, they decided there was no need for another tarp because the difference in size of the two bodies made it relatively easy to separate the bones. They started their second macabre puzzle beside the first.

Kyle jumped from the Tracker and set the basket of cookies on top of the cooler and pulled both from the well. He heaved a heavy breath as he lifted them and headed across the glade to the group working at the edge of the trees. He was out of breath and the veins in his neck were bulging as he reached them, set the cooler on the ground and then took the basket off the top. He handed it to Jake and then popped the top of the cooler open.

"Riva thought you might be hungry," he said as he moved closer to see the trench and what it was disgorging. "Hey, Dr. Richmond," he called, waving at the elderly professor and grinning slightly. "What's happening?"

"It appears we have two bodies that were buried in one grave together," Ellery said, watching as Sandy dug into the ice and began pulling out canned drinks. He licked his lips in anticipation as Jane took a can from Sandy and lobbed it to him. It spewed slightly as he popped the top.

"Yuck!" Andrea said, staring at the bones and then shaking her head as she moved backwards toward the Tracker. "That's gross! Where's Nicole?" She asked, looking around the glade.

Silence fell over the group as everyone stopped what they were doing and looked at Andrea. "What do you mean, where's Nicole?" Jake asked, moving closer to Andrea and lowering his voice slightly. "Isn't she at the Manor?"

"No," Andrea said shaking her head and looking around. "She left about a hour or so ago and Vanessa saw her heading out of the back garden. I thought she would be here…"

Jake drew in another breath and turned to look at Jane. Jake's lips were pursed in a tight line as he stared evenly at Emit.

"I'll head back toward the Manor and see if there's any sign there was trouble on the trail," Emit offered in as matter-of-fact way as he could, turning to stride across the glade.

"Need any help?" Kyle asked, stepping only slightly back from the excavated ground. He glanced over his shoulder and saw Andrea slipping behind the Tracker's wheel and switching the key so the tape player came on. When she saw Kyle's disapproving shake of his head, she turned the volume down.

Sandy loosened a large clod of dirt from the side of the trench and hefted it to the ground. With only a moment's hesitation, Jane dropped to her knees and began sifting the dirt through her fingers. When she came across the next bone, she held it out to Kyle and motioned toward the tarp. He hesitated only a moment before taking it slowly to add the bone to the growing collection. Jane was gaining a respect and fascination for the work.

"Any way to tell how old these remains are, Professor?" she called, reaching for the next clod of dirt to reduce to moist little lumps.

"Not outside of a lab," Ellery called over his shoulder. "But I'm beginning to think they might not be all that old."

"When you say 'old'," Jane asked, breaking up a particularly stubborn clod between her hands, "are you talking decades... or centuries?"

"Oh, certainly not centuries... and I doubt decades... only years," Ellery said, nodding his head. He reached for the skull, again beginning to brush the drying dirt away.

"Gee," Kyle sighed, watching Sandy turn the next shovel full of dirt out onto the ground, "I think there is something there other than bone. Look at that odd shaped clump beside you."

Jane spread the broken clods out across the ground, peering intently at them. Something caught the sun and she picked up a small clod that looked a little too symmetrical.

"Where is that water Emit brought from the river?"

"By Jake's car," Sandy said, hefting himself from the trench and crossing the clearing to the parked cars. Jane carried the clump in a securely closed fist and followed him.

Ellery dropped his spade and slowly straightened himself, catching his breath as the arthritis he suffered grabbed at his stiffened legs and streaked into his spine. He shook each leg slightly before stepping forward to join the group gathering around the car.

"This is pretty exciting," Kyle said with the enthusiasm that only the very youthful can pull off.

Jane let the comment pass as she glanced at Sandy. He was pouring his coffee out of his thermos and he then submerged it under the water. She heard a plop as she dropped the clump of dirt into the thermos and Sandy began swishing it gently around. They soon heard a definite metallic sound hitting the inside of the Thermos walls.

"That's not bone," Jane said softly, moving to stand beside Sandy. She cupped her hands together, holding them out toward Sandy. As he tilted the Thermos, muddy water splashed out, spattering Jane's uniform as she allowed the water to run through her fingers. As the Thermos emptied, Sandy shook it slightly and a chunk of metal fell into Jane's hand.

Sandy handed her a cloth from the trunk and she began cleaning the mud from the object. As she worked, finding clean areas on the rag to wipe the object, the afternoon sun caught gold. Jane held her hand out flat, a small ring rolled gently back and forth in her gloved palm.

"Oh, God!" Kyle breathed, staring at the piece of jewelry. Horror sprang into his eyes as he spun around, staring back at the opened grave. "Oh, dear God!" he breathed again, swallowing hard, tears burning his eyes and then spilling down his face.

"What?" Jake asked, pushing Kyle slightly to the side to get a better look at what Jane was holding. A small, delicate gold ring caught the sunshine.

"Holly!" Kyle breathed, shaking his head from side to side. "Oh, God!"

Jane stared at the ring, realizing the design was holly leaves with tiny little ruby chips in clusters as berries.

"I was with Cam when he bought this for my sister!" Kyle gasped, raising horror filled eyes to stare at Jake.

All eyes swung toward the opened grave as Kyle's words hung in the air like a tangible object. Emit moved to put a massive arm around Kyle to steady him.

Andrea saw something was happening and left the Tracker, moving slowly across the clearing as though something might jump out to grab her. When she reached them, she eased into the circle, trying to see what lay in Jane's hand.

"What?" she asked hesitantly, obviously not at all sure she wanted an answer. "What is it?" As her eyes fell on the ring, her mouth fell open and then she caught her breath.

"Oh, no!" she cried, backing away from the group, holding her arm out in the instinctive stop command as though she could alter the course of events. "Oh, God! Please no!"

Jane handed the ring to Sandy and moved to intercept Andrea's run from the scene. She caught her arm and guided her toward the squad car, helping her to sit down in the back seat. When she heard the familiar wheeze of hyperventilation, she placed her hand on Andrea's head and pushed it down.

"Put your head between your knees, baby," she said calmly, "and breathe. Just take deep breaths and breathe very slowly."

Jake reached for his radio, taking a couple of steps away from the group and pressing in a short code and then hitting the transmit button twice. Lifting the unit to his mouth, he spoke into the microphone, barely above a whisper. "This is the Sheriff," he said quietly, "come in."

"This is the back gate," a voice came through the speaker into his ear. "Go ahead."

"Start a relay," Jake said, referring to the chain of transmissions used in the areas where the signals were disrupted by the mountains. "Call the chopper to the Plaza. Get Gregory Emerson and Richard Weston to the Manor as fast as you can. Repeat," Jake commanded.

"Repeating," the detail on the gate replied. "Order the chopper to the Plaza to bring Gregory Emerson and Richard Weston to the Manor."

"That's affirmative," Jake said, "STAT."

༺༻

Gregory Emerson sat behind his desk and stared out over the expanse of valley and mountains that stretched in a panoramic view from the penthouse suites as far as the eye could see. Garret sprawled across the leather sofa and Richard sat quietly in the chair between father and son. In the conference room next door they could hear the subdued voices of Joan and the team of FBI agents ensconced in the Plaza.

They had been waiting the better part of the day for the follow up call. Joan was a shaking mass of nerves and Cheryl Coolidge had her work cut out for her to keep her focused and calm for the call that might or might not come. They needed her here to verify it was the same caller if and when the call came in. The kitchen crew kept the food and beverages coming, removing most of it untouched as the minutes ticked by and the hours accrued.

"What do you make of the call?" Garret asked, closing his eyes as he used the sofa's arm as a pillow for his head. His long, lean body took up most of the sofa and he was clearly showing the strain of the last few days. His ruddy complexion was sallow and he pressed his fingers against the bridge of his nose to rest his eyes.

"I don't know," Gregory said, sighing deeply and shaking his head, pulling his gaze from the mountains that had always been a comforting beauty to him in their relentless refusal to be tamed.

"What did you tell Mom? She's going to wonder why we rushed out of the house and haven't been back."

"Just that I needed to attend to some business here and I would be back as soon as I could."

"Are they going to resume the search on the river?" Garret asked, opening his eyes and turning his head to look at his father. "They can't just accept this call as legit and not look for him…"

"Until the waters recede and the winds calm a bit, it's a moot point," Gregory said, sighing again. "Then it's Jake's call."

"I think it's a hoax," Richard said as he stood up and crossed the room to the bar where an urn of coffee sat. "Anyone?" he asked, looking back over his shoulder and then shrugging slightly as both men shook their heads.

"I hope you're right," Gregory said, even as he realized there was more hope that Cameron was alive if he had been kidnapped than there was if he had gone over the cliff with the Jag.

"I really need to take care of some matters in my office, do you mind?" Richard asked, turning to look at his father-in-law and waiting for his response. "With Sadie and Ben here, the Zurich office has called quite often."

"No," Gregory said, shifting in his massive chair and shaking his head. "We'll call you if we hear anything."

Gregory watched as Richard crossed the room in several long strides and then closed the door quietly behind him. He paused only a moment outside the hall door to the conference room. He sighed deeply, casting a sweeping glance through the inner glass wall and into the lobby across the atrium. The place had become an armed camp with so many of Malcolm's security details posted throughout the Plaza and the FBI on the premises.

He made his way to his office, breaking his stride only briefly as he passed his secretary and she held out a couple of pink telephone memo slips. He shuffled through them as he paused at his office door.

"Email me the daily reports and then I don't want to be disturbed unless it's Gregory," he said as he stepped through the door and closed it softly behind him.

In the conference room, Garret got up and moved toward the connecting door between it and his father's office. He took a deep breath as he twisted the knob and opened the door.

Joan seemed to shrink a little as the door creaked slightly but the agents didn't blink an eye. Cheryl was still at her post at Joan's side, Jack Stanley was leaning over the technicians manning the electronic equipment they had in place and Terrence McNatt was standing at the window speaking quietly into a two way radio.

"Nothing at all?" Garret asked, unable to mask his frustrated impatience.

"Nothing," Cheryl answered, reaching out to place her hand consolingly on Joan's trembling hands as her tears sprang forth again.

"Is this unusual? Shouldn't he have called back by now? You think he hasn't called back because he knows you're here?"

"There's really nothing unusual about not hearing right away," Cheryl said. She was the designated spokesperson for the team. "The hardest part with something like this is the waiting. Joan, are you sure you can't eat something. I think you would feel better if you tried."

"I don't think I could keep anything down," Joan whispered, shaking her head and dropping it into her hands.

"You need to try,' Garret said, crossing the room and picking up a house phone and pressing the kitchen extension, grateful for something concrete he could supervise.

"What about some soup?" Cheryl suggested, looking from Joan to Garret.

"Hold on a sec," Garret said when the chef answered, and he turned to Joan asking, "What kind of soup do you like, Joanie?"

"Mr. Garret, I really don't think…"

"Just give it a try," Garret encouraged, lifting the receiver back to his ear. "What kind of soup you got down there, Chef?"

Joan sighed deeply, watching as Garret nodded while listening to Chef Michael's recitation. "Hold on," he ordered again, turning back to Joan. "Minestrone," he said in an impressive Marlon Brando impersonation. "Next," he said into the phone and then looked back at Joan. "Clam Chowder," he changed the accent to a Kennedy Boston twang. "French Onion," he offered with a French accent and bowing effusively at the waist. "What?" he asked into the phone, an incredulous look spreading across his face. "Chicken noodle soup! What can I do with chicken noodle soup?" he demanded and asked in the same breath. He turned to Joan, rolled his eyes and shrugged. "Chicken noodle – cockle doodle do!"

"The chicken would probably be the safest," Cheryl said, laughing softly as she saw Joan's spirits lift a bit as she smiled at Garret's antics.

"Chef," he said back into the phone, "bring us a pot of the chicken noodle…"

Gregory was standing at the door watching as Garret completely captivated the room and changed the atmosphere. He sighed deeply as he crossed to the outer wall, again staring out over the vista to the distant mountains.

There was a knock on the door and Garret crossed the room to answer it. Expecting to see a kitchen aide there with a catering cart, he was stunned to see Lee Malcolm.

"Mr. Emerson," he said, stepping slightly into the room when Garret's backwards step invited him to do so, "Jake asked me to let you know that you and Mr. Weston are needed at the Manor – immediately."

Even as he spoke, they could hear the chopper's drone increasing steadily as it made its approach. Something in Lee's expression prevented either Garret or Gregory from asking any questions.

"Let Mr. Weston know," Garret said as he followed his father out of the room and toward the elevator.

❧

Trevor caught Nicole's unconscious body up in his arms before she slid to the cabin floor. He lifted her almost effortlessly and carried her to the sofa. After laying her down, he pulled a pillow under her head. He stared down at her for a moment wondering what he was going to do next. Everything was getting completely out of hand.

As he walked through the open door of the cabin, seeing her stalking across the room with the unsheathed knife in hand, images scattered through his mind like buckshot from a shotgun. All of the suspicions he repressed came flying from the recesses of his mind and his reactions were more instinct than conscious thought. He knew Nicole had not climbed those boulders and taken aim at her own car, but he had seen her with a knife raised to strike with his own eyes.

He just wanted to make some kind of sense out of the events of the last hours. From the sniper's fire that sent Nicole's car flying off the mountain into the river to her standing in the cabin with hunting knife in hand. His world was plunged into a nightmare of confusion. How had it all happened? Why had it all happened? Who was in danger here?

Trevor was used to taking on the enemy. He was trained by the best to become the best. Fighting the enemy was something he was very good at doing. Give him a mission and a target and he was known as one who would get the job done – no matter the cost. He was impressive in going after and taking down the enemy; but as he stood over an unconscious Nicole he realized he could not identify his enemy in this.

He was haunted by the images of Nicole and Richard in the back gardens of the Manor. He had seen them so many times from his eagle eyed view of the trails overhead and never gave it a second though. But now! Was it so innocent? He assumed it was a close friendship but what if it were something far more sinister and deadly? Was she capable of cold blooded murder by act or complicity? The thoughts both shamed and frightened him as he watched her beginning to stir.

"What are you doing here," Trevor demanded, causing a frightened whimper to escape from her lips as she jumped and tried to find him through her distorted vision and the pounding in her head.

Nicole struggled to sit up, but Trevor's firm hand kept her where she was on the uncomfortable sofa. She could feel the coarse piles on the worn yarn pressing into her back and tried to sit up again. His hold on her was controlled and his eyes were so intense she shrank back in fear.

"Just stay still," Trevor said, pushing her back down. "What are you doing here?"

"I needed to see you," Nicole said, casting the large gray eyes sideways at him and seeing the dark expression on his face. At this moment, through the throbbing in her head she could not remember why.

"And so you came calling with a knife in hand?" Trevor countered.

"What?" Nicole asked, turning her pounding head sideways and lifting it off the soft pillow under her. "No! I… ah… it was here."

"Looking for this?" Trevor asked, holding up the hunting knife for her to see.

"Oh," she said, allowing her head to fall back against the pillow and then cringing. "I thought I heard something."

"And so you what…?"

"I called you," she said, closing her eyes against the blinding pain and laying her thin arm across them to shut out the painful light. The flames from the fire were like shards streaking across the room into her eyes. "I called you over and over. You didn't answer. I saw your samples but didn't see your test case or your rifle so I was going to wait for you, but I heard something."

Trevor stood looking down at her, trying to determine if what she was saying made any more sense than any of the other events of the last day and a half. Suspicion was so thick in the air it could be cut with the knife he held in his hand.

"Are you sure no one is here?" she asked, looking over her shoulder toward the back of the cabin.

"Who do you think would be here?" he asked, stepping backwards without taking his eyes off her to lower himself to the hearth.

"I don't know," Nicole breathed in slowly and then exhaling as slowly. She took another few breaths and then leveled her gaze on him. "I don't know what's happening, Trev," she sighed, shaking her head slightly and then catching her breath as the throbbing grew more intense. She was now sobbing heavily. "The whole world has gone crazy!"

He rose and crossed to the kitchen, pulled a Mason jar from the dish drain and then filled it with water standing in an old pitcher. He returned to the main room and caught her gently by the arm, helping her to sit up. He handed her the glass and watched in silence as she sipped at the cold spring water.

"There's a killer in the mountains," Nicole whispered, as though she were sharing a secret with him. "How could this happen?" She leaned sideways, then backwards, curling her legs under her and covered her eyes with her arm again.

Trevor remained silent, continuing to watch her intently. He slipped the hunting knife back in its sheath and tossed it to the hearth. He watched as tears appeared from beneath her thin arm and travel down the side of her face into her raven black hair. A pitiful shiver wracked her small body.

"You need to go back to the Manor," he said quietly. "Everyone is going to be concerned if they can't find you."

"What happened to me?" she asked, the pounding in her head increasing as she stood up reaching out for him and catching hold of his arm to stop the spinning.

"I'll take you back," Trevor said without answering her question. "It will help if you walk around a bit to regain your balance."

"I fainted," Nicole decided, taking the hand he offered her. He did not contradict her. Instead he helped her out of the cabin and to a lawn chair on the porch. "Stay here," he commanded, and returned to the cabin, closing the door behind him.

Nicole sipped at the water in the glass and looked around her. There was a corner of the shed visible around the mountain side of the cabin. The door was slightly open and she could see an axe sticking up from an old stump. Beside her, the stream scurried over the smooth rocks embedded in the riverbed as the waters scampered along the way to the river. Under other circumstances, she could sit on this porch and while away the afternoon in pleasant serenity.

Trevor returned and pulled the cabin door behind him, latching it securely. He held his hand out to her and she stared at the two aspirins in his palm. She took them, put them in her mouth and then took a drink of the water, tilting her head to help the pills slide down the back of her throat. He kept his hand outstretched and she stared at it a moment before handing him the glass. He set it on the window sill and reached for her, pulling her to her feet.

"Can you walk?" he asked, steadying her on her feet.

"My head is killing me," she muttered, taking a few steps with his hand firmly under her elbow. "If I say 'no' are you going to carry me?" she asked, grasping hold of him as she made her way back down the steps.

He inhaled deeply, glad to see her wit returning. The walk from the cabin was slow going. Several times Nicole stopped to catch her breath and leaned heavily on him as they moved.

She walked as quickly as she could, memory flooding through the confusion of her mind. She remembered the sense of overwhelming fear that gripped her as she heard the strange noises coming from the back of the cabin. As she walked along the well worn trail out of the woods to the new road, a chill ran up her spine, causing her to shiver uncontrollably.

She caught Trevor's quick glance at her sideways and felt the same fear creeping into her mind. She did not look at him. She was beginning to realize that an arm came from behind her and wrapped around her neck in a choke hold. It had to have been his. The fear seemed to energize her and she quickened her step. Trevor kept pace beside her, saying nothing. It was totally unnerving. By the time they reached the roadway and the clearing where the Jeep was parked, she wanted to scream.

The sound of a helicopter growing closer brought her to her senses. She paused beside the Jeep and stared into the sky, watching for the familiar sight to dispel the strange atmosphere around her. The chopper swung like a giant scorpion into sight and she threw her hands over her eyes as it passed overhead. Sodden leaves, loose gravel, and small bits of debris swirled up around them as the downdraft from the chopper blades engulfed them.

Trevor grasped her arm firmly and guided her toward the Jeep. She could sense his impatience as she grappled with the hand holds while trying to hoist her weak body into the front seat. Before she was settled comfortably, Trevor slipped behind the wheel, started the engine and threw the Jeep into gear to follow the chopper along the gravel road.

Richard isn't at the Plaza," Lee said quietly as he and Gregory stood with their backs to the activity going on in the glade and stared out over the rushing river.

"Do we know where he is?" Gregory asked, looking across the glade to Andrea who stood sobbing uncontrollably beside the cruiser.

"Not yet," Lee answered. "We don't know yet when he left the building but he's not in his office or his apartment. He's not returned to the Manor and he's answering his cell or responding to his pages."

"*Richard!*" Gregory said softly, his eyes narrowing as he turned to watch Sandy and Ellery as they continued the work of exhuming the remains. "Kyle," he called just slightly louder than he spoke to Lee. "See if you can calm your sister."

Since the discovery of the ring among the remains, Andrea alternated between being almost catatonic and hysterically weeping. Kyle stood behind Emit who returned to the glade in response to Andrea's screams. He and Jake divided up the territory between the glade and the Manor for the search for Nicole to commence as soon as the additional security teams arrived. Nicole was now deemed missing. She was seen leaving the Manor by Vanessa and never reached the glade.

"You might want to take her back to the Manor," Gregory added as Andrea seemed to be overcome with a rush of new tears.

"Dad," Kyle protested, not wanting to be left out of what was going on. "You don't want her going home and getting Mom all upset. She'll be okay. You know how tenderhearted she is. Just let her cry it out."

"Well at least see if you can calm her some," Gregory sighed, watching Kyle as he moved away from them toward his sister, aware of his resentful strut.

Gregory leaned over Jake's shoulder once again, listening curiously as they talked about grids and search patterns. He and Lee moved a little farther from the others as they turned their conversation back to Richard.

Jane was transferring the bones from the tarp into plastic bags and carefully noting the evidence information in the white blocks on the tags with a felt tip marker as she loaded them one by one into the back of the Ranger under Sandy's watchful supervision.

Andrea sank into the front seat of the cruiser again, burying her face in her hands that muffled her sobs. Kyle glanced over his shoulder when she grew quiet and cast a furtive look at his father. He and Lee were farther away from them, toward the river and deep in conversation. He drew in a deep breath and exhaled slowly, moving in slightly closer as Emit began folding up the map; he and Jake turned to stare at the path leading back across the mountain to the back gardens.

The glade was eerily quiet as Andrea got out of the cruiser again and began pacing back and forth between it and the Ranger. She shoved her hands into her jeans' pockets and tried to piece together her memories of the last time her sister came home. How could this have happened to their fun loving, carefree Holly? When had this happened to her? She turned on her heel and strode back across the stretch of earth. How ironic life could be. Here they were, facing the loss of Cameron and Holly's body is uncovered in the glade where they played as children.

Richard! Andrea's mind returned in sporadic jumps to her initial thoughts. Her head shot up and she dropped back into the front seat of the cruiser and stared out across the glade in confusion. Richard! Richard flew to Paris just this year to meet Holly and celebrate their anniversary.

"Dad?" she breathed, whirling around to look across the glade to find him. "Daddy," she called a little louder as a cold finger of suspicion played at the recesses of her mind.

Andrea stared unseeingly across the glade, piecing together the facts they had and the conclusion they offered. Holly and Nate did not run away together. They died together here in this glade. The tears clouded her eyes. "Richard killed my sister!"

She reached up and brushed the tears away, blinking several times to clear her vision. Movement across the glade caught her attention and she took a deep breath, wiping her tears away with the back of her hand. The squeal began as a low whine, growing in intensity and volume until it rang through the trees and spread out over the glade much as her mournful sobs, but there was something animalistic in the sound.

It so startled Jane that she dropped the delicate gold ring she was depositing into an evidence bag and fell immediately to her knees to retrieve it from the grass. She then jumped to her feet, her hand moving instinctively to her empty holster and then her cruiser where she left her weapon. She glanced quickly around the glade to take in the situation with professional skill. Ellery Richmond straightened up from where he was bending down beside Sandy, who shot to a stance with hand instinctively going to the safety release on his holster.

Gregory and Lee, engrossed in their conversation, turned to see what the commotion was and began walking back toward the center of the glade. Jake and Emit turned from the pickup, staring intently at Andrea as she bolted from the cruiser and the scream dissolved into hysterical sobs again. Kyle cursed out loud, turning to glance at his father to see if Gregory realized he failed in his assignment to calm his sister.

Andrea screamed again, and it almost sounded like hysterical laughter as Sandy jumped from the trench, watching with tense confusion as Jane dropped the bagged ring into the evidence pile and headed after her.

"Andrea," Kyle shouted, sprinting across the distance between them to stop her as she ran headlong toward the open footing. "Hey!" he called as she pushed past Sandy, nearly knocking him off balance.

"What the devil?" Jake muttered, lifting his hand to shade his eyes against the bright sun.

"Nicole," she cried, rushing toward the approaching Jeep.

Trevor pulled the Jeep to a stop and watched Emit take giant steps across the glade to the passenger side of the vehicle. With one swipe of his enormous arm, he swept Nicole from the Jeep and deposited her on the ground.

"What were you thinking, girl?" he asked, his exasperation evident at the sight of her.

"Excuse me?" Nicole stammered, placing her thin hand against her temple and trying to sort out this new assault on her senses.

"We were just about to send out a search party to look for you," Jake said, joining Emit at the car and placing a restraining hand on his arm.

"I'm not missing," Nicole replied dully. "I…"

"She got turned around on the trail," Trevor said, swinging himself from behind the wheel and moving to take a place at her side. "She's fine. She's just a little dehydrated and fatigued."

Nicole looked at him strangely, still suffering from the trauma of being choked unconscious and unable to think quickly enough to dispute his words.

"What's going on here?" Trevor asked, taking in the activity around them. "Professor Richmond! What are you doing here?"

"I was called to unearth what we thought to be ancient remains," Ellery said as he moved from his place toward his star pupil. "But alas, it's appears to be terrible, terrible news."

"What's going on?" Trevor asked again, moving toward Gregory and Lee.

He watched as Lee jerked his head slightly and walked away from the group. Trevor moved in the same direction. They met at a point where their conversation would not be overheard.

"It would appear that we have found the remains of Holly Emerson and possibly Nate Caulder," Lee said in a low voice.

"But... what?" Trevor snapped, not at all prepared for a new level of confusion and unanswered questions.

Fatigue and frustration clouded his thinking and he was unable to put all the pieces into place. "But, Holly is in Europe. Richard went to Paris just this past…"

Lee watched as Trevor began to connect the dots. He was silent as Trevor turned to take in the scene in the glade.

"Richard!" Trevor breathed, and the tone of his voice and the look that came into his eyes would have startled Lee had he not known what little he did about Trevor's background. "Where the devil is he?"

"Unable to locate," Lee said quietly, grabbing Trevor's arm to prevent him from taking action that would not be at all advisable at the moment.

"It was him! He tried to kill Nicole!" Trevor breathed as his chest heaved with the rising anger. "He's the one that sent Cameron into the river!"

"Steady friend," Lee warned him quietly. "We need clear heads."

Trevor was staring almost unseeingly at the activity going on in front of him. His nostrils were flaring and he hung his head, shaking it slightly from side to side. He ran his hand through his hair and inhaled deeply.

"Mr. Malcolm, I have something to tell you," Trevor said as he leaned toward Lee so closely he could whisper and Lee could hear him. Lee's face became strangely blank as Trevor spoke and he inhaled deeply. Lee was silent as he watched Trevor make his way to where Emit was helping Jane finish up.

Emit," Trevor called in a hoarse whisper as he leaned over to carefully survey the evidence bags, "I need your help."

Lee watched them closely and saw the strange look in Emit's eyes as he straightened up and stood looking at Trevor. He saw the sheen of sweat that popped out on Trevor's forehead and felt the careful self control in the two men as they turned and walked too casually away from the glade under these dire circumstances.

෨෯

Emit and Trevor said nothing as they entered the cabin and Trevor pulled his backpack, rifle, and test case from the closet and watched as Emit moved toward the back room. He set his test tubes back into their slots in his case and glanced around the cabin.

"You have any idea the hell that's about to rain down on you?" Emit asked him, leveling his steely gaze on the young man.

"I do, sir" Trevor said, not meeting the older man's gaze. "I'm sorry to get you involved in this but I need time now…"

"I know," Emit sighed, shaking his head sadly. "Know where you're going?"

"More or less," Trevor answered quietly, positioning his gear on his back. "There are shelters on the other side of the river I can use for a while. I just need time to think and regroup."

"Know anything about the route to the high country from here?" Emit asked him.

"Only that it's that a way," Trevor said with a sardonic laugh, jerking his head toward the back of the cabin.

"You think you can get to the Lodge from here across the mountain before dark?" Emit asked quietly.

"I think so – yes," Trevor sighed. "But you don't need to get mixed up in this, Emit."

"Go to the Lodge. Tell Rosemary I said you aren't there. Eric will know what to do."

"I can't run," Trevor said as he shook his head and ran his hand through his hair again. "I did what I did. I can't leave. I have to finish my thesis. I have…"

"That's what I said. Go to the Lodge and wait until I get there."

Emit stepped out on the porch and watched as Trevor disappeared along an animal trail into the mountains going in the opposite direction from the glade. Emit could hear men moving along the trail from the new roadbed and quickened his pace to be well out of site before they reached the cabin as well.

As he reached the edge of the glade, Emit saw that Jane and Sandy were just finishing up the collection of evidence. Professor Richmond was knocking mud from his boots against the bumper of his car and Kyle and Andrea were standing with Gregory at the edge of the makeshift grave that held Holly these last four years. Andrea was sobbing softly, her head against Gregory's shoulder with his arm tightly around her.

Emit crossed the glade. The large sheet of black plastic was rolled up and folded over. It lay on the ground beside Sandy's cruiser. Jane lowered the lid trunk, watching carefully as she did. They helped Ellery into his car and watched as he backed away, found a place to turn his car around and disappeared down the road.

"I guess that's it," Sandy said, picking up the plastic and stowing it in the trunk before slamming the lid.

"I guess it is," Jane agreed, turning as Emit approached.

"Not quite," Emit said, shaking his head and peering over their shoulders. Jane glanced at him curiously and felt a strange feeling creep through her at the look on his face.

※※

"What's going on?" Jake asked casually, following Lee's away from the family members. "Looked like something serious,"

"It is, Jake," Lee said, turning to motion to his men who were carefully watching the unfolding events around them. "I need you to come with me, but we need to take Nicole with us."

Jake watched with pursed lips as Lee strode across the glade to the squad car where Nicole was sitting. He leaned over her and spoke into her ear. Jake squinted, but could not see her face because the sun was behind her, but her body language was unmistakable. Lee helped her from the car and to one of the black Emerson vans, almost lifting her into it. He nodded his head toward his men, who all returned to their vehicles.

Jake hurried to his own cruiser and saw Lee nod towards him and jerk his head in a "follow me" motion.

Jane glanced up from where she was still tagging evidence and started to get off her knees.

"I'll be back," Jake called as he slid in behind the wheel and followed the line of Emerson vehicles back down the road.

"Can you help me find the cabin?" Lee asked Nicole as they led the parade of cars away from the glade.

"Trevor's cabin?" Nicole asked slowly, turning to look at him curiously. "I think so."

Lee said nothing and let her contemplate the question. "I can," she finally decided. "If you know where Trevor parks his Jeep, the trail is there, I think I can find my way back. Why?"

As Lee caught sight of the widening of the new road, he swung the car off to the side, getting out of the car and going around the front to help Nicole out. She was still a little wobbly and Lee caught her elbow, holding her gently as the other cars fell into line behind him.

"What's going on?" Nicole asked as she leaned back against the car door.

Lee did not answer her. His mind was racing. He motioned to Jake who was making a bee line towards him. "Give her a hand," he said, turning Nicole over to Jake and making it impossible for him to keep pace.

Jake inhaled deeply, watching as Lee's men crowded around him and nodded solemnly. Two of them followed Lee to the trail and two of them returned to their cars, pulling radios out of their pockets.

"You gonna tell me what's going on?" Jake called as he hurried Nicole along the trail into the woods.

"I think we are going to find that out together," Lee said off handedly. He felt a sense of mounting tension as he moved along. Jake's progress was impeded by Nicole's frailty and slowed pace, which was exactly what Lee intended. His job was to protect not only the Emersons, but their best interest as well. That always involved an advance team. If ever a situation needed an advance team this one did.

CHAPTER EIGHTEEN

Lee stopped suddenly as he made his way into the back room of the cabin. The afternoon sun struggled through the dingy glass to get through the only window, casting a strange filtered light on the scene. It was almost surreal as he crossed the room and pulled the still cool cloth away from Cameron's swollen eyes. Cameron recoiled and Lee dropped to his knees beside the cot.

"You're going to be okay, sir," Lee said quietly. "It's safe to take you out of here now."

He sighed deeply as he saw the tear seep out of the horridly swollen eyes and down the side of the badly bruised face. Lee rose and turned to move back into the main room of the cabin. He pulled his radio from his pocket and clicked the button twice.

"Where are the choppers?" he asked into it.

"I can hear them," the voice of one of his men on the road came through the speaker.

"Then wave them down and send the medics and the stretcher in ASAP."

Jake and Nicole were coming through the cabin door. Lee could see the frustration in Jake's frown and the confusion in Nicole's eyes as she sank onto the sofa after pushing the gnarly Afghans out of the way.

"What's going on, Malcolm?" Jake demanded, pausing as he looked around the rustic room.

Lee held up his hand with a conciliatory tilt of his head and nodded toward Nicole. He jerked his head toward the door behind him and as Jake moved across the room, Lee moved to distract Nicole.

"How are you doing, Mrs. Emerson?" Lee asked, kneeling in front her and taking her hands in his. His actions caused her to swing toward him as Jake disappeared into the back room.

Jake stopped dead in his tracks at the sight of Cameron. An IV tube ran from the shunt in his left arm to a saline bag hanging from a nail in the wall above him. On a small table beside the cot were bandages, syringes and surgical items. If his surroundings were not so rough and remote he could easily have been at Mercy General.

He crossed the room to stand over the semi-conscious man and breathed deeply. He could hear Lee's voice as he spoke to Nicole.

"Mrs. Emerson," Lee said gently, taking her hands in a firm grip. "Cameron is here."

Jake heard her startled cry and the angry words pouring from her when Lee prevented her from rushing into the room.

"He's badly hurt, Mrs. Emerson," Lee cautioned her, "but Trevor has been taking good care of him – really good care. You have to let us get him out of here. You mustn't touch him. I will let you see him but you must promise me you won't try to touch him. I know you have the right, I wanted you to be the first to know... but you have to be very careful with him. Do you understand?"

It took a few seconds for everything that Lee said to her to seep through the fog of confusion still filling her mind and body. She looked over Lee's shoulders as she processed what she heard.

"He's alive?" she whispered, returning her gaze to look intently into Lee's. "He's alive... really and truly?"

"Really and truly," Lee replied with a weary smile. "But, you must be careful."

"I promise," Nicole said, rising to her feet as the words finally spun into clarity. She took a step toward the back room and reached for Lee's arm.

Jake watched as the unrecognizable Cameron reacted to Nicole's voice. He moved and then cried out in pain. Jake stooped down beside him, and cleared his throat.

"It's mighty good to see you, son," Jake said simply, tapping the floor twice with his knuckles. "We're going to get you out of here, okay?"

"You must steel yourself for what you're going to see, Nicole," Lee said, dropping any formality between them. "He looks bad. He looks awfully bad, but what has been done is what medics are trained to do on the battlefield. Did you know that Trevor is a SEAL? Did you know that?"

"Please let me go," Nicole pleaded, trying to pull free of Lee's firm grasp. "Please, please let me see him."

"You have to expect the worst and think the best, okay?" Lee insisted, refusing to let her loose. "We don't need two of you to carry out of here on a stretcher; understand?"

Suddenly Nicole went limp, falling against him. She took a deep breath and turned to look at the door leading to the back room. She did hear something this afternoon and Trevor prevented her from going into the back room. Now she was beginning to understand.

"Why did Trevor do it?" she whispered aloud, shaking her head in confusion.

"Because he is wounded," Lee said, not realizing that Nicole's mind was replaying the events of the afternoon with Trevor. "We have our men coming to get him right now. It's just a matter of minutes."

"What?" Nicole asked, turning her gaze to him and closing her eyes to try to ward off the headache that consumed her thoughts.

As he spoke, a commotion began at the open front door. Two of Lee's men who were trained medics came through the door hauling equipment with them and paused only long enough for Lee to point toward the back room. Nicole watched them as they entered the room and stood up.

"I will see my husband now," she said with a determination Lee had no intention of standing down. "I understand what you are telling me, Lee. May I see him now?"

"Of course." Lee kept her hand in his and led her toward the back room. As he anticipated, the sight of Cameron caused her to sway and he quickly slipped a supporting arm around her waist.

"Cameron," she gasped, moving toward him as the medics assessed his injuries and checked the bandages before loosening the restraints Trevor had in place to minimize involuntary movement. He then motioned for her to come near.

"Oh Cameron!" she cried, falling on the floor beside him, and laying her head on the edge of the cot, carefully avoiding touching him or causing the cot to move.

Lee stood quietly by. The room fell to a hush as Cameron's arm moved and an agonizing moan filled the room. The medics stopped what they were doing. Jake glanced at Lee and then lowered his eyes. Lee watched silently, fighting the emotions that threatened his composure as Cameron moaned deeply, but lifted his arm and then caressed her face with bruised and swollen knuckles. Nicole remained still, tears falling from her cheeks to the wooden floor below her. She lifted tortured eyes toward Jake and sobbed deeply.

The cot vibrated against her and Cameron moaned again, causing her to go limp, frustrating anxiety consuming her. "What can I do?" she pleaded. "Someone help him!"

One of the medics interceded and carefully lifted the dead weight of Cam's arm from her shoulder and secured it again with the restraints. He turned to his partner and motioned toward the straps that were secured around the stretcher they brought.

"We need to take him out on this cot," he said, looking at Lee and then Nicole. "It's not going to be pretty."

"I have to get back to the Plaza," Lee turned to speak to Jake. "There are FBI agents I have to get out of the office now."

"Nicole," Jake said, taking the silent cue from the medics and reaching down to pull her to her feet. "Let's get you out to the chopper. You can ride with him once they get him out of here, but you'll have to be in first. That way, when they get him there, all they have to do is load him in and take off."

"I want to stay with him," Nicole said, standing up and looking at the men around her.

"It's not going to be easy on him, Nicole," Lee said gently. "You are weakened yourself."

"I understand," she said, inhaling deeply as she heard Cameron's moans filling the room as the medics continued their preparations for transport. "I don't care," Nicole said evenly, looking back at her husband. "I go when he goes."

ঔ৶

Gregory paced along the side of the road a short distance, stopped to glance into the woods and then paced back to where the Emerson security team waited further instruction. Emit leaned against the back of his pickup, more than aware of the confusion that was flowing through his cousin. It would take time, but eventually he was sure that Gregory would understand all that occurred. Trevor's instincts and actions were what prevented this from being a greater tragedy.

They heard movement along the trail and all heads turned as Lee emerged from the woods. He scanned the waiting group and then nodded toward Gregory. They walked away from the others out of ear shot.

"What do you want to do?" Lee asked Gregory.

"What do we need to do?" Gregory asked, not as much from confusion and exhaustion as from instincts.

"Gregory, you need to prepare yourself for the way Cameron looks," Lee said looking over his shoulder to the trail opening. "He's in bad shape but he's stable and been in good hands. He wouldn't be alive without Trevor's efforts. You have Trevor Cantrell to thank for Cameron still being alive. In the coming hours – no matter what happens – don't forget that."

"Why didn't he just tell us?" Gregory demanded, the flash of his fury showing in the rugged face.

"He's a SEAL. When you understand fully who he is, you will understand what he did. He didn't know who the threat was and he kept Cameron safe from *all* harm."

"Where is he?" Gregory looked around.

"I don't know. We need to not know, Gregory," Lee said quietly, growing impatient with the single focus that was uncharacteristic for Gregory. We have to deal with the FBI, the press, Cameron's condition as well as Richard's involvement in this and his disappearance. We need to not know some things at this stage. Are you listening to me?"

"I'm listening," Gregory snapped at him, his voice hardly more than a hiss.

"Then, sir, are you hearing me?" Lee asked, glancing down at the new gravel at their feet and inhaled deeply. He slowly exhaled, trying to purge himself of some of his own exhaustion and frustration.

"Are you hearing me, sir?" Lee repeated, looking at Gregory and seeing the slight change of expression on his face. "Trevor is not the enemy here. Trevor has acted to protect Cameron at all cost. You have to understand and you have to stand to defend him. If you don't – given all that is happening – this is going to be taken out of our hands and get very ugly and very public very quickly."

The tone of urgency seemed to seep through the exhausted confusion and anger that was consuming Gregory. He nodded silently and ran his pale, wrinkled hand over his forehead and sighed.

"I hear you," Gregory spoke with a quiet authority that was a relief for Lee to hear.

"Is there any family still at the Plaza?" Lee asked, inhaling deeply as he realized he once again had Gregory's acute attention.

"Garrett, Sadie and Ben," Gregory nodded.

"If you will agree," Lee continued, "I'll leave the press to Sadie. Garret doesn't need to get in the mix of this with his campaign looming and I'll deal with the FBI."

"Agreed," Gregory said without hesitation.

"I want you to also consider something else," Lee said quietly, inhaling deeply before he spoke.

"What?"

"I think it wise if you have Cameron taken to Edgewater's trauma center rather than Mercy General. I can arrange for him to be admitted under an alias and prevent the press from hunting him down. One of the things we don't need to know right now is where he was discovered. Given the river and that storm it could have been anywhere. He will probably be able to be brought home before morning and then I think we need to consider keeping all of this in house."

For the first time since the morning before, Gregory was able to gather his thoughts and turn his mind to an understandable task. As

Lee talked, Gregory was able to focus on the bigger picture. He no longer felt helpless and powerless. He was once again in control and could do something concrete. They needed time to decide how to proceed. He began nodding as Lee continued with the details of his plan.

"He's been in the care of a trained SEAL, Gregory," Lee sighed, too overwhelmed himself with the circumstances unfolding around them. "By morning, we can have all the medical personnel and equipment needed set in place at the Manor. We have two major dilemmas on our hands with the discovery of Holly and whoever else was buried with her. He needs to be identified and his family notified before the press gets wind of all this. With Richard's apparent hand in it, we need more time. We need time to form a united front and have a plan. We need a plan, Gregory. Who could have imagined any of this?"

"I agree," Gregory said, the mention of Holly's name bringing tears to his eyes. "You're right. Do what you think best. Send Garret home as soon as you return and then meet with Sadie and Ben when you get to the Plaza. This is your call."

"Decide the best place for Cam once he's back at the Manor and get it ready. I'll make arrangements for the equipment, arrange for nurses and contact Dr. Newman. I will keep the family name out of it for tonight."

"The nursery wing is the best place," Gregory decided, his attention consumed with something he could actually turn his mind to now. "Andrea and Kyle being close by should be helpful. If not, they can move upstairs."

"Whatever is best, but lock down Richard and Holly's room and don't let anyone in."

Gregory nodded and turned toward the trail leading to the cabin. Lee patted Gregory's shoulder twice before reaching for his radio.

"Where are the choppers?" he called to his team at the mouth of the trail.

"They set down in the glade," one of his lieutenants called.

Without a word Lee strode to one of the cars, found the keys in the ignition and was headed toward the glade.

Sandy and Jane looked up as the car came careening into the glade, throwing the loose gravel from every wheel. The two EI choppers were at opposite ends. The pilots remained inside, dark glasses making them unrecognizable behind the bubble of glass. The rotors turned slowly in idle. They were used to just about anything on this strangest of days.

Lee switched off the car engine and left the keys dangling from the steering post. He inhaled deeply at sight of Jane and Sandy. His mind was racing to decide how much he was going to tell them as he opened the car door and got out. Before both feet hit the ground, they were moving toward him.

"I don't have but a second," he said, signaling to the chopper pilot and raising his voice as the rotors began to spin faster as the pilot prepared for takeoff. "Cameron has been found. I'm headed into the Plaza to deal with the FBI and the press."

"He's...?" Jane breathed sharply, unwilling to finish her own sentence.

"Alive but badly injured."

"Where?" Sandy demanded as Lee headed across the glade to the revving chopper.

"It's a long story," Lee called. "I'll fill you in on all the details when I can," he promised with a direct look toward Jane. She pursed her lips and shook her head slightly but then nodded.

"Cantrell has something to do with this, doesn't he?" Sandy shouted above the chopper's rotors, reaching for Lee's arm and catching the cloth of his shirt.

"Yes," Lee said simply, jerking free of Sandy' grip.

"I knew it," Sandy said, hitting the palm of one hand with a fist of the other. He turned toward Jane who was watching Lee move in a bent position toward the helicopter.

"I wonder why we do that," Jane called over the noise as the chopper lifted off, hovered for a moment and then swooped over the mountain and disappeared. The second chopper whirred behind them, still in idle mode.

"Do what?" Sandy asked in exasperation.

"No one is tall enough to be hit by those rotors, but everyone bends over when they get in and out of a chopper."

Sandy made a noise that pulled her from her thoughts. She turned to look at him and then started back toward the squad cars. He slapped his hands against his thighs and hurried to catch up with her.

"Are you kidding me?" he shouted, far louder than necessary to be heard with the departing chopper. "Of all the things that have happened today... *that's* what you wonder about?"

ও৺

"Oh, be careful," Nicole cried as Cameron's scream filled the room and tears spilled from her eyes and flowed down her cheeks. She placed her trembling hands over her mouth and closed her eyes.

"I'm sorry," she whispered toward the medics. "I'm so sorry."

Cameron's injuries were accessed and the medics decided it was best to not try to move him from the cot, but they had to secure him for transport. They removed the straps from their stretcher, buckling them around him as carefully as they could, but still the ordeal was taking a toll on them all.

"You're going to need some help getting him out of here on that thing, aren't you?" Jake asked, speaking to the medic who seemed to be in charge.

"Such as?" came the young man's response, glancing over his shoulder to Jake.

"I have deputies about a half mile from here and there are still the Emerson men at the end of the trail. My deputies are trained in search and rescue."

"Then call them in," the team leader said, pausing in his effort to secure Cameron to the old cot.

Jake stepped out of the room, reaching for the radio on his hip and began trying to raise Sandy and Jane. He walked through the front room and onto the front porch and heaved a sigh of relief when he heard Jane's voice coming in.

"I need you at the cabin," he said without preamble. "Tell Malcolm and his men they are needed back here."

"Lee just left here on a chopper," Jane's voice came over the air.

"Then look for the security team. I'm sure they are still at the mouth of the trail. Follow it straight about a quarter of a mile. It will bring you to the cabin. We're bringing Cameron out and need all hands."

"Cantrell's cabin?" Sandy's voice overrode Jane's. "I told you so!"

"Sandy," Jake heard Jane's voice muffled by her hand over the radio, "focus!"

"On our way," Jane spoke into the radio. "Over and out."

Jake turned to see Nicole standing behind him, leaning against the wall, her face deathly pale. He clipped his radio back onto his belt and moved to her. Her breathing was shallow and he took her arm, leading her gently to the chair on the porch where her strength failed her and she dropped into it.

"I don't understand," she whispered, leaning forward to brace her elbow on her knee and dropping her head into her hands. "I don't understand any of this."

"Don't try to, dear," Jake said, lowering himself carefully into the other chair. He barely knew this young woman beside him and was a little unsure of how to handle her. He reached out and patted her shoulder awkwardly. "Just focus on what you do understand. Cameron is alive and he's going to be okay."

"Promise?" Nicole asked, raising tear filled eyes to meet his.

"I promise," Jake said, more comfortable with his effort to comfort her. "He's badly injured, but there's nothing life threatening."

"Why didn't Trevor tell us?" Nicole asked, glancing over her shoulder through the cabin window as another painfully unnerving groan came from the back room.

Jake pursed his lips and shook his head. He wasn't going to be the one to tell her that she was Trevor's prime suspect. She was the unknown factor in the equation that encompassed the Emerson clan. Richard was the trusted child, she was the interloper. He would leave it to someone else to spell all that out for her.

"How long do you think it will take to get him out of here?" she asked, changing the subject and not noticing the relieved sigh that exploded from Jake.

"It will take as long as it takes, Mrs. Emerson," Jake answered. "These men are highly trained. We need to just stay out of their way, do what they say and leave it to them."

"Will you do me a favor?" Nicole asked, turning to meet his questioning gaze and reaching out to touch his hand.

"What can I do for you?" Jake asked, discovering the charm and elegance of the young woman who had captured the prince's heart.

"Pease call me Nicole."

"My honor, Nicole," Jake said with a broad smile, patting her hand and then squeezing it encouragingly when the moans from the back room filled the air around them.

~~

Gregory turned to watch the two patrol cars coming to a stop behind the line of vehicles along the new road. He moved to greet Jane and Sandy as though he was in his study at the Manor, instinctive habit compensating for the fatigue, fear, and confusion that was the only alternative.

"Mr. Emerson," Jane said, taking the hand he offered and shaking it. "We've come to help."

She turned to the two security men and nodded a hello. "We've heard from the Sheriff. Help is needed to bring Cameron out. Can you follow us about a quarter mile down that trail?" she asked, pointing to the narrow break in the dense woods.

Both men looked down at the leather loafers they wore. She sighed and shook her head in sympathy and then turned her head to hide the smile that played at the corners of her mouth. She was impressed when they moved to their car and pulled sturdy hiking boots from the trunk. One pair looked brand new and she cringed at the thought of what that guard would suffer if he had not broken them in. She would not want to be in those shoes in about an hour.

She and Sandy headed into the woods, leaving little time for the Emerson team to change shoes and catch up with them, but it happened about half way to the cabin. They must have double-timed it behind them. Jane found the clearing at the base of the cliff beside the babbling brook fascinating. She paused only a moment when she saw Jake and Nicole on the front porch before mounting the stone. When Jake merely jerked his head toward the door, she stepped inside, taking in the scene in one sweeping glance.

Sandy and the Emerson guards followed on her heels. Their attention was drawn immediately to the sounds coming from the back room. Jake joined them in the room. He pulled Jane to the side speaking softly into her ear and she began to nod her understanding.

The medics appeared at the door of the back room, obviously feeling the strain of the task at hand. The team leader pulled the hem of his undershirt clear of his waistband and leaned over, using it to mop the sweat from his brow. His partner used the sleeve of his shirt. They looked around at those gathered in the room.

The lead medic turned toward Nicole, who followed Jake back into the cabin and made his way to where she had dropped onto the hearth in front of the fire. He kneeled in front of her, taking her wrist in his hand and found her pulse. "How ya doing, Mrs. Emerson?" he asked her with a quiet smile. As he did, he took her pulse and checked her for shock.

"I'm fine," she insisted, meeting his concerned eyes with a steady gaze. "I'm stronger than I look."

"I can see that," he smiled, touching her cheek with a professional caress. "My name is Russell." He continued, reaching for her wrist again.

"Thank you for being here, Russell," she said, tears brimming in her eyes.

"My privilege ma'am," he said, rising to his feet in one effortless move. "I need you to do something for your husband," he continued, moving his fingers from her wrist to her hand and pulling her to her feet.

"What?" Nicole asked eagerly. "May I see him again?"

"I'm going to let you see him briefly, but then I need you to go ahead of us and get to the chopper." He saw the rebellion rising in her eyes with the flush of her face and wrapped a brotherly arm around her shoulders. He looked around and spotted Jane, sending her a silent request with the slight jerk of his head.

"I know how you feel," he assured her, watching as Jane threaded her way among the men standing around until she was beside Nicole. "I do. But if it were me in there with the trip ahead of me like Mr. Emerson has, I wouldn't want to have to worry about my wife while I was making it."

"But…" Nicole started, casting an uncertain look over her shoulder at the door to the back room. Jane saw the confused hesitation and made a move.

"He's right, Nicole," she said, reaching for her and taking her hand. "It's going to be a rough trip and Cam needs to conserve his energy and strength and be able to focus on doing what the medics tell him, not worrying about what you are thinking or going through. He would want this. I'm sure."

Jane felt a measure of shame as she watched the tears escape from the large gray eyes and trickle down Nicole's cheek. Nicole continued to stare at the open door, her indecision clearly showing on her pale face.

"I can see him first?" Nicole asked, turning back to Russell.

"Yes," Russell said, turning to cross the room as the others there opened a path for them. Jane took Nicole's hand and followed the medic into the back room. She was stunned at the sight of Cameron, strapped to an ancient army cot with a combination of straps removed from the gurney along with adhesive and duct tape.

Nicole fell to her knees beside him, careful not to disturb the rickety cot. She leaned toward Cameron, unable to check the tears that flowed heavily. She was murmuring in his ear, words that no one but he could hear. Jane turned away in embarrassment and waited for Russell to reach for her, pull her to her feet and guide her gently toward her.

Jane took Nicole's hand, wrapping an arm around her waist and steering her out of the room and toward the front door. Nicole had no fight left in her. She realized she was outnumbered and knew that the men behind her were going to do what was best for Cameron, no matter how difficult it might be for them all.

Jane moved with Nicole across the front porch and down the steps. They made their way across the clearing and along the path. By the time they reached the new road and the waiting arms of Gregory, Nicole was stumbling, barely able to put one foot in front of the other.

"I'll take her to the chopper," Jane said evenly, helping Nicole into her cruiser and then slipping behind the wheel.

CHAPTER NINETEEN

Lee Malcolm hopped from the chopper to the roof of Emerson Plaza and crossed to the elevator where his lieutenant waited with the elevator held open. Their unbuttoned jackets were caught in the updraft of the chopper as it settled into idle. Both men absently saluted in the direction of the chopper.

"Talk to me, John" Lee said as the elevator doors closed and they were bathed in welcomed silence.

"He's gone," John said as the elevator eased to a stop and the doors slid open to reveal Richard's apartment door standing open and three of his men waiting. "We have the security tapes showing him walking out the front door and getting into a cab. We've talked with the cabbie. Richard got out three blocks from here."

"It looks like he just walked out and left everything behind." Lee said, walking through the apartment. "You are checking our security tapes and asking for help from surrounding buildings?"

"We are," John confirmed. "Our tapes show him getting in the elevator and going straight out the front door. If he took anything with him, he had it in his pockets."

"Document everything with photos and make an inventory list. Leave it in my office. Put a security camera on that wall," he said jerking his head to the wall adjacent to the door to the apartment, " and have it monitored twenty-four/seven. When you're through here, search his suits at the Manor. Same thing… photographs and inventory list. I'll let them know you're coming. Take your most trusted men, John. I don't want to see film at eleven on any of this until it's our film."

"Yes sir," John replied, turning his attention to the search his men were conducting as Lee reached into his pocket and pulled out several sheets of the small notebook he carried with him. He handed them to John and watched as he scanned the list.

I need you to contact Dr. Newman. She's called in an order of medical supplies and equipment at one of the supply houses. She'll tell you which one and under what name when you call her. Rent a truck if you need to but I don't want any connection to me or EI. Get it to the Manor as soon as you can."

"Yes sir," John said as Lee left the apartment and headed back to his office.

Lee reached for his cell phone and pressed a speed dial code. Almost immediately, a pager went off across town in the news room at the police station. By the time Lee got to his office, his cell phone was ringing.

"Talk to me," he barked, settling himself at his desk and taking the time to draw in a deep breath. "What about the press?" Lee asked, leaning back in his chair and wishing he'd made a trip by the coffee maker on his way in. "Any buzz or stirring?"

"Nothing so far," the reply came over the phone from Mary Johnston, one of the few women on his team. She was one of Lee's best. She had been with him almost five years. Hired as more of a security assistant to Sadie, she quickly became one of his most dependable assets when she decided to stay stateside during the expansion. Once Holly's remains were discovered, he dispatched her to keep an eye and ear out at police headquarters.

"That can't last much longer. Leak a little tease that Cameron may have been found on the mountain. Leave the scent toward Mercy. Then I need you back here ASAP."

"Understood," he heard her say as he ended the call.

Lee heaved a heavy sigh and decided to get that cup of coffee before he did anything else. He was operating on autopilot so much of the day he had not taken time to process all that was happening. Holly Emerson was dead. The thought brought a sick dread to the pit of his stomach. At some point in time he would have to revisit all the moments of the last four years when they should have picked up on Richard's deceit and didn't but today there more pressing matters at hand.

Little had changed in Gregory's office as he entered from the back hallway. Cheryl and Joan were still manning the incoming lines together. Terrance McNatt was seated on the leather sofa in Gregory's conference area and through the open door into the conference room, Jack Stanley was sitting on the corner of the cherry conference table, one leg swinging slightly as he watched the technicians watching their equipment. He spotted Garret on the sofa and jerked his head slightly toward the hallway.

"Cameron has been found alive and is being brought from the mountain," he said quietly. "Your dad wants you back at the Manor as soon as possible. The chopper is waiting for you."

"What happened?" Garret asked with the same simplicity he would have asked about the dinner menu.

"We're still piecing it all together. Your dad will explain what we know at the moment."

"Very good then," Garret smiled broadly, slapping Lee on the shoulder as the relief spread through him. Lee watched as he headed toward the elevator. He would let Gregory decide how to tell Garret about his sister.

"Ladies and gentlemen," Lee said as he returned to the conference room and glanced directly at Joan. He watched the surprise fill her eyes as he winked at her and smiled slightly. "I am very relieved to report to you that Cameron has been found alive and is, as I speak, being brought from the mountain. You may all get back to whatever you were doing before this crazy afternoon came along."

Joan's rush of tears and emotional sobs took immediate control of the room. She leaped from her chair at him and he caught her in his arms, discovering her uncontrolled emotion was a release for him as well. He inhaled deeply and watched over her shoulder as McNatt and Stanley exchanged glances and Cheryl Coolidge stood up and started toward him. Stanley said something in response to a technician behind him and the techs began to pack up their monitoring equipment.

"Where did you find him?" Terrance asked quietly and Lee could see the wheels turning in his mind.

"We don't have all the details yet," Lee said easily, walking across the room and standing behind Gregory's desk.

"Because if there was a ransom paid…" Terrance began but was silenced by the raising of Lee hand.

"There was no ransom demanded and no ransom paid," Lee answered with a shake of his head. "Looks like that might have been Crazy Cotton after all."

"I have to file a report…" Terrance continued, intimidated only slightly by Lee's stance behind Gregory's desk. Lee hadn't expected much advantage but any intimidation was all he needed to get the FBI out of the EI house for the time being.

"I realize that you do," Lee said with a conciliatory nod. "That is your concern."

"Did Gregory know when he left here…" McNatt started but Lee cut off the question.

"No! He was needed at the Manor on another matter. I assure you, the good news about Cameron was not known when he left here. The family will be issuing a statement at the proper time."

"We will need to meet with Cameron…"

"No! You don't," Lee said emphatically, establishing his control of the situation. "I'm sure the FBI is embarrassed by this rush to a false assumption, but at this time Cameron is unable to tell us much. He has suffered concussion and isn't totally clear about the events of the accident."

"False assumption!" Jack replied, his offense apparent.

"Accident!" Terrance almost spat. "Are you forgetting about the bullet in the tire?"

"*Now* you want to talk about a bullet found at the scene?" Lee commented quietly, watching as the flush crept out of McNatt's collar and into his face. "I thought you were convinced there was a kidnapping. We have it on record that we asked you to let the Oak Meadow Sheriff's Department to conclude their investigation before rushing into any unwarranted action, but you insisted, remember?"

Cheryl lowered her head and then turned back to Joan who was still sobbing but was regaining her composure as he spoke. Stanley turned his attention to his technicians who had their equipment packed up and were filing silently out of the conference room.

McNatt retreated as gracefully as he could from the topic and pulled a card from his inside jacket pocket. "Call and let me know when I can interview him," he demanded with more pomp than authority.

"I don't have any authority over Trevor Cantrell," Lee said with a slow exhaling of breath and tossing the card back. "I do suggest that you respect the family and their privacy in this matter. They have been through a great ordeal."

He reached for the phone on Gregory's desk and pressed in an extension. After a quiet, quick conversation, he looked up again at the two agents. "Someone will be here shortly to escort you out."

"I know the way out," McNatt said brusquely.

❧

Gregory paced back and forth between Jake's car and edge of the forest where the trail reached the road. The chopper arrived, setting down in the widened area on the new gravel and the rotors slowed to a stop. The pilot sat ready at the controls, watching the scene as Cameron was brought from the woods by the rescue team.

Gregory heard them coming and waited impatiently as he finally caught sight of them. There were medics in the front and back, keeping a close eye on Cameron as Jake, Emit, and the security team carried him out. The cot was placed gently on the road and the medics again checked Cameron's vitals as they glanced around, taking in the scene.

"Cameron," Gregory cried, dropping to one knee beside the cot. Tears overwhelmed him as he looked into the bruised and battered face.

"He's in and out of consciousness, Mr. Emerson," Russell said, looking toward the rescue vehicle they drove in. "It's best. His vitals are stable. I promise you he's just learned to not fight the pain. It's a coping mechanism of the body."

"What is his condition?" Gregory asked, standing up and absently brushing at the muddy residue on the knee of his suit pants.

"We didn't do a complete evaluation because of his discomfort; his breathing is shallow but unlabored. He's suffered several broken ribs but there has been no puncture of the lungs. He has severe contusions and abrasions as well as a broken right tibia and a broken left radius. It appears he suffered acute compartment syndrome and that was relieved by field surgery."

"Field surgery?" Gregory repeated incredulously.

"Yes sir," Russell said with an impressed shake of his head. "By a very skilled hand, I would add. I don't know who's been tending to him, but I'd like to…"

"Well, we need to get him out of here," Emit interrupted. His words seemed to shake Gregory from his confusion and he backed away from the cot.

The Emerson guards were inspecting the chopper to determine their next step. Cameron regained consciousness and the heart wrenching moaning began again. Gregory watched helpless as the medics discussed the best way to transport him from the site.

"I don't think the cot is going to fit on the chopper," Russell concluded as the Emerson team trotted back to them.

"It will if we strip some of the seats out," one guard said.

The ordeal seemed endless. Gregory stood by as Emit and the security team removed three of the seats along one side of the chopper. Emit then crouched down beside the cot and inspected the underside. After a moment's thought, he went to his truck, pulled a hand saw from the back and came back to the cot, indicting without a word that the men should lift it from the ground.

"Hold it up and keep it as steady as you can," Emit said, waiting as the men positioned themselves. Emit began sawing the cot's legs off one by one. He watched Cameron as he slipped back into the relief of semi consciousness.

The pilot climbed into the back of his helicopter and directed the others as they maneuvered the cot and Cameron into place, securing it to the sides of the chopper with bungee cords he tossed to them. Nicole was huddled in the back of the chopper, her legs drawn up under her and doing everything she could to stay out of the men's way.

Once the cot was secured inside the chopper, Gregory started to climb in beside the pilot until one of the security guards caught his arm. He pulled him gently back to the side of the road as two of Emerson International's security medics boarded the chopper and pulled the door closed.

"I need to be with him," Gregory shouted.

"No sir," the guard said into his ear. "You would be recognized and Lee wants the family to stay put until he can get things squared away. We'll take you home, sir. Don't worry about Cameron. Those men were Air Force paramedics."

Gregory started to bark orders, but seeing the glances between the security team he realized he was so far out of his element he needed to let them do their jobs. He nodded slightly, peering into the chopper to get another look at Cameron.

Everyone turned their back as the rotors began their revolutions in a slow spin and gained momentum, pulling loose leaves, dirt, and limbs around them. By the time the rotors were at full throttle everyone had moved to a safe distance huddled in a small knot beside the cars. Emit stood beside his truck watching as the chopper lifted off and headed across the mountains. The black brows were in a deep V across his forehead. He crossed the road to the group and cleared his throat.

"I know it goes without saying," he said, "What happened here today is as confidential as it gets."

"It goes without saying," Jake agreed as everyone headed toward their vehicles and the line of cars became a caravan along the new roadway back to the old highway.

❧

Ben Faraday entered the conference room and closed the door behind him, crossing the room to settle himself beside Sadie and reach over to take a sip from her glass. Word had come from Gregory concerning the events of the day and Sadie's normally rosy Irish completion was pale and drawn under her makeup.

"What a day," she commented as Lee walked into the room and headed toward a chair.

"Indeed," Lee agreed, reaching for a notepad from the bookcase beside the table. "We have to prepare some kind of press statement," he announced the obvious, pulling a pen from his shirt pocket and beginning to make notes.

"What are we going to tell the press?" Sadie asked, looking sideways at Ben and then taking her glass back from him.

"Nothing about Holly," Lee said, adding another couple of words to his last note and then leaning back in his chair.

"Then how do we proceed?" Ben asked.

"We release a statement about the rescue of Cameron. We'll use broad strokes – no details – no follow up questions from the press. He'll be admitted to the trauma unit in Edgewater under the name of a second cousin of mine who I know is out of the country and won't mind. That will buy the family some time to catch a breath. I think you should do the press statement," he finished, looking up at Sadie.

"Can you manage?" Ben asked her, concern evident in his eyes.

"I'll manage," Sadie said quietly. "None of it seems real yet anyway," she added, shaking her head and succumbing to tears again. "I can't believe she's been dead all this time!"

"Gregory didn't say a lot about Cameron's rescue," Ben said as Sadie dried her tears and regained her control.

"We are still putting all the pieces together," Lee said evasively.

"So, what do we tell the press now?" Sadie asked him, collecting her thoughts and getting down to the serious business at hand. She would deal with her own personal loss and emotions later, when she was not the only Emerson in the Plaza.

"As little as we can," Lee said, looking toward Ben for agreement. "So far, only a few know Cameron's plunge off Sutter Trail into the river wasn't an accident. The few who have heard of the remains found in the glade assumed them to be ancient," Lee said, lifting his eyes and then canvassing the room. "At the moment we leave it that way."

"Richard?"

"No idea where he is," Lee admitted. "Cameron's rescue is going to completely consume the next few news cycles. We can release bits and pieces at a time and keep them hungry. That will buy us more time to try to figure all this out. A good response to any question is that the family is relieved and thankful to have Cameron back safely," Lee added quietly, "and the family will make a further statement when the time is right. For the time being, this is a family matter and there will be no comments."

"And you've gotten all this okayed by Sheriff Clairborne and his department?" Ben asked him.

"We have a very close working relationship with Jake and his staff. Only two of his deputies know everything and they are professional and trustworthy."

"I hope you're right," Ben sighed.

"They have to verify what we believe to be true. Every indication is that the bodies found are Holly and that of a university student who was interning at The Lodge that summer. They have to have verification of that before they can act officially," Lee said, reviewing his notes again.

Ben turned his attention toward Sadie. "Are you sure you don't want to let someone else handle this, dear?"

"I'm okay, Ben," Sadie said quietly. "It's sad, but in a lot of ways, we lost Holly ages ago. In the meantime, what about Richard? He just gets to walk with all her millions?"

"Not at all," Lee assured her. "We will certainly deal with Richard."

☙❧

"I don't know what to do," Riva said quietly as Douglas entered the kitchen and shrugged out of his formal jacket he wore while attending the family.

"I know," Douglas said, shaking his head and crossing the room to wrap his arms around her. "Mrs. Emerson is in seclusion in her room," he announced.

"Shall I still prepare dinner?" Riva asked, glancing at the clock and then at the vegetables on the butcher's block and turning toward the oven where her rack of lamb was roasting.

"I would," Douglas advised. "If it is served, I think they will eat."

"I just can't get over all this," Riva said, collecting herself and turning back to her task of topping and slicing carrots. "I've never seen Mr. Gregory look so worn."

Douglas nodded silently, reaching for an apron hanging from the pantry door and tying it around his waist. He collected the hors d'oeuvres and carried them into the butler's pantry where polished silver trays were spread over the counter. As he pulled the plastic wrap away, tears filled his eyes. He was not sure if they were joy or sorrow. It was, indeed, the strangest day the Manor had ever known.

He could hear Vanessa's voice as she and Garret entered the family room next to the pantry. He quickly reached for a dish cloth and wiped his face. He never knew what Vanessa was going to say or do. If she was ready for the hors d'oeuvres and they were not present, she would certainly come looking for them and cause a scene.

Vanessa was unusually subdued Garret noticed as he followed her into the family room. She paused at the wet bar and poured herself a glass of sherry and settled into the overstuffed chair that was beneath the large window overlooking the north gardens. Garret needed something stronger and pulled the Jack Daniels from under the bar and reached for a shot glass in the cabinet behind it.

"I don't understand any of this," Vanessa said, sipping at her wine and pulling her legs under her.

"It doesn't make any sense," Garret pronounced as he knocked back the whiskey and then reached for the brandy and a sniffer. "There is no understanding this."

They fell silent as they heard the hall door open. Kyle and Andrea appeared.

"We thought we heard you in here," Andrea said, her voice hoarse and her eyes red.

Kyle crossed the room to the antique hutch, pulling open the doors to reveal the television inside. He reached for the remote and turned it on. "How do you think Sadie will handle this?" he asked, backing toward the sofa and dropping onto it as the picture appeared.

"As well as she does everything," Garret commented, sinking into the chair beside Vanessa.

"I wonder what she's going to say," Andrea whispered loudly, the tears starting again as she plopped herself down beside Kyle.

"She'll say what Lee Malcolm tells her to say," Vanessa said, the touch of sarcasm not lost on any of them. She fell silent as soon as she saw Garret's eyes narrowing and sipped again at her wine.

The door from the pantry opened and Douglas entered the room, carrying the tray of hors d'oeuvres to the cocktail table behind the sofa. He paused after setting it down as the teaser for the news came on the TV.

"Amazing mountain rescue after an accident on Sutter Trail," the news anchor said, smiling into the camera. "Stay tuned for your local news and a statement from the family."

Douglas straightened the tray carefully on the table and then disappeared through the door toward the kitchen. He closed the pantry door after retrieving the empty containers and carried them to the sink.

Riva's carrots were steeping in a pot on the stove. She turned her attention to shucking fresh corn. Douglas crossed to the small television that sat on the counter near the kitchen table and turned it on. The news was just beginning and he could see the front foyer of the Plaza behind the anchor.

"Would you think Mr. Richard would do something like this?" Riva asked, moving her corn to the other side of the butcher's block so she could see the TV. "How could we have a killer in this house and not sense something?"

"I think the capacity is probably in all of us," Douglas said, lifting the china plates from the sideboard and setting them on the cart that already held the silverware for the family table.

"Do you, now?" Riva gasped.

"There's Miss Sadie," Douglas said as he crossed the room to turn up the volume and sat down at the table. "I could do a little killing myself right now if I come across that man."

Sadie read through the prepared statement several times as they rode down in the elevator to the lobby. Ben accompanied her to the press conference but Lee stayed in his office, wanting to get the effect of the broadcast. She stood behind the bank of microphones clustered around the podium in the foyer of Emerson International.

"Thank you for coming," Sadie said, steeling herself as flash cameras began to go off in her face. "It is with deep joy that we express our gratitude to the wonderful staff and volunteers of the Stafford County Sheriff's Department, Fire and Rescue Units, and many, many volunteers who worked tirelessly in the search and rescue of my brother, Cameron…"

ಞ☙

Lee listened as she read the prepared statement and then regally announced the family would not be answering any questions at this time. He waited as Ben collected her from behind the podium and watched with approval as his men effectively cut off all access to Ben and Sadie as they made their way toward the elevator. He hurried down the stairs and met them as they reached their apartment floor.

Not until they stepped out of the elevator and she saw Lee did Sadie sag against Ben and burst into tears. Lee took a considerate step backwards, making himself as invisible as possible as Ben wrapped his arms around her. Her sobs were shaking her violently as they reached their door. Ben cast a quick glance over his shoulder at him as he guided his wife into the living room.

"Call me if you need me," Lee said, reaching out and grabbing the elevator door to prevent it from closing. He stepped backwards into the car and watched their door close as the elevator doors slide together.

He fished his keys from his pocket and thumbed them absently as he located the one to his own door. Once inside the efficiency apartment, he felt both a flood of relief at the same time his physical strength drained completely from him. He shrugged off his suit coat and tossed it over the back of a chair, reached for the remote on the counter that separated the kitchen from the living room and turned on the TV.

He opened the refrigerator and moved the six pack of Bud Light out of the way and regretfully grabbed a canned soda instead. He had to stay alert and on top of his game until he didn't. He loosened the tie from around his neck and pulled it from under his collar and hung it on one of the bar stools. He pressed the play button on his answering machine to hear Jane's voice asking that he call her back.

He stood staring strangely at the fine silk tie as he popped the top on the soda and almost drained the can in one slug. It had been a gift from Cameron and he chose it yesterday for some as yet undefined reason. He had not planned to change his tie until Cam was found, one way or another.

He inhaled deeply, allowing the breath to fill his lungs and then exhaled slowly. More than sleep, he was in need of releasing the stress that overwhelmed him. As he walked back to the bedroom and collected his gym shorts and a towel, he reached for the cordless phone and dialed the number of the Oak Meadow Sheriff's office.

"Hi," Jane's voice came over the phone after he was transferred by the dispatcher.

"Hi," he responded, laughing silently at such an inane moment in time.

"I've had some thoughts," she said, plunging immediately into her reason for her call.

"I bet you have," Lee said playfully. "You've had quite a day as well."

"Could we maybe meet for a drink?" she asked and he could hear the hesitation in her voice. He closed his eyes in both fatigue and regret and shook his head as he spoke.

"I can't leave the Plaza tonight, Janie" he said inhaling sharply, unaware of the nickname he used. "Sorry."

"Oh," Jane said, unsure of what to say next. "I just don't want to discuss this over the phone. Can you meet me sometime tomorrow then? I can come to the Plaza."

"Come on now if you want to," Lee said without realizing the words had come from his mouth.

"Now?" Jane echoed uncertainly.

"I can't leave the Plaza, but I do have keys to the amenities. I was just headed to the gym. I have some kind of frustration to work through tonight."

"Oh," Jane replied, her voice stronger and interest obvious, "that actually sounds good as crazy tired as I am."

"There's an entrance to the parking garage off Fourth Avenue." he said, pulling open a side table drawer, "pick a six digit number," Lee said, pulling a pen out and turning his left hand upwards. He wrote the numbers she called out on the palm of his hand. "When you get to the security gate punch in those numbers; I'll be waiting by the elevator on the twenty-second floor. You won't get far before someone is there to help you find your way. Bring a swim suit if you want to."

"I'd have to go home for that, but I've got gym clothes in my car. I'll see you in a few," Jane said before hanging up the phone.

Lee disconnected and then pressed the speaker button. John answered on the first ring and took down the numbers to be programmed into the security system to allow Jane access when she arrived.

"Will you give me a call when she triggers the gate?" Lee asked, dropping to the side of the bed and unbuttoning his shirt. He pulled it off and tossed it into the hamper. He removed his suit pants and tossed them into the corner. They certainly needed a trip to the cleaners. He then set the alarm on his wrist watch and fell across the bed in complete exhaustion. Within seconds, he was asleep.

CHAPTER TWENTY

Nicole stood in the darkened room staring out across the front lawn of the hospital to the distant lights of Edgewater. The flight was a foggy blur with Cameron coming too and slipping back into his semi-conscious retreat as the pilot and the security team alerted the hospital of their ETA. As soon as they touched down a trauma team swarmed the chopper, removing Cam and rushing him into emergency.

Their newly assigned security detail, Carter Reese and Herb Stilman, were waiting at the hospital for her. One of them remained with her and the other accompanied Cameron as he was taken from TRIAGE and then to have X-rays and either a CT or an MRI. At the moment she wasn't sure which was which. She turned from the window as the hall door opened and an attendant turned on the overhead light, flooding the room with blinding light.

She gave them room to wheel Cam's hospital bed through the door and into place in front of the equipment panel. A nurse followed the attendant in, carrying a chart and plastic yellow tub filled with the usual assortment of hospital toiletries. She set it on the edge of the sink and quietly thanked the attendant.

"If you will step out into the hallway," the nurse said, "we'll get him settled in."

For the first time Nicole was able to see him clearly. The crude splints and dirty clothes and assortments of tapes and bandages had been removed and his arm was set in a plaster cast –braced by a pole attached to the side of the bed. An inflated cast encased his leg and he was washed and his filthy clothes were replaced with a hospital gown.

Nicole paused only a moment before moving toward the door where her bodyguards waited. She glanced back over her shoulder as one of them took her arm gently and guided her away from the room.

"There is a waiting room around the corner," one said with a gentle smile. "Can we get you something to eat?"

"No," Nicole said with a shake of her head. "Thank you."

There were several families staking claim to areas in the waiting room with pillows and blankets scattered around them along with coolers, bags and suitcases. Reese, the older of the two and the senior man of the team moved toward the far corner, leading her to a chair beside a stark, bare side table.

"I'm sorry," Nicole said, turning to him and looking into his deep set eyes. "Would you tell me your names again?"

"I'm Carter," the older one said, turning to nod at his partner.

"I'm Herb," the younger said easily.

"I appreciate you being here," Nicole said quietly. "It's been such a strange day."

"Yes it has," Carter said with a slow nod. "Are you sure we can't get you something to eat... perhaps some coffee or a soda?"

Nicole glanced through the glass into the hall, noticing that the nurse was leaving Cameron's room. She stood up and then smiled at Carter.

"Perhaps some coffee," she said, heading toward the door as they stood to follow her, "just a little cream?"

Carter glanced at Herb who nodded and set out in search of a vending machine or refreshment station as Carter joined Nicole in Cameron's room. Cam was breathing more easily now and she moved to the side of the bed, leaning over him and brushing a strand of the sandy blonde hair away from his forehead and leaning forward to kiss his cheek. He stirred, opening his eyes in slits and looking at the ceiling before shifting his gaze to find her.

"Nikki," he whispered, his lips curling up slightly at the corners. Carter turned toward the hallway as the tears sprang into Nicole's eyes and she reached out and caressed his beard roughened face.

"I've never thought I would like you with a beard," she laughed softly, "but you look wonderful to me." The tears flowed down her cheeks and Cameron lifted his right hand and brushed them away.

"It's over," he said hoarsely. "We're going to be okay."

"You have to rest," Nicole whispered, taking his hand in hers and backing into the chair behind her.

Herb returned with a Styrofoam cup of steaming coffee and a vending machine pimento cheese sandwich and bag of chips. She watched as he set it on the table beside her and then joined Carter in the hallway. She settled back in the chair, reaching for the sandwich and pulling the cellophane wrapper off the triangular plastic container. Suddenly the thin, white bread and processed cheese looked wonderful.

She finished half the sandwich and drained the coffee. The door opened and a middle aged man walked in. She set the cup on the table and rose to her feet. She offered the doctor her handshake.

"I'm Dr. Mitchell," he said, turning from her to look at Cameron. "You're Mrs. Emerson?" he asked, turning his attention back to her.

"I am," she said glancing at Cam.

"I don't have to tell you that Mr. Emerson is badly injured. I've spoken with Mr. Malcolm and understand you would like to transfer him back to Oak Meadows?"

"Sir," Reese said as he stepped into the room. "I'm Mr. Malcolm's assistant and given the publicity this will generate we would rather have Mr. Emerson in a more secure location. He has arranged to have a medical suite and attendants provided at the family Estate above Oak Meadow. I have a list of equipment and supplies for your review. If there is anything further that is needed, it will be arranged for before we transport him."

The doctor hesitated a moment before taking the folded sheet of paper that Carter held out to him. He opened it and scanned the list. "Very thorough," he said handing it back. "You have arranged for nursing care?"

"We have," Reese said, taking the list and folding it over again, slipping it into his pocket. "We have arranged home care through Dr. Newman. There will be around the clock nurses and any rehab needed will be arranged as well."

Dr. Mitchell watched Cameron as he slept fitfully and turned back to Nicole. "Depending on the results of the X-rays and MRI, it should be safe enough for you to take him home. He looks much worse than he is."

A nurse joined them and removed the inflated boot around Cameron's leg and stepped back for Dr. Mitchell to take the dressing off the deep gash that ran from just below his knee to above his ankle along the length of the muscle."

"What happened?" Nicole gasped, moving so she could see the leg.

"After a bone fracture," Dr. Mitchell said, leaning in to examine the cut and running a finger over it, "a condition called compartment syndrome sometimes develops when the damaged tissue and hemorrhaging become severe. If it isn't relieved it can cause serious complications."

"Oh," Nicole said, watching as new dressing was wrapped around Cameron's leg and the splint replaced.

"He's going to be fine," Dr. Mitchell assured her, "whoever performed the field surgery did a heck of a job."

The shrill ringing pulled Lee from sleep and he sat up, groggy and disoriented for a moment as he fought through the exhaustion of the day and reached for the phone. He ran a hand over the stubble on his face and lifted the receiver.

"Yeah," he said into the phone, breathing deeply to clear the fog from his mind.

"Deputy Adler just entered the garage, sir."

"Thank you," Lee replied, dropped the receiver into the cradle and crossed the room to the dresser. He pulled a jogging suit from the bottom drawer and slipped it on. He glanced in the mirror and sighed. He meant to only nap a few minutes and then shower and shave. He grabbed his keys from the top of the dresser and headed toward the executive elevator.

The Plaza was in sleep mode. The lights of the atrium were set on timers and a filtered illumination glowed softly among the trees in the atrium. As the elevator reached the garage level, the door slid open and Jane was standing there, still in uniform, a gym bag slung over her shoulder. She smiled and waved slightly, waiting for him to speak.

"Welcome," he said, taking a step sideways so she could enter the elevator.

"Thanks," Jane responded, her eyes falling away from him as she joined him. Lee pressed the button for the penthouse and the elevator began its ascent. He stepped back to lean against the back wall beside her.

"You look like crap," Jane said quietly, then laughed and playfully fell against his shoulder.

"Thanks," Lee laughed, suddenly feeling as though a weight had been lifted from him. He glanced at her sideways and saw the dark circles under her eyes and realized her day had been as difficult as his. "It's been a long day."

"It's been a long two days," Jane corrected. "And I still have more to do than I've already done."

"Me too," Lee sighed, lowering his head.

They fell into a comfortable silence as the elevator ticked off the floors. Finally it came to a stop and the doors opened. Lee waited for her to exit the car and then took the lead. She paused for a moment to look down to the atrium below and then hurried after him.

"Are you hungry?" he asked as she fell into step beside him. "I've not eaten since breakfast."

"Starving," Jane admitted. The Emerson's sent some snacks to the site but with all that was going on…" she fell silent and he glanced at her sideways. She had paled slightly.

Lee led the way through the maze of halls until he came to the service door of the executive kitchen. He selected a key from the ring he carried and unlocked it, pushing it inward to total darkness. He reached inside and with the flip of a switch the florescent lights came to life, flooding the large receiving area with almost blinding light.

"Right through here," Lee said, moving around crates and boxes that were delivered that afternoon.

They stood in front of the open doors of the double commercial fridge. Lee pulled several covered containers out, handed one to her and grabbed another, motioning toward the prep table in the middle of the massive kitchen.

"These look like they are for a specific occasion," Jane said doubtfully as Lee pried plastic lids from containers. Lee pulled plates from the shelves under the table and serving tongs from the drawer.

"They are for a board meeting tomorrow that's not going to happen," Lee responded, lifting the appetizers onto the plates. "Chef Bekka won't mind. She'll be peddling them in the executive dining room before noon."

Jane studied the open containers, plucking a delicate pastry from it and popping it into her mouth.

"What to drink?" Lee asked, standing at another built in commercial cooler stocked with everything from bottled water to cold beer.

"I need coffee," Jane sighed.

"What brings you all this way, Janie," Lee asked as he found the Bunn coffee carafes and set one under the spout. He pulled a premeasured coffee pod from the drawer below and dropped it in the filter before pressing the "on" button.

"I've been thinking," Jane said, sniffing at one of the appetizers from the plate and closing her eyes in appreciation. "This is lobster," she whispered loudly across the room to him.

Lee smiled, watching as the coffee began to seep through to the carafe. He glanced at her curiously as she popped the canapé in her mouth and moaned softly. He felt his emotions stirring and turned his attention back to the coffee.

"I've spent the better part of the evening cataloging and logging into evidence what would appear to be the bones of Holly Weston and Nate Caulder. It's going to take a forensic team quite a while to sort them all out."

"I'm sorry you got caught up in this," Lee said, pouring two mugs of coffee.

"It's what they pay me to do," Jane said with a shrug of her shoulders. She was holding lobster canapés in each hand and after a moment's hesitation, realized her mouth had gone dry.

"That doesn't make it easier," Lee said, grabbing a handful of sugar packets from the holder. He crossed the room, grabbed prep stools in each hand and set them at her side, dropping onto one as she eased herself onto the other. "What can I do to help?"

"I've been wondering what now," Jane said, ripping open a packet of sugar and watching as the crystals poured into the black brew.

"Now, we wait for positive identification," Lee answered, reaching for the second container that held an exotic curry chicken salad. Using one of the spoons he pulled from the drawer he spilled some onto a plate.

"And then, once you've got positive ID, you loose the hounds of hell onto Richard Weston," she said, picking up a fork and taking a bite of the salad off his plate.

"Of course," Lee said and she did not miss the dark look that flashed through his eyes.

"I've been thinking that might not be the most productive thing to do," Jane said, reaching for the container of chicken salad and spooning out some on her own plate.

"Why?" Lee asked, the forkful of chicken salad he was about to put into his mouth dropping back onto his plate. "What else is there to do?"

"Well," Jane continued, leaning forward and putting her elbows on the table in front of her and waving her fork in his direction like a maestro's baton , "it occurred to me that this isn't something that Richard hasn't had ample time to think through and plan. He got away with Holly's murder for four years by creating the illusion she was still alive. *Four years, Lee!*"

"A quick look at the books indicate he's slowly siphoned off the funds from the different joint accounts they held," Lee admitted, shaking his head slightly. "My guess is when we check her trust funds they will be drained as well. You have to admit the guy was cool about it all."

"He's not just cool," Jane said, looking at Lee and nodding, "he's insidious and devious."

"Is there a difference between those two?" Lee asked with a slight smile.

"I think so," Jane answered as she heaved a heavy sigh. "You can bet he's got a very well thought out escape plan."

"So, what's your idea?"

"A controlled release of information designed to assist in the search without admitting there's been a crime," Jane said in a rush.

"I'm not following," Lee admitted.

"Once we confirm that it's Holly's remains, then release a vague announcement that she has been found dead but don't disclose when or where; the fewer details, the better. There have been reports for four years now that she's been traveling in Europe so no one's going to ever think it being anywhere around here. We don't really know exactly when or how she died – technically – so use that to your advantage."

"How?" Lee asked, leaning forward on the table and pressing his fingertips together.

"Don't identify Richard as a suspect. Instead, report him *now* as missing and offer a reward for information leading to his whereabouts and safe return. I made some calls. It's going to take months to identify those remains officially. *Months!* By the time she's identifies, maybe you will have run him to ground without tipping your hand first."

The silence that engulfed the room was complete. Jane sat on the stool and realized she could once again swallow so she reached for another lobster canapé, not sure how her suggestion would be received.

"I understand the gut reaction of the Emersons to hunt Richard to the ends of the earth," she continued when she saw hesitation, "but Richard knows that too. He's too smart not to have carefully made provisions for his disappearance when this time came. There's no way he could have believed he could get away with this forever."

"Let the public hunt for him," Lee said with a slight laugh and admiring glance toward Jane.

"The Emerson name will drive the interest indefinitely. You can keep this story hot as long as it takes! The story is irresistible."

"That is brilliant, Jane!"

"The minute he's a suspect in Holly's murder he has rights, Lee. We in law enforcement have restraints," Jane replied matter-of-factly. "But, as the missing beloved son-in-law of the Emerson family there will be no restrictions on your search."

She could see the wheels turning in Lee's attractive head and looked around the kitchen inquisitively. "So, got any bread or crackers?"

Lee sat silently staring at her and trying to find his equilibrium in the conversation. The brilliance of her suggestion astounded him and he wasn't sure exactly what to say. He hesitated a moment, then started the search for bread or crackers. He found a basket of individually wrapped crackers inside the walk-in pantry and brought them to the table.

"Why did you turn me down?" he asked, sliding the basket across the table to her.

He saw the shock in her eyes before she blinked quickly and spent a few seconds studying the crackers and then selected a packet of whole wheat.

"What?" she asked, lifting her eyes to meet his and inhaling deeply.

"My job offer... why did you turn me down?"

"I had my reasons," she answered, finding the seam in the wrapper around the two crackers and ripping it open.

"Which were..." Lee pressed.

"Not something that I choose to share," she said softly, meeting his gaze confidently. She just hoped he could not see or hear how hard her heart was pounding. "You mentioned the gym?" she asked, turning the conversation away from anything personal.

"Yeah," Lee said, taking the plastic lid she handed him and helping her put the food back in the refrigerators.

"We can come back and raid it again later, can't we?" she asked as they reached the door and turned the lights off behind them.

੧੦੦੪

"They are through with all the tests and are awaiting the results," Gregory said, dropping the receiver into the phone and turning to Helena. He heaved a sigh of relief and slipped his arm around her waist. He felt as though he had aged decades in the last two days. Nothing in his career prepared him for the personal toll this had been. The loss of Holly was a distant reality that was impossible to truly absorb since she ceased to be an everyday part of their lives long ago. She had been more like a comet that flashed across their sky every few years.

"How long?" Helena asked, dropping into her chair and leaning her head against the back cushion. It was after midnight and the house was still ablaze with lights.

"Dr. Newman didn't say. Nicole promised to call when she hears something." Gregory answered as he patted her shoulder and looked up to see Douglas bringing a fresh pot of coffee into the study.

A strained look deepened the creases around his eyes but otherwise, he was as impeccably mannered and dressed as always. He set the silver pot on the table beside the fireplace and glanced inquisitively over his shoulder. "May I get you anything else, ma'am?"

"Thank you, Douglas," Helena replied, closing her eyes and nodding her head. On cue, Douglas poured two cups of coffee and added sugar to hers and cream to Gregory's.

"There are refreshments in the pantry," he said as he turned toward them, "and we are just about finished downstairs. The delivery men are getting the larger pieces in and Miss Andrea has cleaned out the play room."

Gregory nodded and sank into the chair beside Helena. He stared into the fire that was dancing around the imitation gas logs and sipped at the coffee. Helena held hers, untouched, in her lap.

"Taking him to Edgewater instead of Crystal Springs was a stroke of genius," Gregory commented as he stood and began his characteristic pacing.

"Dr. Newman suggested that?" Helena asked to keep the conversation going. She was unable to completely absorb everything happening in the last two days. Faced the possibility of Cameron's sudden loss, the discovery of Holly's remains in the glade was still not reality to them.

"No," it was Trevor's," he said quietly. "He suggested it to Emit when he admitted he had Cameron at the cabin. Emit mentioned it to Lee who signed off on the idea and made the arrangements. This would have quickly turned into a media nightmare."

"It still will, you realize?" Helena replied, propping her elbow in the arm of her chair and leaning her head into her hand. "I don't understand any of this," she admitted, raising the delicate china cup to her lips and sipping at the cooling coffee.

"Neither do I," Gregory agreed. "We'll get to the bottom of it all eventually."

They were interrupted by a light tap on the door. Gregory crossed the room in long strides and opened it to find Garret leaning against the wall. Gregory stepped back and left the door open as Garret spotted the coffee and crossed the room to pour a cup.

"A word of warning," he announced, throwing a long leg over the arm of the chair as he sank into the chair Gregory vacated beside his mother. "Kyle and Andrea have taken charge. Riva is supervising and there has been some minor damage getting that hospital bed around corners. I fear that these guys are getting caught in the fallout of everyone's frustrations. If Riva calls to complain, Dad, give them a break. It's after midnight and they worked al full day before all this."

"Absolutely," Helena agreed. "Do I need to go down?"

"I don't think so," Garret sighed, all but draining the dainty cup of black coffee. As a heavy thud was heard from the lower floor, Helena closed her eyes and slowly shook her head. Garret laughed as Riva's disapproving voice floated up the open stairwell followed by

Kyle's deeper voice.

"I do think someone should report them to their supervisors," Kyle said, staring out the open door of the nursery wing at the white van with "Radcliff's Home Health" emblazoned on all four sides. Underneath in flowering script were the words: "Supplying all your home health needs." One of the two EI security teams was beside the truck. Another was in the house supervising the crew delivering and setting up the equipment.

"You must be careful," Riva cried as she examined the scratch in the paint on the door frame once the men finagled the bed through it.

"Sorry," one of the delivery men called over his shoulder. "Where do you want this?"

"As near to that bathroom door as you can get it," Andrea said, taking a box one of the EI guards was holding and carrying it to the table they had played around as children. She pulled the invoice from it and began the meticulous comparing of items to invoice.

The windows were open to air out the room and the entire wing was chilly, but as the men pulled the posts for the grab bar from under the bed as though it were a magic trick, beads of perspiration were popping out on their foreheads. They encountered some difficulty getting one of the posts into the bed frame before they attached the grab bar between the two.

"I think that's it," one of the delivery men said to the other as they stepped back and surveyed their finished product. One pulled his own copy of the invoice from his pocket and unfolded it as the other hopped onto the bed. He reached up and grabbed the bar, pulling himself off the mattress completely to test it.

"We have a bedside commode, a wheel chair, a walker and bath bench..." the other said, turning to look first at the guard and then Riva.

"You can leave those in the playroom," Andrea spoke to the men as she pulled a fitted sheet from the box and snapped it opened to spread it over the bed.

Kyle and Riva watched with a new dread as the equipment for an invalid was pulled from the van and brought into the house. Andrea felt the tears rising again and Kyle moaned impatiently as he glanced at her.

"Andrea!" he breathed, shaking his head sharply. "Don't start."

"Thank you for coming out at this time of night," Douglas said as he escorted the men to the back doors.

"You're welcome, sir," they said together.

"I'm sure your supervisor has spoken to you concerning your discretion." Kyle heard the security guard saying as he walked with them to the van. As they moved across the stone terrace, Kyle watched as he pulled two envelopes from his jacket pocket and handed one to each delivery man. "The family is very appreciative of it."

❧

Lee stepped from the elevator and led the way from the back corridors to the lobby, pausing for a moment to survey the number of press vans and reporters loitering around the entrance. He knew the outer floodlights created a reflection that prevented seeing through the smoke colored glass. He punched in the administrative security code to the gym and heard the door unlock. Lighted low wattage bulbs glowed softly from behind the vents around the room, allowing him to see the light switch on the wall.

"Unbelievable," Jane said moving around him as the florescent lights hummed to life. It was a full service, professional gym and she moved around the room from one exercise machine to another and then headed toward one of the benches along the walls. "Seriously?"

"One of the perks of working for EI," Lee said, pulling his sweat shirt off and tossing it against the bench. It landed briefly and then slid to the floor. "What do you want to do first?"

Jane hopped onto an elliptical and took a couple of rounds before hopping off. She checked out a treadmill and touched a button, watching a panel of controls spring to life. She moved farther into the room, checking out everything that was offered. She spotted the mats in a corner and sighed in sheer joy as she headed toward them.

"I think a few stretching exercises is all I can handle right now. I'll be lucky if I can fall out of bed in the morning."

"Ever had a duty like today's" Lee asked, giving her the opportunity to talk if she wanted.

"Never," Jane said, falling into silence as she opened her bag and pulled her workout shorts and T shirt out. She glanced around the room.

"Ladies locker room is around that corner," Lee pointed, moving toward the weights.

When she returned, he was sitting on the weight bench closest to the floor mats. He was lifting hand weights, but his attention was on her. She moved to the mat and dropped to her knees, assuming the Yoga table pose and moving through the cow position to stretch her back.

"Have you?" she asked, glancing at him between her arm and leg. When his gaze dropped to the weights in his hands, her head bobbed slightly and she resumed her position. "Okay, enough not said. What is your background? Military?"

"Yeah," Lee said readily. "I enlisted in the Army and wound up in the Rangers."

"And along the way?" she asked, dropping into the child's resting position and laying her head on her forearms so she could look at him.

"Along the way," Lee repeated. He didn't answer for a moment and she thought he wasn't going to until he inhaled and exhaled several times with the lifting and lowering of the weights. "Along the way… I decided to take the path not chosen."

"Well that's cryptic," Jane said, changing to the lotus position and inhaling deeply.

Lee merely shrugged his shoulders and decided to get on the treadmill closest to her but far enough away to prevent continuing the conversation. She watched him for a moment and then moved to an elliptical, pressing the power button and personalizing the settings.

For the next half hour they concentrated on their work out in comfortable silence. As the end of her session, she stepped off the machine and headed toward her bag for her towel. Lee was not far behind her.

"The only thing this place doesn't have is a track," she said.

"Doesn't mean we can't run," he told her, turning to flash a relaxed smile.

"Meaning?" she asked, glancing around.

In answer, he took her bag from her and started trotting in place. After he raised one eyebrow and gave her a reproving look, she followed his lead. He headed toward the back of the gym through the stairwell door and began taking the stairs. Jane paused at the sight of the underside of the stairway rising farther than she could see.

"Seriously?" she called as she began her upward trot. She heard him laugh from the next level overhead and picked up her pace. She tried to recall the button he pressed when he met her in the elevator. To the best of her recollection, it was somewhere in the twenties.

As they took the third level of stairway, she caught up with him and was relieved when she saw him standing with the door open to the hallway. She slowed her pace and gratefully moved into the deeply carpeted hallway. Lee pressed the elevator button and walked in circles around her as they waited for the doors to open.

In the elevator he continued to jog in place and when Jane sighed and leaned back against the elevator door, he stopped, reached out and pulled her into his arms in a gentle embrace. After a shocked moment, Jane felt the dam of resolve she had held firmly in place all day begin to crack.

"Let is go," Lee said softly in her ear, rubbing her back and holding her close. She began to cry, the tears rushing from the reservoir of her emotional core. She heard the soft bell ring and the doors slide open but Lee did not move. Soon the doors slid closed again and she stood in his arms, allowing the stress and frustration of the last days to overflow.

She didn't know how long they stood there, but she finally was able to catch her breath and go limp against him. He held her at arm's length, looking down into the blue eyes with the beautiful green specs.

"Feel better?" he asked, causing another wave of tears that were mixed with Jane's embarrassed laugh. She wiped at her face with the towel slung around her neck. Lee pressed the open button on the panel and the elevator doors slid open again. As they stepped out into the hallway, Jane realized they were once again at the kitchen door. With a mischievous grin he unlocked the door and they headed back to raid the refrigerator a second time.

❦

Nicole listened carefully as the doctor went over instructions to be followed once Cameron was home. She was mind weary and emotionally numb at the moment. She glanced at Carter as he held her elbow and whispered, "Did you understand all that?"

"Yes ma'am," he assured her.

"And they have written instructions as well," Herb commented. They were moving along the dimly lit corridors of Edgewater's Memorial Hospital to the service elevators. An orderly and the emergency room nurse guided the gurney. She and Dr. Mitchell walked behind.

The EI chopper with the logo discreetly covered was waiting on the roof when the elevator came to a stop and the doors slid open as though it had been there all night. Nicole stepped onto the roped off walkway across the roof, was hit by the sharp cold wind and ducked back into the heated shelter of the elevator foyer until Cameron was loaded into the chopper and the rotors began to turn.

As Nicole hurried across the roof and Herb all but lifted her into the chopper, she spotted Carter beside Cameron in the seat she was crouched in during the flight just hours ago. She dropped into the seat that was indicated as the rotors revved up and the pilot prepared for flight. The moon was nothing more than a thin promising light in the western sky as they lifted off and headed home.

Conversation during the thirty minute flight was impossible. Nicole tried to concentrate on what was going on around her, but the whirl of the rotors, the vibrations of the chopper and her exhaustion were overwhelming. She fell into a fitful sleep and confusion of dreams. She was moving through the mountains looking for Cameron and could see him in a distance, but was unable to get to him.

She tried to reach him, moving along the mountains almost as though she could fly, rising above the natural terrain and leaping over the river as though it were a mere rain puddle. She never lost sight of Cameron but each time she grew near to him, Trevor would appear, either snatching him out of sight or standing in her way and not allowing her to move.

She was jolted awake as the chopper banked sharply. She opened her eyes to see floodlights shining down as the pilot used the river to navigate to the Manor. She could see the dark waters and a chill ran through her. Moments later, the Manor appeared, every light in the house seemed to be on and as they banked again she caught sight of the landing lights clearly marking the helipad on the south side of the house. Minutes later, the chopper bumped to the ground, eliciting a moan from Cameron.

Nicole heaved a heavy sigh as she saw Helena and Gregory emerging from the gate surrounding their courtyard. They moved with a sedate purpose across the lawn toward the helicopter as the engine was stopped and the rotors began their slowing of rotation. Helena stopped a distance from them but Gregory was at the door as Carter jumped out and moved toward him and Herb hopped out of the chopper and began pulling gear from the storage compartment.

Nicole closed her eyes and steeled herself for the difficult transport from the chopper into the house. They all stepped aside as Carter and Herb jumped back into the chopper and checked Cameron before removing him. One of them checked his blood pressure and the other his heart and pulse rate, jotting notes onto a clip chart as they worked.

Nicole sat patiently on the side bench, making herself as small as possible. As Cameron was removed from the chopper she finally stretched out and shook her hands slightly. She seemed to be so stiff and her body would not react as she intended. She was aware of the medic team moving off the helipad and toward the back of the house.

As she reached the door she was almost lifted from the chopper by the pilot himself and she turned to look at him. She could see the empathy and concern in his eyes as he slipped a supporting arm around her waist and helped her across the lawn behind the procession.

"Are you alright, Mrs. Emerson?" he asked as he adjusted his gait to hers. "You've had a long few days, I know."

Nicole nodded, tears welling in her eyes, unable to deal with the gentle sympathy and concern. He escorted her to the back entrance and stepped aside to allow her to enter the children's playroom. She caught her breath as she realized it had been transformed into a hospital room.

"Thank you, gentlemen," Dr. Newman said, dismissing the team and turning her attention to Cameron after they transferred into the bed. As one collapsed the gurney, the other gathered their bags and they both left unceremoniously.

As Nicole moved to the side of the bed to brush the still bloody and grimy matted hair from Cameron's forehead, Dr. Newman nodded toward Gregory and Helena who were waiting patiently across the room. They moved to the opposite side of the bed as Nicole stepped back and Dr. Newman pulled her toward the sofa and guided her down.

"You've got to be exhausted," she said as she sank on the sofa beside her. "You can't take care of him if you don't take care of yourself. You need to get some sleep. I'll be here until the nurse gets here. Go get some rest."

Nicole nodded slightly, watching as the other family members began filing in and gathering around the bed. She leaned her head against the side of the thick, plush sofa cushions and the tears began trickling down her face from the sheer let down At some point, Cameron would have to be told of Holly's murder, but for the moment he was safe in the arms of family, sublimely ignorant of the gruesome truth.

As her eyes fluttered closed in the security of knowing that she could rest and the family would care for Cameron, she realized that at some point during the horror of these last two days, she had truly become an Emerson. She was now a member of this massive family of contrary personalities and opposing family traits. She slipped into a deep sleep, the sounds of her family washing over her with a warmth she had not realized had been missing.

༄

Consciousness filtered through the deep sleep that had overtaken Nicole and she tried to stretch, only to discover she was still on the sofa. She rubbed her eyes and sat up, watching for a moment as Cameron slept in a drugged peace. She threw the comforter someone spread over her off and searched for her shoes.

She slipped them on and eased herself off the creaky sofa and around the hospital bed.

As she stood by the bedside, a young woman in a white uniform appeared at the door to the bedroom just off the playroom. She moved toward Nicole, smiling at her slightly and glancing at Cameron and the monitors that were beeping almost imperceptibly.

"I'm Ali," she said to Nicole, barely above a whisper. "He's doing fine."

"I'm Nicole."

"You were resting when I arrived," Ali said with a broader smile. "Can I get you anything?"

Nicole inhaled deeply, glancing around at the changes in the room and then shook her head slightly. She touched Cameron's hand briefly and then ran her hand around the nape of her neck, pulling the long tresses over her shoulder. There was a hair band around her wrist and with one unconscious movement she had the hair in a pony tail that cascaded down her back.

Nicole took the back stairs, discovering a strange energy in the house. Although it was quiet she sensed that no one was really sleeping. She made her way down the hall and eased into her rooms. Mae was on the love seat, but as soon as the door opened she jumped to her feet and rushed to wrap her arms tightly around her and held her close.

"Mae!" Nicole said, hugging her back. "You should be sleeping."

"What time is it?" Mae asking, glancing at the clock on the wall.

"It's almost morning," Nicole answered.

"How are you holding up?" Mae asked, following her through the sitting room and bedroom to the dressing room.

"I'm very confused," Nicole admitted, sinking onto the love seat. Mae lowered herself into the chair beside her.

"Is it true that the skeletons in the glade are Holly and a young man?"

"It seems so," Nicole sighed, leaning her head back against the sofa cushions.

"But... when... how?" Mae asked, crossing her arms over her chest and shaking her head.

"I don't know," Nicole admitted.

"And Richard?" Mae breathed, the idea of a murderer being so close to Nicole was terrifying.

"It seems so," Nicole repeated.

"And Trevor was involved with Cameron's rescue?" She saw the strange look that came into the gray eyes and tilted her head in alarm. "Nicole?" she asked, leaning forward to rest a hand on her knee. "What's going on?"

"I don't know," Nicole replied candidly, rising from the sofa as though a spring had propelled her and heading into the bedroom.

Mae sighed, getting out of the chair and following her through the bedroom and into the dressing room. She watched as Nicole reached for a brush and leaned over, pulling the band off her hair and letting the dark tresses fall forward. She began pulling the brush through, forcing the knots and tangles out with a controlled determination.

"Cam is alive and will heal, but Mae," she said, raising up and throwing the heavy hair backwards, "his sister and a young man whose name few seem to recall are dead."

"I know," Mae said, taking the clothes from Nicole as she stripped them off.

"I don't know what to feel," Nicole admitted. "I feel so relieved that Cam is safe but I feel such dread and sorrow that his sister is dead. I'm never going to meet her!"

"I know," Mae whispered, emotion also stirring in her.

"I feel relieved and guilty at the same time. It would seem that a man I trusted and loved like a brother not only killed his wife – my husband's sister – but also tried to kill Cam – or me!" Nicole said in a rush as she turned on the shower.

"What?" Mae asked quickly, opening the top of a hamper in the corner and dropping the clothes into it.

"Nothing else makes sense," Nicole said, running a thin hand across her eyes and then crossing to the vanity to wash her face.

"It would seem," Nicole said, slathering her face cleaner on and then leaning over the lavatory to splash it off, "he was desperate to shut down the construction in the glade. He knew that if we kept on, Holly would be discovered."

"Oh," Mae cried softly, pulling towels from the cabinet and setting them out close to the shower.

"Mae," Nicole whispered, turning frightened eyes to her childhood nanny, "no one knows where he is!"

CHAPTER TWENTY-ONE

Jane felt more than a little uncomfortable as she and Lee drove the Trail to the Manor together the next morning. By the time they finalized the plans for the day the night before they had consumed the better part of a very fine bottle of chardonnay from the Emerson wine cellar, which turned out to be a climate controlled room resembling a bank vault behind the chef's kitchen.

Jane going along for the ride to the Manor this morning seemed much more sensible in the glow of the wine's aftermath then than it did in the cold light of the new day. They stopped by her apartment and she changed into a pair of slacks and a bright copper colored print blouse since it was her day off. This was one day she did not want to be in uniform or on duty.

Douglas greeted them and just as they stepped into the majestic front foyer he leaned close to Lee and whispered something into his ear that Jane couldn't catch. She just saw the change of expression in Lee's face and the flash of emotion in his eyes before he headed toward the study behind Douglas. Jane noticed the assortment of fruits and cheeses on the credenza under the window before she noticed the three FBI agents.

Jane hesitated a moment, paused slightly, looked across the room to Lee and caught his slight nod. Feeling as though she was not only missing something but also was somewhere she shouldn't be, she picked up a china plate and concentrated on choosing her fruit and cheese with intensity. The tenseness in the room could have been cut with one of the ornate sterling silver knives on the cheese tray.

"Agents?" Lee said with a calculated tone of confusion in his voice. "What can I do for you this morning?"

"Mr. Malcolm," Terrance McNatt took the lead and kept his stare firmly on Lee.

"This is unexpected," Lee continued with a bright smile on his lips but his eyes clearly conveyed opinion that their appearance was an intrusion as he took a seat behind Gregory's desk. "I must have missed your call at the office, otherwise why would you be so inconsiderate to be here at the Manor at a time like this? What can I do for you today?"

"We need to speak to Mr. Emerson," McNatt said decisively.

"Which Mr. Emerson would that be?" Lee asked evenly. "They are all the Manor this morning given the most joyous family reunion. None of them, however, is receiving guests, let alone taking any meetings."

"Cameron," McNatt said, his eyes never leaving Lee's face and ignoring the not too subtle rebuke. "We need to see Cameron Emerson."

"Nonsense," Lee said simply, squaring his shoulders and leaning back in the chair.

Jane knew how the atmosphere changed when two bull-anything squared off. She remembered camping with her dad one summer when they came across two male elks posturing for territorial battle. The air itself changed and it was a moment she found both fascinating and terrifying. As McNatt and Lee stared at each other across the table she sensed the very same change in the room.

She grabbed a bunch of seedless red grapes before actually slinking across the room to lower herself onto the leather sofa. She resisted the urge to laugh as Lee continued his intense gaze. She wasn't sure he was even breathing. She then realized she wasn't either. She set her bottle of water on the floor at her feet and exhaled loudly remembering how her dad made a loud racket to startle the moose that long ago summer. It worked again.

McNatt blinked first as he pulled a leather-bound notebook from his satchel and opened it in front of him. She almost clapped her hands but caught herself just in time but not before her movement caught Lee's eyes. Her mouth fell open in disbelief and saw the amused twinkle in his eye before he focused again on McNatt. They were beginning to know each other well enough to almost be on the same thought wave.

"We have reason to believe that Cameron was kidnapped and a ransom was paid," McNatt announced, glancing from Lee to Jane.

"You would be mistaken," Lee said quietly. "There was no kidnapping and there was no ransom paid."

"I would prefer to hear that from Cameron Emerson," McNatt replied.

"Your preferences are not my concern," Lee said, finally lowering his gaze. "If and when Cameron feels it necessary to meet with you, he will let you know. I should warn you Terry that I am pretty sure he will see no need whatsoever."

"Then we need to speak to Trevor Cantrell," McNatt said as he pulled a pen from the inside pocket of his jacket and a soft click was the only sound in the room. Jack Stanley and Cheryl Coolidge also set notebooks on the table and prepared to take notes.

"Trevor Cantrell doesn't live here," Lee said with an absent shake of his head, his confusion over their comment exaggerated by his comical dismissal of the question.

"Where is he?" McNatt asked, his voice beginning to show his irritation.

"Nothing concerning Trevor Cantrell, his actions, or his whereabouts is any part of my job," Lee laughed, his contempt for the agent in charge no longer a subtle expression. "Mr. Cantrell is neither employed by nor obligated to Emerson International in any way. He doesn't report to me and I do not supervise or monitor his activities. But if I did, you have seriously overstepped your authority to demand anything from me or EI here."

"But you know where he is," Jack interjected, ignoring Lee's tirade.

"I do?" Lee asked, turning his gaze toward the junior member of the team. The steely look that flashed into Lee's eyes caught even Jane off guard. There was only so much Lee was going to take from the over zealous team who interjected themselves into the situation before it was called for. Now they were scrambling to justify their actions to superiors who were going to have more questions than the trio would be able to answer.

The agents fell silent and studied the pads in front of them. Jane watched as Terrance McNatt blinked quickly, thumbing through several pages of notes and then staring a moment at the pen in his hand. He inhaled deeply, clicking his pen again and leveling his gaze across the room towards her.

Jane almost choked on the grape she just popped into her mouth and chewed quickly as she reached for the bottle of water on the floor under his intense scrutiny.

"What about you, Deputy Adler," he asked as she tried to nonchalantly unscrew the top off the bottle but found it stubbornly difficult. She tilted her chin upward as though she might have to deflect a sucker punch. It was the same feeling she sometimes had on patrol when she wasn't sure what direction a show down of authority was going to take.

"I neither work for nor am obligated to Emerson International either," she said after a moment's reflection, her eyes widening in an innocent expression that caused Lee to bite his lower lip to keep from laughing aloud but did not try to keep them from seeing his amusement. "… and this is my day off," she added, finding enough anger at his impudence to twist the top from the bottle of water. "The county doesn't pay me overtime and I'm not on duty today. So, just call me Jane."

"You have no idea where your suspect in the kidnapping of Cameron Emerson is at the moment?"

"If you are talking about Cotton Prater, then check with the nursing home on the south side of Oak Meadow," Jane said, finally having enough of this entire exercise in foolishness.

"In fact, this was an idea fabricated completely by the FBI. Sometime, when I'm on duty, I'll take you by to meet Cotton. He's the one whose tip you guys jumped on from the tip line. He'll be able to tell you where the gunman from the grassy knoll is while you're there. The last I talked to Cotton, he thinks he's living in a condo in Havana. Crazy Cotton got his nickname for a reason, agent – but just between you, me and the lamppost you'll get more out of him if you wrap your head in aluminum foil that day."

Lee lowered his head even further as McNatt and Stanley exchanged glances. Jane noticed that Cheryl Coolidge seemed a little embarrassed. She raised her gaze to the other woman and smiled slightly, shaking her head in contempt.

"There was a call," Stanley insisted. "Gregory's secretary, Joan, took a call…"

"Yes, there was a call," Lee agreed. "It's as big a mystery to us as it is to you. There has been a suggestion that it was a dropped cell phone call between some of the rescue squad team members discussing the search and rescue plans following the storm. Several people were conferencing a call from Oak Meadow to the Plaza. Crazy cross over on the lines can happen when we try to do that."

Jane sat staring at Lee in admiration. He was handling this impressively. He was carefully avoiding looking at her and she made note of that as well. She glanced away from his stone face to the agents and saw the moment of defeat as it hit Terrance McNatt that he had royally messed up this career hunch.

"There was no abduction of Cameron Emerson," Jane said, scooting to the edge of the sofa cushion and trying to be sympathetic to the agents' predicament and short stop the ill will she saw sprouting in front of her. "The Stafford County Sheriff's department is still investigating the incident on Sutter Trail, and at the appropriate time, the department will have a statement to make as well," she said as Lee stood, leaving no question that the meeting was over.

"We would like to speak to Mr. Gregory Emerson," McNatt repeated, not moving from his place at the table.

"Call his office and make an appointment," Lee said abruptly, making no effort to maintain a polite tone. "This family is celebrating the recovery of Cameron after what could have been a devastating tragedy and they would appreciate a little time to rest and recover from the last two days. Anyone with a modicum of professionalism would not be sitting in that chair at this moment. I find it reprehensible that you are here unannounced and uninvited."

Jane sucked in her breath and fell back against the sofa cushions. So much for tact and diplomacy, she thought as she struggled to get off the sofa.

"Ah… gentlemen," she said, stepping across the room and placing herself in the space between Lee and McNatt just as Terrance rose from his chair. "This is a small community. We need to play nice… all of us. We just never know when we will have to work together again. Let's not start setting bridges on fire here. I've seen bridges around here… they are not so easy to rebuild."

Lee moved from the table to the door and as he opened it, Douglas appeared. "Douglas will show you out. I'm sure you have the number to Mr. Emerson's office. My guess is he will be back at the Plaza tomorrow or the next day."

Jane stood where she was, meeting Terrance McNatt's gaze with a calm tilt of her head and question in her eyes. Her look seemed to convey her message. Was this really the hill he was ready to die on? Taking on the Emerson machine was never a good idea. He inhaled sharply, lowered his gaze from hers and reached for his brief case. She sighed deeply, and then took a position beside Lee as the FBI agents exchanged glances, decided that retreat was the better part of valor at the moment and collected their things to leave. Lee and Jane watched them exit the room and the door close behind Douglas.

Jane stared at the closed door a moment and then glanced sideways at Lee. He was staring at her with obvious admiration as she set her plate and water on the table.

"A cell phone signal getting crossed with an encrypted phone line?" she asked, her disbelief causing the beautiful blue eyes to widen sharply. "Seriously? Are you kidding me? Where did that come from? The state of seriously delusional?"

※

Trevor heaved a heavy sigh as he shifted the test case on his shoulder and began the final push through the upper quadrant of his test area. The fragile sun was making little headway in dispelling the gloom left behind by the storm or the dense surreal mist that hovered just above the ground. There was another threat of rain in the air and a gusty wind that for the most part stayed in the upper branches of the trees but would occasionally rushed downward, sending the sodden winter leaves scattering about in muddy clumps and chasing the mist into deeper recesses of the mountain.

He topped the last crest above the Manor and sighed deeply as he contemplated returning to the cabin. Emit appeared before dawn and hiked with him out of the high country and warned him of what to expect when he got there. He was moving as fast as he could through his test route and trying to maintain his research schedule. He knew he was a wanted man but felt confident he could evade anyone who might be out and about on the mountain.

He slept like a dead man the night before in the Upper Lodge knowing that Cameron was no longer his responsibility. It was his first chance to actually sleep since the night before the attack. He never slept very deeply, combat sleep now an ingrained part of him, but it had been a long time since he actually stood guard over a wounded buddy in hostile territory. The last time had ended badly. Only two of their team survived.

He neared the cabin and breathed in a heavy sigh of resignation. There was evidence of the frantic activity of the day before. Footprints left in the muddy trail coming and going from the cabin. He was caught completely off guard as he walked upon the porch and discovered the dark shadow at the far end. Instinctively, Trevor dropped the sample case to the ancient wood of the front porch and the rifle swung with military precision into his hand and then to his shoulder.

"Don't shoot," Nicole said, getting out of the rough hewn chair where she had been watching for his return in the utter joy of the forest symphony and calm after the storm. She moved toward him, her arms raised in surrender.

He exhaled sharply and dropped the rifle from his shoulder and then leaned it against the outside wall as he exhaled slowly. As she moved into the sun filtering onto the covered porch he could see the dark circles under her eyes and the unhealthy pallor the exhaustion brought to her already alabaster skin.

She was dressed in a fuchsia colored jogging suit and her hair was pulled back into a pony tail, which she had then twisted into a loose knot on top of her head. He knew he would have many questions to answer and actions to defend but he thought he would be able to choose his own time and place. Nicole was the one he dreaded facing the most.

"I knew you would come back for your test case," she said simply.

"Nicole," he said, waiting to see what her reaction to him was going to be. He would not blame her or be surprised if she crossed the porch and attacked him. He could understand the resentment and suspicion he created in everyone.

He watched as she lowered her arms and moved slowly toward him and waited. She stopped as she neared him and then leaned against the log railing of the porch.

"How are you?" she asked quietly, cocking her head slightly as she studied him.

"How am I?" he replied, taking a step forward and leaning against the wall opposite her. Of all the questions and emotions he was expecting, her concern for him was not one of them. "How are you?"

"Cameron's home and alive," she replied simply, "so I'm good."

"I knew he was going to be okay, Nikki," Trevor said quietly watching her, "I wouldn't have kept him here if I wasn't sure he was going to be okay."

"Air lifting him into Edgewater was a good idea. Gregory said you suggested it."

He still wasn't sure what it was she wanted from him. She could just as easily have come to tell him off as any other reason. Airlifting Cameron away from Crystal Springs and the mass of reporters and news coverage just made sense. In Edgewater, he was able to be treated and released under an assumed name before news of the recovery was announced.

"It was a good idea," she said, crossing her arms over her chest and glancing around her. She watched him as she spoke, trying to get a read on him. This was the man Cameron had never seen before, as Cameron kept saying to her in the moments they spoke alone between examinations, X-rays, MRI, and treatments. This Trevor was someone none of them had ever seen before. This was a man in full combat mode, ready to face any enemy and do whatever he had to do to accomplish a mission. He both intrigued and scared the wits out of her.

"Cam told me what he remembers," she continuing, leveling intense gray eyes on him again. "He just doesn't remember much of it."

"That's the body's way of coping, Nikki,' Trevor said simply.

"After what I've learned about it all – I'm grateful. There are no words to thank you for saving him for us."

As she fell silent, watching him closely, he still said nothing. She sighed deeply, looking toward the cabin door and then back at him. "Do you have any coffee in there?"

"Oh," Trevor said, losing his composure over the normalcy that was reclaiming their lives even though nothing was ever going to be the same. "Of course, come on in."

He turned, scooped his sample case to his shoulder and headed toward the door. He released the hasp and swung the door inward, standing aside to allow her to pass in front of him while holding the old door open with his free arm.

"You're not going to put another choke hold on me and take me down again, are you?" Nicole asked, stopping at the threshold and peering inside with an exaggerated carefulness.

"I promise," Trevor said, exaggerating the shameful hanging of his head.

Nicole stepped into the cabin, her eyes moving immediately toward the door in the back. She was trying to absorb so much through the confusion and exhaustion that still overwhelmed her.

"We got Cameron back to the Manor sometime in the wee hours of the morning," she commented, dropping into one of the mismatched chairs around the kitchen table as he pulled the old, battered, coffee pot from the sink and half way rinsed it out. He shook coffee grounds from an opened bag and as much went into the sink as fell into the inner basket. After filling the pot with water he slipped the shaft on the circular aluminum base into the coffee holder and then laid the top over it before lowering the assembly into the pot.

As he set it on the old stove he reached for a box of matches and lit the pilot light. There was a whiff of propane gas around them before the burner beneath the pot burst into a ring of blue flame. Trevor sank onto the chair beside her and crossed his arms over his chest as he inhaled deeply.

Trevor avoided her glance and watched as the pot began to vibrate almost imperceptibly as the flame heated the water inside. He had slipped into Iraq under the cover of darkness, taken out the enemy on its own turf and lived the horrors of battle as many warriors for centuries, but he'd never felt the fear that was bubbling up in him under the unblinking stare of this slight woman.

"Last night seemed like it lasted for days," she said as she watched him rise nervously to his feet and return to the sink. He pulled two cups from the drain and squirted soap into one of them before pouring water out of a jug on the counter beside the sink, washing it out with intense concentration – anything to not have to discuss this with her.

"The events of these last two days kept replaying over and over in my mind," she continued, shifting in her chair so she could see his face. "It wasn't until we got home and Cameron was settled in that it hit me."

She fell silent, her eyes dropped to the floor and as Trevor glanced tentatively at her with a quick sideways glance, the coffee began to perk in the pot behind him. As she lifted her eyes from the floor to his he could feel the blush flooding through his face.

"Why did you think I would try to kill Cameron?"

※

When Ben and Sadie opened the study door Jane was sitting at the table with her second plateful of the delectable slices of kiwi, tangerine slices, and a wonderful cheese spread she could not identify. Lee was standing at the window, watching as the duty nurse emerged from the Emerson car at the front walk and Douglas appeared to help her with her bag.

Ben headed toward the cart which held the coffee urn and Sadie dropped into the nearest chair. She pushed a strand of hair away from her pale face and closed her eyes a moment as Jane watched her and then dropped her eyes to stare at the plate in front of her. She stood up and carried the plate to a side table; set it down as inconspicuously as she could and then returned to the table and her bottle of water.

A slight clattering could be heard as Ben carried two cups of coffee on saucers across the room and set one down in front of his wife. As he lowered himself into the leather chair beside Sadie he reached over and took her hand. Jane noticed that Sadie's was trembling and Ben was watching her with careful attention. The stress and physical demands of the last hours was catching up with them all.

"I'm so sorry for your loss," Jane said after clearing her throat slightly. Suddenly, the gruesomeness of her afternoon before joined them in the room. For the last few hours she was able to distance herself from the ghastly discovery in the glade. Sitting in the study with the next of kin of one of the murder victims put everything back into the unnerving perspective that she was avoiding; just hours before she had pulled the bones of this woman's sister out of a muddy grave.

As Lee, Ben, and Sadie talked, Jane watched Lee, wondering if he deliberately set a stage for her to be able to release the pent up emotions and stress she brought with her to the Plaza. Her mind drifted back to the moments the night before, from her stressed arrival to the lighthearted moments she and Lee shared as they moved through the Plaza. First raiding the refrigerator in the kitchen, then letting off steam and tension in the gym and finally losing themselves in the fine bottle of wine.

She and Lee were able to distance themselves and deal with the grizzly work they were called to do the day before, but for this family, the day was a confusion of emotions and their ordeal was only beginning. Two Emersons were removed from the mountain the day before. Two missing Emerson children were found yesterday. One was known to be missing, the other wasn't. One was found alive and the other in a shallow grave in the woods, evidently killed by a man the family loved and trusted as one of their own.

"Is there any word about Richard," Sadie asked, raising the china cup to her lips and sipping the coffee.

"No," Lee said directly.

"How are we going to handle all this?" Sadie continued, leaning back in her chair and heaving a heavy sigh.

"You were wonderful on the news last night, Sadie," Lee told her. "We can handle the follow ups through my office now that the press has heard from one of the family. I would suggest you call in outside consultants on this one. The EI public relations department is wonderful handling the release of news concerning acquisitions, mergers, and grand openings, but this is a different matter and another type of PR."

"Agreed," Ben said readily. "The family doesn't need to have to deal with these matters in full public view. Have you got any recommendations?"

"I have," Lee assured him. "It's rather unorthodox but I really think we should bring in Chet Driscoll and his team."

"Never heard of him," Ben said with a shake of his head.

"His isn't a PR firm. They handle more complex matters of security. I think you will be pleased with what he can do for the company."

"Will you make the initial contact, Lee?" Sadie asked.

"I will."

"Douglas herded us into the family room to avoid an encounter with the FBI," Ben announced. "That would have been a disaster. What are we going to do? Jake need to make a statement as soon as possible."

"Where is he?" Sadie asked, glancing out of the window.

"He'll be along shortly," Lee spoke, glancing from Ben to Sadie. "He was told this meeting is to begin about ten o'clock."

"Oh?" Ben asked, his brows raised in question as his gaze shifted toward Jane.

"I wanted to have a few minutes with you before he got here," Lee admitted, heaving a heavy sigh and exhaling loudly. "We have to find a strategy that will serve justice and protect the family."

"What kind of strategy is there with this?" Sadie asked, unable to keep her emotions in check. "Holly is dead and Richard killed her."

"Of course Holly's death must be reported," Lee said evenly. "I just wanted to talk to you a moment about how we report it."

"You're not suggesting we protect Richard in this!" Ben almost bellowed.

"Not exactly," Lee said, turning to look at Jane.

"Not exactly?" Sadie repeated, shaking her head as she wiped her eyes with a tissue from the pocket of her morning coat, "then what exactly?"

"Jane has a suggestion that I think you two should consider," Lee said as he motioned for Jane to speak up.

"Well," Jane said, leaning forward and putting her crossed arms on the table in front of her, "it occurred to me that this isn't something that Richard hasn't had ample time to think through and have a contingency plan for. He got away with Holly's murder for four years by creating the illusion she was still alive."

"He just walked coolly out of the Plaza yesterday after the call about the discovery of the remains came in," Lee said evenly. "He didn't go by his apartment, he didn't go to his car, he just walked out of the back door of his office and then left the Plaza through the front door and hailed a cab with as much calm as he would if he had been stepping out for a bite to eat."

"He's not only cool," Jane said, looking at Lee and nodding, "but he's a planner. You can bet he's got a very well thought out escape."

"So, what are you proposing?" Sadie asked with a sigh, pushing a hand through the thick dark hair that was escaping the French knot at the nape of her neck.

"A controlled release of information designed to assist in the search without admitting there's been a crime," Jane said in a rush.

"What?" Sadie asked, her carefully plucked brows taking a dive toward each other over the bridge of her nose. Suddenly she reminded Jane so much of her father that Jane recoiled slightly.

"First," Lee stepped in to give Jane a moment to regain her composure, "before you report the discovery of Holly's death file a missing person's report on Richard. We should do everything we can within the law to keep his disappearance separate from Holly's death as long as we don't know where he is."

"Why?" Sadie asked, obviously more confused than before.

"It will take time to identify the remains," Jane said regaining her confidence in the idea that seemed crazy at first thought. "In the meantime you can use the circumstances to your advantage in the hunt for Richard."

"How?" Ben asked, leaning forward on the table and pressing his fingertips together.

"By Richard being a missing member of the family rather than a suspect in Holly's apparent murder. From what I saw on site yesterday, it is going to be impossible to bring him to trial. The evidence just isn't there. Offer a reward for information on his whereabouts and his safe return."

The silence that engulfed the room was total. Jane sat back in her chair, not sure how her suggestion would be received. "I know the gut reaction of all of us is to hunt Richard like the murderous animal he is, but Richard knows that too. He is too smart not to have carefully made provisions for his disappearance if this time ever came."

"Let the press and public hunt for him," Ben said with a slight laugh and admiring glance toward Jane.

"The Emerson name will drive the interest indefinitely," Jane continued with an almost whimsical shrug. "You can keep this story hot as long as it takes! The story is irresistible and will sell itself to every paper and magazine. Use the media's money and resources instead of the family's."

"As a suspect in Holly's murder he has rights and law enforcement has restraints," Lee added matter-of-factly repeating the logic Jane used the night before. "But, as the missing son-in-law of the Emerson family there will be no restrictions or suspicions about the methods of any search."

Sadie glanced toward Jane and then leveled her gaze on Lee. She was getting a second wind in the demand for her action on behalf of the family. She sighed heavily, lowering her gaze to the table.

"Deputy Adler, forgive me," Sadie said quietly, not looking at Jane.

"Mrs. Faraday," Jane said quickly, "forgive me for interrupting you but I need to make something very clear here. This is my day off, please, call me Jane. I am not at all here in any capacity related to the Stafford County Sheriff's Department. Please understand that. I could very well lose my job if this is repeated outside of this group. I can have no official capacity here whatsoever."

Sadie raised her eyes to meet Jane's honest gaze and then glanced at Lee. She caught some strange look in his eyes that she could not read but looked back at Jane as her mind worked through the information given and the suggestions made.

"Jane," Sadie finally spoke. "Welcome to our home, and please call me Sadie."

CHAPTER TWENTY~TWO

"Nicole!" Trevor said, trying to decide how he could begin to explain what he was thinking as he pulled Cameron from the river and went to ground. He reached for a roll of paper towels and pulled off more than needed to dry out the inside of the cup he washed for her and shook his head. "I wasn't thinking like that."

"You weren't thinking like that?" she mimicked him, propping her elbow on the table and leaning her head on her closed fist. "So, what were you thinking? I would like to meet this Navy SEAL everyone is buzzing about. Tell me – what were you thinking?"

Trevor inhaled deeply and turned away from her unflinching gaze to gather his thoughts. "I don't know that you would like him and I'm certain you would not understand him," Trevor said with a simple shrug.

"I think you-re wrong," Nicole said as she stared at him quietly. "I think I've at least earned the opportunity to be his friend."

He grabbed a tattered hot pad, folded it in half to compensate for the thread-bare spots and then pulled the pot from the stove, pouring coffee into both cups and setting the pot back on the burner, turning the gas off.

"Why didn't he tell us he had Cam," Nicole asked, taking the sugar bowl he handed her and staring for a moment at the clump of coffee stained sugar that had dried on the side of the spoon. She decided she didn't need sugar and handed it back to him.

"Someone tried to kill one of you, Nikki," Trevor replied, the pain and exhaustion that was wracking his body causing him to drop into the chair beside her at the table. "I heard a shot – I saw a car coming off the cliff – I saw a man falling from the car and I reacted as I was trained to react. I don't know if I can explain why. It's just who I am. I didn't know where the shot came from and I didn't know if one had anything to do with the other. I didn't know if the threat was gone or someone would be coming after us. I just knew I had to get both of us out of hostile territory and somewhere safe."

He leaned his head against the back of the old wooden chair. It wobbled under him and multiple colors could be seen in the scratches and scars on it. He closed his eyes and his legs stretched across the floor in front of her. She stared at the heavy boots, caked with the mud of the mountains and could feel the emotions that he was trying to conceal.

"Then they discovered the Jag in the narrows with a bullet in the tire. I learned you were safe at the Manor with the entire Emerson security team watching over you. Cam was at risk out there. I didn't know what was going on, Nikki," he said barely above a whisper. "There was just something in the air… there's always something in the air that you can just feel and smell… when an enemy is near."

She fell silent, absorbing his words as she stared into the coffee, blowing into it gently to cool it. She raised her eyes and looked at him, tears welling in the gray pools and slipping down her cheeks and she shook her head slightly as though to clear the images his words evoked in her mind. They were more than she could grasp in the context of her life experiences.

"You thought it could have been me," she said again, lowering her head as she sipped the hot coffee.

"That's not how thought happens under those circumstances," Trevor said, closing his eyes as he raised his arms and put them behind his head. "I wasn't thinking about who it was as much as what it was, Nikki," Trevor said with a heavy sigh. How could he possibly explain to a civilian all that was now so entrenched in him? "I just concentrated on keeping him alive, keeping him safe, and determining the level of the threat."

"I don't understand…" she said, shaking her head.

"I know," he agreed, "and I don't know that I can explain it. Even if I could, I don't know how you could understand."

They fell silent and Trevor pushed the memories of the cold water and Cameron's limp body in the struggle downriver to the safety of the bank. He knew that he was going to have to answer everyone's questions but at the moment he was still fighting his personal debriefing and decompressing from the dark moments on the mountain.

"You couldn't trust *me*?"

"It wasn't a matter of trusting or not trusting, Nikki," he said, lifting his head from his arms and leaning forward. "That's not what it's about out there. All I could do was keep him alive, treat his wounds, and keep him safe," Trevor said with a distant glance out the window across the room. He stared at the wood pile and the axe that was embedded into the huge stump used as a splitting block.

"One Vietnam vet – one of the ER doctors told me it was the most amazing field surgery that he had ever seen," Nicole said, smiling slightly at him and reaching out to punch his knee with an uncomfortable familiarity. They had shared a closeness she felt she had somehow betrayed and she wanted it back. She was feeling uncomfortable when she saw the look in his eyes and could not understand what it was she was seeing. "I guess it is one of those times I'd just have had to have been there, huh?"

She fell silent again, heaving another sigh and staring at him as he nodded, unable to look at her. He could feel her gaze and wished there was something he could say to make her understand. He glanced at her and shook his head.

"I don't know, Nikki," he said with a shrug. "That's all I can say. I can't explain what happened to me when I saw that car going into the river. I didn't even know it was Cam until I got him out of the river."

"You got him out of the river?" Nicole gasped, the gray eyes widening so large that he couldn't help but laugh at the expression on her face. Somewhere in the recesses of her mind where she had not yet gone to sort through her thoughts, she imaged him wandering up on an unconscious Cameron washed up on the riverbank somewhere. "How?"

"I just did," Trevor replied more sharply than he intended. "It was the mission at hand. It had to done, so I did it. Failure wasn't an option. It's about accomplishing the mission – no matter what."

Nicole saw the strange look that flashed across his eyes. Had she not been staring right at him she would have missed it. It was deep, it was sad, it was pain she realized she could not comprehend. She felt as though somehow she had seen something she had no right to see. She glanced away feeling a guilt she did not fully understand.

"Cam kept saying, 'I'd never seen him before,'" Nicole said, reaching out and deciding the strong brew needed sugar and ignoring the clump on the spoon. She leveled off a teaspoon and watched as the sugar crystals fell into her coffee and then swished her cup slightly to dissolve it.

"Everyone at the hospital who didn't know the facts think some crazed woodsman had him." Nicole commented softly, looking at him with a slight smile. The atmosphere was lighter and her comfort level with him was improving. Still, she was worried things would never be the same again.

"Some crazed woodsman did," Trevor said with a self-deprecating laugh. "You are looking at me like I've grown two heads."

She laughed abruptly and then fell silent again; knowing there were things he wasn't telling her and realizing there were things she was never going to know. She sipped at the coffee and then plunged on.

"When I came yesterday…" she said, setting her cup on the table and watching the dark liquid slosh gently as the table rocked between them on unlevel legs.

"Yeah?" Trevor replied, shaking his head with pursed lips, "About that…" He might as well get used to the questions because they were not going to stop any time soon.

"You knocked me out!" she said accusingly.

"Yeah, I did," he said, reaching behind him to the counter and grabbing something. As he slammed the now sheathed knife on the table, sending the unsteady legs into a rocking frenzy beneath then, causing the remaining coffee in her cup to slosh over the rim, he crossed his arms in front of him and met her stunned gaze. "When I saw you creeping across the room with that in your hand, what did you think I would do?"

"You *did* think I was trying to kill him!" Nicole accused, raising her large eyes from the knife to him.

"The thought crossed my mind," Trevor admitted with a laugh. "And what would you have thought if you saw me stalking across a room toward where you knew Cam lay helpless with this?" he asked her as he pulled the knife from its sheath and the sun caught the metal.

She gasped, realizing for the first time what she must have looked like to an exhausted, on edge trained SEAL. She raised her eyes to his and began to giggle. Trevor raised his eyes from the knife to her and began to laugh too. When Nicole realized Trevor was also laughing, her giggling grew into full blown laughter.

She laughed until tears were in her eyes and rolling down her cheeks. She took the paper tower roll he handed her and looked at it, finding only more humor in it as she pulled some off and covered her face. Her laughter was the catalyst to release the pent up emotion in them both.

Nicole would catch her breath and think she was regaining her composure, only to feel the giggles bubbling up in her and would then begin to laugh again. Trevor would stop and then her contagious laughter would start his up again.

She covered her eyes with her hands and laughed and then lowered her head to the table, her entire body shaking with the uncontrollable laughter. By the time they were able to reign in the overwhelming emotions and exhaustion, Nicole leaned back in her chair, breathing deeply and stared at him.

"You saved his life," she said between the gasps trying to regain her breath.

"That's what we do, Ma'am," Trevor said with a mock salute and leaned back in his chair. "Mission accomplished."

"He almost died, Trevor," she whispered, her emotions swinging in an arc so wide Trevor didn't see it coming. "Holly is dead! Dear God, I trusted Richard! He was the best friend I had in that house and he killed his wife and tried to kill me!"

As suddenly as the laughter had come, the tears flooded through her. She was sobbing uncontrollably as he stood up, pulled her into his arms and held her tightly.

"I know, Nikki," he said, stroking her hair and trying to calm her. "I know." When she seemed unable to regain her composure he held her at arm's length and shook her gently. "It's going to be okay. It *is* okay now. You can calm down, everyone is safe."

"Are we okay, Trev?" she asked, leaning back to look into his eyes. "You and I? Are we okay?"

"We're okay," Trevor promised her, patting her back again and then pushing her gently out of his way.

He sank onto the stool and pulled off the heavy hiking boots and carried them to the front room, dropping them on the floor beneath the table holding his test kit. As he did, some of the dried mud fell off onto the floor surrounding them. He grabbed a pair of sneakers and put them on, tying the strings with a harsh jerk.

"Come on," he said, taking her hand and leading her toward the door and then off the front porch, "We'll run back to the Manor. That should help get you under control."

"You've got to be kidding me," Nicole sobbed, wiping the tears from her eyes with the back of her hands. "I'm pregnant."

"Then we will walk quickly. I'm really not kidding," Trevor said, heading off through the woods, leading the way along the trail that would carry them back to the Manor. "You'll be exhausted and you'll be able to rest. I promise," he called over his shoulder. Besides, he thought to himself as he glanced at her to make sure she followed him at a struggling but steady pace and adjusting his pace to hers, "I've got some 'splaining to do."

◈

The sun was just topping the crest of the mountains as Nicole and Trevor reached the back gardens and slowed their pace to a cool down walk. Trevor was right. The physical exertion of the slow jog through the mountain trails both exhausted and exhilarated her. As they entered the formal gardens she took the lead and headed toward the back wing. As she paused at the back door she leaned over a moment, hands on her knees, and took several deep breaths.

The playroom was still shuttered as she entered, causing her to stop in her path towards the bed and instead, begin to raise the shades to allow the morning light to flood into the room. The day nurse appeared in the hallway from the bedroom, obvious alarm in her face.

"I'm Nicole, Cameron's wife," she announced softly, offering the older woman her hand.

"I'm Lorie," the uniformed woman said glancing over her shoulder in concern as Trevor moved toward the bed.

"It's okay, Lorie," Nicole said, pressing a gentle hand to the nurse's arm. "He's family. How is Cam?"

"Stable and resting," Lorie was quick with a professional response.

"He's about to be better," Nicole smiled, patting the woman's shoulder. She could see the edge of a house tray she was familiar with. She knew that Riva and Douglas would be ever present to meet any need. "Finish your breakfast."

Hesitantly, Lorie glanced over her shoulder and then back at her patient. When she saw Cameron stir and then reach for Trevor's arm in a brotherly grip she returned to the room that had been assigned to the nurses.

Nicole moved around the bed to stand on the other side. Cameron's color was better this morning and as she approached he raised the broken arm slightly to caress her lowered cheek. The swelling in his face was going down even though the bruises over his body seemed to be getting blacker. She was warned at the hospital that he was going to look worse than he felt for some time to come.

There was little to be said as the three stood silently together. Cameron began to drift back into his drugged sleep and as Nicole stepped away from the bed Trevor followed her. Once they were out of the playroom and headed toward the front of the house Trevor felt the sickening feeling in the pit of his stomach. As they reached the family room the door opened and he turned to see Douglas.

"Mr. Trevor!" Douglas said, and Nicole and Trevor were both surprised as tears spring into his eyes as his emotions overwhelmed him. Douglas paused for a moment, clearly uncertain of his next words or actions. Finally Nicole watched as Douglas made a concerted effort to regain his composure and nodded formally toward them both, but could not restrain himself from embracing Trevor.

"The family is in the study with Lee and Deputy Adler," he finally managed before stepping quickly out of the hallway.

"You're his hero," Nicole stood on tiptoe to whisper into Trevor's ear.

"I hope others feel the same way," Trevor replied with a slow shake of his head as they turned toward the foyer.

"It's going to be fine, Trev," she assured him as they reached the grand staircase. As she headed toward her suite to change clothes Trevor took several deep breaths and walked down the hallway toward the study.

He was stunned to see Douglas standing at the study door as he approached. As he neared him, Douglas looked over Trevor's shoulder down the hallway and then behind him toward the kitchen and then clasped Trevor's shoulder with an affectionate grip again, offering him his hand.

"Thank you, sir," Douglas said so quietly Trevor could barely hear him. Again he saw the gleam of tears in his eyes. Trevor could only nod and then shrug, feeling a lump in his own throat at the emotion in this pillar of protocol.

As he entered the study he tried to size up the room as quickly as possible. He wasn't sure who would be waiting for him but only Ben Faraday and Lee Malcolm were in the room. Ben was standing at the window behind the desk and Lee was sitting in the leather winged back chair. As the door closed behind him Ben nodded to him and then lowered himself into Gregory's chair as Lee motioned for Trevor to take a seat beside the desk. Trevor glanced at the two men for the briefest moment before drawing in a deep breath and dropping into the leather chair that flanked the sofa.

"Gregory has suggested I represent you unless you have someone else you would prefer," Ben said evenly, meeting Trevor's eyes with a calm reassuring smile when Trevor shook his head.

"No, I don't have anyone else to call," Trevor said with a shrug of his shoulders. If the Emersons decided he was the enemy, it didn't matter who his attorney was.

Ben pulled the top few pages off the legal pad that Richard left on top of the desk and then looked up at Trevor.

"Now, just take a breath, relax, and tell us what happened," Ben continued in the calm, comforting tone that was one of his greatest assets.

જ∽∽જ

Silence fell around the three men. Trevor seemed to be in a trance as he opened his eyes and looked from Ben to Lee. He blinked slightly, looking from one of them to the other, wondering what he should do next. Ben and Lee exchanged glances and Ben tapped the legal pad in front of him watching as Lee's brows creased over his eyes as he studying Ben's face.

They heard the voices of Jake, Jane, and Sandy in the hallway as Douglas led them into the formal salon. As Ben picked up the tape recorder from the desk and pressed the button to conclude their session, Lee realized he was right to tape it. There would never be a telling like this first telling of what had happened on the river.

"Now what?" Trevor asked, not sure how the men were reacting to him.

"I would like your permission to share this with the family, Sheriff Clairborne, and Deputies Adler and Wade." Ben said lifting the cassette tape from the recorder and holding it up. "We have a strategy we feel is best."

"I guess so," Trevor sighed as he glanced again from Ben to Lee. "I just hope they understand…"

"They'll understand," Lee sighed quietly.

Ben found it difficult to look away from Trevor and his unassuming courage. Lee stood and the warning in Chet Driscoll's words not to underestimate Trevor Cantrell rang in his mind. He wondered what was omitted from Trevor's classified military records.

"Today?" Trevor asked resolutely. "I've gotten behind quite a bit in my testing. I'll lose my place in the master's program…"

"Not today," Ben decided, pulling open the desk drawer and setting his note pad inside and pushing it closed with his knee.

"Thank you, sir," Trevor said as his eyes moved to stare out over the mountains. Lee was conscious of the change in his expression and wondered again where he had been and what he had experienced.

"Can Trevor and I have the room a minute?" Ben asked turning his gaze on Lee.

"Sure," Lee answered, crossing the room with a swagger that was not lost on Trevor. It was distinctive and instantly recognizable between special ops. As the door closed behind Lee, Trevor inhaled deeply and slowly let it out. Army Ranger. They had to show it off.

"Coffee?" Ben asked. He left the desk and moved to the cart holding the urn. There was an empty cup in his hand and he was looking at Trevor with raised brows in question.

"Ah, yeah," Trevor said, heaving a heavy sigh and leaning back more relaxed in his chair. "Black."

There was silence between them as Ben filled a heavy mug with the still steaming coffee and carried it to him.

"There was apparently a call from the Oak Meadow area," Ben said, as he moved back to the desk, picked up his cup and refilled it from the urn. "It's the one thing the FBI won't let go of, Trevor. Do you know anything about it?"

He turned to level his gaze on Trevor and then settled his long, lean body in the chair beside him. The mood of the room was relaxed, nonthreatening. He saw the look that flashed into Trevor's eyes and the shield that dropped into place.

"Jake's department won't be a problem there, but the FBI is another matter," Ben said sipping at his coffee. "You may not know but it was that call that prompted them to insert themselves into the matter. When that call came into the tip, they interpreted it to mean someone might have kidnapped Cameron and was going to call back for ransom. They've been left with a good bit of egg on their faces and they have already been here this morning."

"I know," Trevor said with a short sideways jerk of his head. "That they were here. I saw them on the Trail earlier. I didn't know it was about any call."

"It wouldn't be a big thing," Ben said, setting his cup on the table between them and linking his fingers together over his chest as his gaze returned to Trevor, "except it came into Gregory's office on a dedicated, encrypted line. Do you know the private number into Cameron's office?"

Trevor's gaze did not shift or lower from his which told Ben more than a verbal denial. He could see Trevor's intense, steady gaze and smiled slightly. "I will take your silence as a yes," Ben said evenly. "I am not going to ask you if you made that call."

He saw the slightest change in Trevor's gaze as the mug was lifted to his lips and Trevor's gaze lowered to the black brew in it. He was a very well trained operative Ben realized. He had done a stint in JAG during his tour in the Air Force and knew that look.

"I'm sure the FBI will," Trevor commented off handedly.

"Why do you think such a call would have been made?" he asked changing the tactic of questioning his client, reaching again for his cup.

Trevor was silent a moment staring at nothing in particular and shaping his answer carefully. He drained his cup. There was a rather lengthy silence as Trevor considered his words. Finally he raised his gaze back to Ben and inhaled deeply.

"With a search and rescue team like the one around here and given the fact they have a dedication to their service as well as a devotion to this family, some of them might be inclined to disregard their own safety and ignore the high winds and the threats of the flooding river to resume the search. I would think someone might not want that to happen if there was no need to resume a search."

"I see," Ben said quietly, nodding his head. "Well, we will need to deal with the FBI. I will give the matter some thought and you should take care that you are not especially easy to find for the next few days while I am thinking."

"I have days of collected samples to test and log," he said with a note of dread in his voice. "It will take me some time to catch up. I'll be around the cabin until it's all done."

"Will you be adding to that collection?"

"I have to maintain the schedule or I will lose my place in the master's program," Trevor stated evenly.

"I can speak to Dr. Richmond," Ben said quietly. "I would think some consideration could be given…"

"*I* can speak to Dr. Richmond," Trevor said with an irritated sigh. "That doesn't alter the need for continuity in the sample collections. The spring rains have already started."

"I understand," Ben said quickly, reaching out to place a calming hand on his wrist. "We can work something out. Just give it some thought. You have a map?"

"Sort of," Trevor answered with a touch of defensiveness in his voice. "I still have to plot it out for the final submission."

"I understand," Ben answered. "Is it complete enough for Emit or Eric to be able to follow for a day or so?"

"I should be able to get away with an abbreviated route for a day or so," Trevor admitted after a moment's consideration.

"Then you will be able to stay close to the cabin?"

"I can," Trevor agreed.

"How would someone make such a call?" Ben asked him without warning. "That call to the tip line?"

There was another long moment's silence as Trevor glanced away from him. He shook his head slightly and then inhaled sharply, letting his breath out in a deep sigh.

"If you had to take a guess," Ben asked calmly.

"I might *could* answer that," Trevor finally said shaking his head, "but it would be considered a breach of National Security in some circles if I did."

"And a court marshal offense in others?" Ben asked. "I did a stint in JAG."

"Then you understand," Trevor sigh in relief.

"Let me think about that for a while as well, then," Ben said, uncrossing his legs and standing up. He took the empty cup from Trevor and turned to carry it to the cart. "It's going to be okay, Trevor," he said, turning back to offer his hand to him.

"Thank you, sir," Trevor said as he stood and shook Ben's hand. He looked about the room as though something should be different and then met Ben's calm, steady gaze again.

"I would think there are some questions the FBI would not know to ask," Trevor finally said, glancing away from Ben and then back to meet his gaze. "Sometimes, equipment is – ah – lost on missions…"

"I see," Ben said, nodding slightly. "I don't need to know anything about what you think might have happened and neither does the FBI. What they know and what they may be able to guess are two different things. Stick with what they know."

"Yes sir," Trevor said evenly.

"I don't have to tell you how grateful we, as the family, are for your actions. You can rest assured that we will stand to protect you. Gregory and Helena asked me to express to you their eternal gratitude for what you have done. They are eager to see you themselves when things have settled down around here and you have time."

"What about Richard?" Trevor asked, and Ben saw the unguarded look in his eyes. The last thing they needed right now was a rogue SEAL on a self appointed mission.

"Nowhere to be found at the moment," Ben said evenly. "I want you to not concern yourself with Richard. I have accepted what you have told me this morning and you can trust me with it. I need to accept that you can trust me that this matter with Richard is being handled. I ask that you be as discrete about Richard's involvement and the discovery in the glade as I will be whatever lost equipment may have been used to make a call to the tip line."

Trevor starred at Ben for a moment realizing that it was a promise as well as a warning. The Emerson family could be as formidable an enemy as they could be a lifelong ally. He nodded slightly and turned toward the door.

"Trevor," Ben said quietly.

"Yes sir?" Trevor paused to turn back to him.

"Just think of this all as your debriefing. Everyone is on your side here – the family - Sheriff Clairborne and the deputies who were at the glade yesterday. They just need to know what happened."

"Yes sir," Trevor muttered. "Thank you, sir."

"Just don't be surprised by anything you might hear on the news in the next few days," Ben commented off handedly. "You might want to leave through the courtyard," Ben reached for the pull cord that opened the heavy drapes hanging over the French doors. "And if you have anything that needs to be kept private…"

"*HUA*," Trevor said, turning the knob in his hand and feeling the chill of the morning rush into the room.

"Sheriff," Lee said, offering a firm hand shake as Jake entered the library with Sandy. "Deputy Wade," he nodded, turning toward Sandy.

"Malcolm," Sandy nodded, spotting Jane on the sofa behind him. "Janie?" he called, lifting his hand in greeting. "I thought this was your day off."

"It is," Jane said easily, not moving from the comfort of the sofa cushions.

"I asked Jane to be here," Lee said, crossing the room to the table and returning to his seat.

"Ben is going to represent Trevor Cantrell in this matter," Lee informed them. "I know you will have questions and you can contact Ben about a time to meet with his client. "Were you paid a call by the FBI on their way down the mountain?"

"We were," Jake said with a gruff, dismissive laugh as he inspected the tray and picked up a plate. "Is there coffee?"

"In the urn," Lee said, tapping the stack of papers into a neat pile and jerking his head to the cart near the pantry entrance to the room.

He shot a quick glance at Jane and then left the room. Jane inhaled deeply and leaned her head back on the cushions. She knew the first interrogation of the day was about to come from Sandy and it wasn't going to be about Trevor Cantrell.

She was relieved beyond measure as the door opened and Gregory, Emit, and Garret walked into the room. She sat up straight and began formulating her explanation of her presence out of uniform as Gregory and Garret greeted first Jake, then Sandy and turned to her. If her slacks and blouse were even noticed, the entrance of Helena, Kyle, Andrea and Sadie prevented any mention of it.

"We just want to express our appreciation of all the respect and consideration shown to us as you retrieved Holly's remains from the mountain," Gregory said solemnly as he crossed the room and stood before the crackling fire.

Helena and Sadie joined Jane on the sofa, Helena smiled softly and patted her hand and Sadie offered hers in a firm hand shake.

"Mrs. Emerson, Mrs. Faraday," Jane said, standing up and greeting them formally. Suddenly she wished she had the security her uniform offered. She felt the need to explain her casual attire but knew that would only make things more awkward at this point.

"Please," Helena said with a slight raising of her brows as she reached for Jane's hand. "Please, sit here beside me," she said, patting the sofa.

Jane licked her lips self consciously and then lowered herself back down on the sofa. She glanced at the bottled water in her hand and as inconspicuously as possible, set it on the floor beside the sofa leg.

"We need to make a statement, sir," Jake said quietly. "The FBI agents were in my office this morning wanting answers to questions I don't have. We can't put them – or the press for that matter – off much longer."

"I understand," Gregory said, glancing at Garret who stepped forward and took the room.

"We will, of course, have a further statement," Garret began.

Ben entered the room followed by Lee and Nicole. Lee ushered her across the room to a chair beside the window that looked out over the east lawn as Ben moved to the opposite end of the table and pulled the tape recorder from his pocket.

"Before anything else is decided or done," Ben said as Garret settled himself into the chair at the head of the table, "I want you to listen to this."

There was a distinctive click in the room that caught the attention of them all. From her vantage point, Jane saw Nicole glanced out of the window, but as Trevor's voice filled the room, she paused, turned and leveled her gaze on the recorder.

As the tape began to move over the heads of the player, Trevor's voice eerily filled the room. As she listened, she remembered the look on his face earlier at the cabin and realized that what she saw in his eyes was the horror of remembering what he lived through and what they were all learning now.

As with Ben and Lee, Trevor's words floating from the whirring tape seemed to strangely transported everyone in the room to the moments along the river a little more than forty-eight hours before. Nicole closed her eyes and leaned her head against the back of the tall chair.

"I heard the shot but didn't pay much attention to it at first," Trevor's voice filled the room around them. "But then I heard the tires screeching and knew there was a problem..."

As the words swirled around them the room seemed to fade away. In their own ways and through Trevor's words, they all could see, smell, and feel what he experienced. They could see him in their mind's eyes making his way along the trail, hearing the sounds of the sniper's bullet – but unlike him at that time – knowing the end of the story.

Ben's quiet questioning was lost in Trevor's recounting of the rescue of Cameron. Although his questions moved the testimony along, Trevor's voice was the only one they really heard as Ben skillfully guided him through the last two days.

Trevor heard the screeching of metal ripping against something else as he made his perilous way along a deer trail, half running – half sliding down the mountain. The seconds it took him to stumble and slip to the river's edge seemed much longer than the few seconds that actually passed. He grabbed for the trunk of a thin tree, praying it would hold his weight. As he was jerked to an abrupt halt there was another unmistakable sound of metal against metal and then total silence.

He held tight to the sapling and leaned out over the river staring upstream in the direction of the sound. His mouth fell open as he saw a car chassis appear over the river. He watched silently as the car sailed out over the water with the driver's door hanging open and someone fell from the car.

The impact as the car hit the river was louder than the rifle shot and without conscious thought as to what he was going to do, he threw off his parka and rushed into the river, stepping off the bank and relieved he went under without hitting any underwater hazard. He surfaced, shaking off the shock of the cold water.

He swam against the current toward the lifeless figure that resurfaced behind the now floating car. He watched as the current of the river caught the open door of the Jag and spun it like a top in slow motion. The twisted front door swung closed as the car turned against the flow of the current. His eyes moved back and forth between the car and the body. It was also floating in his direction and thankfully on his side of the river.

He continued to tread water as the river brought the driver towards him. He positioned himself to the best advantage and waited. By the time the car reached him, it was halfway submerged. He could see the mangled passenger side and realized the first commotion he heard was the car sideswiping the rock face along Sutter Trail. He swam into the path of the body, treading water against the current to maintain his position. He knew he would not be able to fight the powerful current long so he waited until the last moment before moving toward the middle of the river.

He was knocked under by the body as he grabbed hold of an arm. By the strange give, he realized it was broken. Within a few seconds he shifted himself and the body, flipping it over and hefting it out of the water and against his chest, letting the river carry them both downstream while he consider the circumstance now. His eyes moved over the river bank as he tried to orient himself. He knew he had to get out of the river before it carried them to the rapids. He also knew someone was higher on the mountain with a sniper's rifle.

He maneuvered the body into rescue position and then began moving strategically toward the riverbank. His feet hit rock and began feeling for anything solid. His legs hit against sharp rocks underwater but he was unable to find a foothold to stop his downstream rush. As he glanced over his shoulder and spotted a tree trunk protruding from the river, he tightened his grip on his rescue and began an all out effort to free them both from the river's current and propel them into the outer calms directly toward the submerged trunk.

The collision into the trunk was as painful as he expected it would be but it stopped his downriver rush. As he slammed into the branches he felt them breaking and stabbing into his back. He grabbed hold of one of the branches and it to shift the weight of the body from himself.

He shifted, realizing his heavy shirt was not torn but his back was cut and scratched through it. He then paused to take several breaths, calming his senses and waiting for the adrenaline kick he knew was coming.

He felt the rush and began pulling them both away from the midst of the tree limbs and toward the shore. He felt a sharp pain as his shin hit a rock and he kicked tentatively forward. Using the tree as support he managed to make his way to the shore.

Once out of the pull of the river's current and secure in the make-shift harbor of the tree's shelter, he looked down at the body. Cameron floated lifelessly in front of him and the nausea that overcame him was replaced as quickly with the taste of adrenaline as it rushed through him again, giving him the strength he learned how to tap into during his SEAL missions.

He pushed Cameron toward the shore, using the buoyancy of the water to support him and the branches of the trees to leverage himself away from the massive trunk. He hefted Cam onto the bank and then climbed out over him. Once on dry land, he began accessing Cameron's injuries. He checked his pulse and then sighed deeply. It was slow and thready but he had seen worse.

He stood up, breathing in deep gulps of air and then walked a few feet along the bank, shaking out the revolt of his now cramping muscles and trying to get an idea of where they were and what to do next. He stared downstream but could see nothing of the car. The river had sucked it under and along with it the answers to questions that were whirling through his mind. Somewhere in the back of his mind the shot he heard and this moment connected. He scanned the mountains across the river, looking for any telltale reflection from a scope or movement among the trees.

He returned to Cameron and realized he needed to get him to shelter. They would both suffer quickly from hyperthermia. With the skills he learned during training and experiences in far away and hostile lands his hands moved over Cameron's body. He was dealing with numerous broken ribs but Cameron's steady if shallow breathing assured him there were no punctures to the lungs; a broken left tibia and right radius were evident along with some degree of concussion and possibly some internal injuries.

He unsnapped the sheath on his belt and pulled his knife out, using it to rip Cameron's suit pants' leg up to mid-calf. He pulled two limbs from the felled tree that had been their safety net out of the river and shaved the rough bark off with his knife. The saturated limbs were pliable enough to shape around the calf. Trevor then loosened the soaked silk tie from around Cam's neck and used it to wrap around the limbs, shaping them against the leg as a splint.

Trevor took off his belt and slipped it under Cam's arms before pulling him into a sitting position against the tree trunk; the deep, guttural protesting moans were a welcome sound. Cameron was semiconscious. He checked his pupils again, relieved that they were the same size and contracted slightly as he pulled the eyelids open.

Leaning Cameron forward, he pulled his knife and slit open the suit coat along the back seam, put the knife in his teeth and then pulled it off each arm in two pieces. Blood was seeping through his shirt and he unbuttoned it slightly to inspect the deep scrap on his shoulder. It was bloody by not serious. He ignored the burning pain from the injuries on his back. He pulled his knife from his teeth, slitting open his sodden jeans legs to reveal the jagged, bloody gashes along his shins. With practiced skill, he ripped the denim material into strips, wringing out the water and tying them securely around his bleeding legs.

Trevor sank down onto the ground and leaned against the tree trunk beside Cameron as he ripped the fine Italian silk jacket into shreds and began tying the strips together. He heaved a heavy sigh as he scoped out his surroundings. He didn't know where he was, but he knew he had to get both of them away from the river. Someone was going to come looking for Cameron and Trevor had no idea who would be friend and who would be foe.

He found another sturdy limb and used the coat strips to cushion and splint Cam's broken arm. With another deep sigh he pulled Cam's belt out of his pants waistband and using it with his own, buckled the two together. He tethered them under Cam's arms and then hefted him over his shoulder. The low, animal like moan that escaped from him was another good sign. Cameron was in pain and in moments like this, pain was a sign of life. All things were relative, Trevor learned in those far away and hostile lands.

Seconds seemed like minutes and minutes seemed like hours as Trevor carried his buddy's dead weight along the trail. He headed upstream, keeping his eye out for an animal trails that he could follow. The trek through the rough undergrowth was both taxing and painful. Experience taught him that the beasts anywhere around the globe were the best guides. He found what he was looking for and paused for a moment before he pulled himself and dragged Cam up the riverbank by using roots and bushes, listening to Cameron's uncontrollable moaning and unconsciously humming along as at this time – in this moment - it was the music of life.

He knew Cam could endure more pain than he would ever image. His training taught him that he could do more than he thought humanly possible. Through the combination of who he was born to be and who the SEALs trained him to become he would be able to handle the mission this had become; get Cameron to safety and keep him from whatever enemy was near.

He did not think much farther than the next step, the next hurdle up the mountain or the next breath that was now burning his lungs. His shirt was sticking to the bloody wounds on his back and refusing to allow them dry and scab over. He pushed the pain from his mind and just moved determinedly away from hostile territory and toward safety.

He stopped periodically to check Cam's pulse and heart rate as well as to listen to the forest around them. Bruising was beginning to show. It took Trevor almost half an hour to get Cameron from the river's edge up the embankment to a point where he was just trekking along the deer path on the mountain.

Half an hour later he intercepted another trail. He began to spot landmarks and realized he had reached his test area and he made his way toward the side trail where he dropped his gear. He left Cam on the trail and plunged down the embankment, locating his rifle, test case, and back pack and climbed back to the trail to discover Cam coming too, moaning deeply.

"Easy friend," Trevor said, dropping down to his knee beside him, "You're hurt. I've done all I can for the moment but you are going to be safe, do you hear me? You are going to hurt like hell but I am going to keep you safe." As he spoke, he moved his hands over Cameron's abdomen, checking as best he could for signs of internal injuries.

Cameron was beginning to show signs of the impact. His eyes were swollen almost closed and bruises were appearing over his body. His arm and leg were swelling. Trevor reached for his test case and pulled a small flashlight from it. "Look at me, Cam," he ordered, grabbing him under his chin and shaking his head slightly. "I'm sure you've got some concussion, while you still can, open those baby blues and look at me."

Cameron did his best and Trevor pulled back his eyelids, shining the beam into each one. The pupils were still the same size and responding to his light. He clicked off the flashlight and returned it to his bag.

"Follow my hand," Trevor said as he moved his fingers from side to side and watched Cam closely. Cam was a little slow to respond to him but he was able to when Trevor repeated his command.

"What happened?" Cameron asked and caught his breath sharply.

"You took that turn on Sutter Trail a little too fast and wound up in the river," Trevor said, watching his reaction closely. "Don't you remember?"

"No," Cam whispered, the exertion becoming too much for him.

"What do you remember?" Trevor asked as he shrugged out of his soaked clothes and didn't even cringe when the shirt pulled drying blood off his back and the searing pain washed over him.

He pulled on a pair of jogging pants and sweat shirt he carried in his backpack. The soft fleece of the shirt was relief to his back. He wrapped the wet shirt around Cam's arm and then secured the wet jeans around the leg as cushions.

"I don't remember," Cameron responded slowly.

"We're going to get you out of here," Trevor said quietly, looking around. There was a sniper in the woods and his urgency was pumping adrenaline through him. He stooped once again beside Cameron. "You need to try to stay awake, Cam," he said, checking the bindings around the splinted leg and arm. "You're right leg and left arm and a couple of ribs are broken, you need to stay awake for a half hour or so now. Can you do that?"

"I can do that," Cam repeated, trying to look at Trevor through the now blackening eyes.

"We don't need to attract the attention to our handicaps here," Trevor said, looking around purposefully. "We don't need to have to face down any curious bears or hostile creatures, do we?"

"No bears," Cameron responded. "No creatures."

"So we move as quietly as we can."

"Quietly," Cameron agreed.

Trevor pulled a limb of a bush close by and clipped it off with his knife. He shaved it clean of bark and then held it in front of Cameron. "When you feel like screaming... and I promise you that you will, bite down on this instead. Can you manage?"

"I'll manage," Cam resolved. He opened his mouth and reached for the stick with his right hand. Trevor handed it to him and was relieved to see he could put it in his mouth and his coordination was normal – a very good sign in light of possible concussion.

"I'm not going to try to get us back across the river right now," Trevor told him casually. "There's a storm moving in and I don't want to get caught in it. I know where there is a cave that will offer you temporary shelter. I have some field equipment that will prevent hypothermia. It's not much comfort but it's enough. In the mean time, your clothes should dry some on the way. Okay?"

"Okay," Cam agreed, watching as Trevor put his backpack on backwards. He watched as Trevor adjusted it below his chin and pulled the harness tight around to his back and snapping it closed. "It's going to be hell, isn't it?"

"More for you than for me," Trevor agreed, pulling Cam up and over his shoulders in one determined movement. The wounds to his back reopened. Cam groaned deeply again but he didn't allow it to carry very far.

※

As the tape played, Jake, Sandy, and Jane moved to a corner of the room away from the family and quietly pulled chairs from around the table. Each one began jotting down notes as Trevor's voice swirled in the room around them. Gregory took Jane's place on the sofa, pulling a sobbing Helena into his arms to comfort her. Kyle and Garret moved to the table where the tape recorder was playing, closer to the speaker and listened intently.

Emit moved across the room and stood at the window, looking out across the lawn and meadow to the mountains beyond. He'd known there was something Trevor was not telling him, but he had not dreamed it was the battle for Cameron's life it had been.

Nicole rose from her chair, leaning against the wall, silently gasping for breath and Sadie crossed the room to her and pulled her close, slipping her arm around her waist and helped her to the sofa beside her parents. Nicole was crying softly, covering her face with her hands with tears slipping unrestrained through her fingers.

"Wow," Garret breathed, not raising his eyes from the speaker as the tape whirred on, no recorded words left to hear. "Wow!"

"What?" Vanessa asked from the doorway, brought to a complete stop by the sight of those in the room.

Garret jerked his head to the doorway where she stood, looked from Sadie to Nicole and then his parents and just shook his head. Sadie laughed a short, nervous laugh and sank into the matching chair across from Nicole.

"I think you can scratch him off your list of suspects, Sandy," Jane whispered, tapping Trevor's name on his note pad and stifling a laugh at the irritated look he shot at her. She caught sight of the smile that split Emit's black beard and watched him as he stood staring out of the window, wishing she could read his thoughts.

Emit was watching Trevor as he made his way up the mountainside and slipping into the forests. He turned from the window and slipped out a door that Jane had not noticed before. Curiously, she got out of her chair and took his place at the window. She watched as he hurried across the meadow. She saw him raise his hand and then heard the slightest note of a whistle through the heavy leaded window. That was when she caught sight of Trevor, making his way along the far side of the upper meadow. Emit's whistle carried on the wind and the distant figure stopped and turned to look back down on the Manor.

Jake and Sandy exchanged glances and then turned back to Jane. After what they just heard they certainly needed time to rethink the interview they were planning to conduct. They also had to deal with the remains of Holly. Jake stood up and turned to Gregory, jerking his head slightly and moving toward the door. Gregory followed him out and then led the way to his study. Ben and Lee were deep in discussion at the conference table. They fell silent as Gregory and Jake entered the room.

"Gregory," Jake said, we need to make a decision about Holly's remains. I ran a check late last night and there is a missing person's report on Nate Caulder with the Boulder, Colorado PD."

"I see," Gregory said, dropping into a chair beside Lee and running a hand through his snow white hair. "Lee?"

"Sheriff," Lee said, leveling his gaze on Jake, "We would like to delay the announcement of Holly's death until the remains have been positively identifies and here is why," he said, launching into the plan that Jane had proposed and seeing both relief and admiration on the faces of both Gregory and Jake as he laid out the details.

CHAPTER TWENTY~THREE

When Jake entered the interrogation room Ben stood up and motioned for Trevor to stay seated. Terrance McNatt, Jack Stanley, and Cheryl Coolidge were seated on the opposite side of the table. There were legal pads in front of each one of them and Terrance was sitting in the middle. Connie was at the end of the table with both a steno pad and a tape recorder.

"Mr. Cantrell is prepared to make a statement now," Ben said, taking up a position just behind Trevor's chair.

Trevor hesitated only a moment. He was aware of Terrence McNatt placing a recorder on the table and pressing the record button. He took several deep breaths. Almost instantly Sandy placed a glass of water in front of him. He took a small sip, feeling the water trickle down the back of his throat.

"I was on the river day before yesterday and heard the rifle shot and saw the car come over the cliff," he said, looking directly at Jake.

"What were you doing on the river?" Jake asked, leaning forward and looking toward Connie to make sure her tape recorder was running too. The assault on Cameron was in his jurisdiction and he was determined not to let the investigation get out of hand.

"Just enjoying it," Trevor said with a laugh. "I had picked up a stream I'd never seen before and decided to follow it to the river. Sometimes I do that when I have extra time – just to get a lay of new terrain."

"Okay," Jake said with a nod, crossing his arms across his chest and leaning back in the chair. "Go on."

"I heard the shot and really didn't think a lot about it when it happened, but then I heard the squeal of the brakes and the car came through the guardrail. Almost over my head..." he said shaking his head as he remembered the incredulous sight. "I could only see the chassis and the open door, you know?"

"I do," Jake agreed.

"Could you tell the direction of the shot?" Agent McNatt asked after clearing his throat slightly to inject himself into the interrogation.

"No. I didn't really think much once I was in the river. I just reacted."

"Let the record show that Trevor Cantrell is an inactive Navy SEAL," Ben intoned quietly.

"I went in after the driver," Trevor resumed after a brief silence wasn't broken. "I don't really remember a lot," he said, meeting Ben's eyes with a sheepish grin. "I've tried to recall details but I just know the river was cold, the current was wicked, and it seemed to take me forever to get to him."

Trevor fell silent. Being evasive around brass was something the SEALs taught well. "I checked his injuries and they were pretty serious but nothing immediately life threatening. I guess it was then that the rifle shot and the car in the river connected in my mind and I started evasive tactics in case someone did shoot at the Jag and then saw me go in after him."

"Your SEAL training just kind of kicked in automatically?" Jake asked.

"Yes," Trevor said, running a hand through his unruly dark hair.

"Why didn't you get him medical help? Why conceal the fact he was alive and well?" McNatt asked when Trevor fell into silence again.

Trevor cast a quick glance at Ben and took a deep breath. He could hear the soft sound of the recorder as it caught every word spoken in the room. He thought for a moment and then chose his words carefully.

"He was alive," he finally answered, looking evenly at the agent, "but he was far from well... or safe for all I knew. It was hard getting him out of the river and to a safe place before the storm."

"Do you realize the manpower that was extended in that search and rescue?" Jake asked with the expected seriousness.

"Yes sir," Trevor sighed and nodded his head. "But that car had to be brought out of the river to know what happen. That would have been done even if Cam had walked away unharmed."

"And yesterday morning, when you thought the rescue squad would resume the search, did you place a ransom call to Mr. Emerson's secretary, Joan?" Terrence McNatt asked in a careful monotone.

"No sir," Trevor said with an emphatic shake of his head. "I never made a ransom call to the Plaza."

"So it wasn't a ransom call," Jack Stanley said, leaning aggressively across the table towards Trevor. "But you did call Gregory Emerson's office from a phone in Oak Meadow and inform his secretary that you had Cameron to delay the search and give you more time."

"No," Trevor said with a slight laugh and another push of his hand through the dark curls. "I didn't make such a call from Oak Meadow."

"Did you use a cell phone?" Stanley followed up.

"I don't have a cell phone," Trevor answered honestly, his irritation becoming more evident.

"I don't believe you didn't make the call," Terrance said, leaning back in his chair.

"What you believe or don't believe isn't my concern, sir," Trevor said leveling a gaze on the agent.

Suddenly, everyone in the room saw the man no one had seen before. Everyone in the room could hear Trevor's deep breath as he shook his head slightly and then stood up.

"That's my complete statement," he said, moving toward the door. "If you have any more questions, then submit them to my attorney in writing."

Ben leaned back in his chair and locked his hands together. Terrance McNatt rewound the audiotape as he was slipping it into his coat pocket. Jake and Sandy exchanged glances and then waited for Terrance to say something. He was the only one who might be inclined to pursue this but Ben was pretty sure that he could not take the chance of being wrong again.

McNatt cleared his throat and then leveled his gaze on Ben. "There are several indictable offenses here, Mr. Faraday," he said, leaning back in his chair and drawing in a deep breath. His words brought Trevor to a halt at the door.

Ben straightened up and braced himself in for the first battle. "What charges would those be?" he asked quietly.

"Obstruction of justice for starters," McNatt almost snarled. "Then there's tampering with evidence … I believe I could make a case for kidnapping and extortion… Cameron Emerson was not in any condition to consent to being kept from his family and allowing them to believe he was dead…"

"I can assure you that not only would Cameron disagree with you there, Agent McNatt," Ben said and Trevor was surprised his tone had not changed with the expression on his face. "Trevor, I know you have things you need to attend to. We are through here. You go on and take care of your business."

The room fell silent and Jane watched as Trevor hesitated only a moment. She could see in his stance and expression he wanted nothing more than to take on the Special Agent in Charge one on one. She glanced at Sandy and saw the almost wicked smiled flickering around the corners of his mouth. For a moment, even McNatt seemed a little nonplused.

"There was no tampering of evidence," Ben continued as Trevor closed the door behind him and Ben reached for the pad and pen from his brief case, "he actually led the investigators to suspect there may have been a crime if my understanding of all this is correct. Had he not been there, I believe this might have been assumed to be an accident. What do you think, Sheriff?"

Jake drew in a deep breath and did not look at McNatt as he nodded slightly. "He was also the one who drew our attention to the missing bolts in the guardrail," he added with a nod. "He and Emit located the ambush site… this doesn't appear to meet the level of kidnapping to me. As soon as there was the opportunity to bring Cam safely out of the mountains, Cantrell jumped on it."

"There is our defense on any obstruction allegations," Ben said, looking candidly at the FBI agent. "And, extortion? I understand that Joan said from the beginning there was no demand for money and never thought it was Trevor and she is very familiar with his voice. She is prepared to testify that she informed you all of that fact as soon as you walked through her door. She told you repeatedly that she didn't recognize the voice."

"Your wife called us in," McNatt almost spat across the room at Ben.

"She did. She did report the call," Ben said, nodding slowly as he made careful notes on his pad. "She also recalls that not once did she call it a ransom call. That classification was yours, Agent, from the moment you heard an anonymous call on the tip line. You were the ones who connected those dots ."

McNatt drew in a deep breath and was about to say something when Jake's deep resonant voice filled the room.

"The boy has the heart of a warrior," he said quietly. "You aren't going to find anyone around here who'll appreciate this attitude from the F-B-I." His pause between each letter clearly conveyed his contempt for the Special Agent in Charge.

"What?" McNatt asked, obviously on the verge of laughing out loud at the small town sheriff.

"Ever been in combat, Agent McNatt?" Jake continued.

"I don't see any relevance…" Terrence began but was cut off by Jake.

"The young man is a warrior," Jake repeated, locking his intense eyes onto McNatt. "You think you could've gotten Cameron out of that river and do what he did? If you do, then you're a better man then I." Jake didn't blink as the deep flush rushed from McNatt's collar and into his face.

Jack Stanley started to speak but thought better of it and Cheryl Coolidge lowered her head. Jake sat perfectly still, staring unblinking at the agent.

"We don't need the cooperation of the Oak Meadow Sherriff's department to conduct an investigation," McNatt announced.

"You sure 'bout that?" Jake asked quietly. "You have agents you can call in who know these mountains well enough to get you in and out without assistance? Don't think you're going to find the Stafford County Rescue squad all that accommodating to you."

"Agent McNatt," Ben said, standing up and taking a step between Jake and McNatt. "I need to ask you a question."

There was silence in the room again as Ben waited to have McNatt's attention. Finally his furious gaze left Jake and shifted to Ben. "What?"

"Actually," Ben continued with a self deprecating laugh. "I guess it's a question you need to ask yourself."

"What!" McNatt repeated, standing up as Ben knew he would.

"When I was with JAG it was a question we asked ourselves every time we decided to take on a fight with a hero. Is this really the hill you want to die on?"

McNatt was breathing heavily as he glanced furtively at first Cheryl and then Jack. He stared at his notes so long Ben wasn't sure what was going to happen next.

***

"It is him,' Jane agreed, peering at the grainy black and white security-cam photo in her hand. "Where was this taken?" she asked, waving it slightly toward Lee.

"From an ATM on the corner of Mills and Oak; a cab dropped him off three blocks after he left the Plaza."

"What is that building?" Jane asked, handing the photo back to him and settling back in the chair.

"The back of the Rosemund Office Complex," Lee answered, nodding at the server as he set coffee in front of them. "A maintenance man came across him in the basement boiler room. He said Richard claimed to have taken the wrong elevator from the ninth floor and was trying to get to Second Street. The very accommodating maintenance man helped him through the basement to an alley between The Rosemund and the bank next door."

"So, what now?"

"I brought Chet Driscoll into the matter," Lee said as he spotted their server returning to the table with their meal.

"Never heard of him," Jane said leaning back to allow the server to place a plate in front of her.

"That's sort of what he does," Lee laughed.

"Not being heard of?" Jane asked, intrigued immediately.

"Yeah," Lee said looking up at her. "He is a securities expert. He's a genius with computers and business and at one time worked with the federal government doing something no one ever talks about. He teaches classes at the university."

"You mean Professor Driscoll?" Jane gasped. "Really? I thought he was with the psychology department."

"He is," Lee shrugged.

"Ok – never mind. So what now?" Jane asked, picking up her fork. Lee watched the look of delight that was in her eyes as she studied her plate as though wondering, *where to begin... where to begin?* This was a girl who certainly enjoyed her food.

"First we start the search for Richard," Lee said with a deep sigh. "It's proving more complicated than I would have thought. We need a plausible timeline and that has become problematic."

"Because...?"

"Because we have to report that he is missing. There may be some questions about and why no one noticed before."

"Right," Jane nodded. She could see his dilemma. Richard's disappearance should already have been noticed.

"So, time is of the essences. We have to act immediately. Then we get Holly officially home," he continued with an unexplainable sadness. This entire matter had affected him on a level he was unable to absorb. He never met her but somehow was caught up in the enchantment and charm that made her famous. No matter how exasperating and maddening she might have been, she didn't deserve to die at the hands of someone she loved and trusted.

"Driscoll has arranged for the DNA testing in Europe. Once we have verification that the remains are hers, they will be cremated overseas and returned to the family with a great deal of publicity. Then family can go into proper seclusion at an appointed time.

"Wouldn't you love to be a fly on the wall when the news breaks of whatever hole Weston crawled into?" she sighed, reaching for her coffee.

"I would," Lee agreed, shaking his head in consternation in the way it was all playing out. "The remains of Nate Caulder will be held until we have DNA results from a lab in the capitol and then we will notify his family that his remains were discovered in the mountains, which is true. Driscoll has seen the remains and is sure the medical examiner will list the cause of death as unknown."

"And if Richard Weston is located?" Jane asked, pursing her lips and tilting her head slightly. "What do we do then?"

She saw rather then heard the heavy sigh across the table and could see the dark expression that flashed over Lee's face. He looked from his plate to her and simply shook his head. She felt a chill run over her and decided that was a conversation better left for another time and was surprised when he continued.

"We have nothing as far as evidence. We may *know* that Richard killed them but nobody can prove it. There's been an internal audit by Driscoll's forensic team to determine exactly where the trust fund went. We think we have a better chance going after him down that road."

"So, he gets away with murder," Jane said softly, staring at him intently.

"He gets away with murder for the time being," Lee corrected her and fell silent. Jane watched him closely, realizing how much this outcome was eating at him. She reached across the table and brushed the back of his hand with hers and when he looked up at him, she smiled sympathetically.

"These things have a way of working themselves out," she told him. "Sometimes, poetic justice is much more effective than anything we can do."

"Maybe so," Lee said quietly shaking his head.

"And in the meantime?" Jane asked, setting her fork on the edge of her plate and reaching for her iced tea. "As long as he's out there…" she left the words hanging in the air between them.

"The family could still be in danger."

∽✧∼

Richard Weston stood at the deeply scarred and battered wooden case studying the tourist pamphlets on display. He selected a number of them and thumbed casually through them as he walked leisurely out of the visitor's center and stopped at the collection of vending machines in a shelter to the side of the building. He waited as two small boys struggled to reach the coin slot and debated what drinks to buy and then stood back to let them pass, smiling playfully at them. He slipped a dollar bill into the soda machine and pushed one of the dirty panel buttons. He heard the can release and then drop into the dispenser.

He collected his change and popped the top of the can as he crossed the parking lot just outside of the visitor's center and made his way toward the back of the rest stop. The front lot was designated for cars and the back for trucks, trailers and RVs. He strode across the manicured grounds and slipped a key into the driver's door of a slightly faded and obviously used RV. Sliding behind the wheel, he turned over the engine and adjusted the sun visor as he drove away from the rest stop. Pulling back into the highway traffic he adjusted the radio and then reached for the sunshades that were on the console between the two front captain's chairs and slipped them on.

His naturally light brown hair was now almost black and Tan-N-A-Bottle darkened his complexion to a ruddiness that still bothered him. The Just for Men packaging was still in the small bathroom of the motor home. He reached for one of the brochures and snapped it open, spreading it across the console to see the map to the campground at the next exit. He veered off the interstate and spotted the sign for an out of the way campground almost as soon as he turned onto the two-lane highway. Several miles farther into the rural area, he saw the collection of mobile homes, travel trailers, and RVs in the middle of farmland as far as the eye could see.

Within half an hour, he was checked in and was set up with electricity and running water. All the creature comforts of home, more or less, he thought as he pulled the privacy curtain across the windshield and walked toward the back of the vehicle. He slid a cupboard door sideways to reveal a small TV and retrieved the remote control from the side pocket of the only chair in the living room section. He lowered himself into it and turned on the news.

The story of Cameron Emerson's rescue from the mountains by Trevor Cantrell was nothing more than a brief item on the evening news. The incident was reported as a traffic accident and Richard stared at the screen long after the commercials had run and the weather report started. He expected and was prepared for a manhunt once the bodies of Holly and Nate were uncovered in the glade. He was now thrown off balance.

With a resigned sigh, Richard reached toward the small sofa that stretched the width of the RV's rear end and pulled the smart leather briefcase with tapestry accents into his lap. As he snapped open the clasps he shook his head slightly. On top of papers and personal effects that belonged to Holly was the document that became her death warrant; the divorce action for her review and signature. He came across them when he went through her bags the last time she had come home.

Richard and Holly had an agreement. The marriage was never more than a business arrangement for them both. It provided the illusion she needed to appease her parents and convince them she was maturing and changing her ways. Two years after their marriage, Gregory released his hold on her trust fund. The partnership agreement was that he enjoyed the prestige and benefit of being in the inner circle of the Emerson family and he would make no demands that she change her ways. His success at Emerson International was a happy coincidence and he was content to let her live her life as she chose.

He'd known her attraction to Caulder was different from the outset and sensed the threat. That was the reason he'd begun to keep a closer eye on her financial transactions through her accounts and began going through her things. When she suddenly developed an interest in hiking he took up jogging and finally discovered them rendezvousing at the glade.

Everything would have been fine had Holly and Nate just taken off together as everyone assumed they had. If only she hadn't reneged on their agreement she would still be alive. Given her flagrant behavior he believed he could have remained in not only the company employ but the family graces as well. That would have been enough for him. He didn't know what would happen during a divorce, though. She brought this all on herself.

There was never a question in his mind that he would kill her once he discovered she was going to divorce him; it was only a matter of when and where. He'd dug the grave in the shelter of the trees days before. Then he discovered Nate's passport in Holly's briefcase and knew he would have to kill Nate as well. Nate would have sounded the alarm. He would have known Holly had not just taken off without him.

A discrete investigation into Nate Caulder's background suggested he was a man with few ties to family or friends. He'd been partially right. A missing person's report was filed in Nate's home town, but the police department made a few inquiries with the university police.

Richard made a call to the dorm at the university and told the RA that he was Nate and he was going to Spain. When the CSPD followed up on the missing person's report and learned of the call, they informed the Boulder Police Department that their investigation led them to believe Nate left the country. Richard thought all was well.

He was concerned the graves were not deep enough to prevent wildlife from disturbing the corpses and kept a watch on the site for quite a while until he was certain nothing was going to become suspect. For a few days, vultures circled overhead, but then an early winter brought the earliest snowfall and harshest winter in more than a century.

He only had to devise some plan for Holly to die later, somewhere overseas, remote, and in some manner that the body would either never be recovered or could not be identified. His plan was the former. He'd been in no hurry because no one at the Manor really seemed surprised that Holly was not in touch. He decided to wait until some prominent person's plane went down or yacht sank and then claim Holly was with them. It was a risk, but he had a sixth sense in knowing how to exploit situations. He'd been doing it all his life.

He thought he would have more time. He was a little alarmed when Trevor Cantrell began roaming the mountains but soon discovered he stayed along the waterways. After a few weeks, he realized Trevor was no threat to him or his secret buried in the glade.

AS a living member of the family, the company dividends continued to be directly deposited into their joint account and he knew he let his greed overpower his good sense. He continued to transfer money from Holly's accounts in what was her normal extravagant expenses. He'd been able to move his entire salary through Holly's accounts after their marriage and that was now safely in the Caymans.

He became very adept at moving funds through the global financial institutions and soon discovered the more accommodating ones that were not as particular about protocol and financial procedures. Once the origin of the funds was sufficiently obscured, he converted them into other more portable and convertible commodities, diamonds being his first choice.

Richard folded the divorce papers into a tight square and then got up to retrieve the Just for Men box from the small bathroom. He shoved the divorce papers into the box, closed the flap and then added the box to a small paper bag of trash under the small sink. He closed the briefcase and set it back on the sofa before heading toward the rear door.

Outside he paused to take in his surroundings. It was still a little early in the season for vacationers and the park seemed to be filled with migrant workers and senior citizens. He pulled his keys from his jeans' pocket and unlocked the storage area at the back of the RV and pulled out a canvas lawn chair, a small portable grill, charcoal and lighter fluid.

He positioned the chair in the shade of the trailer and stooped down in front of the grill. He piled the charcoal in the center of the grill and doused it liberally with the lighter fluid. Reaching into his pants pocket for a book of matches, he struck one and tossed it into the grill and then leaned backwards slightly as the lighter fluid ignited.

While the flames were at their highest, he pushed the small paper bag of trash under the grill and picked up a stick to hold it down. He watched in satisfaction while the flames licked at the bag as though taste testing it and then began to consume it. When he was sure the fire had taken hold, he returned to the small kitchen and pulled a package of hotdogs off the icebox door. He used the same stick that held the only evidence of motive for murder in the fire to roast two hotdogs.

As he grilled the hotdogs over the dying flames, watching as the red skin began to blister and turn dark, his mind turned to the last few weeks and how badly he'd botched things. If he believed in God he would think there was one watching over Nicole Emerson. The ironies of his two failed attempts to bring a halt to the construction in the glade were beyond belief.

He carried the scorched hotdogs back into the RV and closed and locked the door behind him. He pulled a package of buns from the small cabinet over the tiny sink along with bottles of squeeze mustard and relish. While he assembled his dinner he turned and pushed the button on the tape player. The monotonous sound of a tutor's voice filled the air. As Richard responded to the language teaching tapes he opened two buns, slathered mustard and relish on them and then slapped the hotdogs on top. He stood at the sink and ate; listening intently as the tapes continued to play.

He knew that the Emersons would be looking for him. With Gregory's clout, he was sure that not only the Emerson security machine but also the locals, the Feds, and even Interpol would be covering every major airport and port of entry throughout the world. He was banking, literally, on the idea that with the millions he'd transferred out of Holly's accounts, they would not be looking for him in his beat up little home on wheels. He would wander around for a while and eventually make his way to the border. At some point he would be able to access the fortune he considered to be his due for putting up with Holly Emerson's humiliation of him. If nothing else, Richard Weston was a patient man.

Charlotte A. Minga

CHAPTER TWENTY~FOUR

Nicole positioned the hospital table in front of Cameron and set the plate Riva prepared for him on it. There were bite sized pieces of his favorite, French toast and a small bowl of syrup. He was beginning to look like her husband again as she leaned across the bed rail and kissed him gently on the cheek. His beard was growing in because of the scabs from the abrasions preventing him from shaving.

He shifted slightly, reaching for the pull bar hanging above and surveyed the plate through eyes that were not as swollen. The steady nursing care of ice compresses and anti-inflammation meds were doing their job. He put a bite of toast in his mouth and grimaced slightly as he tried to chew. He looked at her and sighed.

"Too much?" Nicole asked, choosing one of the pieces and eating it. "It's wonderful," she commented, taking the plate and carrying it to the table beside the sofa. She turned back and reached for the bowl of oatmeal Riva thinned enough to come through a straw and set it in front of him.

"Maybe tomorrow," Cameron said as he reached for the straw.

"Or the next day," Nicole said, dropping to the sofa and pulling her legs under her.

"Have you seen Trevor?" Cameron asked, pushing the oatmeal away and reaching for the spill proof cup with another straw. He sipped at the orange juice and then smacked his lips in contentment.

"Not since yesterday," Nicole said watching him closely. So far he had not spoken of the attack. Dr. Newman advised them to let him deal with it in his own way and his own time. For the time being, Kyle and Andrea had moved into the north wing and they had the lower wing to themselves along with the four nurses who were changing shifts around the clock.

"I was thinking last night," Cameron said quietly, looking at her.

"Well," Nicole said lightly, "given the circumstances that's good news." She was rewarded by the crooked smile and a chuckle.

"Yeah," Cameron laughed. "I was thinking about what brought Trevor here."

Nicole remained silent. Trevor Cantrell was being discussed by many people in many places during the last three days. The mysterious perception that people like Sandy and Jake called "gut instinct" cast suspicion on Trevor from the outset.

With the family's announcement of the accident and the miraculous rescue, all the unanswered questions about Trevor only intensified the façade and mystery around him. If it weren't for the diligence of the EI security teams the mountain would be swarming with reporters and the curious. She could only image what it would be like if the truth ever came out.

"He wasn't supposed to be here you know," Cameron said.

"No?"

"No," Cameron continued with the slightest shake of his head before the pain brought him up short. "He was injured during a SEAL mission that ended his career in the Navy – whatever happened."

"Oh," Nicole whispered.

"He never wanted to be anything but a SEAL," Cameron sighed. "His father was a Navy pilot killed in Vietnam. His grandfather raised him and when he found out Trev wanted to join the Navy he sold the family farm and they moved to San Diego. From that moment on everything his grandfather did he did to help Trevor achieve that dream."

"Wow," Nicole said, not knowing what else to say.

"Don't tell him I told you," Cameron said suddenly. "He doesn't talk about his grandfather much. I think Emit must remind him of him, though. I think that's why they kind of connected."

"I won't," Nicole promised.

"I've been thinking…"

Nicole sat quietly on the sofa waiting for him to process and then voice these deep thoughts. She watched him closely, seeing the emotions that flashed through the brilliant blue eyes as he tried to absorb and sort out the last few days.

"He lost his dream when he was discharged from the Navy. I think that's why he's so…" Cameron searched for a word.

"Obsessed?" Nicole offered.

"Maybe," Cameron said, leaning his head back on the pillow. The effort he was making exhausted him. "But I've been thinking about how we met. I left my keys in my room and had to go back and get them that night."

Nicole felt a cold chill run up her spine as and she inhaled deeply, staring across the room through the window in the back door. She could see the carriage house on the other side of the drive. She realized she was holding her breath as her mind followed the same line of thought as his. "I can't remember another time in my life when I forgot my keys."

"If he hadn't been here," she said, barely above a whisper, "Richard would have killed you," she finished his thought, seeing him nod slightly as their eyes met.

"We can never fail to thank God for all of this, Nikki," he said quietly. "It all is a big puzzle and we don't see the picture until it's done."

"I know," she whispered, taking his hand and she then began to pray as he sighed deeply in exhausted relief.

❧

"It's that simple?" Gregory Emerson asked, looking across his desk to Chet Drischoll. He glanced at Lee who was standing beside the door listening to the plan Chet laid out. The simplicity of it was brilliance, Lee realized.

"And it's legal?" Garret asked from his chair beside Chet.

"Under the present circumstances —that the supposed 'ancient remains' discovered in the glade are as yet unidentified — you can transport them to the facility in Luxemburg for the purpose of DNA testing. The customs document will state that they are unidentified remains discovered on the family estate and you are interested in learning if they are family related. When the results come back and they are as we expect, then we bring her back through customs under her own name and papers to create a record of recovery of Holly's remains and their return to the family."

Gregory scratched the side of his nose as he studied the man across from him and then to Ben.

"Here are the legal cites which you can check to make sure I've not made a mistake concerning international law in the matter," Chet said to Ben.

"What about the boy?" Gregory sighed.

"That is a different matter," Chet said with a shake of his head. "The discovery of his remains will need to be reported and then returned to his family. There will be a formal investigation into the matter under Sherriff Clairborne and we will report exactly what we know about his disappearance. It was believed he went to Spain and no one was aware he was still in the area. It is my understanding from Dr. Richmond that there is no way to determine the cause of death."

"Correct," Ben stated.

"Well then," Gregory said, lifting an uncertain gaze to his son-in-law. "Ben, what do you think?"

"It's legal," Ben admitted. "I'm still not sure it's the best plan but I have no alternative to offer. I think with the resources we have we can find him."

"I understand your desire to see him brought to justice, Mr. Faraday," Chet said evenly, reaching again for his attaché. "But, besides the fact there is not enough evidence to bring charges against him let alone convict him for murders, I think you should consider *this*," he said, pulling a copy of a photo from his case and handing it to him. Lee took several steps forward so he could see the photo over Ben's shoulder.

It was of a young man and the style of clothing and buildings behind him indicated it was a copy of a photo taken some time during the mid to late forties.

"Who is that?" Gregory asked, reaching for the photocopy.

"It's the only Richard Alan Weston we can find any public record of," Chet said quietly. "He died in 1951. The man whom Holly married was using his social security number and paying taxes with Holly as the primary. It was a clever way to be fairly sure his stolen Social would not attract attention."

The room fell silent as Ben and Gregory stared at the photo. Lee lowered his head, staring at the carpet at his feet and shaking his head. Who the devil were they dealing with here? He watched as Chet sat back in his chair and waited for the others to take in and process the bombshell that he just dropped.

"I know this is adding insult to injury, sir," Chet continued quietly. "I will do anything I can to help you at this time. Just let me know what you want me to do."

"What are the details of your plan?" Ben asked, watching as Gregory seemed to age right before their eyes. He motioned for Lee to join them. Lee crossed the room, pulled a chair from the conference table and placed it beside the desk, reaching for the pad and pen Ben held out for him.

"First of all," Chet said, glancing at his notes made the night before as he examined the evidence at Ellery Richmond's lab, "We should get her remains to Luxemburg as soon as we can. A colleague of mine owns the lab. If he can extract DNA from her remains or the clothing found with her, it will take at the very least six to eight weeks for a confirmation. A sample from any family member will be sufficient for comparison but I suggest it be you, Mr. Emerson."

Chet handed Lee a copy of the lab details and then continued. "I understand there has been some kind of misappropriations of funds?"

"Not the company's," Ben said, "Holly's personal trusts. There seems to be no impropriety in the company books. Holly's trust is the only account involved. Even there, they were married and he held her power of attorney."

"I see," Chet nodded. "I recommend you have a forensic accountant do a complete audit but since we are dealing with personal funds that makes all this much easier and less tricky legally. They *were* married and she *did* voluntarily give him access to her accounts. I suggest you use someone not connected to Emerson International."

"Can you recommend someone?" Ben asked from his place beside Gregory.

"We can provide that service for you. You want to keep this as tight circle of players as possible. I have an excellent forensic accountant and she is as discreet as you're going to find anywhere."

"What if there is no usable DNA?" Ben asked, looking up at Chet. He realized that this man was their best weapon in this battle with Richard – or whoever he was.

"With the personal jewelry found with the remains, the clothes, the location of the grave, I will be greatly surprised if there is no DNA somewhere. And – the absence of the man posing as Richard Weston allows you to move forward on the presumption that the remains are Holly's beyond a reasonable doubt. We may be able to have her remains back in the country by the end of next month. Right now, you need to get Richard's disappearance out there and handled."

"We are waiting to determine the best way to do that," Lee said.

"As directly as you can," Lee instructed. "Someone is going to notice his disappearance. As this plays out, it doesn't matter who."

"It's going to look odd if we don't miss him with Cameron's rescue," Garret said evenly.

"Not necessarily. In times like these there is no normal."

"When the DNA comes in, if it's not a match, we'll look at all this again and come up with a Plan B as far as Holly is concerned. Personally, I don't see that as happening or I wouldn't be suggesting this course of action."

Lee glanced at Gregory and saw his face was drained of all color. He cleared his throat, getting Chet's attention and then stood up. "If you are agreeable to moving forward with this matter, sir," he said leaning toward Gregory, "we can take this meeting to my office," he suggested.

As soon as Ben and Chet saw Gregory's face, Chet sighed deeply. "I'm sorry, Mr. Emerson," he said softly. "You have my heartfelt sympathy."

"Thank you, Sheriff for your cooperation in this," Lee said, standing at the head of the table in the conference room.

Chet Driscoll was standing beside him. He looked around the room and met each one's gaze. Garret was at the other end of the table and Emit, Jake and Jane were sitting on the left side of the room.

"You've all met Chet," he continued, jerking his head slightly and glancing at him. "We all know what we are doing here. I'm going to just turn this over to him now."

As Lee dropped into the empty chair beside Jane, Chet stepped to the head of the table and swept the room with his dark eyes.

"Good morning," he said with a slight smile. "I know how difficult this is and I will make this as brief as possible. I don't want any of you to think I don't understand the devastation this has brought to the Emerson family and Stafford County."

"Thank you," Garret said his voice not quite as vibrant or strong as usual.

Jake nodded his head and Jane and Sandy glanced resolutely at each other. It seemed so strange to Jane to see Professor Driscoll standing at the head of this table much as he stood in front if his class. Something should be different, she decided. He needed derby or trench coat – something other than the sweater vest he was wearing. He looked normal. He shouldn't look normal here. She sighed slightly and focused on what he was saying.

"If at any time you have any questions, please do not hesitate to interrupt me and voice them." He watched as they nodded their understanding.

"For security reasons I suggest that you take no notes," he said as he saw Garret pick up a pen and look around the room for a pad. Garret paused for a moment and then nodded, tossing the pen on the table with a slight thud.

"The facts are these," Chet said as he sat down in the head chair and took command of what would need to be carried out with military precision. "This morning the remains of Holly were sent via private jet for DNA testing. That will take a minimum of eight weeks and could take as long as three to four months."

He paused, glancing around the room to see if there were any questions and then took another breath and continued.

"There is no question that the man you know as Richard Weston isn't," he paused as he slid the photo into the middle of the table. "Richard Alan Weston was born in a small town just below the Canadian border February 10, 1936 and died in 1951 at the age of sixty-two. In 1966, a social security card was obtained in his name in North Dakota and the next year a Wyoming driver's license was issued outside of Cheyenne."

"Man…" Garret said, leaning back in his chair and crossing his arms over his chest. The fury that was burning in him was obvious.

"Everything about the man *we* know as and will continue to refer to as Richard Weston is true. He graduated from high school in northern California in 1967 and UCLA in 1972. I've confirmed that with high school yearbook photos. It is the man we know as Richard Weston. He had an educational deferment until the lottery was initiated and his number for the draft was high. He was never drafted. We know nothing about him before 1966. We don't know where he came from and we don't know why he assumed the dead man's name. He made no attempt to assume any part of the real Richard Weston's identity – only his name and Social. After he graduated from college there is a gap of about three years before he resurfaced in the international division of Pan Am as a financial analyst and was in the Brussels office when he met Holly in Paris."

Chet paused again, allowing the tension in the room to ease a bit and taking a sip of his water. He glanced at Jake. "Sheriff Clairborne, I understand a wallet with a Colorado driver's license was found with the remains."

"It was," Jake nodded.

"Is your office comfortable with that as sufficient identification to notify the next of kin of the discovery of Nathan Caulder's remains?"

"Yeah," Jake said with an emphatic nod. "No one else has gone missing in this county and Eric MacIntosh recognized the clothing found in the grave as Nate's."

All eyes in the room glanced at Emit, who nodded silently.

"Nathan Collin Caulder is survived by a cousin. It is my recommendation that you notify the Boulder Police Department of the discovery of his remains with as little detail as you actually have. It is my understanding that Trotter McGee isn't aware of the fact there were two bodies in the grave?"

"That's correct," Jake replied.

"He still believes they were ancient remains?"

Chet paused again as Jake nodded and then met Emit's intense gaze. "Mr. MacIntosh, are you comfortable with a police report that states that Nathan left the intern program without notice?"

"I am," Emit said quietly. "No one likes any of this," he said with a shake of his head.

"No sir," Chet agreed. "And I assure you, we are developing a plan to find justice in this matter. Nate Caulder will not be forgotten.

If I thought for a moment that revealing everything we think we know would bring a quicker justice or comfort to the Caulder family I would not be suggesting this course of action."

Silence engulfed the room. No one was looking at anyone. Chet waited for a few seconds and then plunged on. "Sheriff, if your office will contact the Boulder Police so that the family can be notified today then you can release at statement to the press just before they go on air tonight. Friday is always a good time to slide something past the public. Washington has been doing it for years."

Jake glanced at Jane, who nodded. "I'll draft that."

Chet cleared his throat and continued, "For our own benefit, the incident on Sutter Trail with Cameron and the Jaguar will be referred to as an accident at all times and in all ways. I understand that there will be no comment from the family and the Stafford County Sherriff's office makes no comment on ongoing investigations?"

"Correct," Jake answered and Chet saw Garret nodding solemnly from the corner of his eye.

"I predict that interest in the discovery of Nathan's remains will last no longer then two or three news cycles if that long," Chet said. "We are as certain that the second remains discovered on the Emerson Estate are – in fact – Holly."

Chet paused for a moment and took quick gauge of the room. Everyone seemed to be in agreement. He sensed no undercurrent among the people there.

"Once the testing is completed I will have a plan in place to report Holly's death. All I can tell you at this time is that it will be reported somewhere overseas. I won't know how until an opportunity presents itself. It's a very big world when it comes to this so as soon as something presents itself, I'll use it. There will be a protocol to return her remains and you will be notified through the appropriate channels. Her remains will be cremated as she requested in her will and her ashes will be returned to the family. Until that time, I recommend you move forward as normally as you can."

"Will we have any advanced notice?" Garret asked.

"As much as anyone normally would in life's circumstances," Chet answered. "I strongly recommend that you make no adjustment in schedules or activities whatsoever; if you have a family vacation planned and are in Hawaii when the word comes all the better. Just go about your daily lives. Normalcy is the order of the day – whatever that normal is."

"What about Richard?" Ben asked.

"There has to be an immediate announcement of his disappearance," Chet said with a shake of his head. "This is the trickiest part of all. We have tracked him out of the Plaza and through an office building several blocks from here. As far as we have determined, only a maintenance man in a boiler room at the Rosamond spoke to him. As I understand it, Weston told his secretary he was going to work in his office and did not want to be disturbed shortly after the remains were discovered?"

"Yes," Lee answered for them.

"Did he often stay in the apartment at the Plaza?"

"Often," Lee agreed. "He was pleasant but aloof. He always just did his own thing at the Plaza. He kept his own hours and reported only to Gregory."

There was silence as they watched Chet going through a thought process that he didn't voice. He glanced at each of them around the room and then briefly out the window. "What was his habit in the office?"

"His position was CEO. He was habitual… very habitual," Lee said evenly.

"And at the house?" Chet continued.

"Again – pleasant and aloof,: Garret chose Lee's words and nodded in agreement. "He wasn't ever-present and no one thought anything about him coming and going either at the Manor or the Plaza."

"Then let his secretary notice his absence," Chet decided. "The CSPD should follow the same trail we did. Lee, when the alarm is sounded you should wait a few hours – about the time it took to make calls and check to see where he might be – and then deliver the security tape of Richard getting into the taxi to the police and just let it all play out naturally."

"And if this maintenance man comes forward?" Garret asked, leaning forward and crossing his arms on the table."What do we do then?"

"Nothing. If this man comes forward then we will use whatever he tells the Crystal Springs Police to the best advantage. It's been my experience that once someone sees a spotlight they do one of two things. They either forget exactly what they know or they embellish it for any number of reasons. He may not come forward at all."

"Won't he remember someone asking about Richard?" Ben asked.

"No one asked about Richard," Chet said without change of expression.

"Then how…"

"If this man comes forward we will spin his statement to our best advantage," Chet said with a calm assurance. "Let's not cross bridges…"

Jane found herself staring at him in wonder. She would love to know what was going on behind the scenes and felt like crying that she never would. She glanced at Lee and saw his knowing look. Maybe she could get something out of him, she decided as Chet began to wrap up the meeting.

෴

Ben Faraday filed a missing person's report that afternoon with both the Stafford County Sheriff's office as well as the Crystal Springs Police Department when his secretary could not reach Richard on his phone or pager and he could not be located. When the CSPD arrived at the Plaza they were given complete access to the apartment assigned to him. Lee stood watch as they searched.

The maintenance man called the police and was then interviewed by the local news. His interviews aired once that night. The man hesitantly admitted to swarming reporters that Richard appeared in the basement of his building and he showed him to an exit door into the alley.

Chet made a few calls and started the chatter about the family's concern that the alley where Richard was last seen in an area known to be used by local prostitutes and drug dealers. By the second news cycle, the news anchors were repeating the family alarm that Richard may have met with foul play.

With the son-in-law of Gregory Emerson missing, the report of the discovery of Nate Caulder's remains was a one cycle news event. When contacted by the local news, the MacIntoshes released a statement offering their heartfelt sympathy to the family and their relief that there were answers to what happened to him and there could now be closure for his family and friends.

Jake's office arranged for Nate's remains to be returned to his family in Colorado. He had been a freshman on the university campus and there were only a handful of students there who still remembered him. The Dean of Student Affairs located the boxes that had been packed up in his dorm room and delivered them to the Sheriff's office where Jake entered them into evidence and placed them in their evidence locker should the Caulder family request their return.

In early August, a ferry capsized in a river deep in the Himalayans and a report came from a remote village in Bhutan and one of the victims was identified Holly Emerson Weston. Holly's passport and driver's license were delivered to the authorities in New Deli and with the deepest of sympathy and regret, the Indian Embassy in Washington D.C. notified Gregory of Holly's tragic death. They were deeply saddened that such a tragedy had befallen such a well respected family in their country.

Sitting in her living room listening to the local news report Jane's mouth was hanging open in. She reached for the phone, knocking her book off a side table. She quickly averted her eyes from the TV as she tapped in Lee's number.

"This is unbelievable," she said when Lee answered her call.

"I know," he said from his house across town. "It's incredible, isn't it? But knowing Holly, she would want to die in some exotic place doing something as spectacular as hiking the Himalayas. She would have loved this, as bizarre as that sounds. She definitely would not want Richard to have the slightest victory."

"Lee…"

"Want to meet me for dinner?" he asked quietly.

"Why don't you grab something and bring it over," she suggested. The questions she had and the topics she wanted to discuss could not be appropriate for any public place.

ೂಲ

The memorial service for Holly Emerson was held in the Chapel at the university three weeks after the notification of her death. The Chapel was the second oldest building on campus, donated by the Emerson ancestors more than a hundred years before and just east of Halsey Hall, named after the original grant owner. It stood on the highest point in Crystal Springs; built of the same quarried granite as the Hall and was adorned with stained glass windows handmade in Venice, Italy by master craftsmen.

The steeple could be seen from almost any point in the city and Ralston MacIntosh, patriarch of the MacIntosh clan, commissioned the bronze bell that pealed such a clear, sweet tone that its echo could be heard around the surrounding mountains for miles. Today, it peeled a loving goodbye to Holly Noel Emerson in the hot August sun.

The weather-stained walls were covered with carefully cultivated and manicured ivy. Family legend said it grew from cuttings brought by Halsey and Ralston MacIntosh when they fled Scotland as a constant reminder of the ancestral home lost in the battle between the Tudors and the Stuarts. The interior of the Chapel was of the same rich dark oak paneling milled from the Estate that graced the walls of Halsey Hall as well as much of Hawthorn Manor.

The interior lighting was completely dependent on the tinted light shining through the stained glass windows. Emit and Gregory donated accent lighting outside the Chapel to augment the effect. They were determined to prevent what they considered desecration of the Chapel with electric wiring. Day or night, the angle of the exterior lights sent soft lighting into the Chapel. There was a caretaker, paid through the endowment of the Emerson family, whose only job was to keep the Chapel maintained.

Only a small number of invited guests could fit into the chapel. Candles were set in the holders along the intricately carved spindles on the stairs leading to the tower room overhead, at the ends of the pews, at the altar and in casings around the windows. Curved beams lifted the ceiling high above the mourners' heads into the loft apex and allowed the subtle music of the old organ to flow out across the campus in mournful symphony.

Her ashes were interred in the MacIntosh cemetery on the far east side of the Estate. The tiny one room chapel offered little more than a kneeling rail and an altar; but allowed for prayer and meditation on the grounds. A private wake was held at the Manor.

Although the press respected the family's wishes and kept a deferential distance, coverage of the story was headline news at noon, five, six, and ten o'clock. The wire services picked up the report of Holly's death because of Richard's mysterious disappearance more than two months before.

At Chet's suggestion, Gregory increased the reward offered for any information leading to the discovery of his son-in-law's whereabouts. Holly's jet-setting history gave the story the impetus needed to extend the coverage into the society columns and news magazines. Friends and fans across the globe held memorial services for her and whetted the appetites of the rag sheets anew. Richard's face began to grace the tabloids as well as the legitimate press at every grocery checkout and magazine stand around the world.

"I salute your brilliance," Ben said to Lee as the family gathered at the Manor following the service. "We couldn't have bought this kind of coverage."

"I can't take credit for this," Lee said with an emphatic shake of his head.

"You brought Chet to us," Ben replied. "I did some research on this place – Bhutan. It isn't an easy place to get to and that village where the ferry boat capsized is almost impossible to reach."

"That was the point," Lee laughed. "No editor or news producer is going to sign off on that trip voucher on the chance there is more to the story."

꙼꙼

The autumn air was crisp and the trees were blazing against the morning sky in vibrant reds, golds, yellows, and oranges. The Emerson clan and a few close friends were gathered for the house warming and dedication of Cameron and Nicole's new home. The front of the A-frame house was smoked glass and the late afternoon sun mirrored the surrounding scene as Cameron draped his arm across Nicole's shoulders. She was flushed and smiling brightly as the general contractor ceremonially handed Cameron and Nicole separate sets of keys.

Nicole turned and unlocked the door, gasping as Cameron swept her off her feet and carried her over the threshold to the laughter and applause of everyone present. He put her down in the entryway and then gathered her into his arms.

"Finally, we're home, Mrs. Emerson," he said into her ear and kissed her tenderly.

Vanessa interrupted the brief moment by coming through the door with the camcorder, making a full sweep of the impressive great room with the glass wall that rose three stories high and offered a panoramic view of the newly landscaped glade and the river beyond.

"Okay now," Vanessa said from behind the camera and focused sharply on Cameron and Nicole, "let's get this show on the road! It's time to cut the cake!"

Nicole moved to the circular table that was in the center of the great room and picked up the cake knife. She stood for a moment looking at the cake baked and decorated by Riva and then glanced up at Trevor with a giggle. "Why don't you stand behind me, wrap your arm around my neck and I'll pretend to pass out cold?"

"That's perfect," Cameron called, laughing quietly.

"You're never going to let me live that down, are you?" Trevor asked as he looked sideways at Cameron.

"Not in this lifetime," Nicole said with a laugh as Vanessa trained the camera on the three who had been through fire and emerged with a friendship forged forever.

On cue, the invited quests filed into the room and the party began. After a moment, Trevor glanced over his shoulder and eased himself away from the crowd, making his way discretely out the front door.

"She's going to make an impressive first lady," Jane whispered into Lee's ear as they watched Vanessa with her camera follow Nicole up the sweeping staircase to the open balcony above. "You would think she and Nicole have been best buddies all their lives."

"She is the consummate politician's wife," Lee agreeed, turning to see that Gregory and Helena did not follow them into the house. "The next best thing to being the darling of the press is to be the best friend of the darling of the press. That way, you are always in the shot."

He stepped to the window to make sure all was well. Trevor was wandering across the front lawn to the side of the house and Gregory and Helena were watching him with an expression he had seen often in the last months. They followed him and the three of them reached the same place at the same time.

At the far end of the terrace a small stone marker was discreetly set in the flowerbed. Trevor crossed the terrace and stood staring at the bronze plate secured to the top: *In loving memory of Holly Noel Emerson – cherished daughter and beloved sister.*

After almost six months, there was still no sign of Richard Weston in spite of the massive press. He had embezzled enough money from Holly's accounts to keep him funded for years to come. After much discussion, the rest of the family insisted that Nicole and Cameron build their home as planned. Holly's body would never have been discovered and her murderer never exposed otherwise.

Trevor caught the movement of shadow and realized Gregory Emerson was behind him. He glanced up at the man who was now like a father to him.

"I hear you defended your thesis brilliantly," Gregory said. "Congratulations."

Trevor's thesis was to identify the natural minerals in the waters of the pristine mountain waters of the Emerson Estate. His attempt was to provide a basis for study in the years to come of the effect of chemicals being introduced to the environment. What he uncovered, however, was a toxin in some of the springs and streams feeding the river. The result was an offer to head the newly created environmental division of The Emerson Foundation to discover what the toxin was and from where it was coming.

"Well, I don't know about brilliance," Trevor said with a self-conscious laugh and push of his hand through his unruly dark curls. "But they gave me my master's."

"And we are excited about you joining the Foundation," Gregory continued. "And your thesis for your doctorate has been accepted by Dr. Richmond, I understand?"

"I appreciate the opportunity," Trevor said honestly. I can't find the words to thank you, sir."

"The appreciation is mine," Gregory replied, slapping Trevor's shoulder with a fatherly affection. "This isn't a job for one man. We have a candidate we are looking at to hire as your assistant. He comes highly recommend by Chet Driscoll. He'll be arriving in a week or so. From what I'm told about the toxins in the water, no one needs to be alone in the mountains until we have some answers."

"I'm ready to get to work," Trevor admitted.

"Helena and I," Gregory said, stepping sideways a step and reaching to draw her into their conversation, "want to give you something more."

"You've already done too much," Trevor said, shaking his head slightly.

"We could never do too much. We would have lost not only our son, and perhaps our first grandchild as well," Helena said softly, stepping forward to kiss Trevor's cheek and hug him tightly. He was treated as an honored guest from the moment Cameron brought him home; but now he was accepted as a child of the household.

"When I asked Cameron what you might like he told me how much you love the cabin," Gregory said, taking Trevor's arm and walking with him back toward the house. "Unfortunately, the Manor is entailed in such a way that it cannot be sold or divested, but I'm having a long term proprietorship drawn up that will allow you to use the cabin as long as you or any of your heirs want to use it. For all intents and purposes, it's yours. I've arranged for some renovations and an access drive to be cut across from Cameron's road. We'll add electricity and plumbing and that will give you a comfortable place where you can work while you're on the mountain or just use it any way you choose. I just wish it could be more."

Trevor drew in a deep breath and merely shook his head. "I don't know what to say," he finally admitted, laughing shortly.

"We are just trying to say thank you for all you have done for us," Helena said softly, caressing his arm with her hand, "...and Holly. There are no words for that and there is nothing we wouldn't do for you. We lost a daughter but I feel like we gained another son."

They fell silent as they reached the patio. Cameron and a very pregnant Nicole were reemerging from the house and everyone was gathering around. In a flowerbed beside the front door, a dark green bush with a large red bow attached to it had been carefully planted and cultivated. Tiny berries were just beginning to ripen in the late October air. Nicole held a watering can and turned toward the video camera. Cameron tried to speak, but was overwhelmed with emotion. Nicole took a deep breath, cleared her throat and stepped up to the bed.

"We dedicate this glade to the memory of Holly Noel Emerson," she said, letting the water fall from the spout over the holly bush, "and name our home Glade Holly in her memory."

"We have everything ready for you," the desk manager said, tapping on his keyboard as he completed the application information and waited for the printer to hum to life. "My name is Carlito, so please, let me know how I can be of service to you during your stay with us. Will you be staying with us long, sir?"

"Carlito," the new arrival said with a quick smile. "Nice to meet you, Carlito."

"Thank you, sir,"

"Here ya go," the man standing at the counter said as he pulled a battered cloth wallet from his jacket pocket and fished out several bills and laid them on the counter. "I'm looking for some property so I may be here a while."

"We are honored, sir," Carlito said with a practiced smile as he counted the change over the cash drawer and handed it back to his new guest. He pulled the receipt from the printer and folded it carefully, sliding it in the slot in the welcome packet. He collected the small stack of brochures he gathered for his obviously well to do and generous new guest.

"This will give you information about the area," Carlito said, leaving the folder open and turning it upside down so that his guest could read it. He pointed to each section, explaining as he tapped his pencil beside each one. There was a list of local restaurants, merchants, entertainment opportunities and services.

"If there is anything else you need just let us know."

Carlito then pulled the top copy off a stack of maps to his left. He made a black X over the office and then drew a line along the page to direct his new guest to his lodgings. "Your cottage is down this main corridor and to the left of the cove. You can see the ocean from the living room and the pool and guest services are just around the corner."

"Thank you," the man said, closing the folder and tucking it under his arm.

"I hope you enjoy your stay with us," Carlito said, looking again at the passport before handing it back, "Mr. Caulder."

"Oh, I'm sure I will," Richard said taking the passport and slipping it into his breast pocket. He looked up over the vanity glasses he bought in a souvenir shop along his leisurely journey out of the States and along the Central American coast, "but, please, call me Nathaniel."

ABOUT THE AUTHOR

Charlotte Ann Minga was born in the South at the middle of the twentieth century under the same wandering star as her engineer father and librarian mother. As a child, she traveled extensively with her parents and older brother across North America when it wasn't the national pastime and camped through eight European countries the summer she graduated from high school.

Thousands of miles and seemingly endless hours in the car gave her time to daydream and fueled her imagination. With her writer's memory, she has spent her lifetime collecting memories of the sights, sounds. smells, feels, and ambiances of the people and places she has seen and created a series of novels to share the stories they ignited. *Shadow in the Wind* is the first of The Stafford County series.

Charlotte came to age in the sixties and didn't enlist in the feminists' movement but was drafted. She held firm to her dream to be a wife and mother and raised three children. When her life took the unexpected left turn of divorce, she returned to college, graduating Magna Cum Laud with a legal degree.

She wrote her first novel when she was a teenager. She wrote it again shortly after her first child was born, again when her second child started kindergarten and one more time when her third child left home. When her life blossomed with a second chance at love and marriage, her present husband encouraged her to complete the journey and actually publish her work.

She and her husband retired and while he returned to teaching, she returned to her first love of writing. They live in their country retirement home in North Mississippi with their menagerie of rescued cats and dogs and look forward to the kids and eleven grandchildren (and counting) coming home.

Mother, daughter, sister, wife – is the context of her life.

Made in the USA
Charleston, SC
24 December 2012